DARK
ILLUSION

The Carpathian Novels

DARK ILLUSION	DARK POSSESSION
DARK SENTINEL	DARK CELEBRATION
DARK LEGACY	DARK DEMON
DARK CAROUSEL	DARK SECRET
DARK PROMISES	DARK DESTINY
DARK GHOST	DARK MELODY
DARK BLOOD	DARK SYMPHONY
DARK WOLF	DARK GUARDIAN
DARK LYCAN	DARK LEGEND
DARK STORM	DARK FIRE
DARK PREDATOR	DARK CHALLENGE
DARK PERIL	DARK MAGIC
DARK SLAYER	DARK GOLD
DARK CURSE	DARK DESIRE
DARK HUNGER	DARK PRINCE

Anthologies

EDGE OF DARKNESS
(with Maggie Shayne and Lori Herter)

DARKEST AT DAWN
(includes Dark Hunger *and* Dark Secret*)*

SEA STORM
(includes Magic in the Wind *and* Oceans of Fire*)*

FEVER
(includes The Awakening *and* Wild Rain*)*

FANTASY
(with Emma Holly, Sabrina Jeffries, and Elda Minger)

LOVER BEWARE
(with Fiona Brand, Katherine Sutcliffe, and Eileen Wilks)

HOT BLOODED
(with Maggie Shayne, Emma Holly, and Angela Knight)

Specials

DARK CRIME
THE AWAKENING
DARK HUNGER
MAGIC IN THE WIND

DARK ILLUSION

A CARPATHIAN NOVEL

CHRISTINE FEEHAN

BERKLEY
NEW YORK

BERKLEY
An imprint of Penguin Random House LLC
1745 Broadway, New York, NY 10019

Copyright © 2019 by Christine Feehan
Penguin Random House supports copyright. Copyright fuels creativity, encourages
diverse voices, promotes free speech, and creates a vibrant culture. Thank you for buying
an authorized edition of this book and for complying with copyright laws by not
reproducing, scanning, or distributing any part of it in any form without permission.
You are supporting writers and allowing Penguin Random House to continue
to publish books for every reader.

BERKLEY and the BERKLEY & B colophon are registered trademarks of
Penguin Random House LLC.

Library of Congress Cataloging-in-Publication Data

Names: Feehan, Christine, author.
Title: Dark illusion / Christine Feehan.
Description: First Edition. | New York : Berkley, 2019. | Series: A Carpathian novel
Identifiers: LCCN 2019003736| ISBN 9781984803467 (hardcover) |
ISBN 9781984803474 (ebook)
Subjects: LCSH: Paranormal romance stories. | GSAFD: Fantasy fiction.
Classification: LCC PS3606.E36 D362 2019 | DDC 813/.6—dc23
LC record available at https://lccn.loc.gov/2019003736

First Edition: September 2019

Printed in the United States of America
1   3   5   7   9   10   8   6   4   2

Cover design and image composition by Judith Lagerman
Cover art: Woman © Beauty Archive / Image Bank / Gettyimages

For my grandson, James Clarke, with love.

FOR MY READERS

Be sure to go to christinefeehan.com/members/ to sign up for my private book announcement list and download the free ebook of *Dark Desserts*. Join my community and get firsthand news, enter the book discussions, ask your questions and chat with me. Please feel free to email me at Christine@christinefeehan.com. I would love to hear from you.

ACKNOWLEDGMENTS

As with any book, there are so many people to thank. First, thanks to Anita Toste, my sister who always is up for working on anything to do with mages, spells and poetry. You always have my back and it is so appreciated! This book was fun to write because you made it that way. Domini and Sheila, thank you for your edits, catching all the loose ends. Thanks to Brian for challenging me to write faster, although I have to say, a few times I suspected that instead of writing his book he was playing video games and just taunting me!

THE CARPATHIAN FAMILIES

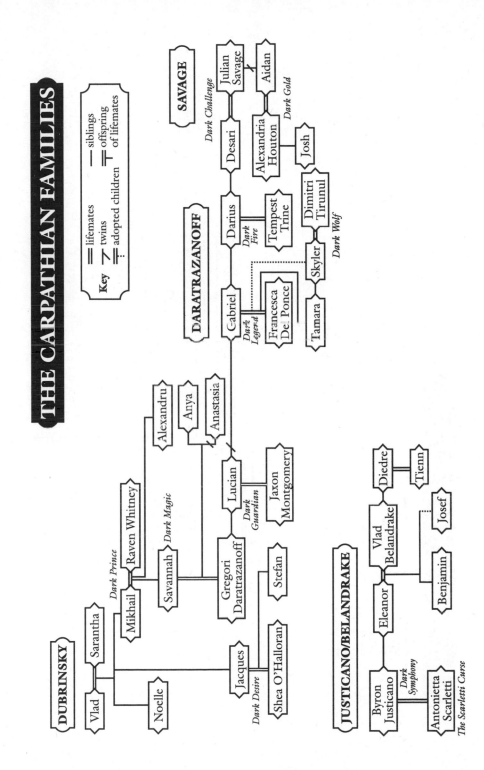

Key
= lifemates
— siblings
⅂ twins
⊤ offspring of lifemates
⊤ adopted children

SAVAGE

Dark Challenge
Julian Savage
Desari
Aidan — *Dark Gold*
Alexandria Houton
Josh

DARATRAZANOFF

Darius
Dark Fire
Tempest Trine
Dimitri Tirunul — *Dark Wolf*
Skyler
Gabriel
Dark Legend
Francesca Del Ponce
Tamara

Alexandru
Anya
Anastasia

DUBRINSKY

Vlad
Sarantha
Mikhail — *Dark Prince*
Raven Whitney
Alexandru
Savannah — *Dark Magic*
Gregori Daratrazanoff
Lucian — *Dark Guardian*
Jaxon Montgomery
Stefan
Noelle
Jacques — *Dark Desire*
Shea O'Halloran

JUSTICANO/BELANDRAKE

Diedre
Tienn
Vlad Belandrake
Josef
Eleanor
Benjamin
Byron Justicano — *Dark Symphony*
Antonietta Scarletti
The Scarletti Curse

THE CARPATHIAN FAMILIES

Key
= lifemates   Y cousins
⤙ twins   V parents not
ᶘ triplets   lifemates
⊤ offspring   ∿ offspring
  of lifemates   * monastery ancients
— siblings   ^ converted male

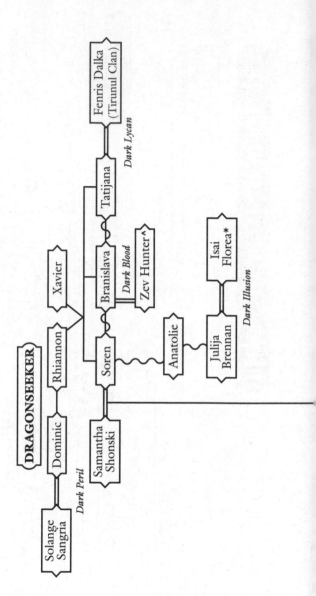

DRAGONSEEKER

Solange
Sangria

Dark Peril

Dominic

Rhiannon

Xavier

Branislava

Tatijana

Fenris Dalka
(Tirunul Clan)

Dark Lycan

Zev Hunter^

Dark Blood

Soren

Samantha
Shonski

Anatolie

Julija
Brennan

Isai
Florea*

Dark Illusion

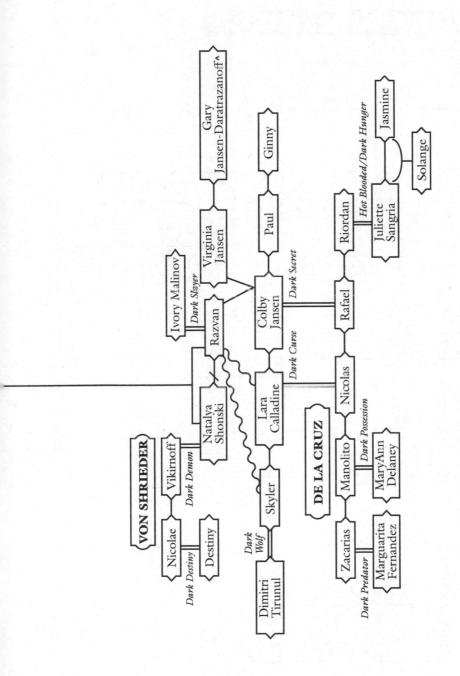

OTHER CARPATHIANS

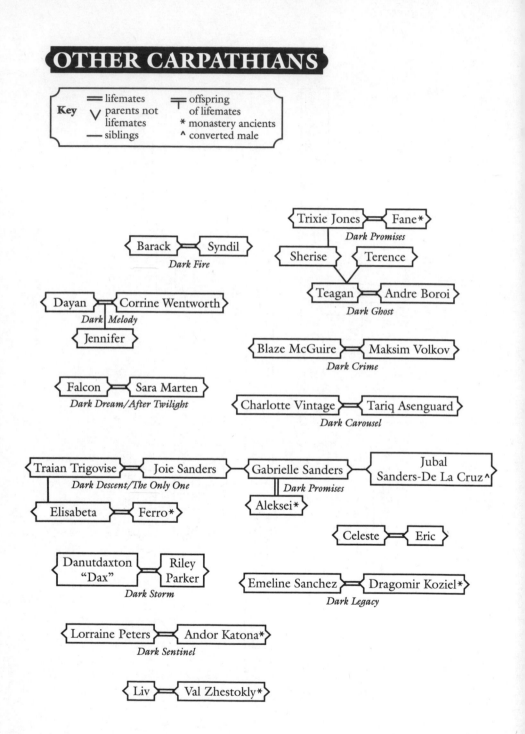

Key
= lifemates
∨ parents not lifemates
— siblings
⊤ offspring of lifemates
* monastery ancients
^ converted male

Trixie Jones = Fane*
Dark Promises

Sherise   Terence

Teagan = Andre Boroi
Dark Ghost

Barack = Syndil
Dark Fire

Dayan = Corrine Wentworth
Dark Melody
Jennifer

Blaze McGuire = Maksim Volkov
Dark Crime

Falcon = Sara Marten
Dark Dream/After Twilight

Charlotte Vintage = Tariq Asenguard
Dark Carousel

Traian Trigovise = Joie Sanders
Dark Descent/The Only One

Gabrielle Sanders

Jubal Sanders-De La Cruz^

Elisabeta = Ferro*

Aleksei*
Dark Promises

Celeste = Eric

Danutdaxton "Dax" = Riley Parker
Dark Storm

Emeline Sanchez = Dragomir Koziel*
Dark Legacy

Lorraine Peters = Andor Katona*
Dark Sentinel

Liv = Val Zhestokly*

DARK ILLUSION

I

Julija Brennan linked her fingers behind her head and gazed up at her unimpeded view of the stars. With the absence of light from cities and the lack of pollution from industry, the sky over the Sierra Mountains was absolutely clear, giving her an unparalleled view of the Milky Way that, despite all her travels, she hadn't seen before.

She barely noticed that she was shivering in the night air. It was cool in the Sierras at night, and with winter coming on, the temperatures promised snow in the next few days. She'd hoped her errand would have been completed before the first snowfall, but that didn't look as if it was going to happen. Any other time, finding herself under the night sky would have been just perfect.

She didn't mind being in a beautiful mountain range far from everyone else. She liked solitude. She even craved it. Unfortunately, she was in the race of a lifetime. She'd been out in front and now she'd stalled. She had no idea where to go or what to do to get back on track. The range was four hundred miles long and seventy miles wide. To find anything as small as a book in it with no idea of where it was located was impossible. Impossible, but it was a matter of life or death, although she hated drama and the last thing she wanted to do was be dramatic, even to herself. Still, it was a fact she couldn't avoid. She had to find the book before anyone else did and there were several looking.

Strange how such a small thing like a book could have the power to destroy lives. Corrupt them. Twist otherwise good people into monsters. Power corrupted. She stared up at the constellations, wishing she could ride on those stars, or slide down the comets instead of trying to find traces of a book no one should ever see or know existed. Riding stars and sliding on constellations might prove far easier than hunting in four hundred miles of wilderness for a mythical book.

She preferred the places in the world closest to the stars with the least amount of people around her. She loved these mountains. The Sierras. Who knew they would rival the Carpathian Mountains for her affection? She was a nomad with no home and she'd accepted that she was a castaway. A traitor. In her world, a criminal. It had taken some time to come to that place of acceptance. Places like this one had helped her get there.

Julija didn't believe she would ever have a home or family. Her one friendship had been formed solely out of desperation. She had seen what no one else could—Elisabeta. A woman held prisoner, beaten into submission, so afraid after lifetimes of captivity to be free. In all those years she'd been caged, no one had ever managed to see through the layers of illusion her ruthless captor had surrounded her with until Julija's sight had penetrated the shields to find her.

Julija had reached out to her in spite of Elisabeta's fears and tried to instill hope. There was no giving the woman anything but that one thought.

Sighing, she closed her eyes to block out the millions of flickering lights overhead. Sometimes, having gifts was more of a curse than a blessing. Finding a friend had been the blessing; leaving her to her fate once she was safe had been a curse. Elisabeta needed her desperately, but she had to complete her mission. She had to. She could only hope that Elisabeta would understand and forgive her.

Julija stared overhead, grateful for the clear night, although clear meant the temperature had dropped. She shivered a little and snuggled deeper into the sleeping bag. It would be nice to be able to regulate her body temperature in the way she knew Carpathians did. There were things she could almost do in the way the Carpathians could, but unfortunately, regulating temperature was not one of them.

Carpathians were a species of people, nearly immortal, who fed on the blood of others but could not kill while feeding or they would become vampire. They slept in the rejuvenating soil and could not be out during the day, but they had tremendous gifts, powers that allowed them to shift shape and become what they willed.

Elisabeta was fully Carpathian and she came from a very powerful bloodline, yet she had been taken at a young age, given up for dead and lived her life at the whim of her captor. That just proved to Julija that she had to be more careful than ever. If someone as strong as a Carpathian could be overcome, then so could she.

She didn't live in a cage in the way Elisabeta had, but in a sense, she was just as much a prisoner as her friend had been—and would probably always be. One couldn't take centuries of conditioning and throw it away because they were free. It didn't work that way. Julija had broken away from her family and friends because what they were planning—and doing—was wrong. She knew it was wrong in every way, but so did they. They just didn't care. Now she had no one and nowhere to go, just like Elisabeta. Freedom didn't always mean free.

A star shot across the sky and fell toward earth, glowing as it raced in a spectacular explosion of glory. The beauty of nature always took her breath, but no matter how stunning or amazing her surroundings, she was still alone with no one to share them with. No matter how right she was, morally or otherwise, she was still alone. Elisabeta, at least, had been left with strangers, but they would all look out for her. It wouldn't be the same as having someone she loved close, but there were people who cared.

Elisabeta had a brother she hadn't seen since she was a young woman and wouldn't recognize after all the years, but at least he would want to take care of her. Julija had two brothers, but they wanted to kill her. More, they would come after her. Most likely, they were already on her trail. They would kill her if they caught up with her—and they weren't alone.

She closed her eyes on the stunning sight overhead, trying to force herself to fall asleep. She loved the night and spent most of it awake as a rule. Until she'd found Elisabeta and eventually was surrounded by Carpathians.

She sighed and turned on her side restlessly. Clearly, word hadn't yet filtered down to those living in the United States that she was an enemy of the Carpathian people. She had desperately wanted to help Elisabeta through the coming months, when she would most need a friend. But she'd run across her while searching for the book, and although she'd been instrumental in freeing her, she couldn't stay. She knew sooner or later word would reach the Carpathians in the United States that she was an enemy. She didn't want to be taken prisoner herself—and the Carpathians were powerful—probably every bit as powerful as she was.

Julija touched the scar running along her throat. Her voice had been forever changed, but at least she had one. She knew, although thankfully no one else did, that her throat had been specifically targeted for a reason. Sergey, the man who had captured Elisabeta so long ago, was well aware of Julija's potential and he hoped to kill her or keep her from her destiny. Neither scenario sounded good to her. She was the mistress of her own fate. She made up her own mind and followed her own rules. She had done so ever since she'd made the decision to split from her family and warn the prince of the Carpathian people what was being planned behind his back.

She'd been too late. Things had already been set in motion by the time she realized the ultimate goal, and now here she was in the race of a lifetime. She accepted that she might not come out of it alive, but she refused to accept defeat. She couldn't lose. There was too much at stake, too many lives depended on her completing her task. Perhaps an entire species of people.

Overhead, the stars stared back at her. A long sweep of what looked like stardust left a comet-like trail through the brightest stars. It was wide and curved gracefully through the night, leaving behind brilliant white specks to mark its passing. Even the stardust had other particles close to it. Neighboring stars twinkled and danced as if talking to the long trail of dust.

"Way to feel sorry for yourself," she muttered aloud when she realized she was comparing her lonely life to the stars overhead. "Sheesh, girl, you've really lost it this time."

She should have gotten a pet. A dog. A big dog. But when the others came looking for her, what would she do with a pet then? Especially a big dog. It would get killed or be left behind to starve. Either way, it wasn't a good scenario for a dog.

The stardust trail seemed to move. It was subtle, just a shifting of the particles to make it seem as if the wide swath of dust began to change course. Her breath caught in her throat. She blinked several times to make certain she had the filmy constellation in focus. There was no question, the entire path of milky stars was subtly veering from one angle to another. The change was happening so slowly she wouldn't have noticed except that she'd been staring up at it nonstop for the last hour.

Nothing could actually change the course of the stars, so the movement *had* to be an illusion. And that meant someone was looking for her. She turned her head very slowly so as not to draw the eye of whoever was searching for her. It could have been anyone. Her family would come after her. The Carpathians would send someone. A shiver went through her. Just a few short days earlier she had been with them, ensuring Elisabeta had others surrounding her who would take care of her. Julija had simply walked away from them, torn throat and all. By now, their prince would have sent the message that she was an enemy and to stop her at any cost.

Her family or a Carpathian hunter? Did it matter which? Both would try to stop her, and she couldn't allow either one to interfere. She inched downward until she was completely covered up to her eyes. There was no fire to draw attention. Campers were everywhere on the John Muir Trail and in Yosemite, but she had known her quarry would never have gone near other people. He would have sought out the wildest places in the Sierras possible.

At first, she had been able to "feel" him. Sometimes she'd known his thoughts. He was Carpathian. An ancient hunter, Iulian Florea, who was the last of his family. He had been searching for his lifemate—that one woman who held the other half of his soul—but by the time he had discovered her, she was already dying of old age.

He'd held her for all of a few minutes and she'd never spoken, never restored his emotions or color, although holding her, he had felt grief. She had opened her eyes and looked up at him right before she passed. Something like peace had stolen into her. So fragile, her body worn with age, but her spirit indomitable, she had given him a half-smile and succumbed. Julija had cried even though the Carpathian could not.

The woman had never married and ended her life alone in a nursing home. Iulian held her a long time, pressing her body to his chest, her face over his heart, before lowering her body with exquisite gentleness to the bed. The workers were busy with their many patients and while they were looking the other way at his command, Iulian had taken the body and disappeared into the night. He'd brought her to a cavern high up in the Carpathian Mountains and buried her deep. He'd stood for a long while over her, and Julija had read in his mind that he'd planned to meet the dawn the next morning.

What had changed his mind? Why had he left the cave suddenly and gone to the home of his prince? What had possessed a Carpathian hunter, a man who had lived honorably for centuries, to suddenly turn on his entire species and put their very existence in jeopardy? He hadn't gone into the thrall when his lifemate died. It was impossible. She hadn't restored his emotions or color, not to mention the glimpses Julija had caught of his mind hadn't been filled with chaos. They had been filled with purpose.

She kept her eye on the constellation above her as she tried to puzzle out what her quarry was up to. She'd been on her way to warn the prince of the Carpathians, Mikhail Dubrinsky, that there was a conspiracy building against him and that she had found out almost too late. Things had already been set in motion and she'd had to adjust within minutes, make a decision and follow it through.

A book of demonic spells had been created by Xavier, the high mage. Every spell recorded in his deadly tome had been the blackest and darkest of what he'd wrought. Death. Destruction of species. Everything he had created over the years to destroy or command every other species. He had wanted complete power, and his spell book could give that to anyone knowing how to use it. She was one of those who could. Her father and two brothers would know how to use it as well.

Julija had abandoned her idea to warn the prince and tracked Iulian instead. That book could never see the light of day. The Carpathian people believed the book had been sealed with the blood of three species—Jaguar, mage and Carpathian—because that had been seen in a vision of Xavier actually sealing the book. She knew it was more than that. The blood sacrifice of a Lycan had been made with a different ceremonial knife. She didn't know for certain, but it stood to reason that Xavier had included the sacrifice of a human as well.

Xavier had grown extremely paranoid over the years he'd been alive. He'd wanted immortality and complete rule over every species living on earth. He'd thought himself superior to everyone, incapable of making mistakes, yet she knew that he had. She'd studied him carefully, brought up every recorded scene she could find from everyone who had memories of him—specifically, her father and two brothers. They had been privy to his work. She was female and expendable. They were not. Still, she'd studied the great mage through her family members. They believed it was harmless to share information with her.

Julija was a mistress of illusion. That was why she knew someone had built that sky to look as if it were the real deal. The constellation, with infinite slowness, was turning toward her location. She countered with her own illusion. She was no lone camper that would draw scrutiny. She was a dark series of low, rounded boulders sitting among so many other larger and smaller rocks. Up on the bluffs overlooking the valleys, beautiful rock formations were everywhere. It wouldn't raise the least suspicion to have a few more. She would have to create an illusion each time she stopped somewhere to rest.

Julija had followed Iulian from the Carpathian Mountains in Romania to the United States. He had traveled in a private jet. She didn't have that luxury. Her family was wealthy, but when she'd broken from them, she'd been cut off from the money as well. That didn't mean she was penniless, she had prepared, but it did mean she couldn't overspend on luxury items like private jets.

Iulian had gotten ahead of her and gotten into the Sierras before she had. She'd connected with Elisabeta and had allowed herself to be captured by those holding the woman prisoner in the hopes of breaking her free. That had taken precious time, and she'd been wounded. Still, she'd gotten on the trail again fairly quickly.

In spite of that she always seemed to be one step behind no matter how hard she tried to get in front of things. Twice she'd made a guess as to where her quarry was going, and both times she'd been wrong and had to backtrack. Fortunately, she could "feel" his presence and the draw was much like a magnet until—unexpectedly—that, too, had disappeared.

Did he know she was following and that she could catch glimpses into his mind? Had he deliberately tricked her? It was possible. She was strong and had endless power and talent, but she wasn't as adept as she'd like or needed to be. Not when it came to dealing with a Carpathian ancient. She was a direct descendant of Xavier, the high mage. Treacherous, greedy blood ran in her veins. She knew Xavier had committed far greater sins than anyone knew about, and she didn't want those sins to come to light, but if it meant being able to stop those in a race to find the book, then so be it. Let the world find out about Xavier and the unholy things he'd done.

She remained very still as she stared up at the clear night sky. The breeze ruffled the hair on top of her head. She made certain it looked as if a small plant had attached itself to the rock just in case that tiny movement brought attention to her. Studying the stars overhead, she tried to find one small thing about the near-perfect illusion that would allow her to identify the one producing it.

She actually admired the work. Both of her brothers were excellent at spells, but illusions, although seemingly easy to do, were actually difficult to use when dealing with anyone skilled in the art of spells. Illusions were simply images that could mislead those who saw them, a misperception of reality—of actual nature. The overhead deception was nearly flawless. If she hadn't been studying the stars, she would have missed it.

The fact was, Julija loved the night and in particular, the night sky. Her family knew that about her. If it was dark and clear, she was outside. She had a very good telescope up on the roof of their home to better study the stars. She could name every constellation. She was a walking encyclopedia of facts about the universe and everything in it. Her brothers would know that, and they would be careful in their choice of what instruments to use to find her.

They also knew she was a master of illusion. She knew there were better, but with the power running through her family's veins, there was a time when her brothers considered her the best within that family. That had changed over the years. Now, they believed she'd been beaten so far down she could barely do any magic anymore. Still, they wouldn't choose the stars unless they wanted her to know they were chasing her. It wasn't to their benefit for her to know. She would make it all the more difficult for them—which, of course, she was already doing.

She knew her brothers were somewhere down below in the valley, looking for her. Not because there had been evidence, but she'd "felt" them in the way she felt the Carpathian she hunted. That was a gift she'd been born with, just like so many others. That was how she knew Elisabeta was close even when she couldn't see her. Elisabeta's captor had put her in a small cage and made her part of the rock and dirt inside an underground chamber. She'd been hidden in plain sight. But Julija knew illusion and she also could "feel" other living creatures.

She could almost always tell just how far someone was from her and in what direction she needed to go to find them. It wasn't always the best thing, but she felt what they did. That was most likely the reason she couldn't go along with her siblings in their plan to follow in Xavier's footsteps and take over the domination of the world.

If her brothers weren't using the stars to find her, it had to be a Carpathian, a very skilled one. The thought made her heart pound faster. She knew what the prince would think once they discovered who she was. She'd been in the vicinity of the book right before it was taken. They might even blame her and think Iulian was chasing her, trying to get the book of black art spells. That would make more sense than the other way around. The prince would know his Carpathian hunter hadn't given in and become vampire.

A delicate little shudder went through her. She'd seen her fair share of vampires and she'd rather deal with a mage any day of the week. Elisabeta had been taken by an old family friend and then he'd deliberately turned vampire. She'd spent centuries in captivity, trained through violence and pain to do whatever she was told. She'd lived. She'd survived.

The Elisabeta from childhood was long gone. In her place was a woman terrified of life. Of living on her own. Of making a single decision. She hadn't dared for centuries and now, just the thought was terrifying and overwhelming. Julija knew she wouldn't be able to do it and would need help. She had intended to help her. Now, she wasn't certain when she could get back to her only friend.

Julija knew the Carpathians were hoping to heal Elisabeta by leaving her in the ground, as was their custom. The earth's properties, especially minerals, aided the species to heal faster, as well as rejuvenated them each day as they slept. The earth might heal Elisabeta's body, but not her heart, not her soul, nor could it help with the emotional toll those centuries had taken on her. She would be utterly lost.

Julija couldn't imagine that any of the omnipotent Carpathian hunters would have any understanding of how completely Sergey Malinov, the man who'd kidnapped her, had shaped her life. Elisabeta had been young and he'd shaped her into a woman who was totally submissive and had no idea how to be anything else. Julija knew the chances of her becoming anything different were slim to none—not with centuries of developing that character.

What was she doing here in the mountains on an impossible quest when the only friend she had in the world needed her desperately? She couldn't help herself. She was telepathic and very, very powerful. Elisabeta was hundreds of miles away and in the ground, but Julija reached out to her anyway, knowing Elisabeta was just as powerful.

Elisabeta. Can you hear me?

The Carpathians were all telepathic and used a common pathway to talk to one another. Julija was well aware of that pathway and wanted to avoid it at all costs. She and Elisabeta had created their own conduit of communication to keep their vampire captor from knowing that they were talking. At the time they'd been focused on Elisabeta escaping. She had been terrified to do so for many reasons.

Julija had only then realized the extent of the problems the other woman would be facing if she got away. She had been cared for since she was only seventeen and before that, her family had watched over her.

Elisabeta remembered that much about her childhood. She'd been so young, and she'd followed Sergey, a childhood friend of her family. He had built a wall in memory of his missing sister and she'd gone willingly to see it. Instead, she'd found herself taken prisoner by a madman.

Julija pushed more power into her query, sending it out toward the location she knew Elisabeta to be in. *Can you hear me? Are you awake? Out from under the ground yet?*

She waited, counting the most prominent stars overhead, wishing on them like a child. When had she been a child? She didn't even remember. Elisabeta was at times very childlike still and yet she'd gone through more than any being should ever have to.

Julija?

The voice was faint, not from the distance—Julija was providing the bridge and she was immensely powerful. She could manage the distance, and it helped that she knew exactly where her friend was. Elisabeta was uncertain. Frightened. Julija didn't like that.

Are you alone, my friend?

Yes. Elisabeta relayed that without hesitation. *Underground. I don't want to face the world yet. Not ready.*

I will come as soon as possible. This errand is taking longer than expected.

There was a small silence while Julija's heart pounded. She pressed her hand, beneath the cover of the sleeping bag, to her heart. She wanted to wrap her arms around Elisabeta. She was still that young girl, never given a chance to blossom and grow into the woman she should have been.

Are you safe?

Julija didn't know why that simple inquiry coming from Elisabeta brought tears to her eyes. Was she? She stared up at the constellation slowly shifting position in the sky. How did she answer that? *I'm not certain. Someone is hunting me. I told you about my brothers and what they wanted.*

The two women often had talked to each other when Sergey had thought they couldn't. Julija had told Elisabeta all about her brothers and what she'd discovered they'd been up to over the years and why. In turn Elisabeta had told her about her life with Sergey. Julija had known she never would have gotten any explanation out of the woman without giving up personal information. She was far too scared to talk to anyone without Sergey's express permission.

And yet you stay on your course. I've never met a woman like you. Julija couldn't help but hear the admiration in Elisabeta's voice.

There are many like me, and many in this world like you.

She knew her statement to Elisabeta was true when she thought of women in other countries without the chances she'd had to become what she wanted to be. Julija had studied at the best universities just because education appealed to her. Knowledge was power, her teachers had always said, and she agreed. They just hadn't agreed on what kind of knowledge gave one power.

The world has changed considerably while you were held captive.

He calls to me.

Julija's heart skipped a beat, then thudded wildly. *Sergey calls to you?*

Yes. I'm afraid I will go to him if I go aboveground. I don't know what to do. I don't know how to be anything but what he wanted from me.

Elisabeta's voice dripped with tears, although Julija knew she wasn't shedding any. That wasn't Elisabeta's way. Tears had been beaten out of her, along with any fight.

You know you can't go back to him. You detest him.

More than anything. With every breath I draw. I just don't know how to live without him. Until I can figure that out, I am staying right where I am. He gave me everything, Julija. I did what he said and in return he would supply me with the blood I needed to live. He especially liked to take my blood, so he would bring me blood from others.

There was a moment of silence. Julija could feel Elisabeta gathering her thoughts, and those thoughts were distasteful to her.

I suspected he murdered those he used for blood. This time the sorrow was not only heard but felt.

Julija hesitated, searching for the right words. *You know you couldn't do anything to stop him, Elisabeta. You still can't. Please don't throw your freedom away. I know it's terrifying, but give yourself time. The Carpathians there can't wait to help you. And you have a brother.*

Everyone tells me that. I don't remember much of my childhood, just bits and pieces, and I'm uncertain if they're real or if Sergey planted those pieces in my head. This time there was reluctance. *If my brother comes, he will expect things from me I can't give him. I feel so afraid and alone. At least I was protected from everyone by Sergey.*

Julija closed her eyes, her distress level rising. She'd hoped Elisabeta was in safe hands, but her friend was hiding from everyone. That made Julija feel all the worse that she wasn't there to shield her and help ease her into some kind of a life. But what? What was there for someone like Elisabeta? The modern world would never understand her. They would expect her to go to counseling and be "cured." That was never going to happen. Centuries of abuse couldn't be swept away. Hundreds of years of submission couldn't suddenly turn her into a fiery, independent woman. Julija knew that and feared for her.

Small steps, Elisabeta. Remember? We talked about this. You can't expect to be on your own right away, if ever. You have to depend on those people who reach out to you, the ones that feel right to you.

There was silence. Rejection. *You didn't.*

Julija cursed the fact that she'd ever told so much about her life to Elisabeta. *I don't know how to make friends easily. I didn't have anyone to rely on.*

She was a direct descendant of the high mage and her parents had never allowed her to forget it. They hadn't wanted her befriending anyone else, mage or otherwise. She'd studied every spell, practiced casting and creating illusions and whatever else her stepmother had insisted on her doing. There hadn't been time to learn how to be friends, or to have a childhood one could look back on and laugh about. Her brothers had often viewed her as a rival, but treated her as a pathetic mage and more of a food source than anything else.

You're afraid of your brothers.

My parents as well. Don't forget them. They were all involved in what my brothers were doing. Breeding cats to make them shadow creatures. It was inhumane and wrong. The cats suffer. They need blood to survive just as you do, but unless they cooperate, they aren't fed.

That's exactly the way Sergey treated me. Some nights I went until I was too weak to see. He would get so angry, he would beat me with a cane or a whip. Then I wouldn't be able to stand. He would come to me, treating me so gently I would be confused. So confused. Not understanding it was the same man.

My brothers did the same with the cats, conditioning them to return to them always after their orders were carried out.

Why are people so cruel?

I don't know, Elisabeta. Money. Power. Just because they can be.

He said I would never survive without a master. He said he made certain of that and then he would laugh so cruelly. He's right, though. I will never be able to survive alone.

No one has to be your master. He's wrong about that. I'll help you as soon as I can return. It shouldn't be much longer.

They are pushing me to rise. There was a little sob in Elisabeta's mind, but not in her voice. *I can hold out against them. I did learn to use silence and to be stubborn when I didn't want to do something. I don't believe they will beat me.*

No, they won't beat you. Why do I get the feeling you are not telling me everything?

There is always more to tell. You haven't told me everything. What is this quest?

Julija tapped her chin with the pad of her index finger. Would Elisabeta worry too much about her if she didn't explain? Probably. Elisabeta had been shaped into a pleaser. She nurtured others—even those who were evil. Sergey had taken all the sweet compassion Elisabeta had for others and amplified and twisted those traits into what he wanted from her. It was possible Elisabeta had always had a submissive nature, but her self-esteem would have been high and her ability to read others and trust them would have developed as she grew older as well.

Elisabeta didn't hurry her decision or try to persuade her one way or the other. Like Julija she was just happy to have a real friend, someone to talk with and bounce ideas off of.

Do you remember hearing the name Xavier? He was the high mage and offered classes for Carpathians to learn spells for safeguards.

Yes, of course.

Xavier was secretly conspiring to bring down the Carpathian people, along with every other species of power. He's pretty much succeeded with the Jaguar race. He turned the men against the women and they have all but died out. The werewolves remain strong, but a war was barely averted between Carpathians and werewolves. That alliance is still shaky at best. Mages are regarded with suspicion by all species.

Elisabeta gave a small gasp. *As if the vampires weren't enough.*

The vampires, under the Malinov brothers, have been forming armies, as you well know. Sergey has slivers of Xavier in him. At least two, perhaps three. He has a sliver of his brother in him as well.

I know this, but how do you?

The same way as you do, Elisabeta. I can feel even the vampires. When Sergey got close to me, even to kill me, I felt Xavier in him. Xavier's presence is very distinctive and I'm a direct descendant.

How?

Xavier kidnapped Rhiannon.

She disappeared. No one could find her. I thought, after Sergey had taken me, that perhaps one of his brothers had her. It was years after for me, but maybe she was still alive, and we'd find each other. I didn't want to be alone. The last was said shamefully.

That is a very natural feeling. Especially given that Elisabeta was still a young girl. In Carpathian years, she was very young. Again, Julija wanted to wrap her arms around the woman and comfort her. Had anyone ever done that for her? *It was Xavier who had taken Rhiannon. He wanted to be immortal. He was able through spells to keep her from calling out for aid, or to help herself. He had three children with her. Triplets. Soren, Tatijana and Branislava.*

Elisabeta sighed. *Poor Rhiannon. I had no idea Xavier was such a monster.*

He kept the children and killed Rhiannon, feeling safer without her conspiring to find a way to kill him. He seemed to have tried to raise them somewhat as his children, but Rhiannon had already told them the truth. He imprisoned the two girls in an ice cave after they had shifted into dragons. At first, he did the same with Soren, but he wanted to use him, so he punished the two girls if their brother went against him. Soren quickly fell into line.

Elisabeta gave a delicate shudder. *Watching someone you love get punished for your sins is very difficult. I was fortunate in that for a long time, Sergey didn't allow anyone else near me. When he finally did, I found it was a nightmare. He liked the results because I could take his beatings for myself but detested when he hurt others.*

Julija knew Sergey had employed that method often with Elisabeta, making her watch him destroy entire families and claiming it was her fault. The human puppets he created ate the flesh from living beings, mostly children. Elisabeta would do anything Sergey asked of her as long as he stopped them.

Xavier kept Soren separated from his sisters unless he needed to punish him. He allowed him to be with a mage, one of Xavier's choice. She gave birth to a son, and they were told the baby died at birth. The infant was given to another mage to raise away from Soren and the birth mother was killed by Xavier in front of Soren because she had "failed" them. A few years later Soren married a human, I think her name was Samantha, another experiment, and Sergey didn't want any children to be more powerful than Soren's firstborn. They had twins, Razvan and Natalya.

Elisabeta gasped. *Xavier is every bit as bad as Sergey.*

I think they are close in their depravity. Soren's firstborn son, Anatolie, was raised to be a powerful mage, one that would aid Xavier in wiping out their enemies. Anatolie married a mage woman of Xavier's approval. It wasn't a love match because I don't think either knows how to actually love. They had twins, boys. The boys were to be their greatest asset, including giving blood to keep Xavier alive.

Mages have longevity, Elisabeta remembered. *But they aren't immortal.*

Technically, neither are Carpathians because they can be killed. Still, to accomplish what they wanted, Xavier had to live, to be immortal. The twin boys were far more mage than Carpathian and their blood didn't sustain the others. The three mages conspired to find a Carpathian female. They set the Malinov brothers on a Carpathian family, killing the male first and then the female. They took the girl. She was no more than sixteen. She gave birth to me. I'm mage and Carpathian. I fed them all with my blood. Apparently, my blood did sustain them.

Julija. Elisabeta breathed her name. She had given blood to Sergey nearly every day of her life since she was seventeen. She knew what it felt like to be used cruelly.

Julija stared up at the constellation. It was directly over her now and she felt as if a thousand eyes watched her. She stayed very still, part of the landscape. She was high up in the Sierras in a particularly rocky area. Large cliffs rose above her and more were below. Her "rocks" were just a few of many. She was usually very confident in her illusions but for some reason, maybe the conversation, she was a little anxious.

Xavier had this book of spells. He had recorded every dark spell possible. It was truly evil and held the means to destroy every species. The book was sealed until Xavier could get in place the powerful mages he needed to aid him. Soren stole the book and hid it in a bog. Xavier sent his demon warriors after him and tortured him to find out where it was. Soren's daughter, Natalya, saw the entire thing in a vision and was able to find the book. In her vision from holding the ceremonial knife, she saw Xavier sacrifice a dark mage, a Jaguar and a Carpathian. The Carpathian was Rhiannon. Natalya thought that provided the entire seal. From things I've overheard, I believe she didn't see anything more because she didn't have access to all of Xavier's prized ceremonial knives.

Elisabeta was silent a moment, trying to comprehend everything Julija was telling her. *Natalya got to the book before Xavier.*

That is correct. The book was given to the prince of the Carpathians.

And destroyed.

Unfortunately, no. It couldn't be opened, which is a good thing, and it can't be destroyed so easily. But the Carpathians thought it safe with Mikhail.

Elisabeta might not want to strike out on her own, but she was intelligent. She put it all together very fast. *The shadow cats your brothers bred. They were bred specifically to get the book.*

Exactly. My brothers took the cats to various countries to train them, so no one would put together what they were planning. They had other mages and humans set up just in case they were caught and in a couple of countries, that did happen, but my brothers were able to get away without ever being seen or suspected. When they were able to get the perfect cat, they sent him to get the book.

Something went wrong.

That guess was easy enough. Julija had told Elisabeta that she was on an important quest, one that was necessary, and now she was saying she wouldn't make it back at the three-week mark.

A Carpathian warrior, one who had just lost his lifemate. Julija's heart contracted remembering how she'd felt the warrior taking the woman into his arms and holding her. How he'd brushed her eyelids and mouth with kisses so gentle they were soul stirring.

His name is Iulian Florea. His intention was to meet the dawn and then all of a sudden, he changed his mind. I had the impression of the book. For a moment I thought he was going to try to bring his lifemate back to life. I didn't want him to try. I knew, even if he could do it, anything coming from that book would be pure evil.

He took the book?

He wounded the shadow cat and took the book. I followed him here. I could feel his presence, that's how I tracked him, but now I can't.

She was suddenly very uneasy. The constellation remained right over her as if somehow spotlighting her. She had the urge to throw back the sleeping bag and run. The need to flee was so strong she found herself gripping the edges of the bag. The compulsion strengthened. She forced herself to breathe through it.

She couldn't tell Elisabeta that she'd been discovered. She didn't know who it was that had found her, but it didn't really matter. Iulian, her brothers and any of their many allies, vampires and their puppets, or Carpathian hunters. They knew she was in the race to find the book. Even if she got there first, none of them would ever let up until they got her. The sensible thing to do was to join Elisabeta and help her. If the Carpathians already had gotten word she was mage and a traitor, she would look innocent helping one of their own.

Julija couldn't abandon her mission. She wanted to, but it was impossible. She couldn't allow her brothers to get their hands on that book. Not now, not ever.

2

Isai Florea stared up at the stars from where he sat on a boulder looking up at the clear night sky. It was beautiful. Without the lights from the city of San Diego, one could get lost in the beauty of the overhead display. After having been locked away from the world for so long, being thrown back into a society he didn't understand—nor would they understand him—so many people and so many homes crammed together gave him a sense of not belonging.

He was given the unexpected duty of hunting for his own brother. He hadn't realized Iulian was alive. He'd searched for him for centuries, long before he'd sequestered himself in the monastery, high in the Carpathian Mountains. He'd been certain Iulian was long gone from the earth just as everyone he'd ever cared about was.

He was grateful he didn't have emotions, not when he was chasing after his only living relative. Not after finding out his brother had stolen something so incredibly evil as Xavier's deadly spell book.

What would be the purpose? Had Iulian figured out how to open it? It didn't matter one way or the other, he'd stolen something of great importance from the prince of their people. That was all Isai needed to know to begin tracking him. More, the little mage everyone had talked about, Elisabeta's friend, wasn't all she'd seemed. She was either hunting Iulian to take the book from him or had aided him in stealing it.

Isai kept his concentration mainly focused on the constellation in the sky. That long sweep of stardust spread through the bright stars. He had re-created it to perfection, every detail, every particle. In doing so, he could see the land below it, miles of wilderness set in valleys and high peaks. He identified campers, not ones on the main trails, but those venturing outside the normal trails within the range.

He was new to the Sierras, but he had studied the topography and devoured everything he could read or hear about the range. That also helped him to find the places he was certain his brother would go. The mage—she was different. He knew very little about her. He'd attempted to speak to Elisabeta, but she remained in the healing grounds, refusing to acknowledge anyone. Isai shrugged. Had he gone through what she'd been put through, he wouldn't want to talk to anyone, either. Nor would he ever aid someone hunting a friend.

He felt it then. A sudden shift of energy. Subtle. So subtle he thought he might be mistaken, but when he stayed very still and allowed all his senses to expand, he felt it again. A steady flow. It wasn't some natural phenomenon the range of mountains had produced. This was created by some*one*, not something. The energy was coming from somewhere and the wielder held great power. The flow of energy never wavered, not for one moment.

Isai couldn't help but admire the efficiency. He focused completely on the energy to trace it back to the caster. Feminine. The flow held a light hand. Delicate almost. He found himself wanting to bathe in that flow of energy. In the sheer beauty of the work. It was unusual for him to react to anything, not like this. It was as if he was drawn to the flow, a compulsion to put first his hands and then his arms in, close his eyes and let the energy consume him. Move into him. Through him. Submerge him completely.

Abruptly he pulled back. The mage then. She held power if she could get an ancient who was part of the brethren from the monastery to fall under her spell, especially from a distance. There were few that could best him. He wasn't arrogant in thinking that, it was simply a fact. Perhaps she was with Iulian. The moment the thought occurred, his heart did a strange stuttering and he immediately found he needed to physically find the flow of energy again and reach for it with his hands.

He took to the sky. One leap and he was shifting, becoming part of the night sky, moving slowly across the atmosphere as part of the constellation he had created. Following the energy was easy enough, and without his physical body he could give in to the compulsion to become part of that very vivid flow.

Looking down, he saw cliffs, great mountains rising, bare of most vegetation, the rocks pushing upward to create beautiful formations. One kept drawing his attention back. He could almost see the shimmer of power emanating from what appeared to be three smaller rocks atop a bare slab.

His heart did that strange stuttering he'd experienced just moments earlier. He'd found her. He examined the slab of rock carefully. There was no evidence of Iulian. The night was still young enough that if his brother was traveling with the mage, he would be close. Perhaps he'd gone off to find a camper, so he could take their blood.

Making up his mind, Isai simply dropped out of the sky, right through the illusion the mage had woven for her safety, and straddled the sleeping bag, trapping her inside. Her eyelids flew open and he found himself staring into wildly furious dark chocolate eyes.

"You are?"

She clamped her lips together tightly and glared at him. She had expressive eyes, so he got it. She wasn't happy with him sitting on her. He had muscle and no fat. She was very petite. Even beneath the sleeping bag he could tell she was small boned, so he could crush her. That didn't stop him from sitting there.

"I can sit here all night. In fact, if I get tired, I'll just lie down on top of you. You're in a great deal of trouble, just in case you thought you'd play innocent."

He made certain to keep her hands trapped. Mages had a way with spells. He knew most and could counter them. When he had come out of the monastery to reenter the world, learning new spells had been the first thing he made a point of doing. Mage spells. He had always been adept, and he knew advances had to have been made while he was locked away. He had studied everything the other Carpathians knew.

She glared at him, her long lashes sweeping down and then back up to allow him to see her fury wasn't abating.

He couldn't help himself. She looked . . . delicious. That was a first for him. He had no real emotions, no real feelings and that included sexual. None. Yet straddling her, he felt a stirring in his body. He went hot. He controlled temperature easily and instantly regulated it. That did nothing to stop the rush of heat through his veins. Flames, a fire racing through his bloodstream to pool in his groin. An ache that fast became an urgent demand and then a real pain.

Isai stared down at the furious little face. Her skin was very soft. Her face oval. Cheekbones high. Her mouth was generous, lips full. Teeth very white. Eyes that dark chocolate color. *Color.* He turned his head away from her to stare out over the cliff into the mist, his breath catching in his throat. It couldn't be. This mage. This treacherous woman? Nothing could restore color or emotion to him but his true lifemate—a woman who held the other half of his soul.

He had been born centuries earlier. Far, far before this time. At birth, his soul had been split in two, giving him all the darkness, giving his other half all the light. He had lost all emotion and color after two hundred years and had begun the search for the one holding the other half of his soul. Endless centuries of . . . nothing. A gray, desolate world of violence. Time passed and more . . . nothing.

He was feeling emotion now, and the first of it, rather than wonder, was anger. A slow, smoldering rage that boiled in his gut when he looked at the stubborn woman. There was no telling her actual age. Mages had longevity and aged extremely slowly. Undoubtedly, she was born in the wrong century. More than one wrong century. She was mage, a mortal enemy of his people. Already she had proven her treacherous nature.

More, she kept her lips pressed together, denying him when she so obviously knew he was her other half.

He leaned down very close, taking in the delicate scent of her. She smelled like peaches and cream. Like heaven. Strands of her hair caught in the dark stubble on his face and his stomach did a slow roll at the feeling of silk against his skin.

His lips brushed her little shell of an ear as he admonished her. "I am your lifemate. Your lord. You belong to me. It does not matter in the least that you fight me on this. You will learn obedience, and you will learn treachery is a very dangerous game to play." He punctuated each word with his tongue, touching her skin, claiming every spot he licked.

He didn't want her answer. He only wanted one thing and he took it. With no warning, he sank his teeth into her neck. She cried out, the sound like music, shattering the silence of the night. Bright colors struck at him, glowing and shimmering behind his eyes. Her blood filled his mouth, delicate and pure, a ruby drink designed for his taste alone. It was perfection. Exquisite. The tang beyond anything he'd ever experienced.

He knew he was changed for all time. Addiction took hold. He would always need this. Waking. Sleeping. Every moment he thought of her. Her taste would be in his mouth, on his tongue. His muscles, organs and bones would cry out for her blood. She had been created just for him and he was nearly drunk—no, euphoric—at the idea of a lifemate. Especially one who would give him trouble at every turn. He would enjoy being with her nearly as much as he would enjoy taking her blood.

It took effort to connect back with reality and realize she was struggling, trying to push him away from her. *You will obey.* He pushed the command deep into her mind. There was a shield there. A very effective one. Her psychic shield was strong, but it hadn't been formed with a lifemate in mind. Nor had she been prepared for a Carpathian warrior as old and as skilled as he was.

Fuck you and the bird you flew in on.

There was pure defiance as well as a hidden note of fear. Good. She would need both to survive and he was going to make certain she did.

That is unacceptable language for my woman to use, especially on me.

In one smooth move, he rolled her over forcing her facedown on the hard rock, trapping her arms beneath her. One silent command and he had stripped the bag from her body, leaving her in her jeans and tee. He brought his hand down hard on her bottom. Over and over. He wasn't gentle about it.

"You are getting off lucky in spite of your cries and pleas. You helped steal from the prince of the Carpathian people. That isn't even your worst crime." He put a little more power into his smacks on her rounded bottom. "You deliberately tried to deny me, your lifemate, what is *mine*. You *belong* to me. I've lived a life of honor. I've risked my life to save every species over and over, century after century. You knew, just looking at me, and yet you childishly and stubbornly refused to open your mouth and give me back emotions and colors."

She sobbed softly, no longer struggling or trying to get him off her back. She lay beneath him, accepting his punishment, her small body shuddering. Abruptly he rolled her over again and pulled her into his arms, looking down at her tear-streaked face.

You will take my blood now. He pushed firmly past her strong shield to force her obedience.

She tilted her head up, her hands going to his shirt. It was already open in preparation and she swept the two edges apart as she pressed her mouth to his chest, right over his heart. Her lashes were wet. Her incredible skin was splotchy red from crying. She hiccupped twice, as if she couldn't quite stop crying, but struggled to do so. He thought she was beautiful. Treacherous, but beautiful.

She turned her face to his chest, nuzzled there. He felt the slow lick of her tongue like a flame against the heavy muscle of his chest. His entire body shuddered with need. Craving coursed through him, hot, almost completely feral, a sexual hunger he'd never experienced before. Heart pounding, he brought up one finger to open his chest, to give her a way to take his blood, but before he could, she bit down, her teeth unerringly finding the vein.

He threw his head back at the pleasure/pain that instantly roared through his body with the force of a freight train. Every cell in his body, every nerve ending focused completely on his woman. For such a little thing, she wreaked havoc with his mind, body and soul. So easily.

Her hands stroked up his chest. She shifted in his lap, turning more fully toward him, drinking his blood, making her own demands. Her own claims. He hadn't ordered her to do more than take his blood for an exchange, but she was definitely going beyond that.

One hand teased at his flat nipples, sending a searing flame through his bloodstream, igniting some explosive chemistry between them. Her other hand slid down his belly to fumble at the waistband of his trousers. He obliged her, waving clothes away from both of them. His breath caught in his throat. Her body was beautiful. She might be petite, but she was a woman and her body proclaimed her as such.

She had taken enough for a true blood exchange. *Enough.*

It will never be enough.

Obey me in this. He pushed more command into his voice, but he didn't physically stop her. He wanted to see what she would do.

She pulled back, licked at the ruby drops running from the twin holes in his chest her teeth had made and then she began pressing little kisses down his chest to his belly button. One hand pushed at him to insist he lie back. He didn't. He leaned for her, but he wasn't putting himself in a vulnerable position. He might want her with every breath he drew, but he didn't trust her.

She stretched out, lapping at his stomach and then his groin, licking the broad, flared head of his cock until he thought he might lose his mind. Still, he let her. How could he possibly stop her when every lash of her tongue felt like a whip of lightning wrapping around his desperate, aching cock?

He ran his hand down her back to her sore buttocks. His handprint didn't show on her skin, but the marks of his punishment did. He rubbed, hoping to take away the sting, but the heavy brush of his palm, the kneading of his fingers, seemed to inflame her more. Her mouth engulfed him.

He threw back his head and let the feeling take him. Euphoria. Nirvana. Her mouth was a tight, hot, wet fist, attempting to suck him dry. He gathered the thick swath of hair away from her face, so he could watch her devour him. Her lips were stretched wide and it was the sexiest sight he'd ever seen—and he'd watched many such performances, many supposedly more erotic, but not to him. He could get off just looking at the sight of her with her lips stretched so wide and his cock in her mouth. Streaks of fire raced through his bloodstream. He wanted to do some exploring of his own.

I want you to stand over me.

I'm busy. You taste so good. I wondered if your cock would taste as good as your blood and it does. It's amazing.

He liked that, but she still didn't understand that when he told her to do something, she had to do it. Not that he could think straight with her mouth sucking the life out of him. One hand played with his balls, stroking the heavy sac, cupping and gently squeezing while her tongue danced and lashed, and then her mouth tightened and she tried to swallow him down.

He felt his seed, hot and wild, raging, scorching, as his balls drew up, tightened almost to the point of pain. His cock swelled. Thickened. Jerked once in warning. Then he was feeding her everything he had. So much. Blasting into her mouth, down her throat. Filling her. All the while he watched her through hooded eyes, his fist in her hair, holding her over him while she swallowed his very essence.

He lifted her head off his cock, the feel of her lips sliding over the sensitive organ nearly setting him off again. It was enough to set his cock on fire. He held her head right there. Waiting. She took the hint and licked up and down his shaft, teasing at the base with the tip of her tongue and then sliding it around the crown. He thought he might lose his mind. She took every last remaining drop from him before turning her head to look at him.

"Stand up. Put your hands on my shoulders." He made it a firm command because she didn't seem to listen very well.

The mage got to her feet in one very graceful move worthy of any of the dancers pleasing the husbands and husbands' friends he'd watched in past centuries. He could imagine her with bells around her ankles and waist and hanging on a chain between her breasts. She would have been a husband's most prized possession. He knew she was already his.

Very slowly, almost as if she was a little afraid, she rested her hands on his shoulders. He slid his hands to the inside of her thighs and urged her closer until she was standing over him, straddling him, her legs wide. He felt her shiver and knew it wasn't from the cold, crisp air. She had bathed in the river and he smelled the snowpack on her. The scent was fresh and mingled with her natural fragrance of peaches and cream, producing a potent aphrodisiac for him.

Very gently he slid his hand up her left leg. Shaping her calf. Caressing behind her knees with the pads of his fingers. His tongue stroked little caresses over her right leg following his hand movements on the left. No matter how hard her fingers dug into his shoulders, and at one point she grabbed a fistful of hair and nearly shook his head off, he kept his movements slow.

He blew warm air between her legs while she squirmed and made delicious little sounds that threatened to drive him mad. His palm caressed her left thigh and he did the same with his tongue on her right. Feeling her skin. Tasting her. She was more than exquisite. He didn't deviate or go faster. He wasn't about to shortchange her—or either of them. He wanted this slow, burning exploration as much as she did. Maybe more.

In the centuries gone past, he'd had time to study every aspect of what a man and woman could do together to pleasure each other. Like his brethren, he wanted to be the best possible lover for his lifemate. He'd studied the erotic arts with the same diligence to detail that he'd studied spells, languages and new technology.

Her fingers found the tattoos flowing over his shoulders and down his back. The tattoos had been made the old way, scarring the skin, but making his vows a part of his body, so that he would never forget. Never dishonor his lifemate or himself. She traced the letters, written in his ancient language to her. To his woman.

He kissed his way up her inner left thigh and then kissed his way down on the right. Her breath hissed out. Her skin was cool to the touch but warming, growing hot under his mouth and fingers.

When he finally reached her hot little spot, she was nearly crying, trying desperately to push her body onto his mouth, seeking relief. He worked her clit gently at first, lapping and flicking with his tongue. She tasted like a combination of peaches and cream, just like she smelled. He used a flattened tongue to stroke and slap, bringing all the nerve endings to life.

Only when she was pleading did he add one finger, sliding it back and forth, collecting the liquid there and then pushing deep. She was tight. Tighter than he had thought possible. Her breath caught audibly when he invaded but she pushed back, impaling herself, seeking more.

"I'm so close. You have to keep going. Don't stop."

He took his finger and mouth away, running his face up the inside of her thigh, using the bristles on his jaw to stimulate her further. All the while colors burst behind his eyes, nearly blinding him. It was disorienting, and he wanted to tell her to stop talking. At the same time, he welcomed the disturbing sensations pouring over him. The colors confirmed she was his lifemate. Traitor or no, she was his.

"What are you doing?" she wailed.

"Starting over." He kept his voice complacent. She would eventually learn what he was all about. She was a little spitfire, but he was in charge whether she liked it or not.

He repeated everything he'd done before, one slow step at a time. His hands were gentle, but his tongue was wicked, drawing circles, lapping at her. He suckled, gently and then strongly. He varied what he did and then added his fingers again. This time he flicked and tapped her clit, until he drove her so close to the edge she was pleading with him. Bargaining. He pushed a finger into her, once more stretching her.

"That burns," she hissed. "But in a good way. Please don't stop."

He added a second finger to help prepare her for him, all the while using his tongue to keep the pleasure to the forefront. Stretching her to accommodate his size was necessary, but if he could keep from hurting her, he would.

He felt the change in her body. The coiling tension. She was so close. He lifted his head, pulling back from her.

"What are you doing? Don't stop. You can't stop."

He used his fingers to flick her clit and rub across her entrance and then lick his fingers. She tasted good, so good her taste was addictive.

"I need more. I need you in me." Her ragged breathing made her demand more of a plea. She looked up at him a little desperately.

"Now you're willing to talk to me." Colors were everywhere. Blinding him all over again. They had come to him slowly at first when she'd been so stubborn, but now, with her little cries and frantic entreaties, he could see every shade of color. He rubbed over her bottom, stroked caresses on her inner thigh. She squirmed in response.

"If you're really my lifemate, you won't just leave me wanting you like this." There was a hitch in her breathing now.

He pressed his finger deep. Curled it into her and stroked while his thumb manipulated her hard little clit. "What's your name?"

She swallowed but didn't pull away. She began riding his fingers, her hands once more on his shoulders. "Julija, Julija Brennan."

"A mage." He stretched her a little more, pressing his second finger deep again, just to make sure. He was *not* going to hurt her.

She threw her head back, closing her eyes, pleasure spilling over her beautiful features. She ground down, working his fingers as if they were a cock. He removed them. The minute she opened her eyes he licked at his fingers and then stuck them in his mouth.

"You do taste good, lifemate. I'm Isai."

"Isai!" She wailed his name.

"Get on your hands and knees." He waved his hand to provide a thick rug for her. He didn't want to damage her knees when he was supposed to give her pleasure.

Julija didn't hesitate. She dropped obediently to the rug. Isai immediately knelt behind her. He massaged her bottom, although he had the urge to spank her again, this time with much more care and not painfully. He didn't. He couldn't. He caught his cock at the base and slid the head across her slick entrance. The sensations on the sensitive head sent shudders of pleasure through him.

"Hurry." She turned her head to look at him. "Please."

He wanted to prolong the anticipation, drive her higher up to ensure she was ready for him. He didn't want her hurt, but his size was going to stretch her limits, and he couldn't stop himself. He needed to be in her as much as she wanted him there.

He invaded slowly, pushing steadily through the scorching-hot petals that gripped him with a thousand fingers. He threw his head back, staring up at the stars, feeling as if, for the first time in his life, everything that had ever come before was worth it. This indescribable feeling Julija's body was giving him was worth every sacrifice he had made.

She chanted softly, over and over, his name, as if by saying it, she could force her body to accommodate his more easily. Her body opened for his reluctantly, but he had to push through that scorching-hot channel every inch of the way. Her breathing turned ragged and he paused instantly.

"No!" She wailed the word. "Don't stop. You can't stop."

He had no intentions of stopping. That wasn't going to happen. He was just being careful with her. His woman was going to experience nothing but pleasure. He caught her hips to still her as she pushed back, trying to take all of him.

"We have to be careful, *kislány hän ku meke sarnaakmet*. We don't want you to get sore." It was extremely difficult to hold back. He had to breathe deeply.

"Sometimes sore is delicious."

Even her ragged panting got to him. He began to move again, pushing steadily inch by inch until he was fully encased in her. Surrounded by her. He could feel her heart beat right through his cock. He took a breath and inhaled her along with the night. He took in the beauty of her, on her hands and knees, head down as she pushed back into him, her breath coming in sobbing gasps. She was spectacular. Stunning. Having a lifemate was worth every single second of those terrible long, endless centuries.

He began to move. Slowly at first, building the burn between them. Moving with deep emotion rather than the lust that stood at the edges of his mind, threatening to overtake him. He felt that dark desire rising in her and his own needs and hunger rose in direct correlation to hers.

He wanted to savor every moment inside her, surrounded by her tight, scorching-hot channel, but she was making unbelievably erotic sounds. Her body kept clamping down on his, increasing the friction that threatened to wipe every sane thought from his head.

Isai held out for a long, beautiful ride beneath the stars, moving in and out of her, increasing his speed until both were right on the verge and then backing off. Again and again until both of them were frantic. He stroked her sides and back, savoring the feeling of her soft skin and female shape, even as he surged forward, knowing the sensations were going to take him. Her body clamped down on his like a vicious vise, strangling his cock, milking his shaft, drawing every last drop so that his seed blasted out of him, coating her walls, producing what seemed like one long, continuous orgasm in her.

Julija collapsed forward on her elbows and then all the way to her chest. Isai held her hips so he could stay inside her, feeling every last sensation, every ripple and quake of her body around his. Her body moved around his, contracting, and then almost strangling his cock. Her channel bit down viciously, sending shocking waves of pleasure/pain swamping his body and taking over his mind. He let himself savor every lasting moment until the euphoria had faded, leaving him with the reality of a wild lifemate.

Very slowly he lowered her hips to the rug and allowed his body to pull out of hers. As he did so, he cleansed both of them. She immediately rolled over to look at him. He couldn't help but admire her feminine form.

"I am grateful you belong to me, Julija." He gave her a compliment, feeling her sudden wariness where before, like him, she'd been riding high on the feelings created by their bodies.

"Women aren't owned." She glared at him, one hand sweeping through her hair in an exasperated show of pure defiance. She sprang to her feet as if she might attempt to flee.

"I didn't say I owned you. I said you belonged to me." He stated it quietly but enunciated each word. "There is a difference." He gestured for her to sit back down.

"If there is, it eludes me completely," she said. She sank down onto the rug he'd provided and pulled her sleeping bag around her like a blanket—or a shield.

Isai scowled at her. "Are you cold?"

"Yes. In case you haven't noticed, I'm naked and the temperature has dropped significantly." There was sarcasm in her voice.

"It isn't necessary to use that tone with me when I'm asking after your comfort. I have not had to look after a human in hundreds of years. In truth, I've rarely talked to one. Fortunately, I adapt very easily, and I'll be paying close attention to your care."

Her scowl matched his. "I don't need anyone looking after me. Not now. Not *ever*. You might be the greatest thing in the entire universe when it comes to sex, but it ends there. Right there. You want sex, I'm your girl. Anything else, don't even think about it."

He studied her furious little face. She truly was beautiful. Silly, perhaps, but beautiful. He liked her fury. He liked her passion. But she didn't make any sense.

"You clearly know about Carpathians, Julija. You know what a lifemate is. You knew you were mine, that was why you didn't speak. I must see to your comfort and care. It is my duty and would be impossible not to carry it out." He waved his hand and she was fully clothed.

Her outfit was lined with fleece and the material was extremely soft. Breathable. High quality. She couldn't help but appreciate that he gave her the best. Still, what mattered to him was the reason he'd come after her. She wasn't losing sight of that for a minute.

"Where is the book you took from the prince?"

She narrowed her gaze, glaring at him. "*I* took? I didn't take the stupid book. I was on my way to warn the prince that the book was being targeted. I don't want anything at all to do with that horrid book. I was doing the right thing and now I'm in this really big mess. It doesn't pay to do the right thing, let me tell you that right now."

"Really big mess?" he echoed. What did she know that he didn't?

"You. You're the really big mess. I took a *huge* risk coming here after that idiot Carpathian who stole the book. I thought he was protecting it, but instead of returning it to the prince, he took off with it."

Isai sat back. She was staring at him and her eyes kept dropping to his lap.

"Do you think you could put some clothes on?" She had a wicked bite in her voice.

"I could if you asked nicer than that."

She rolled her eyes. He could see their life together wasn't going to go smoothly.

"Would you *please* put on some clothes? It's distracting when I'm trying to talk to you about this and it's a serious matter."

He supposed that was as good as it was going to get. She still had the tone. Worse, sarcasm was now a major part of it, but she at least used her manners. It meant she had some. He waved a hand to clothe himself. He could regulate his body temperature, so he hadn't even realized he wasn't dressed.

"Tell me what happened." She could in no way fault his tone. He kept his voice pleasant and calm. Not in the least accusing.

"Do you have to make everything an order?"

So much for keeping calm. He felt a muscle jerk in his jaw. She was going to give him eye ticks fairly soon. "Tell me *now*."

"Ask nicely."

He was on her in half a second, pulling her across his lap and smacking her hard over and over. He knew she wasn't feeling it with the thick trousers he'd given her so, using mind commands, he removed them. There was satisfaction in seeing his handprint on her bare skin. She screamed when he connected. He wasn't being gentle. His hands were large, and she was extremely petite. His palm took up one cheek easily. He reddened them both and only stopped when she was crying. He put her from him, back onto the rug, clothing her as he did so.

"That's twice, you bastard," she hissed. "I'm not without my own power. Don't you dare do that to me again."

"Then don't talk to your lifemate that way."

"Screw you and the lifemate crap. I *knew* you'd be like this. Why do you think I didn't want anything at all to do with the Carpathian people? I would never have gone near any of you. Not even Elisabeta, and she needed me."

He remained silent, watching her carefully. She was mage, and at some point she would try to retaliate. Tears streamed down her face, but she was as defiant as ever.

"Men don't punish their wives anymore. That century is long past. We have equal rights in this world, or in most parts of it. You're like some archaic dinosaur, trying to impose your will on someone smaller than you through brute force. You should be ashamed of yourself."

"Perhaps," he agreed mildly. "You also should be ashamed of yourself. You knew you were a lifemate to a Carpathian warrior, a man of honor. Instead of seeking him out, you chose to hide. Instead of treating him with respect when he finds you, you refuse to speak or acknowledge that you are his lifemate."

He pinned her with a steely gaze. "Are you aware that if a lifemate isn't found, the Carpathian male has no choice but to meet the dawn, meaning suicide, or he turns vampire and can murder hundreds, perhaps thousands of people before he is stopped by—guess who—another Carpathian male risking his life to save others?"

She looked down at the rug, a slow flush creeping up her face. "Yes, I'm aware. Put like that, it sounds far worse than when I was thinking about it."

"That is our reality. I searched centuries for you and then locked myself away in a monastery to keep those around me safe because I was close to being a demon, something far worse than a vampire. I no longer even heard the whispers of temptation, yet you stubbornly and selfishly refused to come to my aid and save me."

Her head went up. "Why should a woman have to sacrifice her life for a man?"

"Why should a man have to sacrifice his life to save mankind? To save that selfish woman?"

She leaned toward him. "He doesn't have to. He can walk away."

"Live without honor? Without doing his duty? Is that the kind of woman you are, Julija? You have no honor? You would refuse to do your duty because it is difficult?" He kept his voice very low, but there was disappointment.

Isai had searched for this woman for centuries, more years than even most Carpathians could claim life. Throughout that time, he had done everything necessary to protect his people and the growing number of humans vampires fed on. His reward was a woman who didn't believe in duty or service? She didn't believe in honor? She had no code? He didn't let it show on his face, but he felt shattered. Betrayed.

Dismissively, he waved away whatever she might say to back up her argument. "Tell me about the book and your part in its disappearance."

She pressed her lips tightly together as if to keep from continuing their argument. He had no intentions of continuing. He didn't want a woman who had no sense of honor. No code. A woman who would let a man become the very thing he had fought against. If she had studied Carpathians, and it was clear she had, then she knew Carpathian women were always happy. Their lifemates saw to that. He might be a dinosaur, but he would have done everything in his power to make his woman happy.

"My family, as you know, is mage. Xavier had a son named Soren. His mother was Rhiannon, of the Dragonseeker family. I know that's a big deal with Carpathians, but I don't know why. In any case, Soren was given a woman, a mage. They had a son, but when he was born, they both were told the baby died. Xavier had the woman killed for not properly taking care of herself and allowing the baby to be weak."

"The baby wasn't dead."

She shook her head. "That man, Xavier's grandson, Anatolie, is my father. My mother was a sixteen-year-old Carpathian girl named Francise. They wanted someone to use for blood to sustain them as they grew older. They used her until I was old enough and then they killed her."

He frowned and rubbed his finger over the bridge of his nose. "You know they killed her, you know this for a fact? You saw the body?"

"Yes. I'm sorry. I know it's hard to think that they would kill a young girl like that, but they did. I wasn't that old, but I remember. They wanted me to remember. Before my mother, my father married a mage, a woman very powerful in her own right. She gave Anatolie two sons. She was on board with him impregnating Francise. Theirs isn't a love match. She wants power just as Anatolie does."

"She isn't a very wise woman. They killed Rhiannon and then Francise. Why won't they kill her when she no longer serves a purpose?"

"I hadn't thought of that. In any case, I overheard them talking about the book and how whoever had it would wield a tremendous power and could destroy any species. It was the chance to rid the world of the Carpathians. My brothers, along with my father, had devised a plan. They were developing a creature everyone refers to as a shadow cat. These cats are part illusion, part shadow and part real. They are trained to slip in where no one can go. They've been training and practicing with them in other parts of the world away from the Carpathian Mountains because they didn't want to tip off the prince that they were coming for the book."

"You overheard them, broke with your family and set out to warn Mikhail."

She met his eyes. "That's the truth. I don't understand why you look and sound as if I'm lying about this."

"Perhaps because sacrifice seems out of character for you." Again, he kept his voice mild. There was no point in arguing. He could look into her mind. She had a shield and it was a strong one, but he had no doubt that he could bring it down when he needed to do so.

She opened her mouth and then closed it, pressing her lips together tightly. Finally, she sighed. "Just because I don't want to be with a dictator doesn't mean I don't do what's right."

"Are you telling me it would be wrong for a woman to save a man? Save a Carpathian male from turning vampire?"

"You're twisting my words."

3

Isai had the most beautiful sapphire blue eyes Julija had ever seen. They were so intense she was fairly certain they could melt the panties right off a girl—or accuse her of being selfish beyond all things. When he looked at her directly, she wanted the ground to open up and swallow her. She supposed from his perspective, she did look selfish. On the other hand, he didn't know one single thing about her life.

"Please continue. It doesn't matter anyway." Isai motioned in the air with his hand as if dismissing the entire conversation.

Julija wanted to defend herself, but how? What could she say? She did know about lifemates and what that meant in the Carpathian world. Their world and their rules were far different than the human or mage world. She *hadn't* wanted to save him, although she hadn't thought of it in those terms. More like she wanted to save herself.

"I can sometimes connect with others if their feelings are overpowering. A Carpathian hunter doesn't feel his emotions, but they are still there—inside of him—sometimes all the stronger because he can't let them out. I found myself caught in the mind of a Carpathian hunter who had searched the world over for his lifemate and like you, had gone centuries looking for her. He found her, but she was dying of old age. She had never married, and by the time he got to her, she was in a nursing home and practically taking her last breath."

Just the memory made her so sad she wanted to cry. She pressed a hand over her aching heart. "He was unbelievable with her. So gentle. He held her and pressed kisses down her face. She couldn't speak but she did open her eyes and look at him before she took her last breath. He took her with him and put her in the ground in some place that was sacred to him. It was a cave. The shadow cat that my brothers had bred was in that same cave."

"Could you tell what he was thinking?"

His voice was strictly neutral, but for some reason, tension coiled in her. She was missing something important. "It's more like I can feel what he's feeling and when it gets intense then I see the images. I saw him become alert, but at the time, I didn't know why. He had planned to stay with his lifemate until the dawn and then he was going to suicide."

Isai shook his head and turned away from her. His hair was the true black of the Carpathian people, mixed now with gray strands. He didn't look at all old, his body in superb condition without an ounce of fat and muscles rippling everywhere. If he'd been walking down the street, she would have stopped in her tracks and stared at him. Maybe she would have followed him. Okay, she would have followed him. She had a strong sex drive beyond imagining thanks to things she didn't want to think about. True attraction for a man had never been so intense with anyone the way it had been with him. Not ever.

"Keep going."

Yes, for certain she was missing something. His voice was mild, calm, but there was an edge to him.

"His name is Iulian Florea . . ."

"I'm aware."

"You are?"

"He's my brother."

Her heart thudded hard in warning. She took a cautious look around her. Would his first loyalty be to his brother? Was it a conspiracy? No. She felt the sorrow in him. She also felt his utter and complete disappointment in her. His rejection of her as his lifemate. It was one thing for her to reject him, but it stung when it was the other way around. She told herself to be grateful that he didn't want her, but she wasn't.

If he didn't claim her, what would that mean for him? She couldn't think about that, but it was already there in her mind and now she wasn't going to be able to get it out.

"He abruptly left the cave and it was clear he was following the shadow cat. I was elated. He would save the day and I wouldn't be involved."

"Of course not," Isai said.

Did she hear sarcasm in his voice? Judgment? She clenched her teeth together and then let out a large sigh. "You're determined to think the worst of me. You're the one who *spanked* me. If you do that again, I'm going to stab you through the heart."

"It won't be necessary to spank you again. In my world, at least during the time I came from, a man treasured his woman. If she needed a lesson as you did, it was his duty to give it to her. He was responsible for all aspects of her care. Times were very dangerous, and obedience was necessary for safety. Others, not Carpathians, over the centuries abused their women and I suppose it became something else. Something not between two people who love each other."

She started to tell him it wasn't love, but then what he said caught at her. "What do you mean it won't be necessary?"

"You are clearly not my treasure."

She frowned and pushed a hand through her hair in agitation. She examined his tone. It was neutral. Matter-of-fact. Dismissive and, unfortunately, genuine. She didn't care. He wasn't making any sense. He was so old-fashioned he thought spanking was caring. People didn't even spank their children anymore to correct their behavior.

"What are you going to do?" she whispered, afraid of his answer.

He shrugged. "Find my brother, get the book back, take it to Mikhail and return to the monastery. Hopefully, my emotions will fade with time."

There was no self-pity, simply acceptance. She wasn't the lifemate he had envisioned. She didn't want to be a lifemate but . . .

"Please continue."

She forced herself back to the main, very important topic. "The shadow cat did manage to steal the book. Iulian severely wounded the shadow cat. It was a terrible battle, but he was able to get the book back. I thought Iulian would return it to the prince, but instead, he took off with it. I knew because I saw the entire conflict in his mind. I didn't want to waste time, so I didn't continue on my journey to see Mikhail Dubrinsky, but instead, chased after him."

Julija pressed her fingers to her eyes. She had run after him without too many supplies. "I had to get a regular flight. I'm also dodging my family. They pretty much want to kill me . . ."

His head jerked up. "What did you just say?"

"I am betraying them and now they know it."

"They can't know it. For all they know you were trying to get the book for them."

"We had a terrible fight before I left. At least, my father and I did. He sent me to my room and put a holding spell on it. The thing is, I'm good at spells. Not just good, *very* good. I can blow my stepmother right out of the water matching her spell for spell. Same with my brothers. My father is used to dealing with them and he underestimated the force he needed to keep me in. I've always been careful not to show all my abilities or power."

"You told him you would warn Mikhail?"

"Yes. He wants the book in order to carry on Xavier's work. They all do. It's been their goal all along. I wasn't privy to it because they felt I had too much Carpathian blood in me and might betray them. Xavier had forced Soren to be with a mage because he needed his own bloodline to be the more powerful of the two in Anatolie. They needed me to be more Carpathian so they could live off of my blood." She gave a little shudder and rubbed her hands up and down her arms. "All of them."

"Where is Iulian now?"

She sighed again. "I was taken prisoner by Sergey. I would have broken loose when he wasn't around but there were children and Elisabeta to free. I wanted to try to find a way to help them and I thought, even being a couple of days behind Iulian, that I would be able to catch up. I'd been in his mind and I had a clear path to it. I just needed to find a direction."

"But?"

She shrugged helplessly. "I did connect with him briefly and knew he had come this way. He likes the high places, the lonely places. He doesn't want to be around people at all, not even to feed."

Isai frowned. He leaned closer. "Julija, that isn't a good sign."

"What does it mean?"

"He doesn't expect to live or fight. If he thought he would need to fight in order to protect the book, he would stay where he could find sustenance. He doesn't intend to have to fight. He lost his lifemate and he determined the book wasn't safe where it was. He is taking it somewhere and he will suicide in order to stop anyone from finding the book's final resting place."

She couldn't tell what he felt. Before, she'd connected with him, but once he determined she wasn't lifemate material, he'd withdrawn and put up some impenetrable shield. She knew, because she tried to get in. He probably knew she'd tried, but he'd kept her out. She didn't like being separated from him. It made her edgy. Uneasy. Incomplete. Still, if she could best a powerful mage, she could best a Carpathian hunter.

"Are you going to go after him?"

"Of course." Isai unfolded his long frame. "I have to find a suitable place to sleep during the day. Your brothers are most likely the two campers I saw not more than a few miles from here. If you want to try to outrun them on your own, that, obviously, is your right. If not, you're welcome to come with me. You need have no fears. I won't try to change your mind, nor will I try to have sex with you."

She should have reveled in his statement, but inexplicably she wanted to weep. She actually felt as if she'd lost something very valuable, and it wasn't the sex even when she tried to tell herself it was. She detested that he had such a poor opinion of her. Again, he didn't look at her when he spoke, and she wanted to remain silent, hoping he would turn those incredible sapphire eyes on her, but she couldn't take a chance that he would just leave.

"I'd rather go with you," she said hastily. "I'd really like to know about the tattoo on your back. It's different. I believe it's in the ancient Carpathian language, isn't it?"

"Yes."

He said it tersely. Clipped. That hurt, but she persisted. "What does it mean?"

"It is for my lifemate alone. No one else."

She stuck her chin in the air, challenging him. "But I can know then. I am your lifemate."

Those blue eyes drifted over her. Remote. Not even judging her. She'd already been judged and found wanting. She found herself shivering and rubbing her arms. Waiting for him to tell her.

"Those words are sacred. To me, they mean something. So much so, I etched them into my body so I would feel them in the darkest of times. So she could pull me through the worst hell. The vows would not mean anything to you. You are not mine and I am not yours."

Again, his tone lacked accusation or inflection. He had stepped back in his mind, so far from her, she couldn't reach him. He was lost to her. Completely lost to her. She found herself so confused she didn't know how to react. She wanted to weep at the loss when she should be celebrating. It shouldn't matter what he thought of her, but it did. To hear him say he wasn't hers was terrible. Each word felt like the slice of a sword in her bones.

Isai suddenly looked up but leapt right at her. Hard hands pushed her down and he hurdled right over top of her. Cognizant that sound carried great distances at night, Julija managed not to scream. He looked terrifying there with the moonlight spilling down on him. He was a warrior and he looked it, looked invincible. Fierce lines were carved deep into his face, and those blue eyes were so intense blue flames seemed to come out of them. He caught something in his arms. It was black, no gray, almost insubstantial, but it was heavy enough to bowl him over backward.

She scrambled out of the way as the shadow cat turned its head toward her. Glowing red eyes locked on to her. It was so evil, her entire body shuddered. She could feel hatred coming off of the creature in waves.

Isai refused to let go and the cat tore at him, shredding his shirt and leaving long bloodred streaks down his chest.

"Get out of here." Isai snapped the command at her as cat and man rolled back onto their feet. The cat took two steps toward her and Isai mirrored the movement, forcing the animal to turn its attention back to him.

Her brothers had found her, or at least their killer cat had. Of course. It would hunt by scent. They had her blood. She would be easy to track. She refused to retreat and leave Isai to fight her fight alone. She lifted her hands into the air and cleared her mind.

That which is shadow and blood scent I bind.

The cat stopped in its tracks.

Sending you back to those who would seek to find.

The cat slunk away, over the rocks, back into the night. Something fierce yowled from out in the darkness a distance away.

Take back that which is shadow, now turn it to smoke.
By the power of air my will be invoked.

Isai sank down onto the rock ledge, looking down at his chest. "You did the majority of that. I was just the convenient weapon."

She hurried to him. "That poor demonic creature tore up your chest."

He held up his hand as if to ward her off. "I can heal the wounds. They're deep scratches, but I'm used to wounds."

"You're very pale. You need blood." Again, she moved toward him, driven by more than the fact that he'd saved her—and he had. If that thing had jumped on her from above, it would have killed her. Isai had sacrificed his body in order to protect her. She detested seeing him injured, and a compulsion so strong it bordered on desperation urged her to help him.

Isai smoothly stepped back away from her. "I'm used to dealing with these types of injuries. The cat has some kind of poison in its claws. Burns like hell. I need to examine it. Do they come in pairs? Whatever yowled out in the distance sounded as if it was calling to it."

"I believe so. When I stumbled across the building where they were housing them, it was horrible, like a place where animals are butchered. Several cats were half formed and had parts missing. Some were starving because they couldn't eat. It was clear some had been fed blood. The place was ghastly, truly out of a horror film. I was appalled and began sneaking in at night to try to help them. Some had to be humanely put down. I hated that, but what else could I do? Let them suffer? I brought water to them every night. They were so thirsty. I think my brothers were instilling hate in them. Once I came in and one had terrible wounds all over it. I tried to get close, but it snarled and warned me off. Eventually, I found a way to make it sleep and I cleaned all the wounds and dressed them. Each night I checked on the big cat and dressed the wounds."

That compulsion in her she couldn't help had her inching forward as she spoke.

"You took a hell of a chance." He moved away from her again, out of reach. "You did tonight as well. Thank you," he said quietly, sincerely.

Julija detested that he wouldn't allow her to help him but that low acknowledgment of his gratitude made her feel a little better. "You saved my life. I'm the one who should be thanking you."

Those blue eyes flared in the darkness, lighting up the night. The sight of them like that, glowing almost, caused a slow roll in her stomach. The sensation was unlike anything she'd experienced. Still, she could see by the blank expression on his face that he wouldn't expect her to thank him. He didn't expect anything at all from her. He had withdrawn so completely from her, shut down any kind of relationship, even friendship, that she didn't know how to approach him.

He rested his back against a rock wall and concentrated on the wounds on his chest. She felt the surge of power. It was incredible. Shocking even. Her father commanded tremendous power, more than any other she knew. Anatolie kept his abilities a secret from most in the mage world. *He* was the well-kept secret. No one was to know of his existence. He was Xavier's secret weapon.

Those with mage blood had scattered since Xavier's death, fearing retaliation by the Carpathian people after the attacks on them by the high mage. Then the truth had come out that he was one of triplets. Anatolie didn't seem in the least surprised, but her brothers were. Their father made it clear they were never to admit Xavier's blood ran in their veins. He said it would make them a target of jealous mages and the Carpathian hunters.

Isai wielded power so easily, as if it was a part of him. He didn't call it up with ceremony, he simply used it. Casually. Easily. The shirt fell away, disappearing as if it had never been. The bloody streaks in his chest were already turning black as if some poison was eating away the flesh. She shuddered, one hand going defensively to her throat. Those claws would have gotten into her. Even if she'd managed to drive them off with a spell, the acid would have most likely killed her.

She couldn't tear her eyes away from the sight of him. He was mesmerizing as he pushed the poison out of his body through his pores. She knew it had to burn, but he never winced. Pale yellow droplets fell to the ground. The beads seemed to have some kind of magnetic attraction to one another and they rolled until they pooled together to form a light buttery-colored puddle at his feet.

"They used sulfuric acid or some combination with that in it," she identified. "That explains why so many of the cats ended up dead with burns on their faces and feet. Somehow the acid leaked out of their venom sacs, right?" She stared in horror at the evidence at his feet. She wouldn't have survived an attack with that acid. He had to be in terrible pain.

"I will be fine. Stand back for a minute. I have to get rid of the poisonous acid."

She moved to the other side of the rock.

"Turn away when I bring this down." He was already looking toward the sky.

Her heart pounded. He was calling down the lightning. It was a feat no other species could do. No mage had been able to wield lightning, even if they could draw it down.

An electrical charge made her hair stand up on her body. She heard the ominous sizzle and crackle of electricity. White-hot and too bright to look at, a whip of lightning flashed across the sky, lashed the pale-yellow puddle of acid and was gone, leaving behind scorched rock. She thought Isai stumbled, but when she blinked to bring him in focus, he was standing straight and tall. He certainly looked invincible. Pale, but definitely omnipotent. The skin where the wounds had been had gone from black to a healthy color again.

"I have to heal these wounds from the inside out just to make certain the cats didn't leave anything behind in my bloodstream."

She hadn't thought of that.

"I will return in a few minutes. I will not be far from you."

Perversely, she didn't want him to go. "Can't you just do it here? You pushed out the poison in front of me." She hoped she didn't sound whiny, but she really hated that he was so remote, so closed off from her. She was used to being alone. In fact, she preferred being alone. She should have been glad to see him go. Instead, she had the mad desire to cling. The shadow cat had shaken her up more than she realized. That was the only explanation.

"Just a few minutes, Julija." His voice was very gentle. "I'll be close in case there is another attack."

She glared at him in challenge, hating that he thought she wanted him there to protect her. It wasn't that at all. "Why? Why do you have to leave?"

"I have to shed my body in order to heal from the inside out."

She knew instantly he didn't trust her with the unprotected shell of his body, and that hurt. Her throat felt raw. Her eyes burned. "You can do it right here." She made it a demand. He really didn't seem to like that tone when she took it with him. Even if it earned her another spanking, which frankly hurt, it was better than his complete indifference.

He just looked at her and then he was gone. He dissolved right in front of her. Shimmering, he looked as transparent as the shadow cat had, but then he was just not there. Julija wrapped her arms around her middle and pressed her forehead against the rock where he'd been standing. That left her looking down at the scorch marks on the rock.

Why had she thought it would be so terrible to be with a Carpathian? She had nowhere to go. Her family and most of those with mage blood would forever brand her a traitor when they learned she'd been on her way to warn the Carpathians. And yet, she didn't know how to live as a Carpathian. She had the ability to take blood, just not to sleep in the ground.

Julija sighed. She didn't know how to trust someone enough to fall in love. There hadn't been one single person in her life that she could remember that she could trust. Not her father. Her brothers. Her stepmother. Not one of them. No friends. Certainly not the man she'd slept with. She had thought him someone special, her friend. Turned out, not so much. A shiver went through her body.

She wrapped her arms around her waist, suppressing the shiver, pushing the memory to the back of her mind where it belonged. *Elisabeta?* She needed something. Companionship. Contact with another being. She was well aware she'd connected very strongly with Elisabeta because she identified in some ways with her. It wouldn't seem so to anyone looking at the two of them, but that awareness of each other was there. Compassion. Empathy. Whatever one wanted to call it, they had it for each other.

She held her breath for the long moments leading up to the stirring in her mind. *I am here. You have need? Are you safe?*

Tears burned hot behind her eyes. Elisabeta was in the ground, healing from the terrible physical punishments Sergey had inflicted on her as well as the mental and emotional scars, yet she was instantly concerned for Julija. That said so much about the woman.

I just need someone to talk to.

We have to be careful. He is always listening at night. Trying to find a way to me.

That alarmed Julija. She knew exactly who Elisabeta was referring to. Sergey would only be able to call to her at night. Julija felt as if she could almost hear him whispering to her friend. She had all but forgotten Sergey in her rush to go after the book. Xavier might be dead, but the master vampire had slivers of the high mage embedded in his brain. She had no idea if those slivers could feel the book had left the relative safety of the Carpathian Mountains and was now vulnerable somewhere close.

I almost forgot that he's doubly dangerous with the slivers of the high mage in him. He was already scary enough. I'm sorry, Elisabeta. I should have been more careful.

Even if the vampire didn't feel how close the book was, it wasn't like something as huge as the evil book of spells being stolen would stay a secret. Sooner or later, the news would get to Sergey and he would start his own hunt for it.

Will your father and brothers help him? Will they have other mages helping?

The anxiety Julija heard in Elisabeta's voice was for her, not the woman who had been caged for centuries and forced to do a vampire's bidding.

I don't know. She hadn't thought of that, either. She knew her father wanted the book for himself. He wouldn't want Sergey to get near it. On the other hand, if it was the only way to get the book back, he might form that alliance. Those slivers of Xavier might actually seek him out to aid him; after all, Xavier was his grandfather.

Julija? If your father is Rhiannon's grandson, he is part Dragonseeker. No Dragonseeker has ever turned vampire.

He is not vampire, but he is evil.

I do not see how that is possible.

Julija knew there was something that was supposed to be extraordinary about the Dragonseeker lineage, but she wasn't certain what it was until that moment. *He bears a mage mark, the same as my brothers. The same as me. But I was also born with a dragon mark low, on the left side of my body where my ovaries would be. When I asked my father and brothers, none had that mark. They couldn't see my mark so they had no idea what I was talking about. It was like the dragon hid from them.*

That had made her feel different, even more apart from the rest of her family when she'd already felt that way. For the longest time she'd thought she was treated differently because she didn't have the same mother as her brothers and her stepmother was jealous of her dead mother.

There was silence while Elisabeta thought what the absence of Dragonseeker marks on Julija's family could mean.

A man has come to me. He says he is my lifemate. Julija thought she might as well tell her friend. *I refused him.*

Elisabeta's gasp of horror was instantaneous. *You cannot. You cannot refuse him, Julija. You have condemned him to death, or worse. So much worse. He could be another Sergey. Is he young?*

He is an ancient. Very much so I think. He was one of a few Carpathian males determined to be so dangerous they locked themselves away in a monastery.

There was another gasp from Elisabeta. *One of his brethren is here. He lies close to me to prevent the constant whispers from Sergey. He's very powerful. He has claimed that I am lifemate to him. I'm terrified, but I would never think to refuse him.*

Of course Elisabeta wouldn't refuse a Carpathian male, Julija told herself. The woman had been caged for centuries, taught to do whatever a man ordered her to do. Every Carpathian female seemed to do her man's bidding. Not that she'd been around too many. Still, Elisabeta's accusation echoed through her mind. *You have condemned him to death, or worse.*

Julija closed her eyes tightly but there was no shutting out the truth of that. *Tell me why a woman must give up her rights but a man doesn't.*

I am uncertain what you mean.

Elisabeta, you were born into a different century. You wouldn't know about women's rights, but we own our lives. No one can tell us what to do.

You speak of a different culture. Carpathian women have those rights and have always had them. We follow our men, but they do whatever it is that makes us happy. It is their duty. I am not certain I can fully explain, but it is imprinted on them before they are ever born. The ritual binding words that tie us. Once said, there is no taking them back . . .

Wait. Julija's heart suddenly beat too fast. *He could have tied us together?*

Yes, of course. Once he says those vows for the two of you, nothing can tear you apart, not even death. You belong to each other. You cannot be without him nor he without you. If you die and he does not follow immediately, he can go into a thrall and become vampire. Otherwise, once tied to you, it is impossible for him to become vampire.

Isai could have taken the decision out of her hands the moment she'd refused him, but he hadn't. He had declared she wasn't worth the centuries of searching for her. Of waiting for her. She almost asked Elisabeta about the flow of ink scarred into his back and what those words said, but it felt as if she was betraying Isai and she couldn't do that. The words he'd put there had been for her. His lifemate. If she found out what they said, it had to come from him.

Lifemates belong to each other, Julija.

You say you have been claimed as well, but your voice trembles when you tell me. You are really afraid, almost more so than you are of Sergey.

That is true. Elisabeta didn't try to deny it. *I am no longer that girl with her foolish dreams of lifemates. I have been with a vampire for centuries. I am . . . altered.*

Again, Julija felt tears dripping down Elisabeta's face, but they were not in her voice. Just that quaver, the one that conveyed so much.

Julija had never known girlish dreams. She'd had the occasional fantasy when she'd watched human women fall in love. When she'd seen human families and the way they'd interacted. Some of them, not all. She'd wanted those things for herself, but she'd been younger than ten. Eight perhaps? She'd already known those things, like love and happiness, weren't for her. There would be no man to love her and no children for her. Her family would never allow such a thing. More importantly, she didn't want to trade one cage for another.

Can you refuse your lifemate? Julija asked.

I suppose it is possible, but if yours did not tie you together, I am certain mine would do so immediately. He is . . . hard. Disciplined. I cannot think about it yet. I do not know how to think for myself. I cannot see how I can please a lifemate.

This time the sob was in Julija's throat, choking her. In her mind. Swamping her. She immediately hugged herself tightly in the hopes Elisabeta could feel it. *I am here for you. You will not be alone.*

I am so lucky to have met you, Julija. Thank you for being my friend.

Julija didn't hear hope in Elisabeta's voice. Not one small bit. Her lifemate had done that. The thought of having one had overwhelmed her friend, not made her happy. Julija was no closer to an answer than she had been before, but she had to help Elisabeta. She couldn't leave her to suffer in terror hiding beneath the ground.

You say lifemates have to make their women happy, Elisabeta.

Yes. The pairs are meant for one another.

Elisabeta fell neatly into Julija's trap. *Then this man has been made for you and you for him. He will make you happy.*

I wish I could believe that, but I am no longer the one who carries his soul.

You must, or he wouldn't know it was you, right?

I worded that incorrectly. I do not know how to say this. I have guarded his soul carefully from Sergey and it earned me my worst punishments, but I was adamant, he could not bring down my shield. I would have suicided first.

Now Julija could hear the terrible screams of agony Elisabeta had made when Sergey punished her for not giving him what he demanded. She shivered, desperate to reach out to her friend. No prisoner of war could have been treated as cruelly as the vampire had treated the one he'd captured and kept for himself.

You are more than worthy of this man who claims you. Was it trading one prison for another? Was that how Elisabeta saw it? That was how Julija saw it for both of them. *Maybe I can steal you away somewhere they can't find us until we sort things out and have the chance to decide our own fates.* She half joked, half made the offer.

That is a wonderful thing to offer me, Julija, but I cannot accept. Elisabeta took her seriously. *I will honor my commitment to him once he knows that I have been changed for all time and we might not fit. He would feel responsible for me once he ties us together, so I hope to get the chance to speak before he does so.*

Just talk to him as soon as you surface.

Elisabeta gasped, clearly horrified. *I cannot speak to him, not without permission.*

Julija went very still, fighting down a surge of anger. *What do you mean? You have to wait for permission to speak before you can talk to a lifemate? Isai didn't tell me that.*

Instantly Julija had the overwhelming impression of shame. Her heart sank. She pressed her fingers to her eyes, wishing the pounding headache would go away.

I'm sorry. It was too late to take back the blunder and Julija inwardly cursed herself for her carelessness. Elisabeta had spent centuries asking permission to speak. She was so conditioned that by now, that law was so ingrained in her that she probably *couldn't* speak without permission. All along, Julija had thought she was the only one who would understand Elisabeta's special needs, but she was already failing her.

There is no need to be sorry. I have told you, and it is true. I am much altered. I believe when my lifemate becomes aware I cannot even think for myself, he will free me. Now her voice shook with terror. *I do not want him to despise me for being the way I am, and yet I must confess to him. He has waited centuries to find me. Gone through so much, and I have nothing of value to give him. I am ashamed and feel sorrow for him.*

Elisabeta took on such a burden, despising who she was and what she'd become because she didn't feel she had anything to give her lifemate, while Julija had turned hers down. She was beginning to feel the urgent need to see Isai. To hear his voice. To touch his mind.

Don't, Elisabeta. Don't think that of yourself.

It is the truth. I cannot blame him if he turns me away, but without someone to guide me, I do not know what I will do.

Julija swallowed hard. *I will come to you.*

You must sort out your life, Elisabeta said. *You are willing to sacrifice yourself for me, but not for your lifemate. Do you have any idea why?*

Julija abruptly pulled out of Elisabeta's mind, slamming the door hard on any memories that tried to creep in. She would not go there. She would not let her past define her as Elisabeta was doing. She sank down, back to the rock, knees to her chest, looking down at the scorch marks on the granite surface. Who was she kidding? Not Elisabeta, and not herself. She was already allowing the past to define her. No one could escape their past.

Elisabeta was forever shaped into a submissive woman who needed someone to gently guide her back to a place where she could feel strong and believe in herself again. Julija needed . . . what? Someone. Someone had come along and she'd rejected him. Not only had she rejected him, she'd deliberately insulted him and the Carpathian culture.

There was no sound, but she knew Isai was there, almost as though by thinking of him, she had conjured him up. When she opened her eyes, he was crouched beside her, looking utterly male, all muscle and hard lines, totally at odds with the way his finger traced a line down her cheek. She realized she was crying and instantly felt vulnerable.

She lifted her gaze to his and the impact of his sapphire eyes caught her right in the stomach like a hard blow.

"Why the tears?"

She shook her head mutely, but the burn behind her eyes increased. So much was lost to her. She couldn't even say lost when she'd never had it. Never. She'd never had love. Or a real family. She'd never had anyone to care whether she was hurt or not. His touch on her skin felt shockingly beautiful. She felt trapped by him, by what he held out to her when she knew it was most likely an illusion. She'd lived in illusions until finally, one day, she'd realized what was happening and become mistress of them.

"Julija, simple politeness requires you to answer."

Her face flamed red and she tried to jerk her head back to get away from his touch. She hit the back of her head hard against the rock. Pain added to the already pounding headache. She let herself cry. For Elisabeta and for herself. Two women trapped in cages they could never break out of.

4

I sai brushed at the tears on Julija's face. His heart clenched hard enough to be painful. The sight of her crying tore at him, caused a completely visceral reaction. She might have rejected him, but while he was with her, he had no choice but to take care of her. The need to stop her tears was so strong he moved closer to her, sheltering her with his body.

"Julija, you must tell me what is wrong. I cannot aid you if you do not communicate with me."

She pressed her face into her hands and shook her head, but the sobs didn't stop. Now his gut was churning. He sighed. "Little mage, you will be the death of me. If you do not tell me what distresses you, you leave me no choice but to extract the information from you."

Her head snapped up and she glared at him. The effect wasn't what she was looking for because her face was splotchy red from crying and her eyes were watery. Her feathery lashes stuck together, giving her the appearance of a drowned kitten.

"You have a million choices, Isai. A *million*. Your last choice should be taking something I haven't offered you."

"At least you are talking, even if what you say is pure nonsense." He stood up and held out his hand. "We have to go now if you're coming with me."

With a show of great reluctance, she put her hand in his. He closed his fingers around it and pulled her to her feet. "You do not have to come with me if you do not want to," he stated. "You want to make your choice, make it fast."

She seemed to wince as if he'd struck her, but she just nodded her head. "I'm going with you."

"If you're going with me, Julija, I will still be the same man you have rejected. I lead. I will always lead. It will be that way until we part ways."

Her long lashes lifted, and she glared at him. "Less talking and more leading would be good." She managed to use her snippiest voice.

For some reason, that made him want to laugh. He didn't, but he wanted to and that shocked him. He couldn't really remember laughter, but he felt it. Without preamble, and maybe just to retaliate and shock her a little, he wrapped his arm around her waist, pulled her tightly into his chest and took to the air.

Julija gasped and pressed her face against him. She felt small and fragile in his arms. He kept her warm, cognizant of the fact that she couldn't regulate her body temperature.

Wrap your arms around my neck.

She did so without hesitation, and his heart jerked wildly in his chest. His body reacted to hers. There was no way to stop it, not even with his tremendous control. She . . . belonged. He closed his eyes for a brief moment, wondering how he was going to give her up. She was born for him. He was born for her. They matched. But how could they? Something had gone wrong.

Over the centuries, whether she had died and been reborn with his soul more than once, perhaps the bond had weakened between them. He hadn't thought that could happen, but she wasn't the woman he envisioned, nor, clearly, was he the man she had. That saddened him. He was finding emotions weren't as easy to cope with as he'd thought they would be. So much time had gone by since he first had lost all feeling that he didn't remember how much trouble emotion could bring to him.

There was a small flutter in his mind. He had forged a connection to speak to her telepathically, and that pathway remained open between them. He was a little shocked that he could feel her exploring it tentatively.

Why are you so sad?

Her voice sounded soft and warm, stroking at the walls of his mind every bit as intimately as fingers caressing his skin. Lifemates didn't lie to each other but he didn't believe he should continually point out his disappointment in her—although once he examined the situation from every angle, he realized the disappointment and embarrassment was with himself. He was too far gone from the modern world and didn't understand her. He couldn't change what he was or who he was. His characteristics were ingrained in him. Deeply. He was a leader and he did expect his woman to follow. That wasn't her fault.

It is of no consequence, but I thank you for your concern.

There was a silence. He felt the press of her face against his chest. She rubbed a little caress there with her cheek as if trying to comfort him. Her fingers linked behind the nape of his neck. He wanted to continue with her across the fading night sky, but knew he needed to take her to the cave he'd found. It was small, but it would definitely protect both of them during daylight hours.

It is of consequence to me.

He liked that—too much. Being in her company was the equivalent of walking through a minefield. One false step and everything would blow up in his face, but the adrenaline was there. Excitement. He felt alive. Truly alive, when he had been a robot going through life on automatic. She made him feel everything.

I do not wish you to think you are in any way at fault because we are not compatible. I am centuries old. I have been locked away behind impenetrable gates for centuries. I cannot change what I am to make myself into someone else for you. I hope you can find a way to forgive me.

The path between them allowed him to feel the rising sorrow in her. She pressed closer to him and he tightened his arms as he took them to the small cave he'd found hidden in the rock. The entrance was a slim crack, which he widened as he dropped down from the sky. Inside the opening blossomed into a large room that enabled him to stand. He set Julija on her feet and waved his hand to close the crack.

"I've got to prevent anything from entering, from innocent man to vampire puppet," he said, turning away from her. She still had tears on her face and he detested the sight. It made him feel weak. The need to hold and comfort her was so strong it was all he could do to turn his back, giving her a semblance of privacy.

"The shadow cat," Julija reminded. "They seem to be able to slip in anywhere. The book had to have been safeguarded yet they still managed to get to it. Once you lay the foundations of a safeguard, I'll add to it."

That brought him up short. He had never trusted anyone with his resting place, other than his brethren in the monastery. Even then, he'd used his own safeguards and changed his exact resting place nightly. Each had their own small place where they kept the façade of a house. That was considered a private place for each and they slept somewhere in the parameters of that area.

He glanced over his shoulder at her, but she was looking around the cave as if she was going to decorate it. "In a minute I will provide seating for you and a bed with a comfortable mattress."

She turned to look at him and then at the slender crack. "If something happens to you, I'm not positive I can get out of here."

"You're mage. You can get out if you need to." His voice carried absolute conviction. He didn't have a doubt in his mind that she could widen the opening enough to allow her body through. Apparently, he said the right thing because she smiled at him, and this time that smile lit her dark eyes.

She waved her hand and sconces with candlelight flickered along the walls of the cave, high up, illuminating the interior. Another wave took the dirt and debris from the floor, replacing it with a thick carpet. She flashed a conspirator's grin at him, inviting him to share her happiness. "Not bad for an illusion."

It was near perfection. "Nice job." He let admiration creep into his tone. He didn't want to like anything about her, not even her sense of fun.

Many women would be complaining after what she'd gone through. The tears weren't even dry on her face, but she didn't grumble at all. In fact, she clearly was trying to make things nice for them.

"Where will you sleep, Isai?" She began to pace the chamber.

The cave was small, but no one had noticed it. There was no evidence of man, mage or Carpathian using it prior to the two of them. Again, he hesitated before answering her. Carpathians didn't allow others to know where their resting places were. But even if he wasn't going to claim her, she was his lifemate.

"Beneath you. Directly beneath you. Should you have need you can reach out to me on the pathway we have established."

Isai turned back to the crack and began weaving layers of safeguards. When he was certain the layers would stop even Xavier himself, he turned to her. "If you can stop the shadow cat from entering, add your safeguards now and I'll finish after you." He stepped back and waited to see what she would do. He was going to layer more weaves on top of hers in order to ensure nothing could get to them.

The shadow cat worried him just for the reason she'd stated. Not only were the caverns protected with the strongest safeguards the prince of the Carpathian people could weave, but the book itself had been protected. Mikhail had contacted Tariq Asenguard, his voice in the United States, and asked that the ancients spread out and look for Iulian Florea and the book, and the mage as well. The moment Isai had heard his brother's name, he had volunteered to go. His blood would call to that of his brother and he would be able to better find the trail.

Julija came to stand right beside him, under his arm, and playfully bumped his thigh with her hip as if she could move him out of her way. Laughing softly, she pushed a second time until he stepped to the side, although her shove hadn't even rocked him.

"Bossy little mage."

"Someone has to get it right."

She lifted her hands into the air and began to weave another complicated pattern. He watched closely, imprinting every graceful movement on his brain. Her voice was musical as she began to chant.

Spiders scurry, spin your web.
Winds that flurry, catch their threads.
Sink them deep within the earth's wall,
Let none who seek hear my call.
Twist and turn, weave and bind,
Set these wards so none may find.

Isai added the closing safeguard to her webbing and then turned to the room. He created two comfortable chairs and a bed with plenty of covers for her. He didn't like that she sometimes shivered for no apparent reason. He was careful to keep her body temperature up yet he'd noted several shivers as if a sudden chill would take her.

"Julija, are you afraid of me?"

Her dark eyes revealed shadows until her lashes feathered down. She twisted her fingers together and he reached out and stilled her hands.

"You are mage and very powerful in your own right," he said softly. "Claimed or no, I am your lifemate. It would be impossible for me to harm you."

She stood very still, almost frozen to the spot, but he felt the tremor that ran through her body and her lips trembled slightly before she bit down as if conscious that he could see that revealing sign.

"Why didn't you use the ritual binding words and tie us together?"

He didn't understand her at all. There was a note of hurt in her voice, as if he had arbitrarily rejected her. "Clearly that was not your desire, and it is my duty as your lifemate to give you what you wish."

"Maybe I just wished you wouldn't spank me." She rubbed her bottom as if she could still feel his hand smacking her.

"I was careful not to hurt you."

"It hurt."

"It didn't hurt more than your dignity," he countered, uncertain why they were even discussing the subject. He thought that was already closed.

"Perhaps you're right. My dignity was very offended. You didn't really hurt me."

The way she said it alerted him. He felt like he was feeling around in the dark for her and only getting the lightest of responses in return. "Has someone hurt you, Julija?" The thought tore at him. He gestured toward the two chairs.

She sank into one of them and he produced a fleece blanket, so she could wrap herself in it. Her smile made him warm inside.

She shrugged. "It doesn't matter. I think we've all been hurt. I see scars all over you, and yet I was told Carpathians didn't scar."

"Not usually. A mortal wound can cause scarring if we are spared. As the centuries go by and we are wounded over and over in the same places, scarring can occur."

He turned his chair around to face her rather than sit beside her where he would be tempted to touch her soft skin. Light was beginning to seep in through the slight crack in the granite. Soon, he would have to go to ground and leave her. In spite of the fact that he hadn't bound them together, he hated leaving her. They'd only done one blood exchange, but he was totally addicted to her taste—to all of her. He wanted her with every breath he drew.

Julija looked down at her hands. "I am afraid," she admitted. "I can feel your power. You hold so much." She twisted her fingers together. "I'm used to my father and brothers. Even my stepmother. They all have power, but yours . . ." She trailed off.

"Would you hesitate to kill them if you had to?" He kept his tone mild, but he needed to know.

She thought it over rather than answering him very quickly. "It's possible. I would hope not. I've never killed anyone, but I believe I would to save myself or someone else."

"You hold the light in your soul for both of us, *kislány hän ku meke sarnaakmet minan*. It is no wonder that you would feel some hesitation. I do not like that you will be unprotected once I leave."

She swallowed hard and looked down at her fingers twisting together in the nervous habit she couldn't quite stop. Her head shook, her glossy hair swinging a little. The candlelight put little gleaming lights in her dark hair. He had to resist reaching out to feel the silk of those strands.

"Tell me about yourself, Isai. What you like and don't like, that sort of thing."

He had been leaning toward her, but he sank back in the seat, steepling his fingers and regarding her over them. It was the first real interest in him as a person she had displayed, and he had no idea what to tell her.

"I like ancient weapons. The feel of a sword in my hand. The way the vibration runs up my arm when the blades crash together. I find battle, hand-to-hand combat, fascinating. For me it is like a dance, the combatants each moving with grace as they watch their opponent for an opening."

"I never thought of it that way. You've hunted countless vampires. Do you get the same feeling when you fight them?"

He gave that thought. "Not exactly. It is more a stimulation of the mind. A newly made vampire is generally easy to defeat because he does not have the discipline necessary to wait for an advantage. Vampires are vain and like their egos stroked, especially a master vampire. Someone like Sergey, or his brother Vadim, *must* have admiration. Deprive them of it and their calm façade of civility disappears."

"I can't imagine what Elisabeta went through for all those centuries at his hands."

"The thought of a vampire having one of our women for even a few minutes, let alone centuries, is horrifying. Their cruelty knows no limits. They crave seeing the suffering of others. How did you two become friends? I hear in your voice that you care about her." He made certain to keep any surprise over that to himself. Julija seemed overly sensitive and he didn't want any more tears when he had no idea how best to deal with them.

She hesitated for just a moment as if she might not tell him, but then she capitulated. "I connected with Elisabeta before Sergey's vampires captured me and brought me to that horrid room where they were allowing their puppets to bite into children."

"She was hidden."

"Yes, but I've studied illusions from the time I was young, so I recognize them. I felt her presence. She's quite strong in spite of what Sergey's done to her. He's made her believe she isn't, but I felt her power. She was trying to get out of the bars that held her in order to save the child. The emotions in her were so intense I locked on her right away and was able to bring the illusion to light. Sergey had made her cage, with her in it, part of the cavern wall. The first time, throwing out power together, we were able to stop the puppet. Sergey was angry, but at the same time he was curious. That saved my life I think."

He liked her voice. It was soothing and peaceful. Even when she was giving him a hard time and she sounded snippy, he liked her voice. He knew he would be able to listen to it for the rest of his life.

"I worry for her. She says she has a lifemate . . ."

Isai frowned. That didn't sound right. Ferro had only told the others two nights earlier that he was Elisabeta's lifemate. "When did you talk to her?"

"Just a little while ago."

He heard the innocence in her voice. She didn't realize that the surge of power would not only draw her brothers, but any vampires in the area. Sergey desperately wanted Elisabeta back. If Elisabeta responded to Julija, he would recognize her energy. He'd held her prisoner for too many centuries not to do so.

The two women also had no idea that talking across a long distance could be difficult for even the most powerful of Carpathians. She spoke of conversing with Elisabeta casually, as if it wasn't in the least an effort.

"Did you contact her first, or did she contact you?" He wanted to know which of the two held the bridge between them.

"The first time I contacted her." She frowned. "Maybe I did each time." She shivered and rubbed her hands up and down her arms. "I feel her. She's so afraid."

"She has reason to be. Sergey refuses to give her up and is calling to her every night, trying to scare her into giving herself up to him. Ferro is with her now. He will make certain, when she rises, that she will be safe."

"You and I both know that is much easier said than done," Julija said. "What happens if she never rises?"

"Ferro will not allow that. He is different. He's always been different.

Of all of us, he is the one most to fear. Perhaps he is Elisabeta's lifemate for a reason. He is the most dangerous, the deadliest hunter, and has experiences many do not. Should he face Sergey and his army of vampires, I have no doubt he would cut a wide path through them."

"Is he a gentle man?"

He could hear the fearful note in her voice and wished he could reassure her. "He will be whatever she needs, Julija." The moment the words left his mouth, he was ashamed. Guilty. He should have been what Julija needed. "Perhaps I misspoke. Ferro, like me, was locked away from the world for a couple of centuries. Time passed us by and modern ways elude us."

"Elisabeta was locked up as well," Julija pointed out hopefully. "She says if she tried to run, Ferro would just bind her to him with the ritual binding words."

He permitted himself a smile. There was no doubt in his mind that Ferro would do such a thing. "That is true."

"How is that different from Sergey caging her? Please don't get angry with me. I'm really trying to find out the difference. Ferro would go after her if she ran, wouldn't he?"

He nodded only because he could hear the frustration and genuine interest in her voice. She was trying her best to understand their culture. "Ferro and Elisabeta are two halves of the same whole. Without Ferro, she will never be happy. Nor will he. There is no one else for either of them. Elisabeta will accept that. She may have been taken as a teenager, but she is well versed in the Carpathian rituals. She would have been told early, from the time she was a child, that somewhere her lifemate searched for her. Ferro knows this and would never allow her to run away from him because she was scared or was trying to prove something to herself."

She was silent a moment, and he could see she was trying to understand. "Isai, what if she *does* need to prove something to herself? Isn't that something he should take into consideration? Or maybe she just needs time to figure things out."

Isai was fairly certain they had gone from talking about Ferro and Elisabeta to talking about them. "Mostly, little mage, she is afraid. Fear is an emotion that can paralyze one or have them run—the flight-or-fight response kicks in."

She regarded him with great suspicion. "How do you even know about that? You've been locked up in a monastery, and yet you somehow can quote flight-or-fight response?"

"We have to absorb all knowledge quickly. It is a gift. It is also part of our culture to continue to learn. The moment we left the monastery, we had to transfer knowledge from other Carpathians to us. We also can gain knowledge from other species as well as through books and now computers. We absorb such things."

"Then why didn't you absorb the part where husbands do *not* spank their wives?"

He refused to smile. He didn't dare, that could get him into a lot more trouble. They seemed to continuously circle back to that particular transgression of his. Still, he couldn't help but like her little flares of temper. It was perverse of him, but every time she got that tone, his entire body reacted.

"If I am to be very honest with you, I will admit I did see that this was no longer an accepted practice. On the other hand, simply because we have that knowledge does not mean we must accept it."

Her dark eyes picked up the candlelight so little twin flames flickered in her eyes. "You are beyond all reason, Isai. You knew you shouldn't and yet you still did."

"You knew you shouldn't taunt me so disrespectfully and yet you still did," he retaliated, refusing to take all blame.

"A war of words is not the same as putting your hand on someone. Especially someone you care about. Child or woman," she informed him in her most chastising voice.

"That is what they teach you now, little mage, but what of the child who refuses to stay away from the water when he cannot swim? Or he runs out in front of a car, disobeying your orders to stay out of the street? How do you treat the unruly child who refuses to listen?"

She flung her hands into the air. "You are making me crazy. *Crazy.* I'm trying to make things right between us, but you are insisting on remaining that man from a distant century. Maybe spanking a *child* because a saber-toothed tiger might eat him would be appropriate, but we're long past those dangers."

"Drowning and getting hit by a car are equally as dangerous as getting eaten by a saber-toothed tiger. Your argument has no merit."

He liked that she wanted to make things right between them. Still, he had to disappoint her. He didn't want to, but he needed to let her know the risk. "Julija, I think it is a good thing that you reach out and befriend Elisabeta. She needs that, and I think you do as well. Unfortunately, you have opened yourself up to Sergey's scrutiny. He will be looking for the mage powerful enough to reach the woman he claims as his own."

She frowned, her dark eyebrows pulling close to each other. "He can't claim her. She isn't his. He had no right."

"No, he did not. As you well know, many people turn ugly for various reasons. Money. Power. Sex. Whatever the reason. They want something others have. Sergey and his brothers didn't want to follow the prince. They felt they were powerful enough to lead the Carpathian people. It isn't about the kind of power they perceive, but they didn't understand that and probably still don't."

"Would sex be the reason for taking Elisabeta?"

"Sergey could not make her his woman, not in the sense of raping her body. He could rape her mind. He could do things to her body, but he couldn't perform the sex act with her in the accepted sense. I know vampires have tried to do so with victims they chose to torture further before draining them of blood, but it would have killed her and Sergey knows it."

"Then why take her?"

"Because she is pure light. Elisabeta brings him what he cannot have for himself ever again. When making the decision to become vampire, a deliberate choice, he prepared by kidnapping her and making her his prisoner. He was very clever. She gave him emotion. She kept his body from decomposing. She gave him Carpathian blood, the strongest there is. Because of Elisabeta, he could take a back seat to his brothers and plot to become emperor. No one would see him as anything but weak. No master vampire would tolerate that kind of disrespect, but Elisabeta gave him that power."

"Will Ferro spank her if she misbehaves?" Her voice was low, and she gave him a look from her dark chocolate eyes that should have melted him. It did, but it was his heart that did the melting.

Isai burst out laughing. "You're never going to let that go, are you?"

"Absolutely not. You'll be hearing about it until the day you die," she assured him.

He wasn't touching that one. "How about we drop this argument for a while and you tell me something about yourself." At first, he had thought to keep his distance from Julija so when he left it wouldn't hurt so much, but for some reason he couldn't fathom, he really wanted to get to know her. Already, everything she said and did just made him want her more. His interest was genuine, and his sincerity came through in his tone.

"I love to play the piano," she offered without hesitation.

He lifted his head to look her directly in the eyes. Her face lit up, and her eyes went bright. Her immediate answer was the last thing he expected from her. He didn't know why. Maybe because of all things, music brought him a semblance of peace when he was so alone. It didn't make him feel anything, so it had never made sense, but when he heard music, everything wild in him stilled.

"The piano?" Deliberately, he provoked her. He found he didn't like Julija subdued. He infused skepticism into his voice. "You play?"

She narrowed her eyes at him. "You do know what a piano is, don't you?"

"I certainly do, but am having a difficult time believing you do. It takes discipline to master the keyboard. You do not have discipline in abundance." The moment the words left his mouth, he felt the sting of an insect on his left cheek, low, by the corner of his mouth. He clapped his hand over what should have been a bug but was nothing but air. He glared at Julija. She sat there looking innocent. Too innocent.

"Did you just zap me?"

She lifted one hand and inspected her fingernails. "I have no idea what you're talking about." The moment the words left her mouth, she felt the smack of a hard hand on her bottom, which was impossible because she was sitting. She jumped and glared at him. "We are about to go to war."

"You fired the first shot, little mage."

She rolled her eyes. "Well, fine, I surrender."

He was almost disappointed. He liked sparring with her better than he should have. "I was teasing about you playing the piano," he conceded. "You're very . . ." He searched for the proper word. *Adorable. Cute.* He didn't use words like that to describe his woman. *Fiery. Passionate. Sexy.* He finally settled on, "I like it, and I shouldn't have baited you." She looked pleased and he sighed with relief that he got something right with her.

"I actually was teasing you a little bit, too," she admitted. "I didn't mind. In fact, I kind of liked zapping you."

"I knew you did it."

She looked smug. "That's just the tip of the iceberg in case you're re-thinking our truce."

He held up his hands in surrender. "Tell me what you like about playing the piano."

"I *love* playing the piano because it gives me a sense of peace. I can go far away from everything and everyone and just fall into the music. It transports me to a safe place. At least it feels safe."

He went still inside. Her statement revealed a lot about her. So far, he'd been more than respectful, not reading her mind but waiting for her to give consent. It didn't appear as if that was going to happen anytime soon. He needed to know everything about Julija.

"Music saved me a time or two," he admitted. "In the high reaches of the Carpathian Mountains, locked away from even those who could pro-vide us with blood, we spent the days pursuing our fighting skills and trying to fill empty hours with other arts. Some painted. I chose music. I studied it as much as possible. There were others who came and went. They would bring back to us supplies or knowledge we needed to continue to grow. They stayed a few years, sometimes as long as a century, and then they would leave us."

"How did you feed?"

Just the fact that she knew to use the word *feed* instead of *eat* told him she was well versed in the Carpathian culture. Unexpectedly, that hurt all over again.

"Fane, the gatekeeper, left us every night to get blood for us." Even as the words left him, he remembered the feel of her mouth on his skin. Her teeth sank into him, connecting them, so they shared his vein. So the essence of his life's blood could flow from him to her. *She* had done that. He hadn't done it for her. He'd barely pushed the command at her. She'd been willing, and not once had she questioned his taking of her blood. Not one single time.

"You have a mage mark." He indicated the mark on her arm. The mark was very distinct. A snake coiled around the belly of a scorpion. The claws and stinger on the scorpion were poised and ready and the mouth of the snake was open, showing fangs, while its raised tail gave warning. "Yet you know about Carpathians and were able on your own to take my blood."

She nodded. "I studied Carpathians because they are the focus of my family. Carpathians are considered the enemy. Xavier wanted them wiped from the earth. And yes, I am able to take blood directly, although I was careful not to show that particular ability to my family for many years."

There was reluctance in her voice and her face flamed red. She looked away from him, but not before he caught a glimpse of distress in her. Whatever memory he had invoked was extremely painful to her.

"Can you explain further?" he asked gently.

"I would prefer not to," she said.

He could see she half expected him to rip her memories from her mind. Instead, he stood up, towering over her. "You really need to lie down. I can feel your exhaustion beating at me."

She stood as well, and he remained towering over her. He indicated the bed and they both walked to it.

"I am tired," she admitted. "I didn't sleep at all last night."

She would have to get used to that if she was staying with him.

"The light is creeping in and I have to go to ground. I really don't like leaving you alone. You're not unprotected." He didn't want her to be afraid, nor did he want to insult her by implying she couldn't handle being alone when she already had proven she could. "You are powerful in your own right, Julija, and you are aware of that power. Still, if needed, wake me and I will give you mine, as much as possible when the paralysis takes me."

She nodded. "I'll be fine. I appreciate the offer. I know it is not given often or lightly."

She knew far more about Carpathian customs than she was letting on. "Before I retire, do you need food? I've put water beside the bed on that little stand. There is what passes for a bathroom in that tiny alcove right there." He indicated the only corner in the chamber that was some-what secluded.

"I appreciate it." She sank down on the bed, suddenly tired. Very tired.

Isai crouched down and began removing her hiking boot. He stripped off one of her socks and did the same to the other one before inspecting both feet.

"I did have blisters, but I was able to heal them," she admitted. "It isn't my strongest suit, but I can do it when I have to."

He massaged her feet for a few minutes. "Get undressed and I'll pull up the sheets."

"I can do that part myself."

"Julija."

"Seriously, Isai. If you're not prepared to have wild sex, then it isn't a good idea for me to take off my clothes in front of you."

His cock jerked at that thought. He wanted her, plain and simple, but now he had a new plan for his little mage. Sex was his backup plan. He could get her addicted since he already was, but he thought perhaps he would win her over faster if he showed restraint in that area. She was right, the moment he saw her body, his discipline would go right out the window. Not to mention, he could feel the effects of the sun on him al-ready. His skin burned, and he was in a cave where the rays couldn't reach him.

He stood up slowly and took her hand, turning it over, palm up, his thumb sliding gently over the scars on her wrist. "The shadow cat was extremely large. Is it possible, rather than to kill you, it was sent to reacquire you?"

She looked up at him and there was a hint of fear in her eyes as if she hadn't even considered that possibility. "How could it do that?"

His thumb slid over the numerous scars on the inside of her wrist. "I am not certain, but it is something to think about. You are their supply of Carpathian blood, right? They need you to continue their longevity. Carpathian blood is not easy to come by and yours is very rich. They hurt you, didn't they?"

A little shudder went through her body. Her gaze jumped to his and held there. He saw fear. He wasn't certain whether that fear was for him finding out some of her secrets, because now he knew she had them, or whether he was probing too deeply into memories she couldn't examine yet.

He brought her wrist to his mouth, his lips whispering a kiss there. She looked confused, but she didn't attempt to pull away. "*Kislány hän ku meke sarnaakmet minan*, I would very much like you to answer me."

There was the briefest of hesitations. "Yes."

The admission was so low he barely heard it, and he was Carpathian, therefore his hearing was acute.

"They will pay."

5

Julija woke to the sound of something scratching at the outside walls of the cave. She lay staring up at the ceiling, her heart pounding. She had never heard the sound before, but she knew what it was. The light in the cave spilling from the crack on the west-facing side of the granite bluff flickered light to shadow over and over as if something paced in front of it, trying to get in.

She forced herself to drag air in and out of her lungs. Very slowly, so as not to make any sound, she sat up and put her feet over the side of the bed. After Isai had gone to ground, she had undressed and gotten under the covers. He had provided an incredibly comfortable bed for her. The mattress was perfect. The weight of the covers just right. The feel of the sheets on her bare skin was luxurious.

She didn't use magic to clothe herself because creatures made up of magic and flesh and bone were particularly sensitive to any surge of power. She pulled on her jeans, shimmying them over her hips, her bare feet on the floor of the cave. Rather than dirt and rock, her toes sank into a thick carpet. Isai was close, and the sun would sink soon. She was grateful she wasn't alone. The shadow cats scared her as nothing else could have.

As she drew the tee over her head, she felt a stab of pain go through her brain, like a sharp needle piercing from one side to the other. She went down to one knee, grabbing her head and holding it as if that could help reduce the agony in her brain.

Julija, I command you to return immediately. Your brothers are waiting. They will turn you over to Barnabas and he will escort you home. They will pursue the Carpathian and the stolen book. You should never have warned them.

Naturally, after the terrible fight they'd had, her father would believe that she had warned the Carpathians and they'd been waiting for the shadow cat. There was no way to convince them otherwise and she wasn't so foolish as to try. The moment she opened her mouth to defend herself, the shadow cats might have a way to lock on to her energy. They had tracked her there, but so far, they couldn't get past Isai's safeguards, let alone her own that she'd added to the complicated weave.

Julija. Her name was a hiss of displeasure accompanied by another, particularly vicious jab. The skin on her wrist suddenly split and blood began to drip to the floor. *You will die there, wherever he has taken you. There is no one that can save you from the things I can do to you.*

She managed to breathe through the pain, but when she crawled the scant foot to the bed to pull herself up, her face was reflected there. Her skin appeared to be sloughing off. Looking down she could see dark spots opening all over her skin. The pressure on her chest was tremendous, as if an elephant sat there. Her heart stumbled, and the air refused to go in or out of her lungs. She fell to the floor, the thick carpet cushioning her fall and preventing sound from escaping.

Julija stilled the chaos of her brain, the images telling her she would die in agony if she didn't comply with her father's demand. She had trained for this day. Was fully prepared. She just had to find a way to get enough air to carry out her plan.

As if Isai had heard her need, dirt and rock spewed into a mini volcano, erupting a few feet from her. He emerged, fully clothed, looking unstoppable. He crouched beside her, lifted her into his arms and took her mouth, pushing air into her lungs. Immediately, the paralysis left her, and she was breathing again.

He grinned at her and winked like a co-conspirator. He waved his hand in the air as if to say, "take over" and then he lifted her wrist to his mouth to capture the ruby red drops dripping from the tear. His tongue slid over the laceration and he licked up the few that were still running down her arm. He didn't see the dark spots or the skin sloughing off her face.

He turned toward the sound of the frantic scratching. He held up his fingers, indicating two. She nodded in agreement. She was confident in her ability to manipulate illusions, to cast them and repel them, and to send them where she wanted them to go. She lifted her hands into the air and began to form a pattern using graceful movements of her arms, wrists, hands and fingers.

Scatter, dissipate, disperse, dispel,
I bind these illusions that were born by air.
Warrior bird, talons of steel,
Within this pattern turn and reveal.
Fire I call you and command you to burn,
All visible threads so none may return.

Anatolie's scream of agony resounded through her mind. She bent her head, ashamed. She had always promised herself she wouldn't use her abilities for anything but good. Hurting another being, even one such as her father, by using her gifts made her feel slightly sick.

Isai wrapped his arm around her waist and bent to brush kisses along the corner of her eye. His hands went to frame both sides of her head. There was a feeling of warmth and the piercing needle was gone, receding with the pain.

"He's in my mind so he knows how to get to me."

"You have a shield that is unbelievably strong."

Her gaze jumped to his face, looked right into those sapphire eyes of his. What she saw there sent her stomach on a slow roll. "But you can get past it, right? I've felt you struggle a couple of times when you wanted to, but you didn't. My father found a way."

"That gives him access to you that we don't want. Can you build one he cannot breach?"

Julija liked that he asked—that he thought she could. She hated to disappoint him. "I've tried so many times. It's like he knows everything I'm doing almost before I do it and he knocks it down."

His hand slid from her shoulder to her wrist and then his fingers closed around hers. Both were ignoring the yowling cats, or at least trying to. Now, the cats sounded desperate, like if they didn't get to Julija, something terrible was going to happen.

"We can build one together if you trust me enough to allow me to help you." He pulled her hand to his chin and regarded her intensely with his vividly colored eyes.

"Yes. I'd like help. If I can keep him out, they'll have a difficult time following, especially if we can get rid of the—" She broke off, her chin jerking up. Her gaze darted back and forth between the crack in the rock and him. "I recognize those yowls. I do. Last night, I heard the same yowl. It was as if one cat was calling to another, telling it something."

"What are you thinking?"

"I helped several of the cats. I was good to them when my brothers weren't. There were two cats in particular I went to every night for over a month. The female was far more receptive than the male. I thought the male was going to kill me several times. He had come back so torn up and wouldn't let me near him at first."

"You mentioned him."

She nodded and moved a little closer to the front of the cavern, careful not to get too close to the crack. Even so, the cats became frenzied, scratching at the rock wall to get to her.

"They both needed blood and I gave them mine. I treated his wounds and the whip marks on her. My brothers amused themselves by hurting the things they created. They said they weren't real, so why not? The cats have substance. They need food or blood to survive. They can be killed. It isn't right."

"No, Julija, it isn't."

She looked at him over her shoulder, seeing the admiration there. His expression made her inexplicably happy. She couldn't help the little burst of joy that spread through her. "I think those two cats are my cats."

The smile was instantly gone from his face. "Julija," he said in warning.

"The one that attacked you was probably paired with the one sent after the book. My brothers tended to train them in pairs. If these are mine, we can keep them with us."

He shook his head. "I am not willing to risk your life."

"The risk is mine to take. They're innocent creatures. They didn't ask for my brothers to shape them into killers."

"Killers, *sívamet*, did you just hear what you said?"

He had been calling her "little mage" and the more possessive "my little mage" in his ancient language, but *sívamet* was an altogether different nickname. It was much more of an endearment, something a male Carpathian might call his love. It literally meant *of my heart* or more loosely translated, *my love*. She found she wished she had the time to dwell on that. Had it just slipped out and meant nothing? Or had it slipped out and meant everything?

"I know what I said. There are two of us. We're powerful and we can stop them together. We're prepared this time. I know it's them, Isai. Trust me. Please."

She could see his decision was swaying in her direction, but he didn't like it. "Even if they don't want to rip you apart, they will want to kill me."

"Then we have to make certain they know you're with me. That you're mine. They understand pairs because they were surrounded by them. When one of a pair died the other proved useless to my brothers. It would either go insane and try to attack them or wouldn't respond."

"Because they were giving them Carpathian traits. Mixing your blood in with their food," he guessed. "When a male lifemate dies, the female can hold on if necessary, but her heart and soul are with that male. If a female dies, the male will either suicide or turn vampire. Your brothers, by giving the pairs your blood, created a similar bond."

The reminder of what lay between them coming out of his mouth so matter-of-factly embarrassed her. She was also shocked at how quickly he'd figured out what her brothers had done. "That's exactly right. I was fairly certain that was what happened."

Isai lifted his hands and began taking down the first few layers of the safeguards. When he reached Julija's work she stood in front of the crack, softly murmured a greeting to the cats and then began to reverse her spell.

Shadows upon me, be trapped by light.
Return to your darkness, never find sight.
I send you back from whence you've come.
Never to cross over or shadows become.

The cats quieted and began to chuff, interspersing the sound with a call to Julija. That was the only reason Isai finished taking down the safeguards. At the last moment, he stepped well back from the entrance and Julija wrapped her arms tightly around his waist, standing mostly in front of him but to one side.

"I don't like you there. Get behind me," Isai said tersely as the cats slunk through the very thin crack.

The shadow cats were long and built like sleek panthers. By turns they were black or gray, and they moved with the fluid, stalking steps of a predator. These were no cuddly kittens. Ears back, they showed their teeth, wicked canines very much in evidence. Their eyes glowed somewhere between a ruby red and a strange amber, going back and forth just as the colors on their bodies moved from black to gray.

Julija broke into a smile, she couldn't help it. She recognized the pair immediately from the scars on them. "Blue and Belle, I missed you." She kept her voice happy and yet pitched very low.

Isai's eyebrows shot up. "Bluebell? Like the flower."

She narrowed her eyes and gave him a look to remind him she was in charge. It didn't seem to work. He gave her a faint grin in answer, and just that expression warmed the sapphire in his eyes to a hot glow. She felt her stomach do that slow roll and she had to hastily turn her attention back to the shadow cats.

Both cats looked from Julija to Isai. She needed to keep their attention centered on her. She wanted to step more in front of Isai to shield him just in case either or both cats decided to attack, but she knew he wouldn't allow it. Twice she tried to be subtle and just take one small step forward, but he moved with her as if he knew what she was thinking. She sent him an exasperated look over her shoulder.

"Seriously? You can see they're friendly."

When she turned back both cats were giving him a perfect view of their teeth. "Oh, stop it. He's a friend. Behave yourselves. Come meet him instead of slinking around acting like you're going to eat him."

She crouched low, but as she did, her hand slid down Isai's arm to his hand. She tried to be casual about it, as if she touched him every single day. Being so close to him was exhilarating. Her blood pulsed through her veins in a rush of heat. She felt so alive, a little scared, but very alive.

His fingers closed around her hand and she actually felt that connection deeper, somewhere in the region of her heart. He had a way of making her feel safe as well as cared for. She was used to doing things on her own, definitely used to facing danger alone. Isai made her feel as if he had her back and would fight for her if anything went wrong.

The female stepped closer, her neck stretched long so she could sniff at Isai's hand, the one wrapped around hers. Her heartbeat accelerated. The male crouched in an attack position, ready to spring on Isai if he made one wrong move toward the female.

The two cats had to accept him. If they didn't, if they attacked him, Julija knew she would have to kill them. There was no other choice. They couldn't be left without direction when her brothers had made certain to make them killing machines needing blood to survive.

Belle, the female, touched her nose to Isai's hand and then tentatively licked at him, tasting his skin. Julija's heart was in her throat. There was no way that Belle wouldn't scent Isai's rich, pure Carpathian blood. He was an ancient and his blood was very powerful. That would call to both cats. This was the telling moment.

The cat pulled back abruptly and regarded him steadily with her ruby eyes. Julija kept watch on the male, but noted Belle's eyes continued to change color rapidly, until, thankfully, they were more amber than red.

The cat once again stretched her neck toward them, and this time she laid her head on Julija's shoulder. Julija immediately scratched under her chin.

"Hey, baby. I missed you, too. You were the one who called the other cat back, weren't you? I thought maybe I recognized your voice. You know they're going to be very, very angry at you for running off and finding me."

Belle pushed against her with her full weight, going from insubstantial to all sleek black fur and roped muscle. Julija ended up on her butt with the cat in her lap. She couldn't help but laugh, ruffling the fur. It was rare for a shadow cat to feel safe enough to become wholly substantial. She'd always felt so sad for them in that horrid room where her brothers experimented on them. The tongue was rough as it lapped at her face repeatedly.

"Okay, okay." She was laughing so hard she couldn't push the cat away from her. "I'm happy to see you, too. You have to stop."

She sensed movement and caught Belle around the neck to try to push her head down, so she could see around her. Blue was giving Isai a wide berth, keeping a wary eye on him, but he wanted to get in as close to her as possible. Over the weeks she'd treated his injuries, he'd finally allowed her to get close without using a holding spell. Once he'd accepted her, he had given her his absolute loyalty. Her brothers never once suspected she was visiting the shed where they kept the animals that lived through their experiments.

"Come sit beside me," Julija invited Isai and patted the spot next to her.

"When I was very young, I came across a mother leopard with three kits. She was dying of injuries inflicted by another leopard. It was too late to save her, but I kept the little ones alive. They followed me everywhere and when I slept, they slept above my resting place. As you can well imagine, for a hunter of vampires, it wasn't an ideal situation."

She reached up her hand to clasp his again. "I'll bet they were a handful."

"They played all the time. I found I spent a good deal of my time rounding them up. I didn't make the best mother to them."

She had to look up at his face and catch his expression. There was warmth there, and a hint of amusement at the memory. It was a good memory. She was happy he had it. She tugged on his hand, reminding him to sit beside her. She knew that would put him in a vulnerable position, and he'd already experienced an attack by another shadow cat. He knew the kind of terrible venom they carried in their claws.

"I'll bet that isn't true. You probably were an awesome mother. These came to me full-grown."

"I think they're coming to you again, Julija. They don't want to go back. Is there a way your brothers call them back?"

"Yes, they use a high-frequency whistle and the cats are taught to respond to that sound. If the cats don't, they use pain to make them return."

"The same kind of pain your father used against you?"

She retreated the way she always did, trying to pull her hand away, but he closed his fingers firmly around hers and sank down beside her, every bit as graceful as she was although he was a big man.

Isai ignored the warning Blue gave him. The male cat snarled and showed his teeth, drawing back from them once again. Instead, he brought Julija's hand to his mouth and pressed a kiss into the center of her palm. "I felt the pain, little mage. It is impossible to go back. We can only go forward. Your family is not just your problem."

"I know." She did know. She'd been conditioned to keep all things mage private, not to mention, it was embarrassing to have a family like hers. They conducted brutal experiments on animals. They casually murdered when someone got in their way. They plotted to kill off entire species for their own gain. Hers wasn't exactly the kind of family you invited your friends to come and meet.

"You cannot possibly survive if you attempt to fight them alone. They will eventually find you, although I do not believe they will kill you. I think they need you alive for your blood."

"That reminds me, you need to feed."

His blue eyes met hers and she felt a jolt of awareness go through her body. His intense gaze drifted over her and she felt as if he left blue flames licking at her skin everywhere his attention touched.

He reached out and gently caught the nape of her neck, pulling her close to him. She turned her head to give him better access, lowering her lashes to savor his touch. She all but forgot the two shadow cats until both pressed closer, watching intently with their wide, amber eyes.

Isai stroked her neck right over her pounding pulse with his tongue. The lightest of touches, but it felt like the burn of a brand. The flash of pain, although expected, did the unexpected. The sensation felt like an erotic arrow straight to her sex. Her feminine sheath clenched, and her nipples peaked. His arms drew her closer to him as he drank. The sensation was intimate, sensual and possessive. She wanted to drown in the feeling, just stay there forever with him.

The cats moved closer, Blue pressing into her so that his nose could nearly touch Isai. Julija knew the ancient Carpathian was aware of the cats, especially the big male. She *felt* his heightened alert, but he finished feeding before running his tongue over the twin piercings in her neck to stop the bleeding.

"I think your pets are looking for a meal."

She stroked a caress over the male's head. The cat didn't take his eyes off Isai.

He leaned toward the animal. "Are you hungry, friend? Didn't they feed you?"

His tone was smooth, soft, even gentle. Very friendly. A shiver of awareness crept down her spine. She found, in spite of their very rocky beginning, there were quite a few things she liked about Isai. He treated animals with respect and compassion.

"My brothers liked to keep the cats hungry. They sometimes fed them human flesh."

Isai frowned. "The cats are natural predators and they clearly tried to make them even more vicious, yet they aren't nearly as ferocious as one would think. Why aren't they attacking me? If they are hungry, by rights, they should be looking at me as if I am their next meal."

"I think, because I gave them my blood on a regular basis—"

"Wait," he interrupted. "Did you take their blood at any time?"

"I had to. I wanted to be able to control them if needed or know if they were hurt. I didn't want my brothers to kill them."

He regarded her for a long moment and then casually bit into his wrist and offered the blood to the male cat. Blue nearly leapt forward and hungrily lapped at the drops of blood.

"What are you doing?" Julija's breath caught in her throat. "You could make it worse. Your blood is far more powerful than mine. My brothers still control the cats with pain. If they command them to kill us, if they find out the cats are with us, they'll hurt them until the animals comply with their commands."

Fear for Isai nearly swamped her. Normally she would have been afraid for the shadow cats, but now, all she could think about was Blue tearing into Isai.

Isai calmly swept his free arm around her. "We are going to prevent that from happening. You are from a lineage known as Dragonseeker. That particular line is legendary."

"Elisabeta was telling me something about it."

"Although you have the mark of the high mage, straight from Xavier's line, you have more Carpathian blood in you than mage. You have converted these shadow cats to Carpathian and they need blood to survive, but they also have taken on the traits of a Carpathian. Your brothers bred them for intelligence, and they have that. It is very evident, even the way they work in pairs. He sent her forward to check me out, but he was waiting to kill me if need be."

"You can't know all that."

"I feel their blood calling to mine. If you are still and you know what to look for in your mind, you will feel it as well. When they are both fed, we will first work on the shield in your mind to prevent your father or brothers from harming you and then together, we will do the same in theirs."

Julija wasn't certain what to think. Could it be true that she was far more Carpathian than mage? She was extremely good at casting illusions. "Isai," she said in protest.

"Think about what you do and how fast you became good at it. Your father is not going to let on to you that you hold the power of both the high mage and Dragonseeker. He keeps you in line with pain because he has no other way. You have dared to break away from him and he *has* to get you back. You are too valuable to them."

Calmly he instructed the male cat to stop drinking from his wrist. The cat snarled at him but backed up to allow the female to take his place.

"Let me, Isai. You'll be too weak for us to build shields or fight enemies. We still have to find the book and get it somewhere safe."

"They both need to recognize that I am head of the family. I will give the orders to them the same as you do. If we keep these animals alive, they have to recognize the authority and obey all laws of the Carpathian people. Turning animals is strictly forbidden, although I have heard that was done with wolves, and now, clearly with these cats as well."

She wasn't certain how to feel when he made himself head of the family, but the fact that turning an animal was against the laws of the Carpathian people and he hadn't killed the two cats outright made her like him even more. On some level, she knew that if he took these cats under his protection, he would fight to the death for them.

"What happened to the leopards, Isai? The ones that slept above you and most likely hindered your ability to hide from your enemies."

He gave her another one of those priceless grins. It was faint, but amusement climbed into his eyes, lighting them, turning them into those gleaming jewels that managed to send a wealth of butterflies winging their way through her stomach. He reached out almost lazily and scratched the top of Belle's head.

"They lived out their lives and I buried the last one right before I lost my emotions. They stayed with me for years and yes, they did give away my resting places and mostly hindered my ability to use flight, but it was worth it." Again, he was gentle in pulling his wrist from the cat.

Julija liked watching his fingers stroke the cat's fur. She found herself mesmerized by the way he murmured softly and reassuringly to the animals.

"You do have a few good traits, lifemate," she said, trying to sound casual. She was opening a can of worms and she knew it. She wasn't certain she could ever accept him and his authority. She had been on her own and there was no way she would ever be able to make herself into a "yes" woman. She liked who she was, other than coming from her murderous family. She laughed at that thought.

He quirked an eyebrow, and she decided to be honest.

"I was just thinking that I like who I am right now. It took me a long time to come to terms with who I am, but then I realized I liked myself in spite of coming from a murderous family. They are not nice people and introducing them to you won't go very smoothly."

His lips did that fascinating quirk that gave away that he was feeling amused. She couldn't help but stare in fascination at the way just that curve to his mouth softened the harsh lines in his face.

"You are just buttering me up so I will tell you what my tattoo says." He held out his hand and pulled her to her feet, once more waving his hand toward the center of the chamber so the two chairs were back. "It will not happen . . ."

Her heart dropped.

"Yet. Go sit in one of the chairs and call the cats to you. I will connect with you first and help you build an impenetrable shield so Anatolie cannot get in your head. You will have to give your consent, little mage, to allow me into your mind. I will not force you."

"This is going to weaken you." She turned away from him quickly, hurrying across the chamber to the comfortable chairs. She didn't want to look at him because she wasn't certain how she felt about letting him into her mind. She was very, very confused when it came to the entire lifemate custom.

She *was* his lifemate. She was certain she was. The pull between them was too strong. It was just that she had lost her ability to trust and he would see . . . She closed her eyes as she sank into the luxury of the chair. He would see into her past. She didn't want to go there. Not ever. She couldn't face that particular betrayal, nor did she want Isai to see how naïve and silly she'd been. How deeply her humiliation had gone.

"Julija?"

Could his voice be any more patient? Any gentler? Why couldn't he sound like the dictator from hell? She tried to conjure up the feel of his hand hitting her bottom, but even that eluded her when his voice stroked over her skin like a velvet rasp.

She touched her tongue to her lips. "There are things in my past I'm ashamed of. If I open my mind to yours and give my permission, you can see the things I don't want to remember or think about ever again."

"I can erase these memories from your mind."

Her gaze jumped to his. She only saw his compassion. There wasn't morbid curiosity. She couldn't imagine him taunting her with her stupidity. She couldn't stop the little shake of her head. "You would still remember."

"I would not care."

"How could you not?"

"You still do not entirely understand the concept of lifemates, Julija. I would protect you from anything, including these memories that make you sad. Right now, the most important thing to do is protect you from your father. He is bound to strike again soon."

"When my brothers get close to this place, he'll do so then to distract me."

"Then let me help you, *sívamet*, before he strikes at you."

Julija had to make up her mind immediately. Either she trusted him, or she didn't. Isai was pale after giving both cats blood. He'd been careful not to take too much of hers because he didn't want her weak. He needed to feed. It would be easy enough to find a camper and then return to her, but she knew he wouldn't until all of them were protected.

"Will I be able to see into your mind?" Her heart beat far too fast and for the first time since she was a young child, she couldn't seem to command it to a steady rhythm.

He heard, of course. He stepped close to the chair, in between the two cats, and very gently used his hands on the inside of her thighs to open them to him. He knelt down between her legs and suddenly, fear and apprehension mixed with erotic hunger and a sense of urgency.

He took her hand and pressed it to his chest over his heart. "Feel that. Let your heart follow the beat of mine. Breathe with me."

His eyes held hers captive and she found air moving through her lungs in time to his. Her heart found the exact rhythm of his and beat simultaneously. She had no idea what to expect, but it wasn't his mind pouring slowly into hers. Nothing had ever felt so intimate. Nothing had ever been so sensual. He found places in her mind, those torn, ugly memories that she couldn't fix in herself and somehow, he just filled those cracks, the shredded places that kept her apart from everyone else.

He didn't feel in the least triumphant, but more a part of her. More as if he wholly belonged right there. Once he was in her mind, she knew it would be difficult to be alone again.

He had left his mark on you. A mage mark, not a sliver of himself. He cannot see through your eyes, but he can reach for this mark. It is uniquely his.

Alarms went off in her head. *Don't try to get rid of it. He will know.*

Kislány hän ku meke sarnaakmet minan, I have been dealing with mages from nearly the time I was born. I am well aware that your father will eventually strike at us. First, we will build your shield so when I remove his mark, he cannot retaliate.

Isai, Anatolie is a very powerful mage. In his own right, he might actually equal Xavier in power. He will not tolerate interference. I had no idea he had put his mark on me. He'll find out about you.

You are not thinking straight. He has taught you to fear him. He already knows about me. The cat returned to your brothers with my blood in its claws.

That was on her. She jammed her fist into her mouth and tried not to rock back and forth like a child. Fear of Anatolie often did that to her, although she'd always kept her terror private and didn't allow it to stop her from her plans to break away. By choosing not to try to kill the shadow cat, she had put Isai directly into Anatolie's path.

He has your blood. Do you know what a mage can do with someone's blood? The thought was terrifying to her.

Yes. Work with me. You are of that lineage, too, Julija.

She knew he could see the chaos and fear in her mind. The cats sensed it and became mere shadows, slinking through the chamber, red eyes gleaming as they tried to ferret out the threat.

You said yourself I am mostly Carpathian.

That does not make you less, sívamet, it makes you more. You are the best of both worlds. You hold the power of both. You do not need me to do this for you or even with you, but you have me, and I am willing to be your protector.

She pressed her lips together and signaled for Belle and Blue to return to her. She didn't want them to become so agitated that they struck out in fear or aggression.

I would much rather we work together. She knew he was an ancient and a Carpathian male. It was ingrained in them to protect their women and children at all times. She had been raised mage and she would always want to stand by his side to aid in the way she could. She was very aware he could see that in her mind. Another strike against her with a man born and bred centuries earlier in a culture where the men took care of their women.

Soft amusement slid into her mind. *That was the ideal in a man's mind, but all does not go the way of the male. Some women aided their partners.*

He didn't have to tell her that. He could have kept that admission to himself. Elation swept through her. She forced her mind and body under control.

I built that shield myself using spells I created without the foundation of any known mage invocation. I don't know how he was able to mark me.

He put the mark on you at birth. He took no chances. Remember, he bred you for your blood, not to be a mage to help him with his plans. He needs you alive. That cat was meant to return you, not kill you.

She knew that, but she hadn't considered just how much her father and brothers needed her. *He knows I'm after the book. He'll think we want to use it against him. I want it destroyed.*

Is there a way to destroy it?

She was silent for a moment, feeling him in her, waiting. Filling her. Making her feel as if she wasn't so alone. *I think it is possible. I'm still working it out in my head.*

Then let's find a way to keep him out. Show me the spell you used for your shield. We will weave safeguards around what is in place. The weave needs to come from both of us, so that each safeguard is intertwined. I will cover the mark while we work and then once it is done, destroy his hold on you.

It sounded so simple. *Do you want me to again invoke the spell to shield me from any intruder I don't wish to give consent to?*

Yes. When you reach the end, you will add to your weave one line and then I will until it is done.

Mirror reflect all hostile intent
Black salt repels that which is negative sent.
I sweep away that which would bind
I call to the directions to wall off my mind.
As air is to earth, fire is to water
None may enter, nor shall they bother.

Together, Julija, he said softly, *I will weave a strand then you.* He didn't wait for her response.

Mind to body
Reflective mirror shall hold.

She didn't hesitate.

Through pain and darkness
Seek to unfold.

He wove the next strand.

That which is pure
Shall remain untouched.

Julija finished the last strand.

Allowing no illusion or falseness to touch.

With her magic he wove his own, so together they were twice as strong.

Isai didn't wait, he shed his body and entered her mind as spirit only. She felt the intense heat. At once he poured everything he was into pure light, concentrating the beam on the tiny dark stain her father had placed in her at birth. The light burned right through the darkness.

The moment the brilliant ray hit the mark, Julija felt Anatolie strike at her. He slashed at her mind with what felt like razor blades. She cried out, but the mark was already burned away and with it went the pain.

The last thing she heard was the shriek of fury her father gave just before the last of the mark was gone. There was a moment of absolute silence as if the earth was holding its breath. Isai returned to his body but didn't leave her mind. They waited. Isai took her hand, remaining kneeling in front of her.

Anatolie struck at her. It was a decisive blow, trying to get into her mind. She felt the contact, as if there was a punch aimed toward her outer temple, but she countered it with a brush of her hand as if she could brush him away. He hit from every angle, over and over. Around them, the bluffs shook, sending boulders crashing down. The cats leapt to their feet with terrified yowls, going from black substance to shadow.

Isai waved his hand to the crumbling chamber, and it remained intact without so much as a small bit of dirt falling to the floor.

Anatolie retreated for the briefest of moments and then struck again, this time at her throat, wrapping hands around her and squeezing. Isai's hands got there before hers, destroying the illusion by simply covering the hands with his and removing them. The two countered illusions and strikes for the better part of an hour, then Anatolie was suddenly gone.

Julija knew it wasn't over and she found herself holding her breath again, looking at the man in front of her. Waiting for the axe to fall on them. She heard the snarl almost before Isai.

6

I sai had given the shadow cats his blood. He felt the difference in them immediately. Pain amounting to agony stabbed deeply at both cats. The two became enraged and looked for a target. He wasn't the target because Anatolie hadn't yet gotten Isai's blood from his two sons. He turned, placing his body squarely in front of Julija's as he rose, pinning the male cat with a predator's stare. He reached for the animals at the same time, mind to mind.

The high mage was in a fury. He struck at the two cats, directing them to find Julija and hurt her. Rip her to shreds within an inch of her life. They could take her life's blood until there was little left. He wanted her alive, but just barely. More, he would not let up on the agony the cats suffered until the job was done.

Anatolie stabbed at their minds over and over, deliberately hurting them, taking pleasure in it. Both cats could feel the mage's enjoyment of the cruel act. He wanted them to know he liked hurting them, and that he would continue until they did as he ordered.

"Merge with me, Julija," Isai instructed. He kept his voice very low, soothing even in an effort not to provoke the cats any further.

She did so without hesitation, filling his mind with—her. She was feminine, but very strong. He could feel her power sliding up against his and then merging completely. Her hand bunched in his shirt at the small of his back. He was utterly aware of her, every breath she took, every small hitch as she fought to maintain their connection when her father's cruelty was torturing the two cats she'd come to care for.

"We are going to concentrate on Blue first. We have to drive Anatolie out of him and build a barrier fast. We will not have much time. He will try to kill Belle, so we will have to be able to quickly get to her and throw him out."

"Isai, perhaps I should take one cat and you the other."

"We will be far more powerful together. Your father is extremely formidable. He is already in control. We have to surprise him with speed and attack."

"Hurry," she urged. "Isai, what he's doing is so painful to them. I *hate* that anyone would hurt an animal like that. It's not right."

He didn't point out that hurting her wasn't right, either, but her father had no problem doing so. Anatolie clearly didn't consider Julija his daughter, not in the way most fathers would think of their child. She was a possession. He had created her for his use, not out of love. In his mind, he could torture her and use her for feeding because she existed to serve him, just as the cats existed to serve him.

"Blue," he said very softly, pulling the cat out of his fight to keep from obeying.

The shadow cat was all shadow and red glowing eyes. It took one reluctant step toward Julija, its body shuddering with the effort to keep from attacking her. The black fur was gone as were the roped muscles, leaving only a shimmering transparent shadow, insubstantial, but very lethal.

"We will stop him," Isai promised.

He took the lead, leaping into the cat's mind, Julija completely merged with him. He caught Anatolie unawares.

That which is bound, acting in pain.
I call to the heart, to that which remains.

The bond that was forged through evil and spite,
I now clear the cord to give you clear sight.
Bound there were two, now become one.
Separate the evil so no harm will be done.

Immediately the two hurried to weave the spell to build a shield for the cat.

Shadows upon me, be trapped by light.
Return to your darkness, never find sight.

Together they intoned the last of the protections so Anatolie couldn't cause Blue any more pain.

I send you back from whence you have come,
Never to cross over or shadows become.

Blue shook his head repeatedly, the red beginning to fade from his eyes.

Belle lifted her head and screamed in agony. Anatolie had done exactly what Isai had prophesized. He'd redoubled his efforts to strike at the female, forcing her to comply with his demands. Belle stalked Julija, trying to get around Isai, who kept turning to face the cat, making sure to keep his body between Belle and her intended victim.

Belle began to whirl about in circles, becoming more and more agitated. Discipline allowed Isai to finish the spell to place a barrier in Blue's mind.

Scatter, dissipate, disperse, dispel,
I free you now from evil's spell.

The moment the shield was there, he leapt into Belle's mind and attacked Anatolie.

The cat screamed and launched herself at Isai, mostly to get through him to Julija. Isai caught her in his arms and tossed her back across the cavern. In her insubstantial form, Belle was light. She nearly hit the wall on the other side of the chamber.

Anatolie fought hard to stay in the cat, directing her back to the attack, lashing at her over and over with stabbing pains through its skull. Belle rushed them again. Blue intercepted, slamming his body into hers to drive her off her feet, giving them a few moments without distraction.

I see you, Carpathian. Anatolie used the shadow cat to speak. The voice sounded eerie and high-pitched.

"Strained," Julija whispered. "He's a good distance away and he's guessing."

"Answer him. Take the forefront. I'll boost your energy, so it seems seamless and easy for you to communicate over such a distance."

"It is easy," Julija informed him with a little sniff of disdain.

Father. It is true I am mostly Carpathian, but you made me that way. You insisted on a Carpathian mother and that gave me the power of the mages and the power of the Dragonseeker. For that I must thank you.

As long as she talked to her father, he was distracted from his brutal attack on the shadow cat. That gave Isai time to study her father's position.

You cannot defeat me, daughter. Come home and all will be forgiven.

I will be punished with pain the way you are punishing these animals for doing exactly as you programmed them to do. They found me and attacked, yet you continue to punish them.

The stabbing pain in Belle's head eased as Anatolie considered how best to answer his daughter. He wanted her to comply, and harming the cat was clearly making her aggressive toward him.

I don't want to hurt you or these animals. You need to come home.

Isai kept very still, studying the other man. He didn't want to give away the fact that he was boosting Julija's energy and that she had the capability to defeat the high mage in the battle for the cat.

Isai knew Xavier had known the threat to him came from the Carpathian people, nowhere else. He had been the one to befriend them centuries earlier and give them the foundation for their safeguard spells. He had thought to always be their benevolent master, but the Carpathians weren't a lazy people. They'd begun to develop the spells themselves, adding to the basics Xavier had taught them. Coupled with their fighting skills and their ability and willingness to pool knowledge, Xavier had begun to fear and envy them.

Xavier's grandson, Anatolie, perhaps his greatest masterpiece, was no different. He had created Julija to serve him. To serve the other mages. They needed Carpathian blood to keep them alive well past years of longevity. He hadn't thought that she, with what he considered to be very diluted mage blood, would become powerful in her own right. It had to have been disturbing to him that she was born with the high mage's mark, but he'd dismissed that as a birthmark only because it suited him. Once he realized that she had the potential to be far more powerful than he was, Anatolie was bound to do everything in his abilities to either get her back or kill her.

You know what will happen if I come home. Crina hates me. She makes my life a living hell. She left me locked up for over a week with nothing to eat and little water to drink. You've seen her, and you've never stopped her.

Isai hadn't considered what it would have been like for Julija growing up with her stepmother. The woman had allowed Anatolie to get a Carpathian girl, one they'd taken prisoner, pregnant.

She continually shows me how she killed my mother. You were there, and you did nothing to stop it. I was a little girl and it was a terrifying ordeal for me. You let her, Father. You watched her hack up my mother as she lay helpless from your spells.

Isai glanced quickly over his shoulder at Julija. Her voice trembled, and tears burned in her eyes, clogged her throat and trickled down her face. He knew she wasn't aware.

Crina had far overstepped her role. She did then and there was no stopping her. Carpathians are our mortal enemy. You know that. She also was jealous. Your mother was a beautiful woman and clearly you remind her of that. If you prefer, I will dispose of her. She has long been a thorn, but she has her uses. If it will make you agree to come home, I will strangle her right now. Or feed her to one of the shadow cats in your brothers' shed.

Anatolie made the offer callously, so casually, for a moment Isai didn't believe what he was hearing. He had a line on him now. Belle had settled since the high mage had begun to try to cajole his daughter into returning to him. Anatolie didn't seem to understand that a woman like Julija wouldn't want her father to kill her stepmother for her as if the death would be a gift.

Isai slid the pad of his thumb across the back of her hand in warning. He was about to strike. She might not want to harm anyone, but he wasn't of the light. Darkness dwelled in him, surrounded him and would for all his days.

In his mind he built an image of everything he knew about Anatolie Brennan. The man was a master of illusion, fitting into his community and yet wreaking havoc on those around him when they got in his way. Isai struck hard, driving his fist through the mage's chest wall, fingers open and scraping through flesh and bone to get at the heart.

Anatolie screamed, and did the only thing possible: he leapt out of the cat's mind. *Barnabas will come for you. You will return with him.*

Julija still had a hold on Isai, her fingers twisted in his shirt. He felt her body jerk slightly at the threat and then a shiver consumed her.

Isai and Julija immediately built the shield for the female cat, a strong enough barrier that would keep Anatolie out, no matter what he did.

Very slowly, Isai turned to Julija. "Who is Barnabas?"

She lifted her feathery lashes and looked up at him with her dark chocolate eyes. There was fear. Trepidation. Wariness. "He is an old enemy who delights in tormenting me. He will do whatever Anatolie commands. Nothing is beneath him." There was contempt in her voice.

She turned her head to escape his scrutiny, but he framed her face with his hands and turned her back to him. He studied her set expression. He was still in her mind and she was holding herself very, very still, as if, when she moved, she might shatter.

"Who is this man to you?"

She couldn't turn her head, but her gaze landed on the center of his chest.

"He is nothing to me."

That was both truth and a lie. She stepped back away from him and abruptly landed in the chair when it hit her in the back of the knees. Blue pushed his head onto her lap, sensing she was upset. Belle came toward them, slinking across the chamber, uncertain of her welcome after she had fought to attack them. Julija held out her arms, and the female completed the last few feet in one jump, her black fur once again sliding over the shadowing body, making her whole.

"It is unwise to lie to your lifemate," Isai cautioned, but he paced across the room, giving her space. She'd already gone through a traumatic situation with her father. He wasn't about to add to it. In any case, she was unclaimed, and he wasn't going to force his claim on her. She had deliberately kept quiet knowing she was condemning him to death or worse.

Julija reached up to her throat and stroked one finger over the scar there, the one that covered the terrible gash that had changed her voice forever. "I hate this scar," she said softly. "Your friend Sandu healed the wound, but it was so severe that it left this scar. Sergey wanted to make certain I was killed, or couldn't speak, so one more male Carpathian hunter wouldn't have a lifemate."

Isai remained silent. She hadn't needed Sergey to do the very same thing, but he didn't remind her of that. He could feel sorrow beating at her, but her emotions were all jumbled up. Shame. Anger. Sorrow. All three mixed together. She didn't look at him but sank her fingers into Belle's fur and rubbed one cheek down the cat's spine.

"I thought I was in love once. A long time ago."

Isai's heart clenched. Not because she didn't deserve to love someone, but because whatever had happened scarred her far worse than Sergey's talon had. He wanted to put his arms around Julija and just hold her to comfort her but from the way she held herself so stiffly, averting her face from his, he knew better. She didn't want to be touched. She was willing to share her body intimately, but not her feelings. She didn't want to care about him or have him love her.

She rubbed her chin on Belle's fur. "I was so alone. And so young. My stepmother was particularly nasty to me and my father was cruel. My brothers had each other, but I couldn't even have friends. Anatolie made that very clear. In any case, who wanted to bring anyone home when you had the stepmother from hell?"

Isai remained very quiet. She rocked herself gently back and forth, unaware that she did so. That small action told him she needed the comfort she rejected. It took great effort not to go to her. He might not have claimed her, but she was still his lifemate and every cell in his body needed to make things better for her.

"Barnabas taught a seminar on medieval spells, useful ways to combine sex and torture to get your victim to cooperate any way you wish. I was the youngest student and the only female in the class. My father was adamant that all three of us, my brothers and I, go to the seminar. He said the understanding of pain combined with sex and how it could be used against one was needed by every mage. Afterward, Barnabas and I went for coffee. I was upset. The things he taught turned my stomach. He was . . . sweet."

He could imagine how anyone remotely nice would appear sweet after the way her family had treated her. He remained absolutely still, afraid if he drew attention to himself in any way, Julija would stop sharing. She didn't want to, and he couldn't imagine why she'd decided to tell him about the man when she had made it clear she didn't want to revisit what had to have been a difficult and painful time in her life.

Isai didn't like the way she'd met Barnabas. Why would her father insist she attend such a seminar? That made no sense to him.

"We ended up dating for several weeks. Just meeting and going for coffee or a drink. I really liked him. He liked animals and just about everything I liked. We would sit and talk for hours. Oddly, I wasn't attracted to him sexually, but I wasn't that attracted to anyone. That didn't seem to matter to him. He treated me like a friend and never once pushed beyond that boundary."

He could have told her she wasn't physically attracted to other males because she held the light to his darkness. Her body was waiting for his. He remained silent.

"In any case, somewhere along the line, I suddenly was on fire, desperate for sex." She rubbed her chin along the cat's spine again, her hands still in the fur. "I burned day and night. I was scared, because to go from being reluctant to have sex to thinking of it every waking minute, I knew a spell had to have been cast. That, or I was drugged, or both."

She fell silent for a long time. Her hands trembled as she petted the cat. The animal was far too big to remain in her lap. He knew the weight on her small frame wasn't good for her, but he kept silent, feeling privileged that she'd told him as much as she had about her past.

"I went to Barnabas because I didn't know anyone else that I trusted. I told him what was happening to me and that I feared it was a spell or drug. I had no one else in my life to turn to and he listened carefully and didn't make fun of me. Or laugh. He was so caring."

For the first time, Julija looked up at him and there was accusation in her gaze. That mixture of shame, sorrow and anger. He didn't like her viewing him like that, but again made the decision to remain silent. What was the use of defending himself simply because he was a man? He needed to know what he was fighting against.

"I let him talk me into being with him. I don't know what I was thinking. I just wanted the burning to go away, and he was always amazing and sweet when everyone around me was cruel and ugly." A sob escaped, and she jammed her fist into her mouth as if that could stop the flow of tears.

The air stilled in the cave and all at once it seemed impossible to breathe. Julija coughed, one hand going defensively to her throat. Isai waved his hand to send a small, cooling breeze through the chamber. He could see the fine sheen on her skin. Tremors rocked her body.

Isai couldn't stand it. She was suffering needlessly. He wanted the explanation for her treachery, for her refusing to allow his claim on her, even more than he wanted his next breath, but her misery and grief were genuine. He couldn't have that. He was so close to understanding her. So close, but there were things far more important than his understanding. Just her physical reaction told him she had a reason for refusing him.

"Julija." He kept his voice low and compelling. "There is no need to continue. I do not want you reliving something that clearly is extremely disturbing to you."

She shook her head, her gaze jumping to his and then back to the other side of the chamber. "You aren't Barnabas and you deserve better. You definitely deserve a lifemate better than me."

He started to remind her that there was only one lifemate, that she carried the other half of his soul, but there was no use. She was too far gone to another place—a place he didn't want her to go.

"The whole thing was a setup. My father despised the fact that I refused to kill using my gifts. It's a requirement in our family. Sacrifice animals. Sacrifice people. Sort of a rite of passage. He was deeply disappointed and embarrassed to have a daughter with the high mage's mark refusing to kill."

She rocked back and forth, a self-comforting motion that broke Isai's heart. Twice she wiped her face along Belle's fur and both times he was certain he caught the gleam of tears.

"All along, Barnabas was setting me up, with my father's full approval. The tactic was to be really nice to me. Gain my trust. Become my friend. None of those things were hard for him because I didn't have any friends. No one was ever nice to me. He became . . . everything."

Isai winced. He didn't like hearing that another man had been her everything, even if it was false. He should have found her. He should have redoubled his efforts instead of going into a monastery. Whatever she was going to tell him—and it was bad—was on him. It was his failure as her lifemate.

"I guess once he accomplished phase one, winning my trust, he was able to introduce the need for sex. By the way, that is a permanent spell. At least, so far, I haven't been able to reverse it. I think he made it that way, so I would have to turn to him no matter what throughout the years. I didn't. He is into extremely cruel, torturous sexual practices and he claimed he needed a subject to demonstrate on for his class."

Isai pressed his fist tightly against his thigh. He didn't want to hear anymore. What he did want was to go find Barnabas and let him know just how he felt about the things she'd told him already. He knew the mage was coming after them, her father had threatened her with him.

"He was still very much the Barnabas he was pretending to be that first time. Then when I said I wasn't certain I wanted to continue the relationship, that I didn't think it was fair to him, everything changed. He took me prisoner. He had a dungeon and kept me down there. It was a very ugly medieval place and he took great delight in torturing me. He would then initiate sex as if expecting me to be grateful. When I didn't do as he ordered—killing small animals—the tortures got worse."

Blue pushed his nose into her and rubbed, a soft chuffing of inquiry repeated over and over until she finally blinked, pulling herself back from the past to look up at him. "I wish I could say things got better, but they didn't for a long, long time. No matter what he did to me, pain, humiliation, and he did it all. Stripping me in front of his class and teaching them whip techniques and quite a few other instruments of torture. He would have sex with me during and after. All the while he told me it would stop if I just obeyed him and killed whatever it was he had there. Sometimes an animal, sometimes a human. Once a mage. I refused."

Julija looked down at her hands. "I knew, even if I did as he wanted, as my father wanted, it wouldn't end. It was never going to end. Barnabas derived pleasure from my suffering. So did my father and brothers and especially my stepmother. It was a very ugly time in my life that lasted for several years."

"*Sívamet.*" He gave her the endearment gently. His heart dropped. Clenched. His gut twisted. Knotted. His lifemate had been tortured and abused. Used for several years in order to get her to comply with her father's demands.

She shook her head. "I can never be your heart. Not ever. I did things that were so wrong. I might not have had a choice, but eventually, the body is taught to respond automatically. I was ashamed of my reactions. I hated myself for years." She looked away from him. "You secluded yourself in a monastery because you believed suiciding was wrong and cowardly. I realize that is your personal belief and you don't visit it on others, but the fact remains, you don't believe in it, and I did contemplate ending my life."

She fell silent, her head bowed as if he would condemn her.

"You think that I would judge you? That I would somehow sit in judgment on you because you were kidnapped and tortured over and over with no hope of escaping? No father to protect you? No lifemate to free you?"

The tip of her tongue moistened her dry lips. "I told you. There were times when my body cooperated." It was a confession, nothing less, and she couldn't look at him. "My brain screamed no, but . . ."

"Julija, you are in no way to blame for the vile crimes committed against you. It is a wonder you were able to have sex with me."

"I *crave* sex all the time," she admitted softly, color creeping up her neck to stain her face. "I burn night and day. I knew you were my lifemate and you couldn't harm me, so it was safe to enjoy myself. But then I felt as if I was using you." She mumbled the last, still unable to look at him.

Isai waited in silence. It took her a long while before she raised her gaze to his. "You are blameless in this matter, Julija. Entirely blameless."

"Barnabas terrifies me. He will come around, and every time he does, he tries to get me to come to him. He casts his net, but I was able to build a resistance. Still, he terrifies me on many levels."

"I am here now. This man will not get to you again."

Her eyes met his and he saw stark fear there. "Barnabas is invincible. With my father's backing, he is even more so. We don't want him to catch up with us. We just have to find the book and return it to the prince or find somewhere safe for it if we can't destroy it."

He wasn't going to argue with her. That wasn't his way. He understood her much better now that he knew what had transpired. She didn't trust with good reason.

"There's something else. Since I'm telling you everything, I may as well let you know, he didn't leave me without scars. He wanted me to always know who I belonged to."

"I have seen your body."

She shook her head, one hand going defensively to her throat, as if she could protect herself from the rip of Sergey's talon, or any other damage another chose to inflict on her.

Isai felt something brutal and vicious in him rise, but he remained expressionless, even serene, on the outside. "You do not belong to this man, Julija. He has cast a spell, in fact it sounds as if he has cast more than one. We will defeat him together. You are incredibly strong. They made you fear Barnabas because they don't want you to know how powerful you are."

"He terrifies me, Isai."

"I can see it on your face. Look at me, *sívamet*." He waited until her overbright eyes met his. "He has done everything he can to conquer you. He's used torture and sex as well as a combination of both. He's used humiliation. He's used spells. This man has done everything he knows how to do to defeat you and he has not. You may not know it, but he knows you are a danger to him."

"I wish that was the truth."

For the first time Isai could see hope pushing through despair on her face.

"I need you to know, I have not been entirely honest about my appearance. I have some scarring on my back and thighs. Pretty bad scarring, even on my arms. Sergey added to what Barnabas did. I covered those with an illusion."

"Why did you do that?" He kept disappointment out of his voice. "There was no need. Did you think I needed you to have the appearance of smooth skin? I want the real woman. I want Julija, not an illusion of her."

"I wear clothes, so no one sees my back or the back of my thighs. There's some scarring on my breasts and one particularly bad scar on my left thigh."

"Julija, I want the real woman," he reiterated. "A lifemate, no matter age or appearance, is always the most beautiful woman possible to a Carpathian male. I do not know what women think when their lifemate claims them, but for the male, she is everything. He does not look at other women. There is only his lifemate."

She bit down on her lip for a moment. "I heard the prince had a sister who was not with her lifemate."

"It happens. There is a sickness that runs through certain lineages. It is in the prince's lineage and a few others as well. It is not in mine and I can assure you, there is no other woman I find more beautiful or sexier than you. Whether that is reciprocated is another matter altogether."

Julija pressed her lips together. "I should have known. I don't think it's vanity. That wasn't the reason I didn't want you to see, although I prefer looking my best around you. It's just that if you saw the scars you would have asked me how I got them. I needed to find a way to tell you in my own time."

"I appreciate that you did. If you hold Belle any tighter, you might strangle her."

She looked down at the squirming cat she had a death grip on. A ghost of a smile lit her eyes briefly as she forced herself to let go. "I'm surprised she didn't bite me. Shadow cats were raised to be vicious."

"Your brothers used torture on your cats, various tortures, perhaps not sexual, but torture the same, which Barnabas taught in his class. You are not vicious, and neither are the cats."

Her dark eyes searched his face carefully. "Isai, I don't want you to think I'm always perfectly nice. I'm not. I have quite a few very negative feelings built up."

"I am very happy about that. I do not wish to have a lifemate who is all forgiveness. I intend to destroy this man, Barnabas, as well as your family. If you do not have 'negative feelings'—whatever that is—you would not support me in this endeavor."

She made a face at him. "Sometimes, when you talk to me, the way you phrase something is so very off-putting, I'm not certain how to respond."

"'Yes' is the proper response," he teased.

He actually got a smile from her and that helped to reduce some of the coiling tension in him. He hadn't realized that just getting her to smile could light up his world. He didn't know how, after what she'd gone through, she could be the woman she was. Courageous, strong and someone who would reach out to another woman in the way she had Elisabeta. He even understood that friendship a little better.

"I don't want you to take any chances, Isai. Before we do anything else, we have to recover that book. We can't take the chance that it will fall into Anatolie's hands. Or my brothers' hands. Or Barnabas's." She gave a little shudder when she indicated the last.

"Would they know how to open the book?"

"They would reverse the order in which Xavier closed it. He sacrificed a life from each species. There is some controversy over whether he only used dark mage, Jaguar and Carpathian, or whether he had a second ceremony before or after that one. That will cause problems, but they aren't insurmountable if you're willing to kill a lot of people."

"You are saying that to open the book one must kill five people in the correct order."

She nodded. "That's the truth of it. The members of my family and Barnabas are very much willing to kill three times that many in order to open the book. And if Sergey gets wind of the book being so close—and he will eventually—he'll do anything to recover and open it. He has tiny bits of Xavier in him. In fact, he would probably know precisely how to open it." She tilted her head back, both hands buried in the cat's fur. "We *have* to recover that book first, Isai."

"We will," he assured her.

"Why haven't you ever questioned that I might be trying to recover the book for my family, or for myself?"

"It is impossible to lie to one's lifemate. You can omit things, but lying will not work."

She very carefully put the large shadow cat from her lap. "Thank you for believing in me, Isai. I haven't given you that much cause to."

"That is not necessarily true. You risked your life to try to help Elisabeta. You could have gotten away and yet you didn't. You allowed Sergey to keep you prisoner so that you could aid her. Have you told her of your experiences with Barnabas?"

"Not exactly," she admitted in a low tone. "She was held prisoner for centuries. It wasn't nearly as bad for me."

"You cannot compare the two, and neither will she. Sergey might have tormented Elisabeta, but I doubt that he tortured her. He wouldn't want her to commit any act that would take away her innocence. It was her light he needed. He might have hurt her in order to get her to comply with his commands and to rely on him, but he wouldn't have sexually assaulted her with the kind of pain Barnabas inflicted on you."

Isai made absolutely certain that he kept his features perfectly expressionless. He didn't want her to know that he was seething with the need to find Barnabas and then her family and one by one wipe them from the face of the earth. He did find it a little laughable that she thought an ancient couldn't handle mages. He had learned so many things in his time on the planet and most of those had to do with battles and hunting vampires. Mages sometimes helped and sometimes got in the way.

He was careful, searching for the right words. She was already wounded. She needed to know she was worth something to him after hearing what her family had done to her. She felt shame and that infuriated him, but he made certain none of his growing anger showed in his voice. "Like me, Elisabeta will admire and respect you for your courage. You truly are worthy of being her friend and my lifemate."

Her gaze jumped to his. For the first time since she'd decided to tell him about her past, she looked pleased. He'd said the right thing. He took a chance. "Perhaps it would be a good thing to talk to Elisabeta. If there is anyone who will understand and not judge you, it will be her. She is a woman of the light, just as you are."

"She is so lost and wounded," Julija protested. "She doesn't need me to dump my troubles on her. She needs me to be there for her."

"Maybe she needs to know she's needed. Would you want to be the one everyone feels sorry for? Everyone tiptoes around? Helping you, even if it is just to listen to you, might be the thing she needs most to start healing."

Julija looked down at her hands. "I don't think it's possible to heal after what she went through. I hate the idea that everyone thinks she'll rise all perfect."

"No one believes that, least of all her lifemate. They were born for each other. He will know how best to make her happy."

Her chin went up. A challenge. "Do you know how best to make me happy?"

"Yes. But you are unwilling to take that chance. Now that I know why, at least I have understanding."

He wasn't certain if that was completely true or not. He wanted it to be. He wanted to do whatever she needed him to do without regret. He was her lifemate and if she absolutely could not stand the idea of it, then he didn't want to force her. They wouldn't work. Some men claimed their women, and he knew they did so because, deep down, their women needed them to. Julija had to make up her own mind. That was as important to him as it was to her.

There was a long silence. He could hear her heart beating a little too fast. Had he already claimed her, he would have immediately corrected that and soothed her. She was upset, and embarrassed, two emotions she didn't need to ever have around him.

"I don't know what to think anymore." There was honesty in her voice. "You're very different than I expected. I was terrified of becoming a lifemate to a Carpathian, now I don't know what to think."

"Terrified?" There had been genuine fear in her voice even when she'd said the word. That seemed abnormal for her. Julija wasn't a woman too many things terrified. "You studied the Carpathian species?"

"Yes, it was a requirement. My father wanted me to know everything about the species."

"Since there are no books on us, how were you informed?"

"We had instructors for our classes. The Carpathian class was taught by my stepmother's brother . . ." She trailed off as he kept looking at her. Her gaze shifted away from his. "So the Carpathians wiping out the mages never really happened? According to the class I took, that was the reason Xavier began to fight back. He had thought they were his friends."

"It never happened, Julija. Is this class taught to all mages?"

"I have no idea. I was privately tutored." She closed her eyes and shook her head. "My brothers were supposed to take the class, but they didn't, and they weren't in trouble for it. I tried to skip out once and my father was furious. I was punished for a couple of weeks."

"How long was this class?"

"Just a couple of weeks, which I thought was strange, even at the time." She shook her head and looked straight into his eyes, realizing the truth. "It was fake, wasn't it? At least fake mixed with truth. Had it all been fake I would have known. I was impressionable at the time and was still trying to figure out why my father was so harsh with me."

"He knew you were Dragonseeker. He knew what that meant. He

wanted to find ways to turn you against the Carpathian people. He knew you were growing powerful as a mage and the longer you lived, the more your Carpathian blood would call to you."

"They all fed off me." She held up her arms for him to see. "Once when he was very angry with me he told me I had been bred just to sustain his life and if I wasn't giving him my blood, I was useless to him."

"How were you fed blood? You must have needed it?"

"I was trying not to use it and that was what made him angry all the time. I didn't like that if I didn't have it, I grew weak. I prefer the night and sometimes, when I was hurt, after he beat me, I would lie in the yard, in the dirt. It soothed my body. Once, my brothers caught me and they told him. He was furious. He said I was acting like a traitor and he would bury me alive if he ever caught me doing such a thing again."

She wrapped her arms around her middle, shuddering with memories pouring in.

"Your father is an ass," Isai declared in hope of making her laugh.

He didn't get a laugh, but he did get a faint smile.

"I suppose you could call him that, although it's mild."

"Julija, we need to get moving to find Iulian and the book. I have to feed again. It will not take me long. You will be safe here while I am out hunting. Are you comfortable with that?"

She nodded. "I can clean up while you're gone."

"When I return, you'll need to feed, you know that, don't you? To keep your strength up." He kept his gaze fixed on her face, reading her every emotion.

She nodded, avoiding his gaze. "I'm well aware."

7

I told him the truth, Elisabeta. It was the most difficult thing I can recall ever doing, Julija confessed in a little rush. *I'm so glad I have you to talk things over with. Just telling him made me feel so sick, once he left, I had to vomit. It was that bad. I was terrified he would look at me and feel disgusted. When I look in the mirror, that's how I feel.*

There was a small silence and Julija held her breath. Elisabeta flowed into her mind, stronger than Julija had ever experienced with her before. Maybe Isai was right and Elisabeta needed someone to want her help.

I assume you told Isai why you are afraid to trust him with your heart.

I did. He's been good to me other than the, you know . . . spanking thing. That was annoying. And it did hurt whether he thinks so or not. He's strong.

Mostly it hurt your pride.

Wouldn't it yours? Julija demanded.

I would have welcomed a spanking, sister. Sergey was very cruel.

Julija was silent for a long time, gathering her courage. In comparison to what Elisabeta had been put through, she felt her horrible experiences didn't count, but Isai had told her perhaps not only did she need to tell

Elisabeta the details, but her friend really did need to be needed. Already she could feel that was so.

Elisabeta was silent, waiting for her to decide. Elisabeta never pushed. Never insisted. In the end, because there was no one demanding, because she had to make the decision, Julija told her everything. The horrifying details that shamed her. The revulsion of being made a subject in Barnabas's classes for others to see. How the torture worsened when she refused to comply and kill someone.

There were times when the spells burned her from the inside out and she couldn't distance herself from what was happening to her. Those times she feared the most, feared she would give in and harm an innocent. Once, they tried to convince her that she had, and, although she was certain they were lying to her, there was a part of her that feared it might have happened. That was the worst, to think she could have sacrificed another being in order to stop her own suffering.

Julija didn't realize she was weeping until she felt Elisabeta surround her with comfort.

Most of those living on earth are made up of balances. Good and evil. Or dark and light. When my lifemate was born, his soul was split in half and he ended up with all darkness, his and mine, while I received his light to safeguard. I had my own light as well. He became a hunter of the vampire. I am incapable of becoming vampire. As are you. There is no way you would have killed an innocent, Julija. It would be impossible.

I feel like I could kill those coming after the book, Julija admitted.

That is different. Those hunting the book are not innocent. Their intentions are to harm others, and the book will allow them to do that. You might protect yourself or those you love, but you wouldn't just kill indiscriminately. Once you allow your lifemate to claim you, the balance is restored. In any case, until your lifemate claims you, it will be difficult.

Julija didn't like that at all. She needed to be able to defend herself and to help Isai. *Are you really going to allow your lifemate to claim you? Are you that certain that he will make you happy?*

I am that certain that I can make him happy if he gives me time. Lifemates will always give their other half what they need.

Julija didn't think Elisabeta sounded as sure as she wanted to sound. She was every bit as frightened of her future as Julija was. *I kind of like him,* she admitted reluctantly, *but it could be just because he's the nicest anyone other than you has been to me.*

You do? Elisabeta encouraged.

He's pretty hot as men go. I hope your lifemate is hot for you.

What is "hot"?

Attractive. You can't resist him physically. Gorgeous.

Amusement flooded her mind. That felt good. Elisabeta didn't often portray laughter to her.

Of course I will find him attractive—um—hot. He is my lifemate. There is no other for me—or for you. Should Isai not claim you, you will never be satisfied with another, Julija.

Sadly, Julija was afraid Elisabeta was right. She was beginning to look forward to his return far more than she should have been. She definitely didn't like the separation. The two cats were pressing close to her, so she dropped her hands into their sleek fur and massaged their necks while she thought about Isai. Was it really so bad to have a partner? Would he be a partner, or would he turn on her?

How can you trust anyone again? Sergey was your friend. He wasn't vampire when he came to you, yet you're still willing to trust a man—a complete stranger at that—with your life. How do you do it?

I am still in the ground. There was shame in Elisabeta's mind.

That admission humbled Julija. She saw courage in the other woman, while Elisabeta thought herself a coward, yet she was determined to rise and allow a complete stranger to claim her, a selfless act, to save her lifemate. Julija tried to tell herself that Elisabeta would do so because she'd been trained from birth to do just that—give herself up for a man—but she knew better. Elisabeta had been taken captive as a young teenager by a Carpathian male, one she'd trusted. One she'd believed to be her friend. Just like Barnabas had taken her, only Julija had been an adult.

She closed her eyes and leaned forward to bury her face in Belle's fur. *Sometimes, Elisabeta, I don't know why someone as extraordinary as you would have me as a friend. I'm so selfish. Really. I want him, but the dream seems too good to be true. I've never had anything in my life be good. Everything that looked that way has been illusion. Sometimes, when I look at him, I wonder if I conjured him up—or if my father did.*

The moment the thought was out of her head and into Elisabeta's her entire body began to shake. She had let out her worst fear when she'd guarded it so carefully. *Elisabeta, my father could do this. He is good at illusions.* She hadn't wanted to examine the idea too closely to tip her father off that she knew what he'd done.

There was quiet. Stillness. Elisabeta thought things over carefully. She didn't just blurt out a denial, she examined the possibility from every angle.

He would create illusions of my mother coming to me when I was just a child. Sometimes I thought I would go insane wondering if he'd really killed her or if that was the illusion and he held her prisoner somewhere. I remember being a child and whispering all my secrets to my mother, all my fears, and of course, it was my father. I learned not to trust anything or anyone. Especially if they were nice to me.

Your lifemate spanked you.

He had done that. Would her father ever have risked that? Anatolie had never spanked her as a child. He was far subtler than that. Far crueler. Wouldn't it be ironic if the one thing she was furious with Isai over was the one thing proving him to be real? She rubbed her cheek in Belle's fur and then sat up, looking toward the slight crack leading to outside. She realized she wanted him to come back.

I can't stop thinking about him, and that makes me more afraid than ever. I don't like feeling like a coward.

Again, soft amusement flooded her mind. *You are chasing after a spell book that could kill off an entire species as well as change the balance of power in the world if allowed into the wrong hands. I do not think you can call yourself a coward, Julija.*

She could never live through the humiliation of giving herself, her body, her heart and soul to another man and have him be an illusion. It would break her. Totally break her. Sometimes she felt held together by the thinnest of threads. She couldn't imagine what life was like for Elisabeta.

There was a faint stirring in her mind and she knew immediately Isai had connected with her. She held her breath and willed Elisabeta not to say anything more.

Are you all right? You feel . . . upset.

It was the last thing she expected him to say. She could feel his worry and it felt genuine. The way he came into her mind, pouring in slowly—like molasses, gently, so as to give her time to shut him out—that alone made her heart flutter. She was so susceptible to him. The way his voice was so intimate, stroking along the walls of her mind. He felt strong and protective—something she'd never known. Could her father be capable of such an illusion? She doubted if he had knowledge of such caring. Of such sweetness.

Sívamet? Now I am really worried. You are afraid.

She was. Of him. Of taking a chance. Of letting someone into her life when they could tear her to shreds. *I am fine.*

You are sad.

So true. She was sad. Sad for herself. Sad for Elisabeta. Even sad for both their lifemates. She tried to live her life in a positive manner, but she didn't know how to handle the present situation.

She had to give him something. Some truth. Even if he wasn't real—and she suspected he truly was—he deserved truth just for making her feel as if he cared about her. *I need to know you're real.*

There was a brief silence. *You believe I am an illusion? Sent to you by this Barnabas? By your father?*

She remained silent, afraid to think or move, frozen, paralyzed by her inability to know for certain.

I am on my way. There was decisiveness in his tone.

Abruptly he was gone, and she let out her breath, not realizing she'd been holding it. *Elisabeta?* She could still feel her friend, so still and quiet. *What do you think?*

He is very real. He is Carpathian. No mage could possibly produce that.

There it was. Confirmation. Julija didn't know whether or not to be relieved, because now she actually had to make up her mind. Already, she'd insulted him and made him think poorly of her as a lifemate. He couldn't possibly understand what her life had been like and why she'd been so terrified of ever opening herself up to trusting anyone, let alone the enemy. And she'd been led to believe Carpathians were the enemy. She just hadn't believed an entire species could be.

I know you have to go. It was difficult to maintain their connection over so long a distance. Elisabeta was very powerful, whether she believed she was or not. *I really appreciate you being my friend.* She needed one. Desperately.

Elisabeta's affection slipped into her mind, warming her. *I have never had a friend before. I like having someone to talk to as well.*

I'll get back to the compound as soon as I'm done here, Julija promised.

I would like that. Elisabeta sounded and felt shy to her.

Before Julija could reply, Elisabeta had slipped away leaving her . . . alone. She patted both cats on the head and stood up, needing to move. She wasn't wholly Carpathian. She could give the illusion of being clean, and she could cast a spell to clean her body and hair if necessary, but it didn't feel like a real shower.

She looked around the cavern. As in most caves, water trickled from the walls. She studied the various paths of water. All led downward in little jagged trails, but one was wider than the others and formed a small puddle at the far end of the chamber. She might be able to do something with that. There was no rock to build up to form a barrier to give herself a pool or bath of any sort.

She was just standing there, frustrated, when she felt him come up behind her. There had been no warning, not even from the cats, and that told her more than anything else could have. They always reacted to her family, mostly slinking away in fear, or hissing their hatred and submission. The shadow cats chuffed softly in greeting and bumped into his legs, winding around them. He was so close, she felt the cats' movements, but she didn't feel him.

"I want to take a shower." She blurted it out like a crazy person, but just his presence was overwhelming when she felt she had told him far too much about her life. She couldn't face him, not with him knowing the worst about her. It was humiliating, and she couldn't think about anything else, vividly remembering the way Barnabas had hurt and displayed her for his class.

"You are Carpathian, Julija," he said softly, his voice whispering against her ear.

She felt her hair move with every breath he took. "I'm mage. I don't understand what you mean."

"If you wish a shower, you can create one for yourself. If you don't want to bother, you simply can freshen yourself and change your attire." He stepped out from behind her and walked in a slow half circle to stand in front of her. "You have already been doing it, probably most of your life."

She shook her head. "I'm mage, Isai. What I do is mostly illusion. I will admit, my illusions are considered some of the best in my world, but I kind of had a knack for it from childhood."

"Julija, you had a knack because your illusions aren't tricks or deceptions, they are real. There is no doubt in my mind that your father is aware of this. Most likely, he discovered it when you were a child. Rather than allow you to realize what was happening, he fostered the idea that you were extremely good at illusion."

She shook her head. "I practiced all the time. I still practice."

He stepped back and indicated the wall behind him. "Build yourself a pool from the rock."

She frowned and circled around him slowly, studying the rock surface and the smaller stones on the floor of the chamber. "I don't understand what you mean."

"Everything around you has properties. You can manipulate those properties. You do it all the time when you're building what you think are illusions. If it was merely an illusion to widen the crack in the rock at the entrance to the cave, how would you slip your body through? If it was illusion to make your body paper thin, how would the reality of it work?"

She frowned up at him. She hadn't thought of that. "I've used magic spells my entire life. They're second nature to me. Magic can create the things you're saying I do as a Carpathian."

"Magic can do a lot of things, but can it build you a pool?"

Once again, she took her gaze from Isai to study the rock. She lifted her hands and began to weave together a spell to gather the smaller pebbles into a basin to begin her build. Before she could utter a single word, he caught her wrist and pulled her hands down.

"In your mind, build what you want."

"I was doing that." She glared at him. "You stopped me."

"You are using magic as a crutch. There is no reason to use it on something so simple as creating a pool for you to bathe in if that is your wish. You can give yourself a shower without taking one. You can change your clothes. Build it in your mind. See yourself clean and refreshed. Design the clothes you want to wear. It all takes place in your mind first."

"I do that."

"I know you do, that is how your illusions are so perfect. You already have built whatever it is you want in your mind and then you come up with your spell. I'm telling you, you do not always need that spell."

"You use it for your safeguards."

"Because we were taught that was how best to ensure we were safe when we went to ground. Over the centuries, all of us have changed those weaves and made them stronger, using our own abilities to strengthen our guards so we can rest easy in the ground. Had we not done so, Xavier would have long ago found a way to eradicate our species."

Julija had to agree with him. She took a breath and once again studied the wall, a tendril of excitement sliding down her spine. Was it possible? Could she do what Carpathians could do? If that were so, then her magic would add to that power . . . She broke off her thoughts, elation causing a little thrill of anticipation.

Isai nodded at her. "You can do this."

Could she? Something very simple. She considered what that might be. She wanted her pool wide enough that she could turn around in it easily. She stared at the rocks, feeling for them, studying how each was formed. Magma from long ago had crystalized. The granite had traces of various minerals such as feldspar and quartz with bits of others as well.

Using the rock, in her mind she began creating her dream pool. She closed her eyes and, keeping the build in her brain, simply manipulated the properties of the rock, heating them so they ran together again, forming a wide, thick wall that was just a little deeper than her waist. She layered her granite there until she had exactly what she wanted.

Julija had always enjoyed creating things and she'd spent hours in her mind, building the things she wanted. It never occurred to her that she could accomplish the things she wanted without magic. In her creation, water ran from the wall into her pool, the temperature perfect for a refreshing shower. She paid attention to every detail, just as she'd learned to do over the years with her magic.

The sound of water falling into a pool grew in intensity. She imagined the spray, tiny droplets, hitting her face as the water entered from where it fell naturally from the wall. She made certain to color the water, that deep crystal blue she always found waterfalls and the pools beneath them to be. The beautiful ones. Her rock formations followed the lines of a natural basin, collecting the water as it ran off the wall. There was natural drainage, a small runoff that took excess water out of the cave, to run back into the ground.

Once again, she stepped forward, raising her hands into the air to aid her near-perfect illusion. Isai blocked her. "Before you do that, look at what you've done."

She could hear the water falling into the pool, the sound as real as the illusion in her mind had been. She'd always been good at illusion because she did pay attention to detail. She turned her head slowly and the basin was there. Solid. Real. She stared at it for a long time and then looked up at him.

"You did something."

He shook his head. "No, little mage. You did something. You created exactly what you wanted to create because you are Carpathian. You are also mage, and that makes you extremely powerful. And dangerous to your father and his followers."

She couldn't help the little surge of hope, but she didn't dare believe him. She would have known, right? How could she not know? It didn't make sense.

"Come here to me. You need to feed. You are very pale. If you are going to continue to create things, you will need your strength. I have fed, although, I do crave the taste of your blood. A lifemate's blood is perfection to him."

She was a little obsessed with his taste. She had continually pushed aside the need that would come at her out of nowhere. Just him making the offer to her brought such a surge of absolute hunger for his taste alone, it shook her. That wasn't right. She recognized that she shouldn't want his blood to the point that everything else went out of her head. Worse, the moment he made his offer, she wanted him to take her blood.

Daringly, she looked up at him, already taking the few steps that separated them, so she was standing in front of him. "I want you to take mine as well."

"That can be dangerous, *kislány hän ku meke sarnaakmet minan.*"

"We both live dangerously," she pointed out. "Just by being who we are." She ran her hand up his body, from his wonderful abdomen with its multitude of muscles to the defined muscles of his chest. Her lips followed the path of her palm. "You taste delicious. Your skin." He did. She didn't care what that sounded like, need was on her. Overwhelming her.

She found his heartbeat and then slid her tongue over the beating pulse just above that. She felt the slide of her teeth and she bit deep. His body jerked. She felt the lengthening of his cock while the taste of his ancient blood burst through her senses. Perfection. Absolute perfection.

She stroked his cock, petting him, wishing his clothes were gone. He couldn't possibly know what she was thinking, so she built that picture in her mind while she drank. Isai. Naked. Her hand around the thick length of him. Shockingly, his clothes were gone, and she found herself with his hot girth in her fist. That was even more perfect.

She drank more and slipped her thumb over the wide crown to smear those pearly drops and use them to help pump him while she consumed his blood. When his hand came up to warn her to stop, she did so immediately, licking across the twin little holes that proclaimed him hers and then licking her way down his chest and abdomen to his cock.

Take my blood. She had to entice him. She could already feel his rejection, the way he was steeling himself to back away from her. He hadn't been able to resist her when she was feeding, the erotic pull between them was too strong, but now that her tongue had closed the twin holes, he was gathering his strength. *Please,* she added.

He murmured something in his language she didn't catch. She was certain she hadn't caught it because there was a strange roaring in her ears. Her head felt chaotic. Her body felt on fire. She . . . *needed.* The taste of his blood was hot in her mouth and she didn't wait to see if he would do as she asked. She bent her head to taste—him.

His breath hissed out in a long, slow trail of desire, heating her blood more. She parted her lips and took the head of his cock into her mouth. Instantly his hand dropped to her head, fingers buried in her hair. She was aware of the pull on her scalp, but whether to guide her or to pull her away, she wasn't certain. Whatever his first intention, as she suckled, he gave in to the pleasure.

Her body felt hot, burning, flames licking at her skin with the same dark intensity as she was his cock. She no longer wanted her clothes and as she concentrated on learning the shape and feel of Isai's cock with her mouth and tongue, she built a picture in her mind of herself without clothes, her skin rubbing along his. She was demanding, not submissive, her fingers digging into his sculpted buttocks as she began worshiping his cock with her mouth. He tasted like perfection. He felt that way. She didn't want to ever stop, but her body burned.

I need you.

You are my lifemate.

She was. She totally was. At that moment she would have worn a neon sign in order to entice him to have sex with her. *Yes. Absolutely.* The thought of another woman with him made her crazy. *I am your lifemate.*

You accept me as your lifemate?

Her mouth clamped down on him, one hand working his cock with her fist, sliding it in and out of her mouth while her other hand cupped his heavy sac and worked much more gently. He was filling her mouth with his heat. His fire. With that addictive, perfect taste she would never be able to replace.

Julija. I have to have your consent.

I need you in me! she wailed. She was burning from the inside out. Between her legs she was on fire. She sucked harder, becoming almost frantic.

Do you accept me as your lifemate? he persisted.

Yes. Clearly, I'm your lifemate. She was beginning to detest that word. She just wanted him. Like *now. Do that thing.*

Thing?

Now she was wild. Out of control. The burning was getting worse. *That thing you do when you bind us together. So there's no going back.* She was going to have him. Take him. Keep him. This man was going to be hers. *Hurry.*

You are certain?

In answer, she sucked harder and took him deeper. His girth stretched her lips and there was no way to get him as deep as she wanted, which was just to swallow him down, but she tried. She was staking her own claim on him.

The hands in her hair became two tight fists. *"Te avio päläfertiilam. Éntölam kuulua, avio päläfertiilam."*

Speak English. I don't know everything you're saying. She should have stopped what she was doing, but she couldn't. Her mouth clamped over his cock like a vise and she suckled strongly, her tongue lashing at him, dancing up and down, needing to know him intimately. One hand began to slide downward along her belly, her body desperate for relief. He caught her hand and guided it back to his balls.

"Ted kuuluak, kacad, kojed. I belong to you."

You do. She agreed with him. No other woman was going to get her hands on him, not if she could help it. She really was frantic for him.

"Élidamet andam. I offer my life for you. *Pesämet andam.* I give you my protection. *Uskolfertiilamet andam.* I give you my allegiance. *Sívamet andam.* I give you my heart. *Sielamet andam.* I give you my soul."

Yes. Mine. She needed to know that he belonged solely to her. She liked that. No, she loved it. No one had ever been hers. She couldn't say she'd ever had a family. She didn't know love. She did know lust, and she totally was in lust with this man. Surely, that was a positive thing. He was giving her his allegiance. He meant it. She could hear it in his voice.

His hands were gentle on her face, slowly lifting her mouth from him. She chased after his cock while his thumb brushed at the tears on her face. "Little mage, you are definitely mine."

"And you're definitely mine." She needed his reassurance.

He lifted her and she immediately circled his neck with her arms, locking her hands behind his head. He lowered her to the bed she'd slept in all day, coming down over her, his knee nudging her legs apart. Heart pounding, she widened her thighs to accommodate him. To welcome him. He brushed kisses over her wet lashes and then she felt him, that thick, broad head pushing into her tight entrance. Her breath caught in her throat.

"*Ainamet andam.* I give you my body."

She *so* wanted his body. She tried to push herself onto him, but she was so tight, her muscles resisted his invasion. She didn't care if he stretched her beyond burning. She needed him. Nearly sobbing, she bucked her hips and squirmed, desperate to take him all the way inside her. The birthmark over her left ovary began to glow, the dragon showing himself.

Isai's breath caught in his throat and then he kissed the mark gently. Reverently. "Mark of Dragonseeker. It is strong in you," he whispered. "*Sívamet kuuluak kaik että a ted.* I take into my keeping the same that is yours."

He surged a little deeper and she almost couldn't breathe. When he bent his head to hers, his sapphire eyes burning his claim into her, his dark hair brushing like fingers over her skin, she couldn't look away. Then he was kissing her with exquisite tenderness. He lifted his head, so their gazes collided, and she was held prisoner in all that blue.

"*Ainaak olenszal sívambin.* Your life will be cherished by me for all my time. *Te élidet ainaak pide minun.* Your life will be placed above mine for all time."

He began to move in her, all the while those eyes staring into hers, as if he could see right into her soul. He held her as if she was the most treasured, precious woman in the world. She felt like she was truly beautiful, cherished, maybe even loved. He looked as if he knew her, and maybe he did, he'd been in her mind.

"*Te avio päläfertiilam.* You are my lifemate. I'm so grateful that you're the one, Julija. That you are mine."

She was more than grateful he was hers. She almost didn't believe it, but it was difficult to refute it when he was looking right into her eyes. She could barely blink. She certainly couldn't look away. "I feel the same," she whispered, praying he was for real. That this wasn't some elaborate illusion or dark, sinister plot against her. She wouldn't be able to live through another one, not whole and intact. "Be real, Isai. Please, be real."

"I am going to be so real most of the time, my little mage, that you will wish me otherwise." His voice was warm with amusement, but it was also a warning.

She chose to ignore that. She found herself lifting her hips to meet his every stroke, urging him on with one hand to his hip.

"*Ainaak sívamet jutta oleny.* You are bound to me for all eternity."

She wanted to be bound to him. Maybe he would drive her insane, but he would be hers. They would fight their enemies together. She needed that. She needed someone to care whether she lived or died.

"*Ainaak terád vigyázak.* You are always in my care."

It was strange, but even with flames spreading like wildfire through her veins and little sparks of electricity dancing over her skin, she felt tiny threads binding them together, weaving back and forth between them. Her light shed over his darkness. In any context she would have thought it hokey, but she had studied Carpathian society. She knew lifemates were a reality in their world. Now she knew it applied to her as well.

He moved in her, welding them together, fusing their bodies the way he had their souls. She clung to him, her nails biting deep. Deep inside she felt the tension coiling tighter and tighter. Her gaze clung to his.

"Isai?" His name escaped. A ragged whisper of sound. Breathy. Needy. A little afraid.

"I have you," he said. "Just let go."

She knew when she did she would be swept away. Julija would be gone and it would always be Julija and Isai. "I'm terrified." She was. Of the unknown. Of needing someone the way she would need him.

He leaned down and nuzzled her throat. "Come to me, *sívamet.* Just let go. You will never be alone again."

Looking into those brilliant blue eyes, with her body on fire and wound so tightly she was afraid she might shatter, she took a breath and did exactly what he said. The tidal wave was massive, moving through her body, washing from her center outward. The feeling spread through her, ripples of shocking intensity that swept her up into a place she'd never been and never wanted to leave.

She took him with her, so that she felt the hot splash of his seed, triggering even more shocks. Each left her breathless. Amazed. Floating. She didn't think anything could ever sate her, not once that horrible spell had been used on her, but somehow, Isai had managed, and he'd been gentle, not rough. He'd destroyed everything Barnabas had ever said about her and her needs for darker, painful sex. She had hated everything Barnabas ever said or did to her, but those nights and days had run into weeks and then months. Perhaps years. She'd been terrified that he was right about her because no matter what he did, or how much it hurt, her body had responded and had been desperate for more.

"Stop, *sívamet*." Isai brushed kisses over her wet lashes. "Tell me what is wrong."

She was sobbing again. He would end up thinking all she did was cry. What could she say? She was so grateful she wasn't completely messed up? "Nothing is wrong. Everything is right. Is perfect."

There was no way Barnabas could possibly have conjured up Isai. Or the bliss she'd just experienced with the gentle, caring intimacy of their sexual encounter. Isai made her feel cherished. Treasured. Important. Barnabas made her feel dirty and disposable. A receptacle, nothing more to him.

She couldn't stop crying, and Isai did the only thing left to him. He kissed her, swallowing her tears, his mouth hotter than a flame. She couldn't think when he kissed her, and she had to respond. She gave herself up to the wonder of his mouth. When he finally lifted his head, she felt dazed, happily so. His mouth wandered over her chin and down her throat, giving her little kisses, tiny stings as his teeth nipped her, then a velvet rasp as his tongue eased that ache. He kissed his way to her breast and right on the upper curve, he sank his teeth deep.

She cried out, her body clenching hard, grasping and milking at his cock, the erotic act triggering a massive orgasm all over again. She circled his head with her arms, holding him as he drank, his body moving in hers, until she felt she had one endless orgasm that tore through her repeatedly.

When he lifted his head, licking across the two holes to close them, his blue eyes smiled down into hers. She let her head loll back against the mattress, desperate for air when her body seemed incapable of breathing properly.

He waited until the last wave had receded before kissing her again. "I think you are beginning to believe I am real."

She nodded, afraid to move.

"Just so I am certain, you are, for the moment, perfectly satisfied, because if you need me to continue . . ."

Teasing. He was teasing her. Playing. Couples did that. She'd read about it. Seen it in movies. She'd witnessed it out in the world—just not in her world. "I am more than satisfied," she assured. "Not that I will complain if you decide you need to make another effort sometime quite soon."

He smiled, and her heart nearly stopped. He was absolutely gorgeous. She wished she didn't have so many scars. His fingers pushed at tendrils of damp hair on her forehead and his touch sent butterfly wings fluttering against her stomach.

"Do you mind if I raise the temperature in the pool? I will carry you in. The hot water will keep you from feeling sore."

She didn't feel sore. She felt delicious. She'd felt his every heartbeat, right through his cock. He'd stretched her ability to take him, yet there wasn't a painful spot on her body. "You didn't hurt me at all. Not in the least."

"Nevertheless, I intend to take care of you."

He lifted her easily into his arms, cradling her against his chest, over his heart. His hands on her body were so gentle she wanted to cry all over again. Instead, she turned her face into his neck and enjoyed the way he seemed to glide across the floor to the short distance where the pool she'd created waited for them.

"I did this." She looked at it with pride.

"You did and it's beautiful. Nice job."

She held his praise to her. It wasn't like she ever got compliments or praise for anything. She would be grateful for anything he noticed. Having him express his approval was huge and she hugged it to her. "I'm glad you like it."

"Very much. It looks completely natural, as if it has always been here. It is efficient and does not take up too much space. You have a good eye. For someone who had no idea she could do this, you created the pool like an expert, which I suppose, technically you are."

He floated into the pool with her in his arms and sank into the heat of the water. It felt like heaven, exactly what she needed.

8

Isai allowed Julija to move out of his arms to the other side of the pool. Before she got there, he waved his hand and she had a comfortable seat, just the right height for the blanket of warm water to hit her just above her breasts. She looked beautiful, all flushed and tousled, as if she'd been thoroughly made love to—and she had.

He'd grown to know her through their telepathic connection. He caught glimpses of her life and it sickened him that he'd been in the world and hadn't been able to protect her. She blushed when he kept looking at her.

"You have to stop. I can't think when you're staring at me like that."

"Like what?"

"I don't know. A hungry wolf. You look as if you might devour me any minute."

He flashed a small enigmatic smile at her. "It is a possibility."

"I'm sorry I doubted you, Isai. Or even acquainted you at all with the likes of Barnabas or my father. I should have believed in my own ability to tell truth from lie."

"Do not apologize to me, my little mage. They conditioned you to doubt everything. You will soon believe in yourself again and in us."

She went underwater to rinse out her hair. He watched the strands floating across the top of the crystal-clear pool. She looked like a sexy water nymph. It was difficult to watch her and not have his body react in spite of the fact that he had just had her. One of the cats mewed and pushed against his arm. Without thinking, he bit into his wrist and offered his blood to the animal. The two had to be hungry to ask so soon. He didn't mind. He wanted his bond solidified.

The shadow cats had shields preventing Anatolie from accessing either one. That gave Isai the necessary time to build the bond, so their loyalty would be absolute. He would also know what they were doing at all times. He couldn't afford one or both cats to go after human or Carpathian blood. They would have to get used to taking what they needed from either Julija or him.

Julija watched him feed the big male. "He genuinely likes you."

She sounded surprised, and he deliberately shot up an eyebrow. "I am likable."

She made a face at him. "I don't know, he hasn't felt your hand on his rear."

He knew she was teasing him, but after discovering the things Barnabas had done to her, he didn't want anything that even came close to reminding her of that poor excuse for a human being. He let the cat finish and then closed the puncture wounds with his tongue.

"I must apologize to you for my behavior," he said. "I had no idea you had this man treat you the way he did. I did not mean to resemble him in any way."

She looked genuinely horrified. "If you think that, you need to look into my mind. I didn't want you to see the things he did to me, but your ridiculous little spanking wasn't even in the same league. Believe me, I never thought that at all."

He stared at her, somewhere between shocked and amused, and with an urge to repeat his "ridiculous little spanking." His woman had a mouth on her. He let the silence between them grow heavy until she realized what she'd said. Rather than react the way he expected, with chagrin or at least some tiny bit of remorse, she burst out laughing. He couldn't help liking the sound. It filled the chamber, a soft, sexy little masterpiece he could listen to for the rest of his life. The sound also made him want to smile. It took a few moments to recognize that the unfamiliar emotion welling up in him was happiness.

He sent a wave of water at her with the flat of his hand. Instantly she retaliated, turning her back and throwing up water with both hands. He cheated, easily building a shield while keeping up a storm of water until she collapsed back onto the seat, laughing. He couldn't help smiling again.

When the laughter subsided, she eyed him closely. "I really created this pool, didn't I? No help from you." She made it a statement, but there was a question in her mind.

"No help from me. Now, when you decide to take to the air, there will be help and you'll be very careful to do exactly as I say and follow my instructions to the letter." He meant it. Absolutely. Then she nodded, her eyes going wide, and all sorts of ideas on instructions came into his head, making his cock jerk. He dropped his hand to the growing length, fisting it casually beneath the water.

Her gaze followed the movement of his hand. "Do you think I could do that? Fly?"

"Why not? I think you are going to be able to do more than most of us can, even when you are fully converted. I think your mage blood will remain just as Lycan blood does."

"A mage is more human than any other species," Julija pointed out. "I don't think of us as being more powerful. We're well versed in the arts, both dark and light, but we appear and are the most human."

"Simply because you cannot shift into another form?" Her reasoning eluded him.

"We live among humans, side by side. Our children grow up in the cities and towns. Most mages have married humans and turned their backs on their gifts."

"This does not mean that mages are any more human than Carpathians. Perhaps it is easier for you to assimilate into their society, but you have to have your own doctors, right?"

She nodded. "Not that I ever went to one." She ducked her head. "Especially after Barnabas. You can see the ugly scars on me if I don't build an illusion."

He dropped his hand from his cock, unfamiliar fury building in his gut. He didn't like it. The emotion was disturbing in its intensity and the fact that he was a very dangerous individual.

"First, Julija, don't do that." He reached across the distance between them and lifted her chin. Her eyes met his and he felt the impact right through the swirling heat and anger churning in his belly. "You have no reason to be ashamed. That is part of their conditioning. They humiliated you and did their best to find a way to bend you to their will. They were not successful. You remember that. You stood your ground. You didn't harm an innocent."

Isai allowed his admiration to show in his voice as well as his expression. He detested that her family had done these things to her, deliberately undermined her confidence and misled her so she had no idea who she was or even what she was.

"You, *sívamet*, are *odam wäke emni*. In case you are not up on your Carpathian, it means 'mistress of illusion.' You are amazing when it comes to illusion, but it is because your illusions are very real, thanks to the Carpathian in you. They do not have to know you have become aware of that little detail. They are going to come at you and you will be able to defend yourself against any attack because you are both. Do you understand me, Julija? You are . . . extraordinary."

Her eyes met his with a hint of shyness. That surprised him. His woman wasn't shy.

"You make me feel extraordinary. I don't know if I can do all the things you think I can, but I'm willing to learn, if you're willing to teach me."

"You know more than you think you do. There's one more thing we have to get out of the way before we go any further."

"Two," she contradicted.

He studied her face. "Two then. You go first."

"I want to know what your tattoo says. You said that belongs to your lifemate."

His heart gave a funny little stutter at the mixture of defiance, challenge and possession spilling into her voice. "Only to my lifemate. These words etched into my back are my vow to you."

He remembered every scar deliberately made on his body and how many times it had to be done to overcome the earth's healing. The brethren had found that once the cut was deep enough, if they inserted the black color even deeper, the design would last on their skin. The creed of the brethren in the monastery flowed in their ancient Carpathian language from neck across shoulders and down their backs. Their creed and a vow to his woman.

"You are the most important person in my life. You always will be. When I realized I had grown far too dangerous to continue hunting the vampire—"

Her head jerked up, her eyes meeting his. "What does that mean? Why would that be?"

He had forgotten, because she clearly was Carpathian, that there would be gaps in her knowledge. "We hunt our own brethren and we do so without color or emotion. In some ways, the lack of both is good because to kill someone we love and continue this practice over hundreds of years would damage us beyond repair. Still, one cannot live that way forever. At first you hear the whisper of temptation, to kill while feeding. If one does that, there is a rush caused by the adrenaline in the victim's blood."

"Really? A Carpathian who had spent centuries being honorable would decide to give up everything in order to feel that momentary rush?"

He nodded. "If you have not felt anything at all for centuries, that rush is a huge temptation. Think of all the males and females who cheat on their partners. It is for a momentary rush. They throw it all away, or at least risk it, for that one moment of nothing but feeling. If a warrior hasn't had anything in his life but gray nothingness, that whisper of temptation grows louder and louder as the centuries pass."

Julija leaned back, forgetting nothing was there to support her but rock. He waved to provide a softer cushion for her, doing so without thinking. She looked startled and then she sent him a sweet smile that struck him like a fiery dart.

"Is that what happened? Why you decided to go into the monastery? The whispers were becoming louder?"

"I wish they had continued, but after centuries, and so many kills, they stopped. Killing, even without feeling, takes pieces out of us. Steals what is left of our soul. At least, it feels that way. Each vampire hunt stole more and more of me and then the whispers stopped and there was only silence. Complete silence."

Her dark chocolate eyes were veiled by long, thick lashes, but he could still read the compassion in them. She turned his heart over. How he thought she wasn't worthy, he didn't know. His woman was definitely worthy of being a lifemate. Everything about her screamed courage and compassion.

"I knew then that I had to end my days of hunting. Should I turn, with my knowledge and skills, it would take several seasoned hunters to slay me. I did not want to risk that happening. I had a few 'friends,' men I knew I could count on, and I told them I did not want to end my life, that if my lifemate was out there, I was subjecting her to cycle after cycle. Once I died, I would have to be reborn and still find her. Our life cycles could be far apart."

"Someday you'll have to explain all that to me," Julija said. "This lifemate thing is fascinating. After what happened to me with Barnabas, I didn't think I would ever find someone to share my life with. Now it feels like we've always been together."

"Because we belong. My friends and I decided to go into a monastery. There was one high up in the Carpathian Mountains. The monks were old and slowly dying as no young men wanted that arduous, lonely life. They showed us the simplicity of the way they lived. It was quite beautiful in a way. We cared for them as one by one, they died. While they lived, we were careful of them, but we took their blood."

"Did they know?"

He inclined his head respectfully. "Yes. We told them what and who we were. They could not communicate with the outside world without our knowledge, so it was safe to tell them. They were good men, very accepting of other cultures and ways, and in our case, other species. They helped us as best they could and in return, we did our best for them."

"I can hear regret in your voice."

"For their deaths. Humans die so young. You must have lost human friends."

"I wasn't allowed friends. I mingled with them, lived among them, but we were always aloof from them. Even the more modern neighborhoods we lived in didn't seem to want closeness. No neighborhood barbecues, that sort of thing. That's probably why my father chose them."

Isai concurred with her conclusion. "After the last of the monks died, we chose the youngest of us, which is kind of funny because he was nearly the same age, just lacked by a quarter of a century, but we referred to him as the 'boy.'" He sent her a small grin. "We did not feel, but we still used humor. We did our best to follow the advice of the monks and using humor, whether felt or not, was one of the things that was told to us. Sandu, one of the brethren, was the best at it, but we all practiced."

"You're good enough," she said, as if knowing he was telling her not to expect him to make her laugh, although he wanted to do so. He craved her smile and the sound of her laughter.

"Fane became the gatekeeper," he continued. "He was the youngest of us, although he was enormously skilled, and we trusted him as our gatekeeper. He was the only one of us to come and go from the monastery. He would find sustenance and then return to feed each of us. It was not an easy job."

"I can imagine, with so many of you."

"During our time there, others came and stayed awhile. That helped Fane. Some stayed half a century or more, others less than a decade. If the call to find their lifemate became too strong, they would leave. Not everyone is suited to such an austere lifestyle. Living there was like living without hope, yet at the same time, we were safe from killing."

"I just can't imagine what that was like."

"We lived for our lifemates. I lived for you. We etched our creed into our backs." He turned around to show her the Carpathian letters flowing down his back.

Her fingers brushed over the first words. *"Olen wäkeva kuntankért,"* she whispered softly. "Tell me the translation, Isai."

"'Staying strong for our people.' We were there behind those heavy gates, the thick walls surrounding us to remind us that the Carpathian people were honorable, and we needed to be strong and fight against the nothingness. That gray void we all lived in. It was like a terrible abyss we had gone into, digging deeper and deeper throughout the centuries until one morning, we looked up and there was no way out. Honor was all we had left."

Her fingers brushed over the second line multiple times. Lingered. Cooled and soothed when he had felt no discomfort but now, forever, would crave the touch of her fingers.

"Olen wäkeva pita belső kulymet."

Surprisingly, her pronunciation was excellent. He glanced over his shoulder at her. Her gaze was fixed on the dark scarring on his back.

"The second line says, 'Staying strong to keep the demon inside.'" Her hand covered the line. He felt the imprint of her palm like a brand. It felt a little as if she was trying to take the weight of his demon from him.

He swallowed down a sudden lump in his throat. "Each of us in the monastery lives with our own personal demon. I know that sounds silly because all people do. The difference is, as the gray nothingness grew inside us, making up our world, it fed the worst of our traits, the killer inside us. Our demons are very real, and they are living and breathing, waiting for the moment we are so weary we are no longer diligent, and they can slip free. We vowed to stay strong, so those demons would never be unleashed. As brethren, we watched one another, just as the monks taught us to do, to help when needed. When one was at a very low point, we all pitched in to get them stronger."

"That's amazing, Isai," she murmured softly.

Were her lips brushing those dark scars? Either he had a vivid imagination, or they were. If so, he wasn't going to turn to see. He wanted her that close to him.

"The monks taught us so much about working together. We had almost always worked alone, tracking and destroying vampires. We were not near our families, or even our people as time went on. We traveled to various countries. Alone. Now, we were living in close proximity to one another and we had to learn to live that way. The monks offered us so much and we were grateful to them."

"And the third line?" She ran her fingertip over it.

He felt reverence in her touch. The lump in his throat grew. "That line is extremely sacred, Julija. To each of us in our own way, that line keeps us and everyone around us safe. When the demon rises, and we can't beat it back any other way, we repeat that line. Sometimes, when it was particularly bad for one of us, we all sat in a circle and chanted that line from sundown until sunrise."

"*Olen wäkeva—félért ku vigyázak,*" she read. "What is the exact interpretation and why is it important?"

"'Staying strong for her.'" He glanced over his shoulder again and this time his gaze collided with hers. He didn't look away. "For you. I stayed strong for you. When all else failed, I knew I couldn't give in because you were somewhere, in this time or another, and you were more important than anything else to me. I might break under any other circumstances, but not as long as my lifemate might need me. I stayed strong for you."

She pressed her lips together and then leaned in to brush a kiss over the scars. "I understand what you meant when we first met, and I refused to open my mouth. I'm so ashamed of that, Isai. I swear, I'll try to be worthy of all that time you spent alone."

"Don't," he said, keeping his voice as gentle as possible. "Really, Julija. I would have been leery as well, knowing your background. Forgive me for jumping to conclusions."

She shook her head and pressed her forehead between his shoulder blades. "You don't. Not ever. I don't want you to apologize to me ever again for that. I won't, either, if it makes you feel better, but knowing what you went through humbles me. I can barely comprehend it, let alone understand how you managed to survive it."

He turned once more away from her, looking toward the sliver of a crack in the rock. They were going to have to move soon if he was going to pick up the trail of his brother. Iulian had the book somewhere in the mountains and he needed to recover it and if warranted, send his brother to the next life.

"The last line clearly says it all for every single one of us. We know what holds us to this earth. We know the importance of our lifemate."

"Hängemért." She'd murmured the word softly. "That means 'for her,' doesn't it?"

"Such a simple word, but meaningful and beautiful. *Hängemért.* For her. That is everything, Julija. You are everything, and always will be to me. There will never be another, nor would I want there to be. As centuries went by, I became aware of you. Everything about you. The way we would fit together. The way your smile would be. The sound of your laughter. Your touch on my skin. The talks we would have, walking together, hand in hand. Each new idea that came into my mind made me realize the importance of you. The need to stay strong, to be honorable and to earn the right to be with you."

"Isai."

She'd whispered his name and he thought he felt the burn of tears dripping hotly down his back. He wouldn't be surprised. His woman was emotional, and he found he liked it. He liked knowing she had a soft heart and that she showed her emotions when he could barely change expression.

"It is true, Julija. The more centuries that went by, the more I understood that my lifemate was to be cherished. Treasured. Put before all things."

"I swear to you, I will do the same for you."

He turned then and drew her into his arms. "This is new for us, but we will find our way," he assured.

"We're already in enough trouble just trying to find the book from hell, but now we've got my family hot on our heels."

He pulled back to look down at her face. "Your choice of descriptions is always interesting to me."

"I forget you're really, really old."

He heard the mischievous note in her voice and he dunked her before taking the long step that would put him on the other side of the pool. He sank down onto the seat. There was one more thing he wanted to get straight between them before they went chasing after the high mage's spell book and his brother, who by all accounts hadn't turned vampire but had stolen something important that threatened the Carpathian people. Worse, he'd brought the book to the United States, in close proximity to Sergey, who had slivers of Xavier in him.

Water sprayed into the air like a geyser, hitting his face as Julija retaliated by splashing him. Her laughter teased at his senses. He loved the way it made him feel. He had gone through his life occasionally hearing laughter, but not really understanding it. He was far too old to remember anything about his childhood or life in their village before he'd gone on his first hunts as a slayer.

"I love your tattoo, Isai," she informed him. "It's beautiful. All the other writings on you? What are they?"

"Silliness on my part," he said hastily. "And for another day."

"Which only makes me more curious."

He sent her a small grin. "We really have to get after Iulian. We do not want any member of your family to find him ahead of us."

"Anatolie has said he will send Barnabas." All playfulness was wiped from her face and tone. There was fear there, although she tried to hide it from him.

"I hope Barnabas does come," Isai admitted freely. "I wish to meet this man."

She gave a delicate little shudder and wrapped her arms around herself. "No, believe me, you do not. He appears to be quite the virtuous gentleman. Very scholarly. In fact, he's almost beatific, but I can assure you, he's the devil himself."

"He is still Anatolie's puppet, Julija," he pointed out, keeping his voice deliberately mild. Every instinct told him to hold her, but her expression was too still. Too frightened.

"Please don't underestimate him, Isai. Please, when you meet him, and you will, don't fall under his spell. He's very good at fooling people. I'm not easy. I see through illusions as a rule. He made me doubt myself."

"That was his purpose, *sívamet*. That doesn't make him more powerful than you. It makes him cunning. You also have to remember, you were set up beautifully. Your father went so far as to include your brothers in that class. Had he not, you might have been much warier, but the fact that he wanted all three of you to take the class caught you off guard."

She rinsed her hair one more time, more he knew to give herself time and separate herself from the conversation than because her hair needed it. Anytime Barnabas came into the conversation, she retreated. Isai would have to find a way around that.

"You said there was one more thing. I said two and you answered my questions," Julija said as she once more sat across from him. "What was important to discuss before we go find that book?"

He nodded, studying her face. She was still holding herself very stiff. He shrugged. "We can talk about it later."

She shook her head. "Not if it matters to you."

"It matters," he admitted. "I think it is very important."

"I'm listening."

He saw that she was. "As a rule, Carpathians do not scar." He plunged right in. "The wounds must be deep for that to happen, but I have scars everywhere. I have lived a long time and been wounded countless times. Some were wounds that would have killed others. I survived, but those times remain on my body. Do you mind the scars?" he challenged. "I need you to tell me the truth. Do you find them abhorrent to look at?"

She looked shocked. "No. Absolutely not. They're part of you. Part of who you are. Your past shapes you, Isai. You might not think so because you didn't feel anything at the time, but your emotions were there, buried deep, and you were affected by every single thing that happened. If you weren't, you would never have entered that monastery. Why would you think that? Have I done something to make you think I can't look at your scars?"

"You seem to think your own scars are so repugnant that you need illusion to keep me or anyone else from seeing them."

She had half risen out of the water, but she sat back so that the water rocked back and forth in the small basin. "It's different."

Isai studied her face. Color had swept under her skin, leaving her naturally pale face a delicate rose. "Why? I do not understand. Those scars are part of you and your past, the past that shaped you, just as mine are a part of me. What would be different?"

She was silent a moment, flicking her fingers in the water so little drops shot in an arcing bridge from her side of the pool to his, almost as if she was flicking him away, or at least his words. She was so close he could have reached out and touched her, given her the comfort she so obviously needed, but he knew she would have rejected him, so he stayed very still. Waiting. Forcing her to think about it. Put her reasoning into words. It took longer than he anticipated.

"I didn't get these scars the way you got yours, fighting valiantly to save the world. I got them in a vile, demeaning way. Strung up by my wrists." She rubbed them as though they still hurt. "In front of his class, whipped until I was bleeding from deep wounds, deep enough to cause scars. At the same time my body was being forced into enjoying sex. It was humiliating. I can barely stand to look at those memories let alone know they're etched into my body."

"Julija," he said softly. Reprimanding her. "You do not think you earned every scar? That you were not valiantly fighting in your way to save the innocents they wanted you to murder? Your father set you up deliberately to be torn down by Barnabas. When you did not break, they took it further, hurting you, humiliating you, and you still did not break. I would say each and every scar you received is a badge proclaiming your unbelievable courage. You should rejoice in them. I would. I know, when you allow me to see them, I will worship these scars, knowing you held out against the dark arts trying to manipulate you. Few can say that, Julija. Very few."

"Did you hear me say they used my own body against me?" she murmured softly, her gaze not meeting his.

He remained silent, waiting until she had no choice but to look at him. There was so much pain in her eyes he winced. "I heard. That makes what you did even more courageous. They did not defeat you. Barnabas getting your body to react doesn't mean anything more than he was skilled at what he did. He wasn't strong enough to break you. Wear your scars with pride, *sívamet*. Your courage humbles me. Believe me, if you allow your lifemate to see them, I will love every inch of you, but those scars will be sacred to me."

Isai meant every word and he wanted her to know that he did. He caught her chin and looked her in the eye. "Come into my mind," he invited softly. "See how much I admire and respect my lifemate."

She hesitated just for a moment, and then, her eyes staring into his, he felt her pouring into his mind. She came gently, a hesitant presence, filling him with her feminine beauty. She filled the darkness in him with light.

He savored the feeling of her. The way she was inside, all that strength and power, tempered with compassion and empathy. There was no greed in her. No need to use her gifts for herself. She didn't have selfish thoughts about acquiring wealth. She didn't want to harm others. She definitely wanted to reacquire the spell book, but not for her own gain. She knew quite a bit about the book, more than he thought most Carpathians, including the prince, knew.

He opened his mind to her a little further. He was dark and shadowed, but her light spilled inside him, warmed those cold places and took every vestige of loneliness from him. He didn't try to hide from her. He had admitted to being a killing machine. He had vast knowledge in most subjects, but he had learned in an effort to be a better hunter. She would either accept him as he was, or she wouldn't.

He felt her moving through his memories. Lingering over some, hastily retreating from others. He knew the moment she found the memories in the monastery. She stayed there for far too long, but those times were the ones where he had sent every message into the universe, unashamedly begging for his woman to be in this time period but feeling there was little hope.

He had, like the others, times over those long years of being too close to the demon, but his brethren had stood with him. Chanting. *Olen wäkeva—félért ku vigyázak.* Hours of chanting. Stay strong for her. She had saved him over and over. So many times. Julija had saved his honor.

She left him after a long while and when he looked at her face, tears tracked down her cheeks. Her lashes were wet and dripped diamond-like tears. He reached out tentatively, but she didn't flinch, so he touched her face gently, following the path with the pads of his fingers.

"*Sívamet.* Do not cry for me. You are worth every moment I spent alone."

Julija shook her head and pressed her fingers to her lips. "I can't believe that's what you think of me. I'm not like that at all."

"You are. I see you more clearly than anyone else ever could. I am in your mind. I know you better than you know yourself. I will never look at you another way. You're perfect to me."

"I have a really bad temper," she confessed.

He smiled at her. "I like your temper. I am not a man who would go through life with a woman who always told me yes. I enjoy putting her over my knee, remember?"

She wiped at the tears running down her face and then laughed, just as he hoped she would. "I'm quite capable of turning you into a toad."

"And you would take great pleasure in it."

"I would," she admitted without hesitation.

Isai deliberately floated from the pool to the chamber floor, dried himself off and clothed himself. He didn't help her. He waited, both cats circling his legs.

"You did that on purpose. You're such a show-off."

He smirked and rubbed Belle's head. "You can do the same."

"You could just help me out and do it for me." She looked all around the pool as if it would give her answers on how to float out.

"I could, but what would be the fun in that? Try."

"I have to know what I'm doing before I can try," Julija said. "Instructions would be helpful."

"I suppose that's true," he conceded. "But not nearly as much fun for me."

He folded his arms across his chest and waited in silence as she walked around the pool and then looked up at him. There was determination on her face, exactly what he had hoped for.

"You have been doing this kind of thing since you were a child."

"They were *illusions*."

"Julija." He said her name gently in reprimand. "They were not. I call you *odam wäke emni* because you truly are mistress of illusion in the mage world. So much so that your own father, rather than encourage you and want you to be the best at it, downplayed your ability. Who are you going to believe? Your father? Or me? It all starts in your mind. You know that. You have power beyond your imagining. Use it."

He kept his arms folded and his expression implacable and just looked at her. He thought she made some very foul gesture under the water, but he couldn't be certain. The thought made him want to smile, but he refused to give in, even to humor.

Julija walked around the perimeter inside of the pool for a second time and then stood in the exact center. She raised her arms.

I call to the element of air, surround me.
I call to the element of light, transport me.
Lift me up like a feather high,
Transporting me to the floor within my sight.

She rose easily and ended up on the floor right in front of him. She flung her arms around him and hugged, rubbing her wet body all over his dry clothes like a cat, and then she sprang away laughing. He caught her arm before she could get away from him.

"Show me."

The smile died instantly, and she gave a half shake of her head. "Isai." It was cautionary.

"Show me."

She turned back to him, almost defiantly, her arms sliding down the sides of her body as if she was disrobing. Instantly he could see the white slashes dissecting her flesh along the curves of her breasts and down her stomach. There were more on her thighs. She turned around and showed him her back, buttocks and upper thighs. There were no raised ridges, only those white and sometimes red lines, some wide, others narrow. All bit deep.

He ran his hand down the curve of her back. "Never hide these, Julija. I will not hide mine. You are infinitely beautiful. Not just to me, but to anyone who sees you. You know I do not lie to you."

"I don't know what to do with you when you say things like that."

Isai gave her a faint smile. "Give me my way in all things."

She rolled her eyes, but she didn't cover the scars with illusion. "I suppose you want me to dry myself off and clothe myself."

"I do not mind you walking naked with me, but I doubt we will get very far. I like looking too much and my body reacts when I do." He was very honest.

Her eyes dropped low on him. "I see that."

She took her time to once again lift her arms, this time a little sultrily, but there was no shame in facing him with her true body, scars and all.

Air encircle me, blow me dry.
Cloths of cotton, weave and tie,
Allowing me to stay warm and dry.

She gave him a faint, triumphant grin. "I'm ready to go, although I really do like this little cave."

"We'll close it up and come back when we are able," he assured.

He signaled to the cats and led the way over to the stone where the thin crack was. He slid through without hesitation. The cats followed him. It took several minutes, but his woman emerged right beside him, a large grin on her face.

"How do you feel about flying?"

9

The world looked very different when one was soaring through the air in the middle of the night. Julija found herself laughing, elated, exhilarated. *I love this.*

Pay attention to what you are doing, kislány hän ku meke sarnaakmet minan. Stay focused.

Was there panic in his voice? Julija thought there might be and that made her laugh all over again. The stars were brighter this far up. Everything below her seemed very small. The cats were running flat out on the rocks below, Carpathian blood calling to them. They would find Julija and Isai before dawn when Isai found a place for them all. In the meantime, she could do a few crazy tricks, like try to do somersaults in the air.

Julija. You will behave yourself. Pay attention. Do you have any idea of all the things that could go wrong?

I want to kiss you right now. She did. Kissing him sounded wonderful. Completing. That was exactly what she needed to make flying the best thing that ever was. She thought about his face. The lines etched deep. The strong jaw. Aristocratic nose. That long hair, pulled back in his braid with cords tying it every few inches. Always neat. Never ruffled. She laughed all over again. *Your feathers seem a little ruffled now.* Her laughter grew. That was true—and funny.

The larger owl dropped down to cover the female with one wide-spread wing. *I think you have truly lost your mind, woman. Stop laughing.*

There was no stopping, not when she was this happy. *Are you crazy? This is—wonderful. Perfection. I can't believe how flying feels. I could do this all night.*

It is your first time, sívamet. There was a hint of a smile coming through the panic along with resignation. *You will tire easily. Please keep your mind focused on what you are doing. If you lose the image, even for a moment, you will fall from the sky.*

She knew that, and it should have scared her, but it didn't. She'd always had the ability to give details her full attention. She was aware of everything around her. She'd had to be. Her father was very exacting of all of them, but of her in particular. Her stepmother was very cruel; knowing where she was in the house at all times had saved Julija from many beatings. She wasn't going to think about her. Nothing was going to mar her enjoyment of flying through the air on silent wings.

Stay with me. Your owl has excellent hearing and vision. We are looking for Iulian's trail. I was searching for him when I discovered you. I tried reaching out to him, but he didn't answer. Neither, when the theft was first discovered, did he answer the prince, Gregori or Tariq.

I felt him up until about forty-eight hours ago. He felt . . . sad. Very sad. His sorrow weighed him down.

You said you connected with him when he was with his lifemate.

She was very tired. She must have been in her eighties or nineties and alone in a nursing home. He held her until she passed.

Isai was silent for so long she was becoming alarmed. In the body of the owl she twisted her neck, although the eyes could see his owl very clearly.

What are you thinking, Isai?

The entire time he was close to you, you could connect with him?

Yes. I felt his emotions, even though he could not. She settled into a pattern, flying close to him, allowing the larger bird to keep her nearly beneath his wing.

Was that common for you? Feeling the emotions of others?

Automatically, her owl observed everything going on below her. For the most part, there was little movement of humans or even mages on the vast acreage laid out below them. Twice she'd seen hikers, but when Isai had dropped low to ensure they were truly hikers, both times they'd been legitimate.

To feel others' emotions, yes. To connect so strongly with a Carpathian male? No. That was the first time and it was extremely strong. I was shocked that he didn't seem aware of it.

You were behind him by several days and yet you were able to pick up his trail again once you were here in Yosemite?

Yes. The pull was extreme again. There was no getting away from it. He was broadcasting sorrow so deep, at times all I could do was weep for him. That was the truth as well. His brother, Iulian, had moved her beyond all self-centered thoughts. Beyond anything. His sorrow was that deep.

Then suddenly that trail abruptly ended?

Again, she twisted her neck to look at him. His voice had been pitched exactly the same, but she listened for any little inflection. Something was off. He was going somewhere with his inquiry, not just trying to find a detail she missed.

I don't believe he was selfishly looking to keep the book. It didn't feel that way to me at all. What are you thinking?

The same thing you are. He took the book to protect it. He had to have had a plan. My blood calls to his, yet it goes unanswered. The book was sealed with the blood of sacrifice. To keep that blood sacrifice from calling to any member of the high mage's family— He broke off.

Julija knew what was coming. She'd entertained the idea she knew was moving through Isai's mind. She wanted desperately to stop him from voicing it. Already she could feel the beginnings of sorrow in his mind. She couldn't stop herself. She had to delay the inevitable, even if it was just for a few minutes.

How close were the two of you? She wasn't close to her siblings at all. She'd tried. They hadn't wanted her, other than to use her for blood. More than once, she was told she was worthless to the family. As she got older, she knew that wasn't true. She had what they wanted most—an abundance of Carpathian blood.

He was born nearly a thousand years after me. I met him twice and only by chance. For a long time, before I entered the monastery, I kept tabs on him. From everything I gathered about him, he was a very good man and an excellent hunter.

Isai's voice was strictly neutral, but she could feel his emotions. The sorrow was growing stronger. She decided to just get it over.

You believe he is dead.

Yes. You lost the connection with him. I cannot feel my connection with him.

They flew together, Julija pressing closer to Isai in an effort to comfort him. The wind ruffled over her wings, but rather than producing turbulence and noise, the effect was an eerie silence. The construction of the owl's feathers allowed it to be a silent, deadly predator.

Do you think Sergey got to him? Anatolie? She didn't want to think it was Barnabas, but it was possible.

I think he sacrificed his life, spilling his blood over the book to hide it. He believed me dead. He thought himself the last of our lineage. No one else would have his blood or a connection to him. His lifemate was dead. He knew he would meet her in the next life cycle. He wanted his death to count for something.

Julija turned the idea over and over in her mind. A blood sacrifice to hide the book? It might work. The book was still in existence and someone could stumble across it, but if Iulian had taken his own life, spilling his blood over the book as he'd died . . . She didn't know. *It might work.*

He would know no one other than the prince would be able to track him, Isai mused to her. *Would that do it? Would that successfully hide the book? From Sergey? From your father? From any with the high mage's mark?*

She wanted to tell him it would. She wanted him to believe that his brother sacrificed his life for all of them and that his sacrifice would count. Be legendary. She remained silent, trying to believe that the book couldn't call out to the slivers in Sergey's brain with Iulian's blood over it. Or that her father couldn't find a spell that would get past the lock Iulian's blood put on finding the book.

The book was magic, and magic left a trail. Those who wielded magic were sensitive to that trail. She thought it was a great idea Iulian had had. His scent would successfully drown out the others, but that didn't mean the magic inside those bloodstained pages would remain there. Over time, the entrails could leak out and once again call to Sergey or Anatolie.

Julija? Isai prompted, looking for an answer.

It would be so much better if the book was destroyed, she said carefully.

She felt Isai's sudden weariness. She wanted to reach out and touch him to comfort him. In the body of the owl, she couldn't do that, so she stroked a caress in his mind.

Do you know how it can be destroyed?

No. But I haven't thought much beyond trying to catch up with Iulian and make certain he wasn't using the book to get something for himself.

Such as?

Bringing his lifemate back.

Isai's owl pushed into her, turning her toward the west. They began quartering the area, looking for backpackers, campsites, any place an enemy might be.

I will admit I had not thought of that, he said. *It makes no sense.*

Of course it does, Isai. He waited a thousand years for that one woman and she's dying when he finds her. Why wouldn't he think he could bring her back?

Carpathians do not think like that.

You don't think that way, Isai, she corrected. *You do not know how he thought.* She detested pointing that out to him, but it was the truth. Still, she didn't believe Iulian had betrayed his people for selfish reasons. It wasn't in him any more than it was in Isai.

I want to explore the theory that he took his life, spilling his blood to hide the book. He was alone, and he believed his lineage had ended. How would anyone find that book?

The obvious answer is accidentally. But there are a few other ways, magic being the most evident. What's that below us?

The male owl broke away from the female and circled the area below. It appeared devoid of all life, just flowers and shrubs clinging to rocks, living out the last of their cycle before winter set in fully.

I do not see anything.

Look in the shadows. Inside the female owl's body, she shivered.

The male made another lazy circuit. Sharp eyes inspected the deeper shadows thrown by large boulders in the silvery moon and multitude of stars.

Let's go, she whispered. *Right now, Isai.*

As the owl passed over the largest boulder, a streak of gray shot from a crevasse in the granite and hooked savage claws into its body. The cat was that fast. Its weight pulled them both to the rock as it sank razor-sharp teeth into the bird.

As the bird fell from the sky into the hungry cat's jaws, a steady stream of what appeared like fog rose back into the sky as Isai escaped into the air.

Do not panic, little mage. I am perfectly fine. This cat is starving. He is one of your brothers' cats, and he's very hungry.

The shadow cat was enormous, the size of a large panther. The animal was very thin, and its hair was patchy, as if nutrition had been an ongoing problem. A second cat crawled up over the top of the large boulder, slinking toward the feeding cat. The larger cat lifted his head, looked around suspiciously and then backed off its kill. As the female approached, the male made a soft chuffing sound and took another step back.

Clearly, he's starving, yet he gives up his food to his hunting partner, Julija said. *See why I wanted so much to help them? They're mostly good to one another. It isn't their fault that my brothers use them to harm people.*

Those two look far more vicious than the two we have, Isai stated, circling the shadow cats.

The female crouched down and began to eat. Her eyes had been glowing red, but that vivid color receded, and she looked around her with jeweled amber. Her fur was more black than gray, and the wind ruffled it slightly.

Those two are called Comet and Phaedra. They are the biggest and most dangerous of his cats. I couldn't get near them. The female in particular would have taken my head off if she could have.

She looks docile enough now.

Julija's breath caught in her throat. He wasn't going to listen to her. *Isai, please, let's just get out of here. Anatolie can lay traps in places like this. The cats are programmed to find Carpathian blood. They crave it. Anatolie craves it. So do my brothers, and now, especially Barnabas. It is only a matter of time before they recognize that Carpathian blood is in close proximity to them.*

Do you believe they are looking for you? Me? Or my brother?

Panic was beginning to fray the edges of her mood. She'd been so ecstatic, now she wanted to run for her life and take Isai with her.

We cannot leave these two with your brothers. They will harm human life as well as mage or Carpathian. If they are left to run free without direction . . .

Their direction is to kill. You. Me. Anyone they find. Come on, Isai. Let's leave here. She directed her owl to circle above the cats, looking for anything that would tell her this was a trap Anatolie or her brothers—or worse, Barnabas—had set for them.

Take a breath, sívamet, they do not know anything about us. They cannot know we are lifemates.

She wanted to curl up inside the owl, small and frightened. She wanted to demand Isai listen to her. Mostly she wanted to gather up every molecule that could possibly be her lifemate and force him to leave whether he wanted to or not.

He knows, Isai. Anatolie knows everything. What he knows, Barnabas will know. I believe he has chosen Barnabas as his right hand. He directs and Barnabas carries out whatever it is Anatolie tells him. She kept a wary eye on the feeding cats.

Then Barnabas is not nearly as powerful as they want you to think. He needs your father's direction and approval. Had he been intelligent, he would know, like your father, that you were the one with the power.

Isai kept telling her that. Over and over. He clearly believed that the Carpathian DNA in her body coupled with the mage had given her some advantage over everyone. She wished it was true. She was beginning, in the back of her mind, to believe him. Just a little.

Sívamet, look to the east.

She didn't want to take her eyes off the scene below. Isai needed her as a guard. Still, she did as he directed and saw Belle and Blue running full out, in shadow form, two gray streaks moving in the darkness toward the cats on the bluffs.

Can you stop them?

Either one of us can. They will obey orders. I hope they can help us with these two. I have a plan.

Whatever you're thinking, don't. She wanted to shake him. *I'm telling you, there is a trap here.*

I believe you. I am not on the ground. I am studying the situation.

She heard the teasing amusement in his voice and she couldn't help relaxing just a little bit. He could make her laugh, no matter the circumstances.

She gave an exaggerated sigh. *What is your plan?*

Plan? he echoed.

A small laugh escaped her. *Our kittens are getting closer. What is your idea?*

I am still thinking.

It will not matter if any of them come for us. I'm going to strangle you, Julija informed him.

She heard his deeper laugh brush through the walls of her mind. The sound was joyful. She loved that. She hadn't heard Isai laugh often, and she hugged that moment to herself, savoring it, letting herself have those few heartbeats of time without worry. Without a negative thought.

She'd been brought up in a world where spells and magic were normal. She found Isai was the true magician. He was magic. She would follow him anywhere.

The owl suddenly jolted hard, pain spreading through the small body. She heard a loud crack as she fell, tumbling out of control, through the air toward the ground.

Float. You know how to float. It starts in your head. Float, Julija. Right. Now. Isai streaked toward her.

Julija closed her eyes to keep from seeing the ground rising toward her fast. In her head, she built the image of a bubble and instantly the velocity of her fall changed, and she was inside a balloon, carried on the wind. Isai snagged her out of the sky and took her balloon down to the surface, the floor of the bluff, a distance from the two cats.

She emerged from the bubble and waited until Isai was in his human form. He was ruggedly good-looking. Every line. He could have been chiseled from the granite they stood on. She stared at him for an eternity, her heart pounding. "You saved me."

He shook his head, a faint smile on his face. "You saved yourself. Your choice was rather unique, but you did that all on your own. You didn't cast a spell, or weave patterns, either. You just became lighter than air and you floated."

He looked so incredibly proud of her. Euphoria hit, but it wasn't the fact that she really had saved herself, or that she hadn't needed to add spells or weave intricate configurations in the air, it was that look on his face. No one had ever looked at her like that before. She wanted to etch that look into her mind for all time. She wanted to be able to take it out and examine it later when she had plenty of time.

"The cats," she whispered. "*Our* cats. Why do you want them here?"

"Look at the two of them, what did you say their names were? Phaedra and Comet? Really look at them. *Feel* them."

She had looked at them. She'd gone into her brothers' experiment shed every night to try to heal the cats that were injured or hurt. Phaedra and Comet were always locked away. They would hiss and leap at her, hitting the doors of their cages, and she would almost pass out. Venom dripped from their teeth. She would be afraid to even feed them.

"You need to look at them," she pointed out. "I love that you have compassion for them, but those two are so far gone."

"Why would they be so far gone?"

"My brothers take turns beating them. They're kept starved. After I found the shed, I fed the animals food, even them, although getting near their cage was taking my life in my hands. They especially hated me. All the cats did. They could smell my family on me. We have to do something now before Blue and Belle get here. I'm going to direct them away from here."

"No, my little mage, let them come. I do not want to leave these cats behind."

"Did you not see my owl shot out of the sky? They are coming after us."

"They were fishing. Even as the owl dropped from the sky, they couldn't see you. They may have caught a glimpse of the balloon, but I pulled it out of the sky very quickly." He turned his head toward the two cats who had run up to them. "Belle. Blue." He rubbed their heads as they wound in and out between his legs, nearly knocking him over.

Each time the cats bumped Julija, they rocked her body. They were big animals and once they took their normal forms, they were the size of panthers—healthy ones, and quite formidable. She petted the two cats, realizing she had missed them in the short time they'd been separated.

"Above us, Julija," Isai cautioned in a low voice.

She didn't tilt her head, but she did lift her gaze and her heart nearly stopped. Comet was crouched in the rocks above them, his body once more shimmering gray. He looked malevolent with his glowing eyes, two red pinpoints of evil staring at them.

"Isai," she whispered, "they can do damage in seconds."

"Yes," he agreed. "I want you to think of yourself as molecules—"

She shook her head. "Absolutely not. I stay right here with you. It happens, or it doesn't. If he attacks, he attacks both of us." She wasn't going to argue with him, but she was shaking like a leaf. She might not have to use spells or weave protections to aid him fighting off the enormous cats, but she was used to it and much more comfortable with the concept.

"Stay quiet then and let me handle them." He lifted his hand and waved it casually toward her as if gesturing to her to stay silent.

She sent him a look that should have withered him right there. "Your bossiness knows no bounds."

He inclined his head, a faint smile in his jeweled eyes. "You have no idea, *kislány hän ku meke sarnaakmet minan.*"

Julija watched intently as Isai lifted his wrist to his mouth and bit down. At once crimson drops beaded up. He held his wrist out to the large cat crouched above them. Saliva dripped continuously from the cat's mouth as it glared down at them.

"Come to me, Comet," Isai said in a low, compelling tone. It was a whisper of sound, but it carried on the wind and swelled with command. He held up his wrist so that the ruby drops slid down his arm in a trail of red.

The enormous cat came to his feet and put one giant paw on the narrow trail that led down to where the two sat with Belle and Blue. Isai held up his hand in a wait command to the two cats who watched Comet warily.

"*Aćke éntölem it*—take another step toward me. I am *Karpatii*. Your brother. I offer you life—or death. You choose. Stay where you are and be treated as a cur, kicked and beaten by those who have no *aka-arvo*— respect. With us, you will be treated as family. You are intelligent, Comet. Choose life or death now."

Julija wasn't certain if she wanted Comet to choose life. He moved one slow step at a time. Above them, Phaedra had taken his place, crouching to watch their every movement, determined to protect her mate. She looked terrible. Her coat was thin and shabby, and when she slipped from her solid form to shadow, there were visible holes in the shadow creature. Her brothers had starved the cats almost beyond salvation. They must have done so in preparation for hunting her.

She shivered and wrapped her arms around her middle as the huge male came closer. Isai sent her a sharp, assessing look. She was grateful that he thought her strong and steady enough to handle the anticipation of the cats' attack on them, but at the same time, a little protection would have been nice.

Isai's blue gaze jumped to her face. "Do you really think I would not protect you? Above all else, Julija, you have my protection and care. If you need to go, or to be invisible, I will aid you to do so, although you are capable of that layer of protection yourself. I suspect these cats would find you. They have some element of Carpathian blood, most likely from the blood they took from you."

She jerked her gaze from the female cat crouched above her and turned her head to stare at him. "I knew they gave them blood. But . . ." She trailed off. What was the use? Her brothers were sick individuals, and they had tried to create the ultimate in a weapon. A shadow that could slip in and out of homes, maybe even dreams, kill when they were told to and return cowed to their masters.

Blue snarled and Isai dropped his hand down toward their cat, offering him the blood trailing down his wrist.

"In our world, Julija, blood is everything. It is what gives life and what takes it away. Our blood heals. It is powerful. We are nearly immortal because of our blood. Xavier was well aware of this and wanted it for himself. Blood was the one thing that always eluded him. Those he used for supply had to be kept weak and near death. I suspect your brothers, once they saw the power in the cats they bred, were afraid of them. They followed tradition and kept them weak."

She swallowed hard. The big male was so close now that Blue's head went up and he stepped back, his body going to shadow, his eyes glowing hotly as he followed Comet's every movement. Comet crept closer, his gaze going from Isai's face, to Blue and then to Isai's wrist.

Isai put the temptation of the twin blood trails sliding down his wrist directly in front of Comet. "Trust is difficult when you have no reason," he said softly. "My little mage had a difficult time trusting me. Belle and Blue did as well. We welcome you and Phaedra to our family. You will remain with us."

She gasped, one hand going to her throat, then she wished she hadn't. Comet followed the movement with his gaze and at once the amber in his eyes receded so that the glowing hot coals of red replaced the cooler color.

"On me," Isai said. "Stay on me, Comet." Again, there was both command and compulsion in his voice.

Julija had to admire him. The cat was moving closer and closer to him and he didn't so much as flinch. At this distance, even if Isai wanted to defend himself, the cat could rip him to shreds. Up close, Comet was even more intimidating than Blue. The cat had weight, height and more roped muscles than she'd ever seen on an animal. His claws were enormous, more like a grizzly's than a panther's, although retractable.

"His fur is a mess," she whispered softly.

"No nutrition. He's hurting. They both are."

She hadn't wanted to let them in her mind because she was certain they would have to kill the pair. Now, because Isai was giving the cats this one chance—and that meant he intended to kill them if they chose wrongly—she decided it was only fair that she suffered, too. She had to let herself feel the emotions of both cats. She knew, once she did, compassion would kick in, and if they had to be destroyed, she would be devastated. Still, it wasn't fair to let Isai do all the hard things.

She opened her mind to encompass the pair of shadow cats. Pain ripped through her immediately, taking her breath. She looked up at the female, crouched and ready to attack should they in any way threaten or harm her mate. She had at least two broken ribs where she'd been repeatedly kicked, and there were torn places in her coat as if she'd been whipped or ripped at with some instrument of terror from the medieval era.

"Isai," she whispered, tears in her voice.

He glanced at her sharply. "You are far too compassionate for your own good, *sívamet*. Stay alert. They want their nightmare to be over. They have listened to your brothers speculating that Blue and Belle didn't return because they stayed with you. They were furious and took it out on Phaedra, stating that if she dared run away, they would skin her alive when they found her. They meant it, too."

"I'm sure they did. Poor Phaedra." She kept her voice low but attached a lure—a gentle one.

Comet was about two feet from Isai and he stopped, angling his body away from Blue and Isai, so his back was more toward Julija. He slowly stretched his neck out as far as possible, his eyes watching Isai the entire time. Twice, just before he tasted the blood, he pulled back, whirled around and ran a few feet away. He crouched there, his body going from solid to shadow and then back again.

Each time Comet retreated, Phaedra snarled and leaned forward as if she might leap down on them, but she backed off, settling on her haunches when Isai looked up at her and murmured soothingly in the ancient language.

"I cannot believe how patient you are," Julija said, her breath exploding out of her. She hadn't realized she'd been holding it. Even with the blood trickling down his arm, Isai didn't try to hurry the cat.

"One of the mantras taught to us that we are never to forget—*türelam agba kontsalamaval*. The saying has great value."

"What does it mean? I can get most things, but you said it fast."

"'Patience is the warrior's true weapon,'" he interpreted for her. "I apologize that I slip back into my language. In the monastery we daily practiced other languages to get the accents right, but we preferred to speak in the ancient language and still do, as a rule, when we are together. Does it bother you?"

"No, I actually love the cadence when you speak. He's about to touch your arm," she added unnecessarily.

Comet was so close to Isai's wrist, her heart nearly jumped out of her chest. He looked even bigger so close to them. Isai wasn't a small man, but even beside him, the size of the shadow cat was shocking.

The rough tongue came out and tentatively licked at the thin streams of blood. All the while those eyes spun from red to greenish gold and back again.

"I welcome you, brother," Isai said after the cat had begun to lick at his arm in earnest. "This is your family. You will travel with us. Hunt with us. Eat with us. Sleep when we sleep. We protect one another."

The cat looked up at him, stepped back and studied his face for a long time before turning toward Julija and subjecting her to an even longer perusal.

You helped the others.

The images of Julija caring for the cats' wounds and secretly giving them blood startled her. She didn't know if it was an accusation or not. She just inclined her head, because there was no denying it. She was there. Comet was there.

There was movement above them, but Julija didn't dare take her eyes from the big cat. Both Belle and Blue had come to their feet. She felt this was a defining moment, but she was unsure what to do so she sat very still. Those strange eyes stared into hers and she felt the cat deep within her. She willed him to see her good intentions. Willed him to see that she wanted to help his mate. After what seemed an eternity, Comet looked up toward the female and yowled.

Phaedra remained where she was. She shook her head and cried, mewling pitifully. Comet bared his teeth and called to her a second time. The female looked around her slowly, tentatively. Julija heard Isai's breath hiss out of his lungs.

I told you it was a trap, Julija said. She wanted to shake him. They could have been halfway out of Yosemite had they taken to the air.

It is only a trap if we are unaware of it, Isai pointed out. *You warned me earlier and I believed you. It was necessary to expose ourselves if we wanted to save Phaedra and Comet.*

The large cat looked at Isai as if he'd heard every word. Once again, he called to his mate. This time she obeyed, slinking down the narrow trail toward them, her head swinging cautiously left, then right.

Without warning, something cracked hard almost against Julija's thigh and then up near her shoulder. Shockingly, cracks feathered out around her as if she were sitting in a glass house and the glass had shattered but held. Isai leapt for the female cat, taking her off the trail as more bullets struck where she'd just been.

"Go, brothers, hide yourselves," he called to the shadow cats as he tumbled down the rocky hill toward the cover of brush with the large female.

Phaedra had been startled enough to rip across his thigh with a hooked, venomous claw, but then realized he was saving her life. She held herself very still as they rolled together. More bullets hit the brush, but Isai had thrown up a barrier to prevent them from being hit.

You could have told me, Julija said, touching the shield her lifemate had erected around her. Clearly, he had been protecting her not only from the large cats should they attack, but all along he'd been expecting her murderous family to catch up with them. They'd shot the owl, so it stood to reason they had a high-powered rifle and would use that in the first phase of their attacks. *Why don't you have a shield around you?*

You are much more important.

Was there laughter in his voice? Maybe not, but certainly amusement. She wanted to shake him. *This isn't a game. Anatolie is very, very dangerous. If you knew Xavier, or heard of the despicable things he did, then you should realize that he raised Anatolie to be as bad as he was. He wanted an heir. He kept Anatolie secret from everyone, so he could teach him everything he needed to know and help him take over the world. That was the ultimate goal. Do you think he would raise someone to be wimpy?*

Wimpy? Now he was laughing. *What does that even mean? Is it slang?*

She was not going to laugh. *You're impossible.* More bullets hit the shield surrounding her and the cracks webbed wider. *Should I run for it?*

Go invisible. Become mist and fade away. Once you have done that, I will follow with the cats. Do not worry, I will be right behind you.

Her heart jerked hard. She took a deep breath and shook her head. *Isai, I can't possibly do something like that. It's too scary.*

The moment she sent the words to him, he flooded her mind with soothing warmth and filled her visually with mist, so it felt as though it was building in her mind rather than outside around her, yet when she looked up toward the stars, she could no longer see them. The mist had crept in, a few long fingers at a time until it surrounded her, thick and impenetrable.

The change always starts in your mind, just as your illusions do. Think of it as an illusion if that helps you, little mage. You must hold two things in your head at all times. You will be mist and you must be lighter than air, taking to the sky to escape. Moist air is heavier than dry air. You can do both.

The moment he said that, she realized he was right. She lifted her hands and began to weave a pattern of mist so that she felt it twisting around her body, those wet, cool, very fine droplets. She began to chant softly.

> *Mist made of water, I call to the light.*
> *Moonshine surround me with your beams so bright.*
> *Take that which is water transforming its light.*
> *So I may transcend, becoming mist and take flight.*

Her body dissolved, a stranger feeling even than when she'd become an owl, or rather had been buried deep in the owl's body. She moved quickly, rising to join the strange, eerie fog that surrounded the large series of passes along the mountain range.

A loud crack followed by a single command sliced through the heavy fog. *Show thyself.*

The air shimmered around her. The droplets went iridescent. Julija had been trained to obey that voice, that command. Without real thought, she started to shift.

Stay with me, Isai whispered. *Feel me with you. He cannot have you.*

Shocked that she'd nearly obeyed her father when she knew better, Julija clung tightly to Isai. *I'm with you.*

10

A series of loud cracks like lightning whips echoed across the sky and reverberated down through the canyons. Isai held the cat low, murmuring soothing reassurances to the huge female. Phaedra had one venomous talon hooked into his thigh, but she'd gone still, realizing they were being fired upon. She'd heard the sound of gunfire before and she'd seen the results.

"That's a girl," Isai praised, his mind more on keeping the image of fog in Julija's brain than on his predicament with the cat. He hadn't yet given the animal his blood, so he couldn't fully read her, but she'd gone docile. She was too thin, clearly starving. "We have to stay here, hunkered down, you might as well feed." He offered his wrist. He hadn't closed the laceration and blood still beaded there.

Phaedra looked at him in much the same way her mate had, studying his face, looking for a trap. These cats had been so abused by their creators that they had little trust—like Julija. His woman. She was in the thick fog moving overhead and he wanted to send her somewhere safe while he dealt with those hunting them.

He'd known there was a trap. He had hoped to get the shadow cats out before it was sprung. He'd protected his lifemate first and then reached out to the cats. He would have killed them both immediately had Comet not responded.

Why are you called Comet? he asked the cat.

In the form of a shadow, the male made his way to Isai and made his presence known by pressing close to his mate. She didn't look up from where she was licking frantically at the blood beading on Isai's wrist, but she did press back against the larger male.

Fast. The image of speed came into Isai's mind. There was no bragging. The cat stated facts.

Isai felt his woman move in his mind. She felt sweet. Compassionate. Wholly feminine. Her touch warmed him unexpectedly. *How are we going to get out of here with the cats? Can you make them like the fog as well?*

He had no intentions of leaving, not until he had engaged the enemy. He knew there was at least one, but more likely two. One to handle the rifle and probably a partner, a spotter. *I will settle you in the distance and return to fight these people. We do not want them biting at our heels while we search for the book.*

Feminine outrage filled his mind. *You will not settle me in the distance. I am perfectly capable of helping you. In fact, I'm probably better at dealing with them than you are.*

He was careful to keep the thought that she hadn't dealt with them ever from the front of his mind. If she'd been capable, her family would already have been annihilated. She might have the power, but she lacked the compartmentalization needed to kill. Also, they had programmed her to believe they were all-powerful. Especially her father.

"Enough," he said regretfully to the female cat. She needed more blood. More food. More care. He couldn't shed his body and enter the cat's while keeping the fog surrounding them and Julija safe. "As soon as we are in a safe place I will see to your injuries," he promised.

Move to the very edge of the fog.

He waited to see if Julija would do as he commanded. They were new. She was more of the modern world than he was. Mage women were powerful in their own right and as a rule were not in the least subservient to men. He wasn't asking for obedience from his woman, but in a battle, he expected to be the general.

He felt her hesitation, but then she moved slowly within the thick fog, going in the direction of the slight breeze. Movement was very slight, and she moved sluggishly, not wanting to draw attention.

Can you spot them?

At once he felt the difference in her. She had thought he wouldn't ask her for help and had been upset, but with that one question, she was once again fully with him.

I see movement. They're trying to use the fog for cover. My two brothers. They have leashes on two shadow cats. The cats are young. I recognize them from the shed. They are from the last litter considered Phaedra and Comet's. The only two to survive.

Anyone else?

They have three mages with them. Males. Their friends. Terry, Sam and Andrew. They always hang with them.

He wanted to ask about "hang with them," but the implication was that they were always together, so he understood enough to know the five men had probably worked together before.

I do not play games when I hunt, my little mage.

There was a small silence. *What are you saying?*

I intend to kill them.

Another silence. She held herself away from him. It was subtle, but it was there. He didn't give in. Her family was the enemy. More, they were her greatest enemy. As long as they were alive, she would never be safe. He was not going to pretend that he wouldn't destroy them. The moment he heard her story of Barnabas and realized her father and brothers had not only allowed such a hideous thing to happen to her but had set her up, he knew he was going to kill them.

Was she silently weeping? He couldn't blame her. She had never really had a family. He touched her mind very gently, working his way around the image of fog she was so valiantly holding uppermost. He felt her fear of the unknown. Her family might be something out of a horror film, but they were familiar to her. He felt her loneliness. It felt stark. Raw. Ugly. He had been alone for centuries, but he felt nothing, certainly not lonely.

Sívamet, you are my lifemate. You are never alone.

I've always been alone.

She didn't feel sorry for herself, nor did she want pity. She was stating a fact. He wanted to wrap his arms around her and hold her safe. He had to kill their enemies. That meant her family. He couldn't take that pain away from her.

I am sorry I must do this, Julija.

I know it has to be done, but I would hesitate. I'm grateful you're strong enough for both of us. What do we do about the cats?

Is their loyalty to your brothers or Phaedra and Comet?

I would imagine their parents. My brothers tortured the shadow cats at every opportunity, believing fear brought results much better and faster than kindness.

Belle and Blue popped their heads up just over the grass to allow him to see them. They had also taken their shadow forms. Only their eyes glowed in the darkness through the fog. The four cats awaited their orders.

You four get to safety. I will hunt alone. Perhaps one day he would use the cats to help take down enemies, but he felt his loyalty to them needed to be proven before he started asking for help, and none of them were in the best of shape.

The cats exchanged some kind of communication he didn't quite catch. He felt the passage of information, but he didn't hear it.

They are talking to one another, Julija cautioned. She was careful to keep the pathway between them very exact.

Yes, I caught that. Keep watching the enemy, sívamet. I want exact positions. I also need to know if someone is backing them up with a rifle.

Andrew is carrying a rifle.

That was one piece of information he had been looking for. The shooter was with her brothers, Vasile and Avram. That was good news.

We are your family. That was unexpected. Firm. And came from Comet.

Isai understood that while taking his blood, they could see his intentions and perhaps even share his mind for small glimpses of what kind of man he was, simply because they were cats and had psychic gifts of their own. Still, it shocked him that just that little bit of kindness had given him their full loyalty.

Why? He needed to know. *Going into battle there can be no switching sides. Not now, not down the line. You have to know what kind of man I am. Ruthless. In battle, I do not hesitate, and I kill. There are no halfway measures. I do not take prisoners. I destroy my enemies. Most importantly, I do not tolerate traitors.*

She is good.

It was a simple enough statement and it said it all. Julija. His woman with her compassion. She was good. That he understood. The reasoning made perfect sense to him.

What are they talking about? Julija sounded confused.

You, my little mage. They are loyal to you.

She was silent a moment, turning that over in her mind. *I treated wounds on some of them. Phaedra and Comet wouldn't allow me near them.*

But they saw your kindness.

I don't want anything to happen to them.

As opposed to me? he teased.

I am well aware you can take care of yourself.

Even though she sounded snippy, he felt her underlying worry. She didn't like him putting himself in the hot zone. *Blue, take the others and get to safety.*

The cat hesitated. *With you.*

He didn't want the cats with him. Not yet. He was used to working alone. He wanted them always to protect his lifemate, but if he said that, she'd fall out of the sky in indignation. He needed to stay in her mind to ensure she remained safe, just as she was.

It would make this battle much easier for you if I had my feet on the ground, Julija pointed out. *Your attention can't be divided.*

She was very astute, or she was more adept at reading his mind than he realized, and he had to be careful when he conspired with the cats to keep her safe. He turned to the four shadow cats. All eyes were on him.

He signaled toward Blue and then pointed toward the sky where Julija was hovering. It took a moment and then the cat swung toward the others, clearly communicating. Isai hoped they got it.

Take position on the bluff about a mile from here. I will need you to tell me where they are. He swept his arm toward the bluff. Three of the four shadows slipped into the fog, sliding around and over boulders. Only Blue remained. Looking at him. Watching. Very still.

Isai wasn't prone to arguing. He had a choice of freezing the animal right where it was, or letting it come with him. He shrugged and began inching slowly down the mountain, moving with the fog, his mind firmly entrenched in Julija's.

I'm good now. In cover. On the ground. You can do your thing without worry.

He would always worry. He would always need to know she was safe. *Do not go to sleep while you wait for me. Contemplate on where Iulian might have gone.* He wanted her mind on something other than the fact that he was going to kill her brothers.

He broke off his connection with her and reached for Comet, Phaedra and Belle. *Guard her with your lives.*

The moment he felt their affirmations, he took to the air, not bothering to hide his trail through the fog. There was no drifting with it. No pretense. Mages didn't force him into hiding, they hid from him.

Below him, the mages were spread out, each finding their way up to the spot where Julija had been sitting. The last they'd seen of Isai was when he'd made his dive to save Phaedra from a bullet.

He would have had Blue call to the young shadow cats with them, but Julija's two brothers had them leashed. That meant he couldn't attack them from a distance in the air, not if he wanted to keep the cats alive. He turned toward the first of the three mages traveling with her brothers. Julija had identified him as Terry. The man was halfway up the side of the steep pass. Isai sent the entire side rolling down on him from above.

Big chunks of granite broke off in rolling boulders, sweeping everything in their path with them as they rushed down the mountain, picking up speed. Terry, warned by dirt, debris and the shaking of the ground, looked up, trying to peer through the fog. The largest boulder hit him dead center, crushing him under it as it rolled over him. Isai dropped down to make certain he was dead or dying.

The body was mangled, dirt covering most of it. Shockingly, although half of his face was gone, the other only had a few specks of dirt and grass. He was dead, his eyes staring up at the fog in a kind of horror.

Isai took to the air to hunt Sam. Sam had felt the movement of the earth and heard the boulders, the sound like a clap of thunder. He dropped low, crouching, using a natural overhang to protect himself from a slide. He was in a good position to defend himself. He was ready, his hands up as he cast a spell. Isai watched intently as the mage wove a protection spell around himself. He listened intently.

I call upon the power of the moon
Sky above
I call upon your energies
Both small and large
I call to the wind to surround me
Protect me from that which cannot be seen
Moon surround me with your light
Let that which would do harm be destroyed
I call to the four directions
Envelop me with your powers
Protect me as I fight.

Above, below and from either side. Isai shook his head. Sam was supposed to be a very experienced mage, yet he'd left a loophole. He had given himself protection from every direction, including above, but he'd been specific, using the sky. Isai dropped down, as light as a feather, standing on the overhang. The one Sam thought protected him.

He paced across the entire overhang. It was very thick, much like the roof of a cave. It felt firm. There was grass and even some small bushes and saplings growing in it, the roots holding it in place. Each featherlight touch of his foot removed the roots and loosened the rocks holding the dirt.

Sam looked up as dirt rained down, small particles of almost dust. Realizing he hadn't completely protected himself, he had to make the decision to step into the open or remain in the enclosure and once again throw up a protection spell. His hands went up.

Isai stood in the middle of the roof, right above Sam, and jumped. The structure collapsed instantly, burying Sam under all the debris. The weight of the dirt, rocks and brush was enormous. Sam was driven to the ground, buried, with only his eyes showing. His mouth and nose were covered in the massive mound of dirt. He looked at Isai frantically, but he couldn't weave a spell and he couldn't breathe. It took only a few moments, but it was a hard way to die.

Isai left him there and found Andrew about twenty feet away. The fog had remained thick, which surprised him. He wasn't the one maintaining it anymore. He couldn't care less if the mages saw him or not. He was almost bored, used to going up against humans, mages and vampires alike. These mages knew they were hunting a Carpathian, yet they took no precautions against him.

You are going to get yourself killed. You may have all the experience in the world, but when you underestimate your enemy, you will lose every single time.

Now he knew who was maintaining the fog. He had recognized all along that the streaming whirls of droplets were feminine, but now they stung his face and neck, sending shocking charges of electricity through him.

You little demon. He didn't know whether to laugh or head back to the bluff to teach his wild mage a lesson. He was afraid the lesson would go badly for him immediately. Worse, he was feeling the cats' amusement as well. Who knew shadow cats could find humor in situations?

Someone needs to wake you up. Not to mention, you're an old man and may have slowed down, especially since they locked you away in that prison . . . er . . . monastery, you call it?

Andrew lay prone in the grass, rifle to his shoulder, finger stroking the trigger of the rifle. Isai, from his vantage point above Andrew and just behind him, waved toward the grass and dirt. Immediately, the earth responded the way it did to all Carpathians. The particles began to fill the rifle. Dirt and grass packed themselves in thickly while Andrew looked through his scope first up toward the steep pass where Julija had been sitting and then sweeping each side slowly in an effort to find a target.

Suddenly Andrew looked down at the barrel, frowning. He reached out to brush a leaf of grass from it, his entire body over the barrel of his weapon. The rifle went off, the barrel exploding. Metal ripped apart, shrapnel slicing into his neck and face. The blast of hot gas engulfed his face, burning his skin, bursting through one eye. He screamed and rolled over, away from the hot metal, unaware that it was sticking out of his flesh.

Isai closed his fist, and Andrew couldn't get air to his lungs. He gasped. One hand went to his throat as if he could remove the fingers he felt there. There was nothing to pry loose. His good eye bulged out as he tried desperately to breathe. Isai was patient, allowing the necessary time to pass until Andrew was still, lying on the hillside, staring up at the night sky with one wide-open eye.

My brothers have separated. Avram is closest to you. He has the female cat with him. She is looking right at you, and Avram has hunkered down just near the rocky section of the ridge. He looks to be building a spell, Julija warned.

Thicken the fog so he cannot see. Isai took a careful look around him. He knew Blue was close. The cat was determined to protect him whether Isai wanted his protection or not. It wasn't easy to spot the shadow, up high, just above his position.

Blue. Can you make your way down to the little female? Is it possible for you to communicate with her? Comet and Phaedra are her parents. She is not your littermate, yet she is of your blood. I do not want to kill her if it is possible.

Six cats were a lot to care for. They would need blood nightly and they would have to be very disciplined. They had been given Carpathian blood already, which meant they would grow even stronger, more difficult to kill. If he didn't take them under his wing, he would have no choice but to destroy them. He wasn't certain if it was entirely ethical to keep them alive, but he felt the cats deserved a chance at a decent life.

Blue sent him the equivalent of a shrug. Before Isai could give the order, the cat was already moving, picking his way down the steep slope, angling toward the ridge. He disappeared immediately into the thickening fog.

Do not expose yourself to danger. Avram is there. He will not hesitate to kill you, or try to reacquire you. Just talk to her. See if she is willing to come with us.

There was no answer, but Isai felt the cat's assent. Communicating with the shadow creatures was different than the paths he forged with Julija or his brethren. Still, he understood them.

He moved away from Andrew's body and began to circle around, coming at Avram from a different direction. No doubt Avram heard the blast as the rifle exploded, accompanied by Andrew's loud, horrific screams. The mage would expect any assault to come from that direction.

"Julija. This is your only chance. Come to me. If you don't, I will summon Barnabas and his hounds. They will track both of you. That Carpathian cannot protect you from all of us. Even now, Vasile has completed the circle of power. You are caught within it."

Isai, I have asked Phaedra and Comet if Barnabas is close and they say no. He has not yet arrived.

Isai didn't like the fact that her voice was shaky. She was truly terrified of Barnabas. More so than she seemed to be of her brothers. They had to be dangerous mages, coming from the lineage they did. Their DNA makeup was more mage than Carpathian. So much so that they were unable to sustain themselves in immortality. Without their sister, there would be no centuries of longevity. They needed her.

They will not kill you.

That is my fear. I would much rather be dead than go back with them. And certainly not with Barnabas. I will not let him take me alive.

Isai pulled up sharply, turning his head toward the bluff where his woman waited. *You will know that your lifemate will always come for you. Always. We have not had time together, but that knowledge must be already stamped into your very bones. It matters little if these people get their hands on you. Even without me, you can defeat them. You are powerful on your own, Julija. Far more than they are. Believe in yourself and always, believe in me.*

She worried him. Her father, stepmother and brothers had drilled into her from the time of her birth that she was less than they were. They'd done a good job, making certain she had no idea what her true lineage made her.

He softened his voice. *There are few, if any, like you in the world. I am privileged to call you lifemate.*

He felt Julija's smile. It burst through him like the brightest star in the universe. *You make me happy, Isai. You do. No one has ever said the kinds of things you say to me. I can't recall ever receiving a single compliment until you came into my life. I do believe in you, and I promise to try to begin believing in myself.*

You are maintaining the fog by yourself. He began moving toward Avram once more.

The fog is an illusion.

The fog is real. You are creating and maintaining the fog because you are Carpathian. The spell you used wasn't necessary, he insisted.

I'm not taking chances with your life. She sounded a little snippy.

He smiled because he liked her snippy. As he neared the ridge, he stepped very carefully, easing his body forward. He felt the light tentacle and dissolved instantly. The tentacle thrashed, reaching out to capture whatever had brushed against it. Finding nothing, it retreated, settling back into its hole much like an eel might.

Can you counter Avram's traps? Mostly, he was concerned for the cat. He could get rid of the traps, although it would take time to unravel them. He wanted to put distance between this place and wherever he would settle for the day.

He felt Julija's presence as she reached out to feel for the strains of magic. *Be very careful, Isai. The entire area there is a minefield of traps. He's using a blanketing spell, creating allies with the insects. He will continue to use them, growing them in strength and size as he has the time.*

Counter it. Take it down. He wanted Julija to realize she could use her Carpathian gifts with her mage talents and do anything she needed to do.

Avram is considered one of the best at these kinds of blanketing spells.

Perhaps he is. Perhaps he is the best of all mages. You are both mage and

Carpathian. You will remove this spell for your lifemate. He decreed it, using an implacable tone.

She muttered something he didn't catch. The words floated through his mind, making him want to smile again. Not words really, her little attitude. She was talking to herself, and her sentiments about her lifemate weren't necessarily flattering. She did that for a few minutes and he realized she was gathering her courage, trying to overcome her feelings of inferiority, of weakness. She repeated his words to her several times and as she did, there was that strength he knew she had, filling her. He felt determination pouring into her. Next was laser-like focus.

I call to those covered by darkness
By your own will I set you free.
Let your wills be regained as I command
Through my will so mote it be.

She took another deep breath as she now had Vasile's full attention, his understanding that she was fighting him on a level he hadn't expected. She had to believe in herself the way Isai believed in her. She couldn't hurry. She couldn't make a mistake. She just had to remain calm and do what came so naturally to her.

I gather that which has been shattered
All remnants do I retain.
I return you now to Mother Earth
So that it is her power that stands and reigns.
Each piece is a part
All elements bind.
By universal power
I propel you now to connect and bind.

Thunder rolled across the valley. Lightning zigzagged through the sky, looking as if it was tearing it open. Colors broke through the dark velvet background of the night. Green and purple shimmered in the sky. The aurora borealis brought to life over the Sierras. More colors flickered through the star-filled sky.

He felt the power of her spell. No—the power of the wielder of that spell. Magic warred with magic. The valley and peaks shone with it. Reverberated with the strands as they were peeled back, reluctant layer after reluctant layer. Each one of Avram's strands were shredded, ripped apart, as Julija's magic prevailed. He could see the black layers infused now with color. The sparks of red and pink ate through the black, leaving holes and then thin strips that floated aimlessly through the sky.

Blue? Isai was on the move, rushing through the magic grid, now torn apart. The colors were incredible, as strands still clashed in small places, Avram desperate to revive his fading spell. There was power in the colors alone. Julija's magic wound around each remaining strand of Avram's and slowly strangled it. The colors were brilliant, sparkling, almost too bright to look at as they consumed the black of her brother's spell.

Isai found the battle beautiful to watch. He could see the feminine power engulfing the masculine one, refusing to relent even when Avram chose to make a stand, pulling his magic back to the immediate area surrounding him. Julija's magic continued to attack, no less strong, bringing each layer of her brother's magic down so that it withered and fell, leaving Isai and Blue a clear opening to reach their targets.

She is receptive but worries for her mate. Vasile has him and will retaliate against her by killing him.

That brought Isai up short. *Julija? Did you hear that? We cannot allow that to happen. They have deliberately separated the cats and will kill the other if one escapes. I will have to free them simultaneously.*

How is that possible? You cannot be in two places at the same time, she objected.

No, but you can battle your brother, keeping him occupied to give me time to free the male. I'm sending Blue to him now.

Isai, have you assessed Vasile's magic? Blue could get caught in his trap.

Blue says no, he is part of Vasile's magic, so he can see the traps clearly.

That is so. Just tell me what you want me to do. Julija's assent was clear in

Isai's mind, confirming that she thought the shadow cat could reach out to the male cat Vasile held.

While I am engaging Avram and freeing the female cat, you throw some of your attitude at Vasile. Do not let him think you can best him. I want him countering your every move. I want him full of himself, believing he can best you and willing to show you.

That won't be difficult. He has a big ego.

You have to keep him fully focused on you, Julija. If he realizes his brother is gone and so is the female cat, he will retaliate against the male. You are the male cat's only chance. Tell me if you think you cannot do this.

I have spent most of my life annoying Vasile. He has spent most of his trying to prove to his mother that I am very, very far beneath him.

Isai couldn't wait to meet Vasile. He inched closer to Avram. The man was average height, and very slender. Almost thin, but not quite. Isai had come across a great many men with such a build and many were extremely strong. Watching this one, he doubted if that was the case. This man relied on his magic for everything, including lifting. He was very pale, and now he was sweating. Isai smelled fear. The fear wasn't of him—but of Julija. Like Isai, Avram recognized that she was the wielder of tremendous power.

"Little sister. Come home. There is no need to test your abilities. You know the outcome and it only makes you feel small. I have allowed you to shred my magic, so you can see I just want you home. You belong with your family. Whatever has happened to cause this rift can be fixed. I will go to our father myself and speak for you."

Silence followed his plea. The sincerity in Avram's voice bothered Isai more than his actual words. The entreaty should have sounded like a lie to his ears, but the voice was deceptive. He couldn't imagine Julija growing up listening to lies couched in sweet, sincere tones. How would she ever be able to trust? How would she be able to trust him? He had not only asked for her faith in him, he had demanded it from her.

I am in your mind.

Her voice was gentle, accompanied by little brushes of her fingers, caresses that were unexpected and intimate.

Yes, you are, sívamet. He couldn't help but send her the way he felt about her. The fierce need to possess her. The overwhelming softness she created in him. Love. He hadn't known what that was, and yet now, the emotion was beginning to encompass him entirely. *I would like you to engage with Vasile while I finish here.* He didn't want her to witness what he had to do.

At once he felt her withdrawal and across the small valley, on the peak closest to where Julija waited with the cats, he saw a sudden ring of green slapped to the ground by a black hand.

He shifted and became a shadow cat, moving swiftly through what would have been a minefield of traps had his woman not disposed of the traps for him. He was fast, sliding in and out of cover until he was beside the female cat. He approached her cautiously, not wanting her to give away the fact that he was close.

Avram built his defenses quickly, trying to surround himself with tougher strands of magic. Unfortunately for him, the enemy was already inside the weave. Isai slipped up right beside the female cat. He nuzzled her with his chin. She trembled and pulled at her collar, but the leash held tightly.

Avram turned toward her scowling. His brows drew together, and he flicked his hand toward her. In his fist a whip appeared, and the lash fell across her back, the tip hitting her left hip. She jumped and yowled in pain. Avram smiled and pulled his arm back to repeat the motion. Isai caught the whip in his hand and jerked hard. The smile faded as the whip turned on the wielder, striking repeatedly, not giving him a chance to regain his weapon.

He screamed his anger and ordered the shadow cat to attack. She leapt forward as if obedient, but the short leash jerked her back to the ground. She went off her feet and rolled over, coming up whining in distress, clearly not knowing what to do.

Isai ducked beneath the whip and went for the man. Avram shouted holding spells, but Isai was already past him, breaking the tendrils of magic before they could be established. He was on the man, his fist driving deep through the chest cavity to reach the heart. Unlike the blackened wizened organ of the vampire, this heart was normal, deceptive in that it didn't show the true character of the man. Avram's mouth opened wide in a silent scream, but Isai ripped his heart from his body and tossed it aside.

Whips of lightning hit all around them, one precisely striking the heart and the other Avram's body. He kept the play of lightning going and then let it die down naturally, knowing Vasile would think that his brother was orchestrating a battle with Isai.

Isai approached the shadow cat cautiously. "Little one, I will free your mate. Stay with Blue until this is over."

Blue watched with his amber eyes flashing red at times. He didn't take his eyes or his focus off the little female. Should she decide to attack, it was clear he intended to kill her.

I will take her to Julija. The cat pushed the images into his head. He was all but telling Isai he would return to aid him. *Come with me now.*

The little female shook her head. *To my mate.*

Blue swiped at her with his paw, making it clear he was in charge and if she didn't do as he said, she would suffer. Or worse. *If you want your mate to live, come with me now.* Blue swung around, not deigning to see if she followed. The little cat followed.

Isai headed toward the other side of the valley, following Blue's progress with the little female.

Her name is Sable and her mate's name is Phantom, Blue supplied. *Comet is coming to meet me to escort her back to the others.*

The blasted cat had outsmarted him. Isai didn't reprimand him. It only went to show the intelligence of the shadow cats. When the mages were breeding, they had deliberately chosen exceptional animals to experiment on and in mixing magic with their choices, they had bred extraordinary creatures. The six cats were potentially extremely dangerous to everyone. It was only the fact that Isai and Julija had managed to gain the loyalty of Blue, Belle, Phaedra and Comet immediately. If they didn't do the same with Sable and Phantom, he would have to destroy the pair. He would regret that to the end of his days.

You will not have to, Blue said with confidence.

Why do you think they will have loyalty to us?

Julija treated their wounds, he reminded. *But that is not what I meant. I will destroy them. It is my duty. If they will not fit in with our family, and follow the pack leader, I will do what is my duty.*

Isai found it interesting that Blue had stepped up to become leader when Comet was clearly the older, more experienced cat. *Will Comet be a problem?*

In what way? He has declared his loyalty to you.

Blue was pragmatic. It didn't occur to him that Comet was going to be trouble. Isai liked that in the cat. Isai spotted movement along the rocks and boulders climbing toward the bluff where Julija waited for him with the remaining cats. Comet slunk around the granite, slipping from one shadow to the next until he made his way to intercept Blue. Sable hesitated when Comet stepped close. She sank to the ground in submission. Immediately, Comet ran his muzzle down her body as if claiming her into their pack.

Blue and Comet touched noses, and Comet pushed his muzzle into Isai's hand and then wound his body around his legs. Isai was certain the show was for Sable, to make certain she understood who her family was. He turned and started back up toward Julija. Blue and Isai began to make their way around the steep bluff to the other side.

At once they felt the pressure of mage magic. It seemed to be coming at them from every direction. Above them, gray and black lines zigzagged like lightning across the sky, lashing at anything that moved. Below ground, something lifted the earth, running like a beast beneath the surface. Occasionally, a large spray of dirt and rock burst upward into the sky.

Isai halted Blue with a hand to his head, fingers absently rubbing in his thick fur. "Look at her, boy," he said softly. "She is just underlying his magic, challenging it, but acting as if she can barely keep up with him. She is amazing."

His woman. He wanted to bask in her power. Her colors were there, bright and shimmering with just an edge of the firepower she could bring. She had her brother fooled. Clearly, he believed she was doing her absolute greatest effort to best him.

Are you ready, sívamet?

I am.

Isai heard the growing confidence in her voice and it warmed him.

II

Julija shrugged off all doubt and stood, facing the direction of her brother. There was no room for hesitation or uncertainty now. Either she could defeat him and allow Isai to get close enough to destroy him, or he would kill her. She knew Vasile was extremely dangerous. Their father underestimated him, just as they did Julija. It would be Anatolie's downfall someday. He counted on loyalty from his followers, but he didn't give them much reason to follow him, other than fear.

She knew her stepmother, Crina, had little loyalty to Anatolie and tried often to get her sons to conspire with her against him. Neither respected her enough to do so. There was little love lost in their family. Crina didn't know how to love. She was with Anatolie because he gave her prestige in the mage community.

They lived in a good neighborhood, in a gated community, one made up mostly of mages. The occasional pure human moved in but was never invited to any of the gatherings. Usually, after some time, they moved on, uneasy, but not ever knowing why.

Vasile was the strongest of the family, aside from his father. He looked up to Anatolie, almost revered him. He would do anything the high mage asked of him, including killing his twin, his mother or her. He was far crueler than his brother, merciless in his quest for power. But even he didn't rival Barnabas, although none of them seemed to know.

"I tire of your antics, little sister. And I'm running out of patience."

She found it interesting that he had engaged with her, defending his grid of magic but not striking at her. That didn't make any sense unless Isai was right, and he didn't want to kill her. Her blood had fed them for years. It had boosted their abilities to produce magic.

She was tired. Maintaining her shape and the fog was just too difficult after time. Her head pounded with pain. She had to keep up the fog because that was what kept Isai safe.

No, little mage. I am perfectly capable of maintaining my cover. Your job is much bigger. This brother of yours feels strong.

He is extremely powerful. I've been testing his grid. There are weak points on the southern side. Just two. If you make your entrance from that side, once I start tearing it down, you'll be able to get inside what he believes is his safety zone. Just know, he will have traps, all of which will be lethal within that grid. I can do nothing about them without seeing them.

I will have no problem with his traps. I am going to send Blue in first to get to Phantom, Sable's mate. If Blue can get him to cooperate, Blue will try to free him. The two will slip away while Vasile is trying to hold you off.

Unlike Avram, he will retaliate by striking at me.

You are out in the open, sívamet.

She spotted Isai making his way to the south side of the field surrounding Vasile on three sides. His back was to the rock. She could make that rock unstable, and as a last resort she would. Yosemite was beautiful. Even if she tried to put everything back the way it was, it would never be exactly the same.

Isai waved his hand toward her. She moved before the air could reach her and surround her with a shield.

Isai, I can't work behind a shield.

You did.

I wasn't fighting against Vasile. I need to be able to move.

She could hear him murmuring something in his ancient language, but he kept his hands to himself. She sent him warmth and then turned her attention once more to Vasile's grid of defense. The entire time she'd engaged with him, she had been testing the strength of his traps. He was far stronger than Avram, so much so that it surprised her. Over the years, Vasile's diligent practice had paid off. Every line in his grid pulsed with energy.

She ignored Vasile's implied threat. It was best not to think about it. Isai had already killed four of the enemy. She had to think of them like that. They were people she had known growing up, but they weren't at all nice and she knew each of them had killed people and would kill more if allowed to live, so they were the enemy.

Little mage, I only wanted you to know how powerful you truly are. I do not need your help in defeating this mage. I have fought many over the years. Let me build a shield around you and distance you from this fight.

She heard the genuine sympathy in his voice. He wouldn't think less of her for allowing him to take over.

You have done your part. Isai meant it.

She looked down the mountain and saw Blue slipping through the magic safeguards Vasile had constructed. The cat ducked under one particular line and immediately flattened himself to crawl beneath the next even lower one.

She didn't want to face Vasile because she wasn't nearly as brave or as certain of her skills as Isai thought she was. It would be so nice to let him take care of her. But what if he got hurt? Or injured? That would be on her. She knew Vasile and his dark magic far better than anyone else unless it was Anatolie, and she was fairly certain she knew more than he did.

Julija had paid attention when they'd studied. She'd paid attention to each spell, even if it was one she never wanted to use. She'd memorized the construction of it, how each word was put together, not so she could use the spell, but so she could counter it. Barnabas, Anatolie and Vasile favored dark illusions. They could turn anyone's dreams into nightmares that turned into reality. They created dark webs of deceit, terror and agony and they reveled in their abilities to do so.

She lifted her hands. *I will bring down the grid.* She poured a confidence into her voice that she didn't feel. Concentrating on that southern tip where her brother had sent out his magic but failed to follow up on his construction, she began to weave strands of shimmering color.

Julija could almost hear Vasile's sigh of annoyance, then a wave of anger hit her, much like a blast of hot air from a vent in the ground. In the distance, she could see dust rising as something came toward her bluff very fast.

Her heart sank. She knew what was in his first attack. She didn't mind scorpions. She knew Anatolie often took their venom, and that her brothers thought her secretly afraid of the arachnids. It wasn't true. She had come to peace with them.

Right now, the birthmark of the high mage reacted, the scorpion squirming in anger that anyone would use scorpions against one born with the mark. The snake loosened his coils, rattled his tail, and the scorpion lifted his stinger as if they could help stop what was coming.

The scorpions moving fast toward her were large, close to twelve inches tall, and positioning as an army. She judged the distance to her. Vasile thought she would run, not fight. She didn't want to hurt them, but Vasile's evil had already invaded. First, she sent her magic straight to the southern tip of his grid. She shot it straight toward the spinning black and gray layers of magic. She made certain to keep the colors as soft as she could, hoping there would be no sparks of energy to give Vasile any clue that she was attacking his defense.

Strands of silver seemingly gray
Attach and weave dissolve evil away
As blackness forms let silver invade
Transfusing evil so light may be made.

The moment she could see that magic had taken hold of the weaker tip, she turned her attention to the army of scorpions crawling up the mountain toward her. They were coming fast, the clicking they made with their legs against the rocks horrid to hear.

She visualized them gone, each one disappearing in a puff of smoke.

Lifting her arms quickly, she wove the pattern she needed, air and water, earth and fire, entwined together, a plaited band she flung out toward the scorpions. As the band moved through the air, it lengthened and widened until it was a large canopy covering the fast-moving insects. Then it dropped over them.

As the canopy settled over the insects, orange and red flames burst into the air, tall columns that turned immediately to black smoke, as if water had been poured over the fire. So many. Too many. The forward charge halted, and a few strays tried to escape the fires, but each time they moved, the flames found them.

"Nice, sister. Very nice."

"I am mage, the same as you," she pointed out.

"You're not the same. You are nothing. I can't believe you'd be so stupid as to defy our father and me. Do you think you will find the book and reign?" As he spoke Vasile gestured toward her with both arms.

Beneath her, the ground shook. Rolled. Cracks appeared along the rock. She countered immediately.

I call to the power of Earth
Hear my call
I stand to fight that which would destroy us
Quiet yourself, Mother, join with me
Let our power be as one
Let us fight together.

Strangely, she felt almost as if she connected with Mother Earth. For just one moment there was a feeling of something old, definitely feminine, rising to meet her as she chanted softly, calling on the elements once more to protect and preserve the beauty of the landscape, but more, to keep it safe for its inhabitants.

She watched her magic eat the black magic, strand by strand, grid by grid. It was slow. She had been careful to keep her true intentions from Vasile for as long as possible. She wanted to open a route for Isai and the cats. Blue had made his way to the other male, staying just out of sight, but where he could dart in and pull the chain loose, so they could both escape. It wouldn't be easy if Vasile noticed. He would retaliate, and that was when she had to be ready.

Blue? Can you wait just until I have opened a large enough path for both of you to run through when you free Phantom?

I am nearly to the mage. Isai made it a statement. *Blue, as soon as the mage turns to attack you, I will strike.*

Vasile was becoming agitated. He flung fireballs at her, one after another. The balls spun through the air, gaining speed and fury. Bright, hot spheres of molten rock and fiery flames. Now he wasn't trying to keep her alive or control her. He'd gone past that to wanting to kill her.

She countered with a simple water spell, turning the fireballs to smoke, dousing them with liquid pouring from the sky. Her magical colors had spread now, going through the layers protecting her brother from any retaliation. He thought himself safe. It wouldn't occur to him that she would find a way to penetrate his defenses and be brave enough to aid in the escape of the shadow cat as well as a Carpathian's attack on him.

The moment Vasile saw his fireballs turning to smoke, he slammed lightning down on her. It cut through the star-filled sky, striking the top of the bluff over and over in an effort to kill her. The white-hot whip struck right over her head and hit a barrier, sizzled and burned, lighting up the shield Isai threw over and around her.

Thanks. She wouldn't have been able to stop that one as quickly as she needed to. Vasile might have succeeded, had her lifemate not been looking out for her.

You can step through it when needed, but keep the cats inside, just to be on the safe side. I can feel his anger growing.

Julija thought that was a mild way to put it, but then Isai was not bothered by the attacks. They were normal to him. The fact that Vasile had turned his wrath toward her might be different, but over the centuries, Isai had seen mage attacks many times.

Belle pushed against her legs uneasily. Phaedra hissed. Comet crowded her until he was pushing her back behind him. Even the new cat,

Sable, reacted, going from her sleek black fur to the gray shadow where Julija could see spots of transparency, as if she was so worn she was starving and perhaps her fur was falling out.

"What is it, Belle?" She dropped her hand on top of the cat's head and took her eyes off her brother for just a few seconds to stroke reassuring caresses through Sable's fur. She realized, the moment she put her hand on the cat's head, that she was totally exhausted. She could barely move her arms.

A hiss answered her inquiry. Julija stiffened. That wasn't a cat's hiss. She stared at the ground. All around the borders of the boxlike shield Isai had constructed were snakes. Large and small, they coiled, hissed and rattled, knocking their heads against the invisible barrier as they did so. Tongues touched the see-through material. One overly provoked snake left streaks of venom running down the side, just about knee-high.

A shudder ran through her. *Isai. Snakes. We're completely surrounded by snakes. It's freaking me out.*

Woman, you make no sense at all. Scorpions didn't bother you, but snakes do?

For a moment she couldn't think. Snakes had never bothered her before. If anything, she liked them. She could even speak to them. She could scorpions as well. She had been born with a mage mark. Not just any mark, but the mark of the high mage. The scorpion and snake were intertwined and there for anyone to see right on her arm.

She ran her finger over the mark. It looked more like a tattoo than a birthmark. The snake and scorpion were very distinct. She'd always felt her affinity with the scorpion because she knew her magic, her stubborn willpower, grit and determination rose from that source. The snake awoke that force of energy inside her so that her gifts and abilities exploded through her entire body, building her strength fast and feeding her source of knowledge.

She looked at the snakes surrounding the small place of safety. Instead of cowering in a corner behind the cats, she stepped to the very corner of the box and crouched low, putting her face level with the snakes.

Watch Vasile, Isai. He knows I am occupied. He will try something new.

I am close to him now. As soon as Blue lures Phantom away, I will strike.

Your counterspell was so efficient I just walked my way in. I am impressed with your skill.

She knew that wasn't exactly true, no way had he just walked through the various traps her brother had devised, but she'd take it. He was alive. In her lifetime, there had been no compliments or acknowledgment of anything she'd done. It mattered little that she was top in her class for practically everything. She didn't have time to bask in his statement, but she let herself feel good.

Julija turned her attention to the snakes. Not wanting to agitate them any more than her brother had already done, she lifted her hands very slowly.

Brothers by birth
Surrounded by walls
Release yourself from evil's call
I surround you with warmth
Return to your dens
Be at rest with no harm to defend.

It was necessary to keep Vasile's attention on her—at least until Blue was clear with the male cat. She also had to be ready to defend Isai should there be need. She intended to steal Vasile's magic. She'd practiced hundreds of hours, but she'd never dared try it on her brothers or father. She had done so with other mages, without letting them know.

Stealing magic could have enormous repercussions, especially if the magic practiced was that of the dark arts. She'd worked up her courage on more than one occasion and stolen Crina's. Her stepmother thought she had done a misstep when casting and had messed up her carefully wrought spell. It had never occurred to her that Julija would ever dare to try such a thing.

Stealing from Crina was one thing, but stealing from Vasile was a far different proposition. Her heart pounded hard with the enormity of what she planned to do. She rose slowly, keeping one eye on the snakes. Most had already uncoiled and begun to slither away, sliding silently across rock and grass to return from wherever Vasile had called them.

She moved out of the box, around one large snake and just narrowly missed stepping on a baby snake. Facing her brother, she stayed very still.

"I am awaiting your next juvenile attack." Provoking him was always the best way to stir him up enough to come at her again. "Snakes? Scorpions? I wear that mark with pride."

"You are Carpathian, not mage," he sneered. "You are to be used to feed, nothing more. You will never be one of us."

"I am one of you whether you want to admit it or not. I am mage, and I bear the mark of the high mage. You can say whatever you wish, Vasile, but the truth is, I am mage, the same as you, and I am able to counter your pathetic spells."

Blue, is Phantom responding? She heard Isai's voice. He included her so she knew what was happening on their end, just as she was doing so he knew she was in position and ready.

I told him we have Sable safe. That was his main concern. He remembers Julija's kindness. I am releasing him.

Julija renewed her efforts to keep her brother's attention centered on her. She lifted her hands. Every muscle in her arms and back protested. Even her lungs felt labored, as if she'd already run a great race and had little left to spare. She was doubly grateful that Isai had taken over manufacturing the fog. It had been the least difficult, pulling droplets of water from the night air to make the heavy mist. She needed every bit of her strength in her fight to counter Vasile's increasingly complex attacks.

Gathering the energy in the mountains and between them in the surrounding valley, she very delicately spread it throughout the distance between her brother's fortress and the bluff where she waited. She didn't have to wait long. The attack came from every direction.

Air. Enormous birds with vicious beaks and razor-sharp talons, wings beating at the air, heavy with hatred and rage, driven by the dark mage's own venomous emotions.

Ground. The dirt and rocks moved, raising and lowering inches and then feet as tentacles erupted, searching blindly for her, or the cats she protected, reaching with greedy claws for anything in their path.

Wind. The force beating at her. Coming out of nowhere, hurtling with the force of a hurricane. Whipping up debris and rock, whirling and spinning, drawing everything into the mindless vortex to throw at her.

Rain. Not just any rain. Acid rain. It dripped from above, burning through everything it touched, including the hideous birds so they shrieked and cried but kept coming at her to attack.

Blue darted in, under cover of the dark and shadows, slipping right past Vasile as he cast his spells, one right after the other, determined to kill his sister. The cat bit down on the collar holding Phantom prisoner. Phantom remained very still, his gaze locked on Isai, who waited patiently as Blue began to chew through the thick leather. His sharp teeth made short work of the tight collar. The moment Phantom was free, Blue slowly ducked back into the shadows, indicating that the other male should follow him. Phantom began to follow and then, at the last moment when he would have found freedom, whirled around and leapt toward Vasile.

The mage whipped around, snarling, his face twisted into a mask of hatred and rage. He slammed pure power at the shadow cat, knocking it from the air in midleap. Phantom screamed in pain and hit the ground hard, to lie there panting. Vasile thrust power a second time, but it hit an invisible shield and bounced back at him. Vasile staggered backward, whirled in a circle, throwing up a barrier between his personal power and whatever or whoever had come to the cat's aid. He took a careful look around.

Phantom just blew it for us, Julija, Isai informed her. *I had to shield him in order to keep him from getting killed. As it is, I do not know how badly he is injured. Vasile has cocooned himself behind a barricade making it impossible to strike at him.*

Are you safe?

Julija had multiple problems and she didn't want to completely annihilate Vasile's spells, which meant when she protected herself, she had to be careful. She couldn't completely destroy or reverse the spells. She needed them. The delicate net that she'd thrown, so subtle Vasile hadn't felt it, was already working to form a circle around each of the spells her brother had cast.

She threw a net over her head to protect herself from the low-flying birds and then added a shelter above the birds to keep the acid rain from hitting them. The wind was less problematic because she could counter that rather easily. The tentacles were more of a difficulty.

She couldn't think about Blue, Phantom or even Isai. She had to concentrate very carefully and make no mistakes. Her magic began to twist around Vasile's. She knew the spells he used, but not necessarily the patterns he wove when creating them. That was the hardest part for her. She closed her eyes to "feel" his magic.

Dark arts were ugly. Vile. The hatred and loathing woven into each strand were difficult to bear. They weighed her down, attempting to steal her spirit, stabbing at her heart and soul. Who could conceive of such malice? She'd always known Vasile was spiteful and mean, that he could be cruel, but she had no idea of the true evil that resided in him. She felt tainted, coated in his malevolence. In the truly immoral code he believed in.

Each dark spell had to be surrounded by her white one—a subtle takeover without tipping the mage off that he was in any kind of danger of being stripped of his power. She closed her eyes, trusting her ability to keep Vasile's attacks from reaching her while she worked. She went over every line for the first spell that he had wrought. The birds had been first, the rain last. She needed to go in reverse order.

She felt for strands of magic, separating them carefully in order to see how the pattern had been woven. Very delicately, so as not to disturb a single layer, she began to reverse the spell, but kept it contained within the circle of her magic. As each strand was stripped from the one before it, the dark ugliness was infused with light. Again, it was subtle, so there was no vibration to tell Vasile his magic was in danger.

Already, her colors had spread through his grid of defense, moving outward from the path she had opened for Isai to travel unharmed through. Now, it widened, moving through those dark weaves to begin a complete takeover.

Wiping the beads of sweat from her face, she began the second spell, reversing the force of the wind. That would actually be the most difficult of all, not taking the spell over, as weather was always one of her fortes, because Vasile might notice and react before she was ready for him.

Can you keep Vasile focused there without too much danger to yourself? Even as she asked, she knew there was no such thing as turning the dark mage's attention on Isai without the danger level going through the roof.

No problem, Isai returned without hesitation.

She couldn't worry about him, not when she had to have the most delicate of touches. He had to take care of himself—which he'd been doing for centuries. He also had to look after the shadow cats. She gave one thought for the injured Phantom and then closed her mind off to everything but finding a way to harness the fierce wind, swallow her brother's magic, all without letting him see she was no longer in danger from the wind or the rain.

Once again, she studied the weave in the dark components. These were much thicker strands. Each cylinder was fatter at the ends and thinning toward the middle. They spun aggressively toward one another, in a counterclockwise motion. The spinning action made it difficult to find a thread to start with in order to unravel it enough to infuse her own magic. She was patient, watching carefully in order to envision the complicated pattern he had used when concocting the spell.

She had no idea of the passage of time. In the back of her mind, she heard the shrieking of the birds and the sound of their continuous pecking, the drilling of their sharp beaks stabbing repeatedly at the barrier she had formed between them, the cats and her. The tentacles erupting through the ground shoved rocks around, knocking them into the boxlike shelter and the barricade. All the while the wind slashed and hurtled debris at her. The rain sizzled with dangerous intent.

She couldn't allow herself to be distracted. Or exhausted. Her arms felt like lead as she once again took a deep breath and began to unravel the strands, picking at them gently until she caught the very end of the weave. Immediately she piggybacked her magic there, doing her best to tone down the bright light so there was no chance that Vasile might see before she could spring the trap.

Once she had infused her magic, the spinning cylinder actually worked to her advantage. The fast motion helped spread her magic like a wildfire. She immediately turned her attention to the tentacles. Time was running out for her. The moment the last of the strands for the wind had been consumed, Vasile would know. There was no getting around that. She had to work much faster in spite of the fact that her focus, her entire concentration had to be complete.

Below her, the fight was on between Isai and Vasile. Isai didn't do anything by half measures. She could see great fireballs slamming into the rock all around the Carpathian. At the same time, Isai was keeping Vasile's focus on him by sending shock waves through the rock surface where the mage had secreted himself. The earth shook and pitched. Small rocks fell like rain, forcing Vasile to protect himself.

Julija began on the third weave, picking it apart, searching for an entry point so her magic could devour his. She had to study the layers of magic to figure out the pattern he had used. These strands were lumpy. Flappy. Each time she thought she had the right construction, the strand would heave upward and then flop downward, changing the angle and giving her a different view. She realized she would have to be patient until the long tubes would show every angle before she started unraveling them.

Each second felt like a million years. Sweat trickled down her body. Her legs shook. Her vison blurred. She closed her eyes against the physical discomfort and visualized the floppy strands. When she was positive she understood the complicated weave, she began to reverse it, using her hands to gracefully pull each thread and filament free of the thick, lumpy strands until she had a bundle of ends.

Did she have them all? She let her breath out slowly. She had to believe in herself. Second-guessing led to mistakes and she couldn't afford any in this battle. She sent her magic, delicately touching the black art. At first, there was a small puff of smoke and her breath caught in her throat. Then the colors consumed the smoke and began to wind through the strange, lumpy configuration.

Julija gave herself a moment to breathe before she turned her attention to the birds. This was his beginning spell. The origin. Most wielders of magic understood that they put their power into that first strand. Each person had an aura. Energy. Their power rose from within. Some thought if they gave up their souls—like the vampire—they received more supremacy in exchange. Others—some mages such as Xavier—believed stealing others' souls as well as binding their souls—or their power—to hell gave them more. To weave layers of magic, that first strand contained the essence of the wielder. She needed to get to that.

The spell appeared simple. It usually was when one worked with actual creatures to create an illusion that took on a life of its own. Julija wasn't deceived. When binding creatures to one, there was usually an exchange of power. Vasile wouldn't give up anything of himself to another living being. He stole souls. He stole bodies. He was ruthless, merciless and vicious.

She studied the seemingly innocent layers. Somewhere inside those neatly laid filaments and thicker threads, all twisting together looking much like thick braids, lay the true start of Vasile's dark spell. She was grateful to Isai that he didn't try to rush her. Even with his experience, removing an entrenched mage from his chosen fortress was nearly impossible—not without bringing down his magic first.

She noticed a tiny little bump on the underside of the darker strands. It was cleverly woven in, but once she'd spotted it, it was impossible to conceal. Each time her light shone on it, the little bulge slid away, trying to hide itself among the thicker strands making up the weave. She refused to let it elude her.

Isai, I'm so close. Make certain he's wholly occupied with you. He can't feel me invading.

She was so close. Her heart beat so hard and fast she feared Vasile might hear.

Count down to zero from five.

She did so, not looking down to see what her lifemate might be planning. She didn't dare. This was it. Either she did this correctly or Vasile could take her magic, steal her power from her. Her soul.

Using the greatest care, the lightest of touches, Julija plucked at that little lump. The strands refused to move at first, clinging together as if they'd been welded that way. She persisted, never changing the light touch, but once she made a little bit of headway in separating them a paper-thin amount, she pushed her magic between them, hoping that even a tiny fragment had opened in the weave. She continued to pick at it.

Without warning, the strands twisted open, so a gap appeared. Vile hatred, malicious, spiteful vindictiveness poured into her. Evil fought with light. She gagged. Vomited. Began dry heaving. It was nearly impossible to breathe. She would have screamed if any sound could be made, but there was no air in her lungs to produce noise—not even a cry.

She felt Isai stirring in her, his strength pouring into her, his breath moving through her lungs. She wanted to tell him to stay away in case she failed, but she knew he wouldn't. He would divide his attention, risk his life, even his soul for her. He might think he was wholly dark, but he had honor. Integrity. He was a man who walked in light even when he didn't see it around him.

Knowing her lifemate was at risk enabled Julija to strengthen her resolve in spite of her exhaustion. She fought back against the evil threatening to eat her from the inside out. Everything she'd ever wanted was dangled in front of her as an enticement. Every vanity she might have had. The temptation of having anything she wanted, anything she wanted to do with no repercussions, it was there in her mind, calling to her.

Julija forced herself to relax into the churning mass of evil. She sank into it, surrendering as if overcome. The moment it closed around her, surrounding her, she threw her magic out. The colors burst through the darkness, consuming all black magic, eating through every spell, ripping power from her brother.

Now, Isai. Attack now. He is not without tricks and illusions, but his true power is gone for the moment.

As she sank onto the ground, limp, unable to move or speak aloud, she heard the dark mage shriek in sheer shock and anger. He had never once conceived that she might try to steal his magic from him. Or that she could do such a thing.

The shadow cats surrounded her, pressing close, turning outward toward any threat, but the birds had disappeared as if they'd never been. The rain was gone. The tentacles fell to their sides and withered. The ferocious wind died down as well as the turbulent tornado it had spawned.

She waited until she could get to her hands and knees and crawled and pulled her body to the edge of the bluff, so she could see below. She didn't have any energy left, but if Isai needed her, she would give the last of everything she had for him. Never in her life had anyone ever come to her aid. Not a single time. Isai had done so without any thought for his own safety or the safety of his soul. He'd spent centuries guarding his soul and yet in that moment, he had risked it without reservation—for her.

Tears leaked out of her eyes, blurring her vision, but she dashed them away and peered over the edge of the bluff to see the man who was her lifemate step out into the open, facing her brother. Her heart pounded, and she tasted fear in her mouth. She wanted to scream to Isai to be more careful. She'd removed most of Vasile's defenses, but he still had an arsenal.

Blue rushed to Phantom as Vasile moved out of his useless stronghold to face his opponent. Blue nudged the fallen cat. She couldn't see if the other male was alive or dead.

"So you think you have won. Clearly my treacherous sister wants Xavier's great book for herself," Vasile said. "She will use you and then kill you as she does every living thing that gets in her way. She's murderous."

Isai didn't deign to speak. He simply threw his right hand forward and took a step toward the mage. Vasile tried to dodge, but the invisible weapon didn't emerge in time for him to see which angle it was coming from. A spear materialized from thin air just before it penetrated his flesh, narrowly missing his heart as he lurched sideways.

He howled in agony as the force of the throw drove him backward. He landed on his butt, hard, the spear vibrating. He ripped at it with both hands, murmuring a hasty spell. At first nothing happened. The spear remained embedded in his body, blood oozing around it. He gripped it harder and yanked, calling out his spell a second time as blood sprayed into the air like a geyser. At his command, the blood stopped, and the wound closed.

He pushed himself up with one hand, glaring not at Isai, but at the bluff where his sister lay. She met his eyes even from that distance. His hatred was venomous. He knew she had opened his defenses, allowing the Carpathian access to him. If he lived, Anatolie and Barnabas would never allow him to live it down that she had succeeded in stealing his magic from him. He flicked her a malevolent gaze promising retaliation as he began to climb to his feet.

Isai hit him again, this time the wave almost casual, as he continued to walk forward. He didn't hurry. He didn't change stride, even when the mage flung a series of fiery darts at him. Isai waited until the last possible moment before knocking each out of the sky as it came within arm's length.

The second spear hit Vasile as he rose, spinning him around, the sharpened tip driving through his throat. His body turned full circle so that he faced Isai directly. Rather than look at the Carpathian, his gaze jumped upward, across the valley to meet Julija's. His eyes had gone red. Leaked blood. Blood ran down his throat and soaked his once immaculate shirt.

Her heart accelerated. She recognized the absolute loathing for her. A single sound of fear escaped, and she tried to push back with her hands, to scoot out of sight.

With his last vestige of strength, rather than make another vain attempt to kill the one destroying him, Vasile turned his malice on his sister. He waved toward the bluff, sending a shock wave across the small valley so it hit the rock hard just beneath the ledge. Isai's blast hit him as the bluff began to crumble.

Julija saw Isai turn toward the sound of the rock as it broke away, tumbling far down to the valley floor. Already the cats were leaping away, scattering somewhere behind her, but it was too late to save herself. She didn't have the strength to crawl, let alone run. She felt the ground give way. Rock. Grass. Dirt. It folded beneath her and then she was falling.

You are Carpathian. Fly. Her lifemate gave the command.

Isai was in the air, but he was too far away. Instincts came alive. She knew what to do. She tried to picture an owl in enough detail to save herself, but it was impossible. She was just too tired. The ground was too close.

Julija felt Isai leap into her mind, taking over. He had never seemed so ruthless or so commanding. So hard. He held the picture for her, forcing her body to shift. The owl pulled up just in time, screeching as it did so, Julija huddled in a small ball somewhere inside. She should have felt like a prisoner because she couldn't get out even if she wanted to. She should have felt elated that she was alive. She didn't have the strength to feel triumph, happiness or even sadness that so many had died this night. She just wanted to curl up and go to sleep.

The male owl joined the female and spiraled downward until they landed on the ground. Isai shifted first and then pushed the command into her brain, the only way for her to come back to her own body. His hands moved over her, searching for any injuries, and then he left her with the cats in order to burn the bodies of the mages.

12

So much for trying to be an evolved male. Isai lifted Julija into his arms and looked around him at the pack of shadow cats. They looked almost as destroyed as she did. Emaciated and far too thin, the cats were haunting in their devastation. He couldn't leave them behind as much as he wanted to get his woman someplace safe and see to her.

He sank back into the soft dirt there in the valley and looked up at the field of stars. One would never know that a battle had taken place just minutes earlier. Even with Julija's help, and it had been incredible, walking through a dark mage's minefield of defenses was a harrowing and dangerous proposition.

Every few feet, the slightest change in even the wind could produce a new monster to deal with. He'd dealt over and over with them as Julija's magic had destroyed the layers of safeguards, allowing him to get closer to Vasile. Because the cats were mere shadows, they didn't trigger any of the mage's defenses. That was how the shadow cat had managed to get past Gregori and Mikhail's safeguards surrounding the book to steal it.

"What are we going to do with all of these cats, Blue? We have a little pack."

Blue pushed close to him. Phantom and Sable watched him suspiciously while Comet and Phaedra waited for his orders.

"Come here to me, Phantom." He thought it best to let the male feed first to show the wary female that he wasn't going to harm them in any way. She would do whatever her mate did.

The instant Phantom moved out of the shadow, out into the open, Sable crouched low in a position to defend him should there be need. Blue shifted position subtly, moving locations just slightly, just enough to protect Isai and Julija. When Blue changed his stance, Belle, Phaedra and Comet did as well.

Isai couldn't help but smile to himself. Already, his little pack was forming strong ties. He had been alone and used to working by himself, and now he was surrounded with . . . family. He would count these cats as part of his family. He used his teeth to open his wrist and offer the bright drops of blood to the starving male.

Instead of pouncing immediately, Phantom looked at him warily, sensing a trap. "It is your choice, boy," Isai said. "But you have to make it soon. I intend to take my woman and get her to a resting place. I want to do that fast. The mages have more coming, which you probably already know."

The shadow cat looked around him and then at Blue. Blue didn't move but remained staring with eyes that went from amber to red, glowing there in the darkness, a subtle warning. Step by wary step, Phantom came forward. His entire body shuddered, but he stretched his neck until he could reach the rich offering. The tongue came out, a rough rasp as it licked tentatively at Isai's wrist. The moment the cat took the first lick, it leapt back, watching Isai, clearly expecting a reprimand.

Julija stirred in his arms, one hand sliding up his chest. She felt small. Insubstantial. "I do not want you to move, little mage. I am uncertain whether you are the bravest, most courageous woman in the world, or reckless, rash and imprudent. No matter which it is, you have taken years off my life."

She rubbed her face against his chest, directly over his heart. "Since you are nearly immortal, it most likely wasn't that great of a sacrifice."

Her tone was teasing, inviting him to share the humor, but watching her nearly fall to her death was still too close. Feeling her body, so light, almost insubstantial, like the cats', as if every bit of her strength had been drained from her, didn't make him see much humor in anything, let alone the situation.

Phantom began licking at the droplets in earnest. He had to feed both cats, Phantom and Sable, before they could get moving. He wanted to find a place to settle before he took care of Julija. They had two blood exchanges. One more and she would be wholly converted. He was certain, because she bore the mark of the high mage, she would always have her mage legacy, but he wasn't absolutely positive. How could he be? As long as he had been alive, there'd been no precedent set.

"I think we are going to have a very long talk about your abilities," Isai finally said to Julija. "This is never happening again."

"'This' being?"

"Your helping me. I intend to lock you in the ground, deep where no enemy can get to you whenever danger arises."

"Is that what you're going to do?" She nuzzled his throat.

There was that hint of laughter in her voice that somehow brought light to his world. The cats had switched places. Sable was drinking the crimson drops while her mate remained on alert. He could see the thin places on their bodies where one could see right through them.

"That is exactly what I am going to do."

"Right now, I would let you," Julija whispered.

The weariness in her voice got to him. She was exhausted. He had fought Vasile's monsters, one by one as they rose in front of him, and he was still fresh, ready to do battle should there be need—all thanks to his woman. She'd borne the brunt of the night's work, taking down the grid of defense, the layers of safeguards that would have taken Isai all night. Dawn would have come, and he might not have managed to unravel the complicated patterns. Nor would he have pulled Vasile's teeth the way she had, stealing his magic. That had been the most incredible feat he'd witnessed.

Stealing magic wasn't only extremely difficult, it was extraordinarily dangerous. He was so proud of her, and yet at the same time, he wanted to shake her until her teeth rattled. He imagined, if he did that, it would be considered right up there with spanking. His arm tightened around her, holding her to him.

"I couldn't watch you as you got closer to him," Julija confessed in a little rush. There was guilt in her voice. "I had to concentrate, focus wholly on his magic. I knew he would have traps set, but I counted on you being able to navigate them. Was it bad?"

Had it been? He didn't think in terms of something being difficult or not. One did what one had to do. He had gone up against monsters for centuries. He shrugged and pulled his wrist from the female shadow cat.

"I did what I had to do to get to him. I would not have succeeded before dawn came had you not brought his safeguards down. He had erected a complicated barrier that was very effective. Inside of it, he had multiple traps."

"The multiple traps are what I'm referring to," she pointed out.

He looked down at her. She was very pale. Her eyes closed, the thick fan of dark lashes in stark contrast to her white skin. "I need to find us a place to rest, Julija. Let us take our cats and go."

The lashes fluttered, and she managed to open her eyes, although he could see it took effort. The dark chocolate appeared soft, melting. His heart turned over. She looked around at the six shadow cats all sitting close, waiting to see what Isai would do.

"What are you going to do with them? You'll take to the sky and they'll have to run the rest of the night trying to find us."

"They all have my blood. They can shift, become shadows on my skin, much like the writing on my back, although I suspect much more insubstantial."

"Because they are Carpathian."

He nodded. "The mages turned them without realizing it. That is the reason they need blood to survive. They will always need blood. That means, my little mage, we will always need to take care of them and make certain they know the rules. They cannot ever prey on humans or we will have no choice but to destroy them."

He turned his attention to Blue. "You make certain they all understand what I am saying to you. I lay down the rules and they are sacred. We do not ever kill when we feed. If that is ever done, it is a death sentence I will not hesitate to carry out."

Blue turned his head toward the others, and Isai caught the wave of telepathic energy. He gathered his woman and stood, indicating to the cats to leap on his back. They hesitated, uncertain as to what he meant. He formed the image in his head. There was a woman in the Carpathian Mountains who had a wolf pack. The wolves rode on her as tattoos, part of her skin. Or they provided a long winter coat for her. Few knew they were actual wolves, turned accidentally when they were quite young. He had taken the idea from her. He could travel with his cats as she did, with few ever realizing they were real.

Blue caught the idea when he turned and showed his tattoos. He was patient. The shadow cats were skittish for a reason. They had no real reason to trust Isai yet, but they put their faith in Blue. Even Comet and Phaedra. Blue leapt onto his back. Claws dug in for a moment, as the extremely large panther-like creature tried to adjust to what was needed of him. He dropped back to the ground and paced for a moment.

Again, Isai didn't hurry him, although they were going to run out of night soon and he still had to find a resting place and take care of his woman. Again, he pushed the images of shapeshifting into Blue's mind as the cat leapt and pressed his shadowy body into Isai's back as if etched there by an artist. The second attempt was far better than the first. Not perfect, that would come with time and experience, but Blue managed to attach himself successfully.

Belle stayed back, guarding Isai as Comet tried next. One by one the cats leapt onto Isai. There were many mistakes and claws ripped his skin, but in the end, he wore all six cats on his back. He wondered what it would have been like for the woman to try to teach her wolves to ride on her. How many times had the heavy creatures clawed her and perhaps even bitten her in an effort to learn to shift smoothly?

Belle had leaned over and licked his face and then done the same to Julija before she'd leapt on his back. That small gesture of affection did something strange to Isai's heart. Belle and Blue were already working their way into his affections.

"Hold on to me, Julija."

"I'll try." She sounded as if she was already falling asleep.

"You stay awake until I get you settled." He took to the air with his little family. Six cats. His woman. His brethren would laugh at him, if they could feel humor. He was not a man like Sandu, who was naturally funny and found humor in everything, even though he no longer felt it. Isai had always been a man more reserved and serious.

The night breeze was cool on his skin. He had a few injuries where Vasile's creations had ripped him open, most going for his belly in hopes of eviscerating him. It was a common practice among creatures created by vampires. He found it significant that the dark mage used the same creatures. Puppets. Beings with no souls feeding on the flesh of others. They were promised immortality and used ruthlessly until their purpose ran out and then they were discarded by their makers, cast aside with no concern that they would prey on humans or animals in an effort to survive.

Which had created them first? Mages? Vampires? Isai knew that Xavier had made an alliance with vampires. That was unheard of, but it had been done. Had he been the one to teach the undead to use puppets to attack during the day when vampires could not? Perhaps. At the moment it didn't matter. It had been a long night, facing and defeating the ghouls Vasile had waiting in his traps.

"Those are awful creatures." Julija gave a delicate shudder. "I wouldn't want to face one. Why didn't you reach out to me? I had no idea. I would have tried to help you."

"Had you seen them before?"

He felt rather than saw the shake of her head. His eyes were on the terrain below them. He had taken them high, so he could spot the best potential spot for a resting place, and if he could be truthful with himself, maybe he could get very lucky and see his brother alive and well. He didn't believe he was alive. He was certain Iulian had sacrificed his life to seal the resting place of Xavier's book of black magic.

"Not until I was captured by Sergey's band of vampires. He had puppets, and they were feeding on children. It was so sickening. It's clear you've faced them before."

"Many times. Too many times. You never saw your father or brothers or even Barnabas create a puppet to serve them?"

"No." That was definite. "Although, any of them are capable of creating something that vile."

Below, there was a beautiful lake, a shimmering deep well of blue in the moonlight. The sight was breathtaking. Now that his feelings were restored, along with his ability to see in color, the sights of nature were wholly appreciated. Isai slowed his speed and circled around, looking among the rising cliffs and boulders for a place that might have an opening in the granite. Even if he couldn't go to ground, burying himself in the healing soil, he needed a safe place no one could get to him during the hours of complete paralysis.

"Turn your head, Julija, look at the lake."

She made an effort to obey him. He could tell her body was just too drained. He couldn't give her blood until they were in a protected environment. Suddenly, he was extremely glad that he had the cats on his back. Blue would guard their resting place while they slept. Instinctively, he knew the cat would guard them with his life. Belle as well. Perhaps, in time, he would have the same faith in the others. He knew he had to win their loyalty completely before he could expect that kind of devoted allegiance.

"It's beautiful, Isai," she whispered. "And do you feel it?" Her body vibrated with something close to excitement.

Emotions weren't his strong suit. He'd just rediscovered them and feeling was at times overwhelming, so he tended to push them to the back of his mind to distance himself from them. "Serenity. What else?"

"I don't know." She had already subsided against him, as if the burst of energy had depleted her completely. "I thought I caught something but it's gone now. I must have imagined it."

He nearly asked what it was, but he spotted what he'd been searching for. It was no more than a thin line that zigzagged through the granite up the length of the cliff. It wasn't even a wide crack, not even a mere inch, but he had been judging such things for centuries. He knew this could open into a chamber, perhaps even a series of them. Sometimes such a crack hid a labyrinth of caves behind it.

He studied it carefully before approaching. He wasn't the only one aware a crack in the rock that size could hide a maze of caves. Vampires and Carpathians alike would know. There was no sign that anyone had disturbed it, but then, there wouldn't be. Carpathians didn't leave traces of where they slept. Vampires were equally as careful.

He waved his hand, and with a groan of protest, the rock separated just a hair. Paper-thin. A couple of millimeters, no more. He waited. Nothing poured out from inside. The movement hadn't triggered a safe-guard.

"Press your face against my chest. We are going inside. I will shift both of us to get us through." He gave her the warning but slipped into her mind almost simultaneously so there was no way for her to protest. He simply took her over.

If the opening was only two millimeters wide, they could only be one. He slipped his woman and the cats through the opening and closed the crack behind him. Inside, it should have been pitch-black and difficult to breathe. It wasn't. A slight touch of cool air came from above and to his right. There were several small openings in the front chamber that told him cracks in the side of the cliff were wider near the top, allowing fresh air and light from the moon in. If the moon could shine in, that meant the sun could.

The chamber narrowed toward the back and seemed to curve. He walked easily upright. The sound of water beckoned him. Just around the corner was a narrow tunnel that branched out in three directions. He chose to follow the sound of water. His woman, although mage and Carpathian, followed the more human ways of washing. Water would comfort her.

The second chamber wasn't nearly as spacious as the first and didn't have the light, which he was grateful for. He lit it using sconces high up on the walls. There were crystals embedded on two sides of the granite and the light spilling over them sent out a rainbow of colors.

He waved toward the darkest corner to provide his woman with a bed. Knee to the middle, he gently deposited her right into the center. She rolled onto her side and curled up. He let her for the moment. He needed to thoroughly investigate before he committed to their resting place, and then he had to set safeguards. He left Belle and Blue on guard with his woman while he went to explore.

The caves went back even farther, right into the heart of the series of cliffs. It was cool, but very stuffy the farther he went in, not at all a good environment for his cats or Julija. They shared the first few chambers with bats. He hoped Julija didn't mind them because there were thousands. He was careful not to disturb them and sent out a message to the cats, they weren't to, either.

He found Julija asleep in the middle of the bed, right where he'd left her, but Belle had climbed onto the bed and wound her body around his lifemate's in order to keep her warm. He thanked the cat even as he scooted her off the bed. Phaedra and Comet were already at the front of the chamber, lying intertwined but blocking the entrance. Phantom and Sable, the smallest and youngest of the cats, the two in the worst shape, were in the darkest corner, as if hiding from everyone. Blue prowled around, checking everything.

"Get some sleep," Isai commanded. "It has been a long night and we have more enemies." More than anything, they needed to recover the book and find a way to destroy it.

He gathered Julija into his arms. She gave a drowsy murmur of protest and nuzzled his chest. "That is right, little mage, you need to feed. You are so pale you look like a ghost." His shirt was gone, leaving his chest bare to make it easy for her.

Isai closed his eyes at the first touch of her lips on his skin. Feather-light. Barely there. Yet he felt that touch like a lightning strike through his entire body. Her tongue slid over his skin, and then her teeth sank deep, an erotic bite that flashed fire through his bloodstream and woke every nerve ending.

She connected them together with her teeth, drawing his life's blood into her. He cradled her in his arms, looking down at her face. Her eyes were closed, those long lashes like two dark fans lying against her cheeks. Dark hair tumbled around her face. He felt the push of her breasts against his bare chest and had to resist the urge to cup the soft weight in his palm. She was exhausted and as much as he wanted her, as her lifemate, he would always put her needs first.

When he was certain she had taken enough for an exchange, he gently pressed around her mouth so she would stop. Her tongue licked at the twin holes to stop the flow of blood and seal the wounds. She turned her face up to him.

"Your taste is addictive, Isai. I could have fed forever. I imagine the cats feel the same way. You can't possibly supply all of us without growing weak."

He kissed his way down the side of her face, from her temple to her ear and farther, finding the pulse beating steadily in the side of her neck. She didn't fear him or his taking of her blood. She hadn't liked it when her family had done so, and he wanted to teach her that there was a very big difference between them and her lifemate.

He let his teeth scrape gently over her pulse. Once. Twice. He kissed her there. Back up to her ear. His tongue did a little foray. "You will help me with the cats when you feel as though you can." He didn't make it an order. He would never want her to do anything that made her uncomfortable. They all needed time to grow together as a family.

He kissed his way back down to her neck, to that little pulse beating there that drew him. Again, he used his lips, his tongue and finally his teeth to tease her. Her breathing changed. Her breasts grew heavy against him. He bit down, and her body shuddered with the pain and pleasure of the erotic bite. He gathered her closer to him and indulged himself, taking the blood that was the best he'd ever had in all the centuries he'd been feeding.

She was born for him. He for her. Her taste was designed to appeal to him. The essence of her poured into him, turning his body harder than a rock, his cock full with urgent demand. He let that sensation fill him as well. He savored the way he wanted her. It was an exhilarating feeling to hunger for his woman. Holding her the way he could. Feeding on her. He would never take any of it for granted, no matter how many centuries they would have together. He had been too long without.

It actually took effort to pull back. He made certain he took enough for a full exchange, although perhaps more than was actually needed. She was already Carpathian. Dragonseeker. The lineage was legendary in the world of the Carpathians. He used the healing agents in his tongue to close the twin holes in her neck and then pressed a kiss over the spot.

He sat on the bed, no clothes, back to the headboard, her head on his thighs as he rubbed the pad of his thumb over the snake intertwined with the scorpion.

"Do you hate that I'm mage?"

Isai frowned. "Julija, why in the world would you think such a thing?"

"Xavier tried to wipe out your entire species. My father would very much like to carry on his work."

"Without Carpathians there would be no vampires. Do you despise me because I'm Carpathian or wish that I wasn't?"

"Of course not. I think it's cool that you're Carpathian. You do wonderful things."

"I think it is extraordinary that you are mage, and more, that you bear the mark of the high mage. That means you hold tremendous power inside of you."

She turned her head to look up at him. "You like that I have power? Why?"

There was a note of wariness in her voice. He wanted to smile, there in the darkness, surrounded by the suspicious shadow cats. Each of them had reason to be leery, but still, they were coming together, giving one another a chance.

"I will always know, should we be separated for any reason, that you are strong enough and dangerous enough to take care of not only yourself, but our children. Tariq Asenguard has the compound in San Diego where Elisabeta is being safeguarded. There are a few women who are teaching the others how to defend themselves. In the old days, many of our women were Carpathian and learned from the time they were young how to fight off a vampire if it was necessary. They didn't hunt, as we do, but if necessary, they could defend themselves. Now, with some human women becoming lifemates, that is not the case and the fear is we will lose them."

She smiled at him. "I'm glad you like that I can defend myself."

"What I do *not* like is you using yourself up."

"What does that mean?"

He heard the genuine puzzlement in her voice.

"Julija, you were so exhausted you would have died falling from the cliff."

"It was more that I haven't practiced shifting. I didn't know I could. I think mage first, so I was trying to think of a spell to give me wings. I'll get the hang of it. I don't know why I never consider that I might be able to shift. I really thought that everything I did was an illusion, not reality."

He brushed a kiss on top of her head. "In some ways, it is both. But the illusion becomes reality for us. Shifting is very real and a skill that would be good for you to practice. You want to become very adept at it. The faster you are, and the more images you can hold in your mind in detail, the easier you can call them up when needed, without any real thought. As a child, a Carpathian starts training almost immediately. No one wants their son or daughter to try on their own and end up in the middle of a rock."

He watched her closely. There was no indication that she was uncomfortable. He had heard that conversion was horribly painful. The impurities and toxins in the body had to be purged. Organs were reshaped. That was an extremely painful process. Sometimes there were convulsions.

He ran his hand down her side, over the curve of her hip to her thigh. She was totally relaxed, her body lying close to his. He kneaded her firm bottom and then traced her ribs.

"You were magnificent today, *sívamet*. I could barely conceive of your courage."

"I wasn't certain I could pull it off, but I knew, even with me taking down Vasile's safeguards, he would have all kinds of traps laid out. I didn't look. I didn't want to know. If I had tried to help you with them, I couldn't focus on taking his magic. To me, that was the far more important obstacle to remove for you."

"You chose right. I had no problems with his many monsters."

She turned her head and lapped at the raw tears in his belly. "They came close."

"You have to get close to monsters to stop them. Then they have to burn to ensure they do not rise again."

"You burned them after. You had to have, or I would have seen the flashes."

"Vasile would have seen them as well," Isai conceded. "I loved what you did, Julija . . ." He trailed off.

"I hear a 'but' in there."

"I am not certain my heart can take you doing it again. Hunting a dark, powerful mage can be much more dangerous than hunting a vampire. You made it easy for me today, I will admit that—"

"We make a good team," she interrupted and then yawned

He rested his hand on her forehead. There was no spike in her temperature. He had been told that in a conversion, the temperature could soar to dangerous heights.

"Yes," he conceded. "We do. I still do not like the idea of you risking yourself like that."

"You said yourself that I have power. I have extensive training as a mage. I also watched my father, brothers, stepmother and so many others. I know their work. If I can learn how to utilize being a Carpathian as well and teach you to learn the way the mage works, we would be pretty unstoppable."

He hadn't thought of her training him. He had thought in terms of him working with her to learn all the things she could do as a Carpathian. She was right, though. If she taught him how to think like a mage, how to perform their spells, the two of them would be a very dangerous force as well as a huge asset to the Asenguard compound. They would be able to safeguard the women and children from the continual assaults by Sergey and his army of vampires and servants.

"You would share your knowledge with me?" That interested him. Greatly interested him. Sharing knowledge was a Carpathian trait. They learned by simply taking those experiences from one another's minds.

Taking anything from his lifemate's mind seemed not only a great idea, but intimate. He had never thought in terms of intimacy.

"You're my lifemate, right? That means we're going to spend our lives together. I think the more we both know, the better off we're going to be. And you have to know, Isai, that I am the daughter of the reigning high mage. By siding with you, I will forever be known as a traitor in the mage community. There will be a price on my head. It will go on century after century, handed down from one mage to the next."

"Then it will be good that not only do we both know how to handle battling an experienced mage, but that we continue to learn."

She smiled and traced little symbols over his thigh with the pads of her fingers. "You rescued the cats, Isai. Thank you."

"I am not certain whether I did the rescuing. Blue did more than I did. He's a good cat. A strong leader." He glanced across the chamber to where Blue's eyes shone at him. The cat was still alert. Still awake. He didn't know how much sleep they required. He had quite a bit to learn about all members of his new family.

"He is." She yawned again and tried to hide it behind her hand.

"Try not to go to sleep yet. We have exchanged blood three times. I do not want you to be sleeping soundly and the conversion start to take place. Pain could jolt you awake and then you might not be able to get on top of it."

"Pain?" Her lashes lifted again, and she regarded him with suspicion. "I don't like how casually you said that."

He shrugged. "Pain is simply an inconvenience, one we can cut off when it becomes too bothersome. You have enough Carpathian in you already to shift, which means you can block pain if it gets to be too much."

"No one mentioned pain to me, or conversion, for that matter."

"You are my lifemate, Julija. You studied Carpathians."

"Carpathians do not have to be converted. At the time I was studying, Mikhail had not found Raven and there was no such thing as conversion. Or pain."

He wanted to laugh. Instead he leaned over her, studying her profile as she lay across his thighs. She hadn't moved. She was still relaxed in spite of the conversation. She wasn't nearly as bothered by what they were discussing as she wanted to pretend. He stroked little caresses into her hair and then across her cheekbone and down the side of her face. Her skin was soft. Her body entirely feminine. She had curves. Lots of them. Beneath all that soft skin was firm muscle.

"Conversion and the way it works is a well-kept secret," Isai conceded.

"Is the secret part that it can hurt?"

"You seem a little fixated on pain."

"Why didn't you mention that I would be able to keep from hurting when you spanked me? That would have been helpful." Her voice was drowsy. Sexy drowsy.

He rubbed her bottom, smoothing over the firm flesh and then kneading and massaging. "I think you are fixated on spankings. Perhaps you enjoyed it much more than you let on."

He felt the fan of her lashes against his thigh and then she turned her head again to look up at him.

"What part of 'I am a badass mage' did you not get when I stole magic from Vasile? Because I could turn you into a toad. Or worse. Something with a tail and ears. A donkey. You might be hot as hell right now, but not so much as a donkey."

"Many people find donkeys quite cute."

"Who? Who finds donkeys cute?" she demanded.

He kept a straight face. "Little girls all over the world."

She rolled her eyes and settled back down. He dropped his hand into her hair and began running his fingers through the silky strands. There was no change in her breathing. Her eyes were clear. Sleepy perhaps, but not a single hint of pain. How long did it take before the conversion started? It didn't make sense that she wasn't already going through it.

"I would like to check your body."

"I'm certain you would." Her tone was very droll.

He laughed softly because he couldn't help himself. She was too funny, his woman. She was going to teach him fun whether he liked it or not. "I do not understand why the conversion is not taking place."

"I'm too tired to move, so as long as it doesn't require me to do anything differently, go for it." She wrapped her arms around his thighs and closed her eyes.

Isai didn't wait. He separated his spirit from his body and immediately entered hers as white-hot energy. He moved through her, examining every organ. There was no warring of bloods. No fight to reshape organs. Her structure was no different than any Carpathian born.

Puzzled, he returned to his body. He caught her arm, studying the mage mark. It was definitely a birthmark. She'd been born of Xavier's lineage. "Julija, did you ever sleep in the ground?"

She frowned. "No, of course not. How would I breathe?"

"You told me you preferred the night and that you sometimes found you liked lying in the soil. Did the soil ever feel as if it rejuvenated you? Has it ever healed a wound?"

Julija didn't answer him immediately. As usual, she gave thought to his questions. "It was a very long time ago, but I remember when I was a child and my father would slap or punch me, or Crina. She was the worst when I was little. She would beat me very badly. At the time we lived close to the forest in mountains. We'd already moved to the United States. I used to have this little fort I would hide in. I remember making a shallow depression and lying in it. I always felt soothed and at peace there. I thought it was because they never found me there. But when I went back, I wasn't as stiff or as sore as I should have been."

Was it possible for her mage blood and her Carpathian blood to give her both worlds? It seemed as though she was both. She clearly wasn't undergoing a conversion. She could do anything a Carpathian could do. He had called her that, but only because he knew she was born with the Dragonseeker mark.

"When Sergey's servants captured you and forced you into those underground tunnels where all the vampires were, did the Dragonseeker mark come to life?" The birthmark of the Dragonseeker—that small dragon—always warned when vampires were close.

She nodded and reached down with two fingers to rub at the little dragon positioned over her left ovary as if guarding the eggs of their future children. "It glowed red and became so warm it was almost hot. But my mage mark came to life as well."

That brought him up short. He went very still inside. He had lived centuries. He had seen that mark before, of course. Of course he'd noticed it on her. She had both. The high mage's birthmark was very distinctive and not all children born of Xavier's line bore it. Most didn't. Only the very, very talented ones.

"Your mage mark alerted you to the presence of vampires as well as your Dragonseeker mark?"

"Yes, it always has. The tail of the snake rattles and the scorpion's tail always pulls up in preparation to sting."

"You essentially have two warning systems?"

She rubbed at his thigh with her cheek and then tightened her arm around his thighs. "That's exactly right."

"Then how in the world did Sergey's army manage to get their hands on you?"

She was quiet for so long he didn't think she'd answer him. Finally, she shrugged. "Elisabeta. You may as well know. We have an extremely strong connection. I could feel her pain. This endless, hopeless despair that cut through me like a knife. I couldn't ignore it. I knew I should have continued after Iulian and the book, but the grief in her was so strong I could barely breathe. I had to do something."

"You allowed yourself to be captured."

"Something like that."

"Exactly like that."

She didn't dispute it.

His woman. She sounded ashamed because she had stopped to help another woman, a perfect stranger, in need. Fully mage. Fully Carpathian. Two warning systems when it came to vampires.

"You are worth every single second of those centuries I searched to find you and didn't," he had to tell her, because it was the truth.

13

Isai woke to the familiar sounds of the night. He lay beneath the thin layer of dirt he'd managed to find in the chamber of almost pure granite. The rock surrounding them was solid in spite of the maze of chambers inside the mountain. Often, in caves such as these, there was plenty of fresh soil, usually filled with rich minerals unused for centuries. Not in this case. Dirt was at a premium.

Julija had protested moving from the comfort of the bed to the ground, so he waited until she fell asleep. Her body was exhausted from the hard-fought battle with Vasile. He opened the soil and stared up at the crystal-covered roof above their heads. In the shallow bed of dirt, his lifemate slept beside him. Curled around both of them were the six cats. While the cats and Isai had been totally covered, he hadn't covered Julija's face, not wanting to take chances.

He had insisted the shadow cats sleep in the soil as well. They had never done so and all were nervous, so once they complied and came to the bed he'd opened in the ground, he had sent them to sleep much in the way he had his woman. The cats wouldn't mind. Looking them over, he could see the minerals in the soil had done their job, already working to repair the damage done to the abused animals. His woman, on the other hand . . .

Isai smiled to himself and rose, calling to Blue to wake. The cat responded immediately, lifting his head, immediately nuzzling Belle and then touching each of the other cats with his nose before touching Julija, as if assuring himself they were all alive. Isai dropped a hand on his neck, fingers moving in the thick fur.

"I need you to watch over them all while I feed. When I return I'll take care of Julija, you and the cats. I believe there are campers around the lake I can visit."

Blue's intelligent gaze remained on his face, those amber eyes meeting his without flinching. They thought alike, two generals ready to go into battle when needed.

"Have you been around Barnabas?" He couldn't help but be curious about the man Julija was so frightened of. She was afraid of her father and stepmother, but she was terrified of Barnabas. Isai couldn't blame her, not after the stories she'd told about the man and what he'd done to her. Not after he'd been in her head and actually seen what he'd done.

Blue shuddered, his back arching, his claws suddenly digging into the ground. *He is very bad. Worse than the others.*

It took a moment for Isai to convert the images Blue sent to him into words. The cats could only use actual images to convey what they meant, but Blue was adept at it and his opinion only confirmed what Isai had already thought possible. This was a man who could deceive mages. Deceive a woman as powerful as Julija. If he could deceive her with his intent, was it possible he was also misleading Anatolie about his loyalty?

"Did you see him with Julija?"

He is very cruel. He liked hurting her and will not give her up. He is waiting. Biding his time. Waiting.

Blue's impressions were very clear. He emphasized that Barnabas was the type of man who had the patience to carry out a long-term plan. It could take weeks. Months. Years. Centuries.

I watched him, and he watched her. When she didn't know, he watched her.

Isai glanced down at Julija's sleeping figure. She was curled up in a little ball. He realized she tended to sleep that way. Each time he'd seen her on the bed, she'd pulled her knees into her chest and made herself very small. Hiding. From Barnabas? Had she learned to hide from his cruelty? He taught how to use pain and sexual pleasure combined to get a victim to do anything for their master. He'd tried to conquer Julija and hadn't succeeded. Had that been a blow to his pride?

Isai wanted to hunt him, but there was no clear direction. He had no idea if Barnabas was even in the Sierras. If Barnabas was aware that Xavier's book was there, Isai was certain he would come.

"Keep her safe, Blue."

The big cat met his eyes with calm determination. Complete loyalty. That humbled Isai. He hadn't done much to give the shadow cat reason to give him allegiance.

Isai left them, exiting the cave quickly, taking the form of an owl. Wings spread wide, he flew across the valleys toward the lake. The night had turned cold, but the owl didn't feel it as it silently made its way to the wide expanse of deep blue. From deep within the owl's body, he scanned everything below him, looking specifically for any sign or feel of his brother.

Sadly, though he had met Iulian, he had no real memory of him. They shared the same parents, but were so many years apart, Isai had already been gone, out hunting vampires by the time Iulian was born. He had traveled extensively and never returned to his home village, although they'd encountered each other a couple of times. He should have gone back. He had no idea what had happened to those he'd grown up with, or even if any of them remained. In his later years, he'd had his brethren in the monastery, but prior to that he'd been alone.

Now he had his lifemate as well as six shadow cats to look after. The weight of that settled on his shoulders and fit perfectly. He liked the idea of the responsibility. Of the cats being part of their family. They were independent thinkers. He could see that in Blue, but they were also intensely loyal creatures. Anatolie had never learned that fear didn't give one loyalty and more than anything, fidelity was priceless.

The world around him seemed to glitter and shimmer in the crisp night air. The water seemed bluer than ever. Deep, a true medium blue, the color dazzling even in the growing darkness of the night. He saw several tents in the distance, none close to another. Just single camps, most likely weekend hikers. He took his time dropping from the sky to inspect the nearest site from a tall pine tree.

The owl folded its wings and sat silently, listening to the night. Mice scurried in fallen leaves. A snake made its way to a rock and slithered beneath it for warmth in the cold air. Sierra garter snakes were often found around the lakes or rivers, even in the higher altitudes. He watched it carefully until it fully disappeared beneath the rock.

The two men camping talked quietly, occasionally bursting into laughter. They appeared genuine campers. Friends. Two men hiking the trail together, their intention to end their journey at Half Dome. Both appeared to be healthy. He touched their minds cautiously. If the two men were mage illusions and his touch was detected, it would remove his advantage. Both seemed to be what they appeared.

He flew over them once more, paying attention to the camp itself and then the closer surroundings, working his way outward in an ever-widening circle. This time he looked for evidence of vampires. His little mage thought mostly in terms of fighting off her family, keeping them away from finding the book. He thought in terms of Sergey Malinov.

The Malinov family had consisted of five very lethal boys and one girl. The entire family was of above average intelligence and highly skilled as warriors. The girl, Ivory, had been left for dead by vampires, betrayed by Draven, the prince's son, centuries earlier. The five brothers, all seekers of power, had used her disappearance as an excuse to give up their souls and become vampire.

Sergey had worked closely with Xavier, the high mage. Although the high mage had been slain, he had left behind pieces of himself. Those pieces resided in Sergey, which meant the vampire had access to all knowledge Xavier had—a very dangerous combination—especially now that the dark spell book was no longer in Mikhail's possession.

Sergey would be after the book the moment he knew it was close. Would it call to him? Isai had no idea whether it would or not, and there was no one to ask. He could reach other Carpathians, particularly the brotherhood of the monastery, over long distances, but not like the connection Julija and Elisabeta seemed to share.

Certain that the two campers were exactly what they appeared, he spiraled down until he was among boulders. He shifted and strode out, backpack on his back, looking the epitome of the lone hiker.

One of the men looked up and gave a friendly wave. "Come on into the camp. We have fresh coffee."

Isai tried a smile. His was fairly rusty, but since he'd been around Julija, he'd found he could not only smile, but wanted to laugh. "Thanks. That sounds good." He walked right into their camp, shrugging out of his backpack. "I have been on the trail since early morning." At the last minute he remembered he should be using contractions instead of the more formal-sounding way he normally talked. Neither seemed to notice. "You're the first I've run into in a day or so."

"Really? What trail are you hiking?" The one pouring the coffee looked up. "We were just saying the place seems overrun this year. We went to school together and meet up every year to hike the trails."

"I live on the east coast," the blond said. "Josh lives on the west coast. We keep in touch, but this is what we do to catch up with each other's life. We were just saying we're getting too old for this."

Both were telling the truth. Isai didn't wait any longer. Waving his hand, he stopped both men from moving or speaking. He didn't want either to be afraid or able to remember him. The less contact they had with him the easier it would be to erase every vestige of the memory from them. If Sergey detected even a small imprint of him, he would torture the two men trying to extract what they would never be able to give him. For all he knew, Anatolie or Barnabas would do the same. He took their blood, removed every memory of himself and left them both lying on their sleeping bags inside their tents recovering.

Coming back to the cave, he again took his time, studying the surrounding area carefully, looking for signs of intruders. He examined the battlefield. Other than a little scarring from the lightning, there was no real evidence of a life-and-death clash between mage and Carpathian.

Julija. Why hadn't she undergone the conversion? She should have. Did that mean she was already fully Carpathian and could sleep beneath the ground? He needed to find out. Could she escape the paralysis of his kind with her mage blood? Could she walk in the sunlight without fear? If he lay out in the sun, it would kill him.

He knew he would take her blood whenever he could. The taste of her was addictive to him. Would her mage blood, over time, allow him the freedoms it allowed her? All good questions with no answer. He would have to be patient and allow those answers to come to him as time unfolded.

The surrounding landscape appeared untouched, and he slipped through the narrow crack. Blue was waiting at the entrance to the chamber where his lifemate slept. The cat greeted him, amber eyes fixed on his face. The steady, focused stare could have been disconcerting, but Isai liked the cat more for his ability to concentrate his attention where it was needed.

"Everything all right?"

The cat nodded and watched him as he carefully woke the other cats one by one and fed them. Six cats were quite a lot. He would welcome Julija's help in caring for the animals, but not this night. When he had fed them all and reinforced the growing bond between them with pets, scratches and murmurs of assurance, he sent them all to the chamber closest to the exit. He wanted to be alone with his woman.

Isai carried Julija to the bed, removing soil and freshening her skin and hair in the way he knew she preferred before whispering the command to wake. Already, heat moved through his body. Just looking down into her face sent fire rushing through him like a freight train. He hadn't known such an intensity of emotions existed.

"Good evening, my little mage," he greeted when her lashes lifted, and he found himself looking into the dark chocolate of her eyes.

Her smile took his breath. It lit her entire face and brought something even more beautiful to her eyes. The beginnings of affection? Was that what he was seeing there? He bent his head and took her mouth because there was no waiting.

He thought that he might devour her. The intent was there in his mind, but when his lips touched hers, it was to gently coax her. A soft brush to tempt her. Back and forth. He savored the way she felt, so soft, so completely his. All for him. His tongue made a little foray along the seam of her lips, enticing her to part them for him.

There was no demand. He didn't want to take from her. He wanted her to give to him. To share the need that burned through him hot and wild. Her taste was there already, teasing every one of his senses. Binding him closer to her. The tip of her tongue touched his tentatively and then she parted her lips.

Isai dragged her closer and settled his mouth over hers, his tongue sweeping inside. At once her taste burst through him like he imagined champagne bubbles would. He felt as if he'd touched a match to a stick of dynamite, and they simply exploded together. Rockets went off. It was silly, but true. He would never get enough of kissing her.

The earth trembled and then seemed to stand still as he explored her mouth, claiming every inch for himself. His veins turned to slow-moving magma, a potent combination of fire and passion. Tiny flames seemed to lick over his skin. Her mouth was scorching hot.

Julija's arms crept around his neck as he pressed her back onto the mattress, letting her take most of his weight. Her body was soft, pliant, giving, her breasts pressing into his chest.

She entered his mind slowly, a soft, sweet, very feminine heat, moving slowly down the walls of his mind, filling every dark or lonely place with . . . her.

Good morning, my amazing lifemate.

Her voice, a whisper of sound, stroked caresses intimately into his mind. His entire body reacted to that sound. To the feel of her. To the intimacy of sharing his mind with her while her mouth moved under his.

Her mouth was hot. Searing him from the inside out. Her hand wandered down his back, the pads of her fingers stroking fire over the vows he had etched into his body—vows to her. *Hängemért.* For her. She traced the ancient promise over and over. Each stroke of her finger across those raised lines added to the molten fire burning through his veins.

Isai found himself acutely aware of her. Every nerve ending in his body had sprung to life. He kissed her over and over and then kissed his way down her throat to the swell of her breasts. Her skin was incredibly soft. There was a melting sensation to it, as if, when he put his mouth to that wide expanse of skin, the heat became so intense, he sank into her beauty.

You have the heart of a warrior, Isai, but really, the soul of a poet.

He wasn't certain what she meant by that, but the whisper in his mind was sensual and breathless, making him feel as if she thought he was her everything.

You're making me fall in love with you. You're definitely becoming my everything.

His mouth closed over her right breast and she arched her back, cradled his head and gave a little startled moan.

You are my everything, Julija. Never doubt that. He meant it. It wasn't just because she was fated for him, although a lifemate was a treasure beyond any price, but everything about her appealed to him.

Not everything, she reminded, her fingers wandering down his spine until she found the small of his back. They pressed there for a moment and then shaped his buttocks.

Everything, he assured. *You were so afraid, Julija, and I did not understand. I should have taken the time to find out what was wrong before I condemned you.* He didn't like to think that he'd failed his lifemate in anything, but he knew he should have shown more patience.

He kissed his way over the curve of her breast and under, found her left breast and drew it into the heat of his mouth. She seemed sensitive, and he was gentle, using his tongue and just the edge of his teeth to build her need of him.

He slid his hand down her belly and over her mound to the tiny little curls guarding the treasure that was for him.

I like knowing you are mine, he admitted. The thought slipped into his head often. He had someone. He wasn't alone. She was his. Julija. She really was everything to him.

Julija couldn't help staring at Isai's face, all those edges and planes. He was strong. He'd seen countless battles. He had an implacable strength and it showed, stamped in that strong jaw and ruthless set to his mouth. Right now, his face was soft, gentle, loving even. His expression turned her heart over.

I like knowing you're mine, too. She still had a difficult time believing he wanted her. There was a tiny part of her that kept expecting her father or Barnabas to jump out at her, laughing cruelly to tell her she'd fallen for one of their illusions.

You will be certain of me over time, little mage, he whispered, reminding her he could read her thoughts easily—as she could read his. It was very difficult to lie to someone or carry on an illusion when that person was in your head.

His mouth was making it impossible to think. Or breathe. He took her every thought away, sweeping her into another realm, another dimension where there was nothing but pure feeling, all good.

She'd never felt sensual or beautiful or just plain sexy. Isai made her feel all three. She heard her own gasps, those little ragged pleas as he made his way down her body, taking his time. It felt as if he was worshiping her. He was almost reverent—almost. The nips and licks became more demanding, more passionate, until she couldn't think at all. There was only Isai, surrounding her with his heat, his strength and the pleasure that bordered on sin.

Then his mouth was on her and she cried out, the sound reverberating through the cavern, sounding breathless, sexy and needy. His hands were strong, stroking caresses over her body. He didn't feel greedy. He didn't feel as if he was simply preparing her body for his pleasure. He felt . . . loving. Stroking love over every inch of her with hands and mouth, with his tongue and teeth. Showing her love.

Isai took his time, wanting to know every inch of her. What made her gasp? What made her cry out? What made her wanton with need? His woman. She needed care when it came to loving. She needed to know the man with her wanted to give her every pleasure and pain wasn't in any way part of that equation. It wasn't about him. This was for her. All for her. His pleasure came with the scorching heat of her body, the sound of her cries, the way her legs wrapped him up and her fingernails dug into his shoulders.

She was his world and she needed to know that. After the deception that had been played on her, the dark world of the mage, pretending to love her, to care about her, and taking her down that dark path out of some spiteful need to see others suffer, Julija needed to be reassured every time he touched her. He wanted her to recognize love when she felt it, so she would never doubt, never ever feel as if she could be touched with anything but love.

"Isai, you have to hurry." She whispered the words aloud in a rush of heat and need.

He kissed the inside of her right thigh, rubbing his gleaming, shadowed jaw there so it scraped gently over her sensitive skin. "Do I?" he asked and switched to her left inner thigh, rubbing like a cat. He blew warm air on her glistening body.

Blood pounded through her, hot and wild. Her hips bucked. His hold on her tightened as he guided his shaft between her legs. The moment he touched her with his heavy cock, she felt fire spreading. He wasn't even in her, but he had taken his time, not missing a single inch of her body and she needed him so much she tried to push herself onto his thick, hot erection.

"We are not in any hurry," he assured her. "We have all the time in the world."

"We don't!" she wailed. "We really don't." Because if he didn't take her, she was going to go up in flames. Burn right there with him probably looking down at her wondering what happened.

A smile broke out on his face. She hadn't thought anything could make him look younger, but all at once, that weathered, rough mask was gone, and he looked carefree. *Hers.* Isai belonged to her.

"Get on with it," she said, clenching her teeth as he held her deliberately still.

"I am contemplating." He held very still, not breaching her entrance.

Her breath hissed out in a long, slow whimper of disapproval. "Now is not the time to be cute, Isai. I'm really going to spontaneously combust."

He moved up her body slowly, kissing the dragon, the mark that told him she was Dragonseeker. Kissing his way up her belly, stopping to dip and swirl his tongue in her belly button. Nibbling on the underside of her breasts. He seemed to get distracted by her nipples, teasing and tugging, his tongue flicking until she was pushing her heels into the mattress, hips bucking, her body desperate to draw him in, to surround him with her heat. He kissed his way from her fingertips to her forearm, then over the mark of the high mage, the one that told him she was a very powerful mage.

Isai kissed her throat and then looked up at her, into her eyes. "I am saying something to you, Julija, something you need to hear. I want you to tell me what I am saying to you."

He kissed her mouth gently, another long, drugging kiss that left her breathless. Senseless. Dazed by his touch. She studied his face through half closed eyes. She could see love stamped there into every line. She could see it in his hooded, mesmerizing eyes. Her heart clenched hard and then seemed to melt. For a moment she felt overwhelming fear. He was wrapping himself so tightly around her heart, merging so deeply with her soul, she knew she would never be happy without him. It was too much. Too intense.

Looking at his face, she realized it might be intense. It might be too much. But that didn't make it any less real. He felt that deeply for her. The same way she was feeling for him. She touched his face with trembling fingertips.

He turned his head to capture her fingers in his mouth. *What am I saying to you?*

You're telling me you love me. She whispered the words into his mind because he shook her every time.

Instantly, his hand was there between them, grasping his heavy cock, sliding it inside her and then, without waiting, he surged forward. Fire streaked up her spine and radiated out from her core to every part of her body. She gasped and clutched at his shoulders, needing an anchor as he began to move in her.

With every stroke, every thrust, she felt the combination, fire and love. Love and fire. She knew he wasn't finished telling her. She was in his mind and knew he wanted it to sink into her bones, be branded there. For eternity.

The fire built hotter and hotter until she thought she might really spontaneously combust. Deep inside, that tension coiled tighter and tighter, desperate for release until she thought she might go insane. Through it all, through the flames and fire, she held on to him. Isai. Then she was crying out, the pleasure streaking through her, passion rocking her world, taking her somewhere she'd never been. Wave after wave crashed through her, completely consuming her.

They lay together, both fighting for air, her body surrounding his, the aftershocks keeping him gripped tightly, feeding both their pleasure. Then his mouth was on her neck, teeth sinking deep, triggering another massive orgasm that swept through her, shaking her, until she was clinging to him, one hand in his hair, holding him to her.

The moment he had taken his fill, he rolled them over, so, still locked with him, she was sprawled on top of him. *Take my blood, sívamet.*

His voice was a whisper of temptation, of erotic promise, a velvet brush of love, impossible to resist. She licked over the pulse beating so strongly in his neck. His cock jerked hard, swelled impossibly. Her teeth sank deep and he moved in her, triggering another hot orgasm that swept through her so intensely it flung her back to that place she just floated in surrounded by his love and nothing but sheer pleasure.

His blood was hot, spicy, the taste exploding against her tongue, spreading through her body to merge with the tsunami building again. When it broke through her, the intensity of it swept Isai along, catching him in the strong waves rushing through her body. She felt the hot splash of his seed. All of it together, the taste of his blood, his release, hers, merged them into one being, sharing the same skin, the same mind. It was beyond anything she had ever hoped or dreamt of experiencing.

Julija slid her tongue over the twin pinpricks in his neck and then allowed herself to collapse over top of him. She couldn't move. She might never move. She was quite happy to stay right where she was. She just closed her eyes and nestled her cheek against the hollow of his throat. She had no idea how long they lay together, just drifting in a world of pleasure. She felt safe, surrounded by his love. It was the best feeling in the world.

She supposed she couldn't spend the rest of her life like that, although she was willing to try. Eventually one of them stirred and she sat up, waited for him to do so as well, and she scooted back until she leaned against him, using him as a headboard. He didn't seem to mind in the least. He just wrapped his arms around her, holding her tight. She wasn't going to try to tell him how much what he'd done meant. She felt too raw. Too shy. But she believed.

"I take it you fed the cats this evening."

Isai dropped a kiss onto the top of her head. "Of course. And then gave them the order to stay in the other chamber. If I hadn't, they would have been driving us insane with their demands to feed and for attention. I thought Phantom and Sable looked better this morning."

"Your blood is . . ." She searched for the right word and finally settled on one. "Potent."

"Potent?" he echoed, a smile in his voice.

She tipped her head back until she could see his eyes. She particularly liked when she could get him to smile. The smiles were so rare. "Very potent," she reiterated. "I'm addicted."

"When you do not get blood to feed, Julija, does it weaken you?"

She nodded. "Very much. I can't really eat regular food, not like the others in my family. Animal blood doesn't help with the craving at all."

"But you never slept in the ground."

"No, I never even contemplated it, but I did lie in it sometimes. I studied your species for years, but I didn't try any of the things I'd learned about them, especially sleeping covered completely."

His chin nuzzled the top of her head. Strands of hair caught in his shadow, tying them together. "*Our* species, Julija. You are Carpathian. There is little doubt. You are also mage. It is unusual to say the least. After we find this book, it will be good to ask questions of others to see if they have heard of such a phenomenon."

"I like that you think I'm a phenomenon, but I don't want a bunch of strangers talking about me. Can't we just keep that part to ourselves? I can tell Elisabeta. She won't say anything about me to anyone."

"Elisabeta is Ferro's lifemate. He told us just before the prince contacted Tariq and asked him to send someone after Iulian. I recognized the name, knew it was my brother and took the job of hunter. It is my duty to make certain our name is lived with honor."

Julija was fairly certain Iulian had been noble as well as honorable.

"There is a small lake, very beautiful. Few campers, although I saw signs of horses when I flew over the vicinity, so I'm certain there are a few people who visit on a regular basis. Hopefully, they are gone at night. We will look closer this eve."

"Evening," she corrected automatically and then felt horrible. She liked his more formal way of talking. It appealed to her and when his accent slipped into his dialect, the combination was irresistible.

"I need you to make certain I fit into this century, and that includes with my speech," he assured her, subtly reminding her that he had access to her thoughts.

"You fit in. Women will be so busy drooling over you when they meet you, and the way you talk is very sexy, adding to that allure." Did she have a jealous note in her voice? She hoped not. She didn't want to lose him to any other woman . . .

"*Sívamet*, you still do not understand the concept of lifemates, and you had better learn quickly, before we go back to be surrounded by others. I am in your mind, just as you are in mine. It is easy to see your insecurities and know the reasons for them, but at the same time, you have to understand it is impossible for me to see any other woman but you. I have searched centuries for you. *Centuries*. There were times I gave up, but in my mind, you were always there. You. Not some other woman. Had I wanted other women, I would have had them. I want you. You are my choice. Lifemate aside, you are my choice."

She hugged his reassurance to her. "Tell me about Ferro. What's he like?"

For the first time, Isai hesitated and at the same time, pulled out of her mind. It was abrupt, so she felt his exit. It was impossible to reach him when he didn't want her inside. For a moment she was hurt, which she knew was silly. She really did have insecurities if she couldn't stand not being alone even for a few minutes.

"Ferro was the oldest among us," Isai said with obvious reluctance. "He is tall, taller even than I am. His shoulders—" He broke off, shaking his head. "Very wide. His eyes are very unusual, the color of iron and yet there are rusty spots within the iron so that his eyes pierce right through you. He always has an aura of danger clinging to him. He is not a man to cross. He was the most respected among us, and yet also the one we all were careful to watch. It is good that he has a lifemate. She will ensure that he cannot turn."

Julija was silent, trying to process how she felt about what Isai had told her. Her friend was very vulnerable. On the other hand, she would need a very tough and dangerous man in order to keep Sergey away from her. Everyone knew the vampire would do anything to get his prisoner back. Elisabeta's lifemate would have to be extremely powerful to match a vampire with splinters of the high mage embedded in him.

"I'm afraid for her."

"That is natural, Julija," Isai surprised her by saying. "You are her friend. You want what is best for her. Ferro will be best for her."

She had closed her eyes and pressed back against him. "You are always so certain."

"They are lifemates," he said complacently.

"Yes," she admitted, "but the course of both their lives changed, which means they have been altered. If the soul was split in half at birth and she has been born more than once, or at least one other time so lived other life cycles, and this time Sergey managed to kidnap and keep her, holding her prisoner for centuries, her life has to be shaped by that. She's different. He's different as well. Whatever they were supposed to be, they no longer are."

He pressed kisses along her bare shoulder, sending shivers through her body. "That is one way to look at it and I can see how it would cause you to worry, but it is truly for nothing, Julija. Her soul calls to his. His soul calls to hers. Each will be what the other needs."

Julija rubbed her fingers along his thigh, feeling the casual strength running beneath the surface—strength he took for granted. He believed deeply in the connection between lifemates. She wanted to believe. Certainly, Isai was an unexpected gift.

"I like that," he teased.

"You would get back into my mind just at the perfect time." She turned her head to give him a mock glare. It was strange. She was so used to him that she hadn't felt his presence. "I want to have that light of a touch."

"You will. It just takes a little practice," he explained. "Just like flying or shifting."

"I love flying," she said. "I used to think, at night, I would fly away in my dreams. If I left my bedroom window open, I could feel the night air surrounding me and ruffling my hair. Whenever I woke, I was always in my bed."

His arms tightened around her. "That kind of thing is very dangerous, Julija. When you fly, you need to know what you are doing at all times. It is called sleep flying. We are never allowed to do such a thing."

"I had no idea it was real, not until I started coming home with bumps, bruises and scrapes." She forced herself to sit up. Staring across at the pool of water, she decided hot would be good. She tried waving her hand toward the pool and thinking of the perfect temperature, but no steam arose. Exasperated, she sketched a quick pattern in the air and chanted.

Energy to molecules,
Liquid to steam,
Bring forth your heat,
To meet my need.

"If you persist in cheating, you will never learn." Isai waved his hand toward the water, and at once it cooled.

She leapt up, hands on hips. "You do not want to start a war with me."

Energy to molecules,
Liquid to steam,
Bring forth your heat,
To meet my need.

She waved toward the small basin of water and started across the room toward it.

"I would very much like to see what would happen if I did start a war," he said and waved his hand toward the pool. Even the room's temperature lowered.

"Isai," she warned. "I need to soak in hot water. You do not want me sore."

"If you get sore, I will heal you."

He had that same complacent tone in his voice. Mild. Nothing annoyed him. She put her hands on her hips and tossed her head back, hoping she could carry off the look even though she wasn't wearing a single stitch.

"I won't have a need to be healed if I can soak in hot water. Do not touch my bathwater." She pointed toward the basin and sent her spell straight to it.

She'd taken three steps and the water cooled, cooling the air around the pool as well. She swung around and pointed over his head.

Warm air rise, bringing forth your clouds,
Combine your cold with air's curling shroud.
Pollen, atmosphere now collide,
Dump your droplets down his spine.

The water poured over his head and shoulders. She spun around and ran to the pool, murmuring her spell for hot water. At once steam rose off the surface. She dove over the thick rock that made up the wall around it.

An arm curved around her waist before she hit the water, and she was pulled up against a hard male body. They both hit the surface and went under, the hot water closing over their heads. She was trying not to laugh and lost half of her air, but it didn't matter because they both surfaced immediately.

"Rain?" he asked, laughing.

She loved his laughter. The sound. That expression on his face. The way his eyes lit up. His mouth curved. She could get caught there, mesmerized just by that look on his face. Without thinking, Julija flung her arms around his neck and, lifting her face to his, kissed him. Hard. Meaning it. Pouring herself and her feelings for him into that kiss.

The moment her arms went around his neck and her fingers locked behind the nape of his neck, Isai wrapped his arms around her and pulled her body tight into his. She was lost all over again, kissing him over and over until she couldn't think. Some time passed before she ever got the soaking in the hot water she craved, but she didn't mind in the least.

14

The night was breathtaking, or maybe it was the fact that he had his woman with him to share it. Isai had never seen the stars so bright, or the moon so beckoning. The small lake was directly below the half ring of mountains. A large meadow crept up to the water's edge on one side.

This was the back country and fewer campers and hikers made their way there, although day ramblers on horseback often used the trails around the lake and up into the mountains. To the east of them was a small camper's resort where a few trekkers stayed, happy to be away from the more popular tourist sites.

Julija walked along the edge of the ledge, making him a little nervous. She could fly and had done so from the sanctuary of their cave, to this spot, but she still thought in terms of building an illusion. She was incredibly fast at it, but a second or two was all it took to be badly injured or killed. He found he watched her more than he should as she moved along the edge.

She looked beautiful with the stars as her backdrop. She walked with fluid grace, occasionally crouching low to pet Belle or Phaedra as both females pressed close to her. Blue and Comet were definitely on guard. The males stayed watchful, pacing along the top of the cliff, eyes and senses tuned for any danger.

Phantom and Sable, the two smaller cats, stood very still, as if expecting a reprimand, or an angry recrimination. They pressed together but watched everyone. Isai wasn't certain what to think of them. These were two cats Julija had risked her brothers' wrath for when she sneaked into the shed they used as a makeshift lab to house the shadow cats. She'd taken care of their wounds and given them blood. Still, of all of the cats, they appeared the most nervous and the most suspicious.

Isai sighed. He couldn't afford any traitors in their midst. Phantom had attacked Vasile, and clearly detested him, but Isai still had a very bad feeling in the pit of his belly. Julija turned her head and smiled at him as she slowly stood, keeping one hand on Phaedra's head, her fingers deep in the dark fur.

"They'll come around, Isai. They were horribly tortured. They haven't been shown kindness unless it was to trick them. Remember, my brothers practically worship Barnabas and employed his methods of torture and fear on the cats, at first being nice and then hurting them. It is very hard to accept kindness for what it is when you are certain you'll be betrayed in the end."

He knew she was speaking from experience. She was reading his thoughts anyway, he might as well have the discussion. "Your brothers, particularly Vasile, were very clever. They separated the cats and used each as a threat against the other, but what if they expected you to rescue them? It would be something you would do, Julija, and they knew that."

She nodded and lifted her face to the wind. It tugged at her clothing, the jeans and T-shirt she wore beneath her puffy vest. He told her he wanted her practicing regulating her body temperature, but she had donned the vest saying she was going without a jacket just for him and it was very cold.

"Yes, they would know," she agreed. "Blue doesn't believe they're a threat or he wouldn't let them near either of us."

He looked at the two smaller cats. They were younger than Belle and

Blue. "Aren't Phaedra and Comet the oldest and parents of Sable and Phantom?" When she nodded her head, he continued. "They didn't seem to acknowledge the relationship at all."

"They weren't born like other cats, Isai," she reminded. "They were made in a little dish. It wasn't like Phaedra fed them. They were given mixtures of blood and milk. They were to be shadows more than alive."

"Some things are much easier without emotion."

She came to him, her eyes on his face, and he read the compassion for him. The understanding. Julija was in his mind and she knew the intelligent thing to do was destroy the two small cats. The animals were in bad shape and needed care. Isai had spent time working on healing them, but they were a question mark and because both were extremely dangerous, not only to Julija and Isai, but any human, it would be smarter to destroy them.

She put her hand on his arm, and leaned into him, letting him take her weight for a few moments. "I know this is a difficult decision. We need to give them a chance. Blue and Comet will watch them. Both are extremely fast. If either of the little ones tries to attack us, they'll stop them. If we win them over completely, the pair will be as loyal as Blue, Belle, Phaedra and Comet, or even more so. Please, let's give them a chance."

She wasn't dictating to him, putting him in a position of making her angry. She was indicating her preference, but still giving support to his decision. He weighed the dangers. If it was only him, he wouldn't have hesitated, but he had Julija to protect.

He reached out to the two big male cats. *Watch the young ones at all times. Talk with them. Both are still nervous around us. If they are shadowed by one of the mages, or programmed to harm us, I need to know.*

He was met with intelligence. Both males turned their heads slowly to look at the smaller cats, taking them in as they huddled together just a little apart from the group. They would definitely be watchful now.

"The lake is beautiful, isn't it?" Julija said. "So peaceful. One would never know that somewhere close is a book of such vile darkness that the spells inside could wipe out entire species, including humans."

"Do you feel it close?" He looked down at her. She was facing the lake again, as if drawn to it. He wasn't certain if she was drawn by its beauty or something far more sinister.

"I feel that Iulian was here. He sat at the water's edge for a long time. Several nights. In the same place." Her voice softened, and her hand rubbed up and down his arm. Her eyes held compassion. "He's no longer alive, Isai."

He had known that. He should have felt sorrow for his lost brother. He'd never known him, but he'd always hoped he was still somewhere in the world. Isai was now the last of his line. Perhaps there was sorrow, but no grieving. There wouldn't be that. His brother had gone honorably from the world when he missed his chance with his lifemate. He hadn't succumbed to darkness or temptation as so many others had.

Something came close to him and he glanced down to see Phantom taking tentative steps toward him. The moment he looked down, the cat whirled around and raced back to the female.

"He was trying to comfort you. He was drawn to you because you felt overwhelming sadness."

"I didn't," he denied.

Julija frowned. "You really don't acknowledge your emotions, Isai. I felt sadness pouring off of you. It is strange that you can't."

"I acknowledged that he met an honorable death," he admitted, "but I didn't feel as if I was grief-stricken. I acknowledge that I love you. I think you should be able to feel that pouring off me rather than sadness."

She smiled, and that soft, sweet smile contained love—enveloped him in the emotion. He slid his palm around the nape of her neck. "I would much rather feel what I'm feeling at this moment, my little mage."

"You often call me that. Sometimes in your language and sometimes in mine."

"I never want either of us to forget that part of you. Being mage is extraordinary, something to be proud of. Just as Carpathians have those who turn vampire, mages have to worry that power corrupts, but for the most part, they are good people with astonishing gifts."

Her lashes fluttered, and she went up on her toes to press kisses along his jaw. "Thank you. I don't come from the best family. It seems my relatives are very interested in power."

"That makes you all the more special." He turned back to survey the campsites near the lake. There was the one with the two friends he'd already taken blood from. Just beyond the lake in a secluded area of trees and rock was one lone tent. No campfire. He hadn't seen anyone come or go from that site. He nodded toward it now. "I do not feel any danger from the camper, but there hasn't been any activity. I haven't seen the occupant."

She turned toward the direction he indicated and stayed silent for a moment. "I feel both men, Isai, but there is no information whatsoever coming from that other area. None. That bothers me."

He was immeasurably pleased with her. She hadn't given it a cursory glance and dismissed it. She'd actually allowed her senses to flair out and she'd studied it. There should have been something there. Humans didn't cover their tracks, not the way Carpathians, vampires or mages often did. Of course, it might mean the tent was set up and whoever occupied it wasn't there at the moment.

Julija caught his thought. "No, it's more than that. Someone's there. Waiting."

"We shouldn't keep them waiting long."

Her eyelashes fluttered again, drawing his attention. He realized she did that when something made her nervous. "It's a trap of some kind, Isai, and whoever it is, is targeting you. They know you're Carpathian and they are hoping to lure you in. It isn't bad odds that you would choose the lone camper versus the site with two men in it. They couldn't know you would be trying to feed six cats as well as your . . . er . . . person."

He burst out laughing. "Person? You are my *person?* Lifemate. Woman. Lover. I can think of several things to call you, but *person* would not have been among them."

"You're not all that funny," Julija declared in a snippy tone, but she started laughing as well. "Okay, you might be. It was rather silly. I started to say 'lifemate,' but the word is so foreign to me. I never thought I'd really be someone's lifemate."

"Why? You knew you were. You hid your voice."

She ducked her head to inspect the toe of her hiking shoes. "When I read about it, the concept seemed so beautiful. I made the mistake of telling Barnabas. I told him a lot of things I shouldn't have. I'm still angry with myself for being so naïve. He taught classes on torture. He couched it in medieval terms, but I should have seen right through that. Sex and pain to bind someone to you? He was a brilliant instructor, mesmerizing. His voice could charm the birds out of the trees. He slept with several of his female students in other classes."

"But not you. You he singled out as special. He became your friend."

She nodded and stepped away from him, twisting her fingers together. "Yes. For weeks. I was comfortable with him, and I let my guard down. It wasn't very smart of me. I'd already learned from being in my family not to trust anyone, but I still did."

Isai didn't like her retreating from him. He noticed both Belle and Phaedra pushed close to her. He'd been keeping an eye on the little cats and Sable lifted her head and took three small steps toward Julija as well. She stopped, her gaze darting around and her body almost folding in on itself as if expecting any moment to be struck.

Julija had noticed as well. She dropped to a crouch and held out her hand for the smaller cat to join the circle of females. Isai stilled. Waited. He noticed both Blue and Comet had gone on high alert and he was grateful to the shadow cats.

Sable edged forward and then stopped just out of reach, stretching her neck as far as she could in order to sniff suspiciously at Julija's hand. Once the cat had scented her, Julija dropped her hand into Phaedra's fur, stroking little caresses there and ignoring the smaller cat.

"It's difficult to think about Barnabas. It was a terrible period in my life. Painful both emotionally and physically."

"Why did he stop?"

She sank back on her heels. "I'm ashamed to tell you, I did actually try to commit suicide. I couldn't see a way out. My world felt hopeless."

Isai froze. It was the last thing he expected her to say. "Julija," he whispered. "You would have left this world and I would never have known you."

"I know. I'm sorry. Despair. Hopelessness. It can creep up on you. Devour you. I felt I was utterly worthless. I hated myself and what was happening to me. I couldn't sleep. It just all became a vicious circle. I couldn't eat, or feed. I just didn't see a way out. I felt so alone."

She ducked her head, so he couldn't see her face. "When I realized the endless centuries you'd endured, Isai, I was ashamed that I hadn't handled my trial with more grace."

"Do not ever say that, Julija," he decreed. "Not ever again. Depression is very real. I could not feel, so in many ways, I had a huge advantage. I joined the brethren, so I was surrounded by others who believed as I did. I had knowledge of a lifemate and I held on to that belief, that someday I would find you."

"I came so close to missing out on you," she whispered and looked up at him.

Sorrow. It was there, and it struck at him. He felt that heavy emotion through her. It seemed to swamp him. Before he could decide whether to hold her or allow the cats to comfort her while they continued the conversation, Sable made up her mind and moved in to press against her. Julija was careful to caress her fur gently, murmuring her gratitude for the caring. She glanced at him triumphantly.

Isai smiled back. "You were afraid Barnabas would trick you and provide a false lifemate for you."

"He was furious to lose me. My father insisted he leave me alone after the . . . um . . . second time it happened. He didn't want to lose out on his blood supply." She tried not to sound bitter.

Isai studied her face. "But Barnabas did not obey that dictate, did he?"

She sighed and sank her fingers into the fur of the littlest cat. It was still fairly sparse. She gently rubbed over the old scars that could still be seen on Sable's back. "No. He whispered to me at night or when no one was around. Telling me I missed him. I couldn't live without him and that I would come to him and beg him for more. Only he could give me what I needed."

He didn't like the shame or guilt in her voice. "You realize he was weaving a spell."

"I was too messed up in the beginning. I was terrified he might be right. You have to remember, that spell to make me want sex raged through me."

"Did you try to counter it?"

"Yes. I honestly don't know which one of them cast that spell. Anatolie, Crina or Barnabas. One of them did. That was truly the beginning of my downfall."

He reached down and pulled her to her feet. "There was no downfall, Julija. Barnabas, Crina and Anatolie conspired to put you under their control. You held out. None of them control you. In the end, in spite of everything they did to you, your strength prevailed."

"I let myself down a million times," she confessed.

"We all do that. It is the getting back up that defines your character, Julija, and you did that." He pulled her into his arms and, putting a finger under her chin, tilted her face up to his. "Kiss me before I go spring the trap on whichever one of your relatives is waiting to kill me."

"Let me go. You can watch from the sky and rescue me if I can't handle them."

He was already shaking his head, everything in him rejecting her plan. "That is never going to happen so do not bother to argue." He cut off anything more she had to say by taking her mouth. Where before he had kissed her so gently, he was much more demanding. She responded instantly, giving him everything. She was hot, addictive. *His.*

When he lifted his head, he stared down into her dark eyes. "I am beginning to think you may have cast a spell on me."

"I couldn't help myself," she teased. "You were so gorgeous it was that or faint from sheer girlish desires."

He laughed. "You are impossible." He glanced down at the little cats. They were back together, almost cowering. It bothered him that they were so afraid. The female, Sable, had tried to comfort Julija, and both had chosen to escape when given the chance. The male, Phantom, had attacked Vasile. Isai had given them his blood. He'd never spoken harshly to them or lifted a hand against them. He could understand them being leery and taking their time to trust him completely, but they weren't even trusting the other cats.

"Something is not right with them, Julija. While I'm visiting our lone camper, I would prefer you in the air. If there is a hidden trap we are not yet aware of involving these two, I do not want you dealing with it alone."

For the first time, he felt Julija was actually listening to him, considering the possibility. "How could we both miss something like that?" There was speculation in her voice.

He went still inside. Watchful. What kind of spies had her brothers planted in their camp? Now, he was more certain than ever that the two little cats were hiding something. "You tell me."

She regarded the little cats. Both stared up at her, freezing in place. She gave them a smile and knelt down, right there, with him close. One hand remained on his leg to keep him from moving.

"Phantom, come here to me." She held out her hand.

The male took a reluctant step toward her. The effort cost him. He began to tremble. She kept her hand extended toward him. There was no suspicion in her voice or on her face. Isai wasn't certain how she could do it, because alarms were shrieking at him. The cat was clearly averse to going near her.

He doesn't want to hurt me.

I am getting that. Julija, you are in a very vulnerable position.

On purpose. You are right here. I can examine him if he will let me. I don't want to invade without his permission and lose any chance of him trusting me.

Isai had the strange urge to shake her. The woman could be totally exasperating. *You do realize that this cat might be programmed to kill you.*

Yes. Of course. It isn't his fault if he is. He doesn't want to carry out the command, whatever that command is. He's had a terrible life, one of betrayal and pain.

He clenched his teeth and dropped one hand into the thick mass of her hair, his fingers bunching those silky strands into his fist. *Do not identify with this creature. That way can get you killed. You have no sense of self-preservation, Julija.*

She smiled up at him and then sank back on her ankles. "Phantom, I am mage. I can counter whatever they did to you. If you let me, I'll examine you and fix the problem, but you'll have to trust me."

Phantom looked back at the female.

"The threat is to her, isn't it? If you don't do as they've commanded, she'll be the one to suffer. Let me look at her. Perhaps I can remove the threat."

Isai wanted to gather his woman into his arms and comfort her. Shelter her. Protect her from the terrible things her family had forced her to live through. They were still doing it in spite of the fact that he'd destroyed them. He had a sinking feeling the cats wouldn't be able to overcome their fear and he would have to kill them. Would she forgive him?

Of course I would forgive you. I can't hold it against you when you're trying to save me, Isai. You haven't indiscriminately decided the cats need to die. You're waiting, even though you know they've been programmed.

How would they have done it? Isai believed in her. He believed in her ability to counter any spell or command they might have given to the cats. He tried sending the shadow cats waves of reassurance.

"I've been thinking about that," she said aloud. "Clearly, they expected us to try to rescue them. That's on me. They know I have a thing for animals. We'd had arguments over the sacrificing of them plenty of times. I gave them that weakness to use against me."

Isai remained silent, but he watched the cats, particularly the male. He was close to Julija, much closer than he'd been just a few moments earlier. His eyes had gone from amber to red and back again, never a good sign. He wanted to yank Julija out of there, away from the cat.

Phantom was the smallest of the shadow cats, but that didn't mean he was small. Most male panthers in the wild weighed between one hundred and thirty pounds and one hundred and sixty pounds. The females were smaller, coming in around seventy to a hundred pounds. These cats were larger than that and yet they could be insubstantial. Nothing but shadow, thin enough to slip through cracks and enter rooms they should never be able to get into. To have those razor-sharp claws and teeth so close to his woman made Isai very uneasy.

Julija ignored the warning signs that the cat was close to attack. She turned her attention to the female. "Sable, are they threatening you? Have they put something inside you that can harm you?" She beckoned the cat closer.

Isai suppressed a groan. Two of them close? *Are you out of your mind? I am not a miracle worker.* Already he was working out how to kill them both before they could touch his woman.

Of the two cats, the female was far more receptive to Julija's overtures. She padded across the short distance and thrust her nose right into Julija's middle. Every cell in Isai's body reacted. He wanted to fling the cat away from her. He looked at the male, who was pacing, his eyes on his mate and Julija.

"I understand what you are feeling, *ekäm*. I want to protect my woman as well." Deliberately he called Phantom his brother. They were forming a family and the shadow cat had to want to be part of it. That meant trusting Julija and Isai to guide the pair through this crisis.

"Can you lie down for me, Sable?" Julija asked, patting the ground beside her. "It will make Isai feel much better."

"But not her mate."

"You will, no doubt, ensure we are all safe from him." Julija didn't look at the male. All of her concentration was on the female. The little panther hesitated and once more glanced at the male before she reluctantly lay down in front of Julija.

His woman passed her hands over the cat's body. She frowned and glanced up at him. *Something is here, but I can't feel it exactly.*

You are much more sensitive to mage magic than I am, and I need to keep on Phantom. He is considering launching himself at you.

Julija's gaze shifted, just for a moment, to the male cat and then she was back concentrating on the female. Once more her hands passed over the cat, this time much more slowly. She appeared to be searching inch by inch for whatever her brothers had placed in the cat. Her hands stayed over the head, and she frowned and moved on.

There is no command in her. She isn't the trigger. Phantom obviously is. But still . . . there is something here.

You are Carpathian, Julija. I can protect your body if you go outside yourself and into her to examine her. He felt Julija's instant excitement the moment he made the suggestion.

I can't do that. I've never even tried. I wouldn't know where to start.

You must be without all ego. Your sole purpose is to serve, and you do so without expecting anything in return. You shed your body and become healing light. Once you do that, you enter the body of the person or cat. He tried for a little humor when he was now wishing he hadn't made the suggestion. *You can examine them from the inside. If the mages left anything in her, you will see it. If you do, come back out and share with me. The experience might leave you very tired and in need of blood.*

Her eyes met his. "I know I can do it. She wants me to find whatever it is and remove it. I can, Isai." She switched her attention to the male cat. "Phantom, I've never tried this before but if it works, she will be free of whatever they left behind. Give me a few minutes to get it right."

He didn't like her sharing anything at all with the shadow cat. He seemed too far gone already. He wanted to protect his female, and the only way to do that was to follow whatever command he had been given.

The male suddenly swung his head away from Julija and snarled, pulling his lips back to expose his teeth. Comet had come up behind him. Phaedra slipped between the male and Julija. Belle stayed right beside Phaedra, closing an invisible gate to Julija. The only hope Phantom had to reach her was to leap over the cats, exposing his belly to them. Behind him, Comet prowled, but it was Blue that worried him the most. The big cat was nowhere in evidence.

"Hurry, Julija, if you are going to do it," Isai encouraged.

She didn't hesitate. Once she made up her mind to do something, she was determined. It took three tries to shed her body in the Carpathian way. It was difficult for anyone new at it to let go of all ego and become pure healing spirit. She had no problem entering the little female cat's body. She was used to merging with Isai and used the same seamless method.

Isai stayed merged with her, just in case she got into trouble. He didn't want her distracted, so he stayed quiet, not giving her any advice, just remaining as an observer. He was impressed with her way of quartering the body, looking for something off. She made her first pass without finding anything, but she was patient and she went back to the cat's spine and rib cage. Her white-hot spirit illuminated the entire skeletal structure.

Do you see it, Isai? There is a dark spot, very thick, on the underside of her spine. It's about an inch thick and three inches wide.

He didn't like the sound of that. He didn't want her to get too close. *Pull back, Julija. If it is some kind of explosive, you might detonate it.*

She didn't argue with him. Instead, she pulled completely out of the cat and wiped at the sweat on her head. She appeared to be reeling, her body trembling with the effort she'd made.

"Let me try something else now that I know where it is." Without explaining, she lifted her hands, one curling around the cat right over the spot, the other waving in the air gracefully. She began chanting.

That which is hidden, now bring to light,
So that I may see what is inside.
Light to dark, dark to light,
Revealing all which would hide from sight.

Once more, she shed her body and entered the little female cat. Isai, merged as he was, continued to keep an eye on the agitated male. His rumbling protest rose as the other cats kept him from his prey and his mate.

The dark spot was once more back in the light. Now, it was no longer just a spot. It was clearly a very tiny bomb placed within the female's body. In his mind Isai heard Julija murmur another spell. This one seemed to access the memory of the inner workings of the bomb.

Shade to shadow, shadow to dark,
Reveal to me your working parts.
Show me that which is hidden away from light,
So I may see your working mind.

For just a few moments, the case was laid open, allowing them to see the contents. The blast would radiate outward in a starburst pattern, at least, it appeared so to him. He could see the simple mechanism that the mages had attached inside the cat's spine. It was counting down. It wouldn't matter what Phantom did or didn't do, eventually the explosive would detonate. There was also a way to remote detonate, but seeing as how both mages were dead . . . He broke off his thought as once again, Julija returned to her body.

She looked up at him with shadowed eyes. He despised that look. "Barnabas," he said aloud and switched his gaze to the male cat. He couldn't help the unfamiliar surge of anger he felt at the cat. Julija looked so lost, very afraid, and he knew she was feeling as if she would never be free of the dark mage.

Instead of ranting, he remained calm. She needed steady, an anchor, and he had to be that for her. "Is it possible that we are seeing an illusion?"

She shook her head. "There would be little point. He wouldn't consider that we would find this. He still has a remote detonator."

"That matters little. It can be dismantled easily."

"He is very good at protection spells." There was despair in her voice.

"I have no doubt he needs them," Isai said. "You are both mage and Carpathian. You are far more intelligent and definitely stronger than he is. More to the point, you do not need his spells. See with the eyes of a Carpathian. You will see the layers of his protection weave. Once you know any strand, you will be able to take it down."

"He could blow the bomb and kill us all."

"He could," Isai agreed. "There are some chances you have to take." She needed to defeat Barnabas over and over until she believed in herself. For Julija, the mage was her greatest enemy, her terror, that monster that couldn't be destroyed. It wouldn't help her if he continually fought off everything Barnabas threw at them—she needed to do so. "Is keeping Sable alive worth the risk?" He had the sinking feeling that this was another test. Barnabas was trying to force Julija to kill the two small cats. He would find a way to shield her, should the bomb detonate.

"Yes, of course."

"Then remove it from her." He stated it with complete confidence, as if there was no question that she could do it.

Julija stared straight into his eyes for a long time. She took a deep breath and then once more shed her body and entered the cat. She had to be exhausted by now. Just the act of removing one's spirit from the body was tiring. She'd done so several times now. Isai turned his attention to Phantom.

"You will settle down. She's trying to save your mate. No matter what, that bomb would explode, killing her and anyone near. It wouldn't matter if you obeyed or not. Is there one in you?"

Phantom had been pacing and snarling, swiping his paw toward the larger males, but now he subsided. He shook his head and just stood. Waiting. Knowing even if he attacked and Isai was not telling the truth, it would be too late. Julija was already inside the body of his mate.

Isai left Phantom to Blue and Comet. He had remained merged with Julija to see how she was going to go about removing the bomb from the inside of the cat. She didn't try to take the device off the spine. Instead, she used what she knew best—her mage spells.

Each word was a command. There was no plea. She didn't leave anything to chance. She went after the parts, taking the bomb apart from the inside out.

Tick tock, sound of a clock,
Show me your workings so I might stop,
That which is enclosed and intended to harm,
Stop now and separate so I may disarm.
Each piece a puzzle, I surround you with light,
I dissolve you away without a fight.

It was slow work, because she feared at any moment Barnabas would find a way to override her, but she did it. When she came out of the cat and into her own body, she was shaking with weakness. Isai immediately wrapped his arms around her and gave her blood. He was going to need to feed before the night was over.

He rocked Julija gently, rubbing his chin on top of her head. "I am so proud of you. I know that was extremely difficult, but you did it."

"It was actually easier than I thought it would be. I just went backward from where he ended and took apart everything. There is no chance it will work. The parts disintegrated, and the casing was being eaten away already by the cat's blood. It was a good thing we found it."

"You found it," he pointed out. He looked out over the bluff toward the lake. "I still have to deal with our visitor this night, and I will feed as well."

She lifted her head immediately. "Not without me. Just give me another minute and I'll recover. I can feel my strength returning. Don't worry, I listened to you. I'll take the form of an owl and stay in the sky until you have things under control."

He didn't argue with her. She was becoming adept at shifting, holding the images in her head. The more practice she got, the better. He nodded and waited for her to get to the edge of the bluff. Both shifted at the same time, spread wings and flew over the campsite set well back from the lake.

Isai studied the camp. Although the tent was lit, it appeared deserted, but he knew better. The illusion was a good one, and any other time, if he had been unwary, he might have fallen for it, but it was too good. The landscape blended seamlessly, yet when he sent the breeze in, the leaves on the bushes didn't follow the pattern or rhythm. He had flown over the tent, only once, not wanting to tip off the occupant that he was coming, but in spite of the fact that he'd been in the air, Blue and Comet followed on the ground. They were already there, in the deep rock, mere shadows, but keeping watch.

The tent was lit, so that shadows should have been thrown on the canvas, but it was impossible to see the occupant. He only knew there was one and she smelled female. Alluring. Deliberately alluring.

He stepped out from the trail side. "Hello to the camp." He was a gentleman and didn't want to startle any occupants. He wore a backpack on his back and made certain to look the part of a traveler just out hiking.

Inside the tent, he could see the woman as she deliberately sat up slowly, thrusting her breasts out, so that the image appeared on the wall of the tent. She shook back her hair and crawled out on her hands and knees, another very sensual sight. Very slowly she stood. She was taller than he expected, very slender, with long legs and high breasts. She wore a ridiculous outfit, one that looked almost like a catsuit. It was one piece and clung to her body, fitting her like a glove, emphasizing every curve.

She put her hand on her hip and stepped back. "Well hello. I didn't expect to meet someone so handsome on the trail." Even her voice was a lure, sexy as hell, a temptation to bring him closer.

He took a couple of steps toward her, stopped with what appeared an effort and let his backpack sink to the ground. "I wasn't going to bother you, but I ran out of food a few days back and was hoping you had some to spare."

She didn't have a campfire going so he couldn't claim he was cold or wanted hot coffee. It had to be food.

"Are you camping for the night? There's plenty of space and I'd be happy to share it along with my food. The animals get close and to be honest, I'm a little bit of a chicken." She laughed, the sound like a velvet stroke over his skin.

"I'm looking for a good place," he admitted, letting his gaze linger on her curves. The front of the catsuit was a sharp vee that stretched to accommodate her generous breasts.

She stepped closer to him so that her potent perfume reached him. Surrounded him. Cocooned him in the alluring fragrance. She was a web of temptation, drawing him to her.

Isai let her come close enough that she was able to run her hand up his chest and look up at him with her wide, blue eyes. She parted her crimson lips. He bent his head toward her and at the last moment, shifted just enough to lock her to him and sink his teeth in the pulse beating so steadily in the side of her neck.

She cried out, a call for help that sounded more like a muffled demand, but he ignored it, drinking his fill, taking as much from her as possible before dropping her to the ground without closing the twin holes. Blood trickled down her neck to stain her catsuit at the shoulder.

"How *dare* you," she snapped and tried to scramble to her feet. She had both hands up as if to ward him off, but she was beginning to weave a pattern. Her strength was gone so she couldn't get to her feet, but it didn't stop her mumbling insults while her hands created a weave.

"No, Crina, how dare *you*," Julija said, striding into the camp. Her hair looked as if it had taken on a life of its own, crackling with electricity. "You know he's mine and yet you tried, pathetically I might add, to seduce him."

She lifted both hands and pushed air toward Crina's uplifted arms. At once electricity leapt from her palms to Crina's arms, snapping and crackling as the sparks bit into her stepmother.

Crina dropped her hands and yelled profanities, glaring at Julija. "You're going to pay for that."

"What are you even doing here?" Julija looked around cautiously. *She would never, under any circumstances, come here alone.*

15

Julija, get off the ground. Isai was uneasy. She thought in terms of mages. It was very possible that Crina was in league with Barnabas, even probable, but so far, Sergey had not made his presence known. There was no way the slivers of Xavier had not felt the call of the book. Every vampire and mage for hundreds of miles would have felt that call, at least that was Isai's way of thinking. So far, no one had felt the call of the book, not even Julija, and she was actively looking for it.

Julija floated into the air, keeping her gaze fixed on Crina. She noted that her stepmother was tapping her finger in a steady rhythm against her thigh. Julija zapped her immediately, sending little sparks embedding into her fingers. Crina yelped and glared at her, putting her fingers in her mouth.

"Calling for your friend will do you no good," Julija said. "But call away. We will be more than happy to get rid of him as well."

Crina's head went up, glaring, her blue eyes filled with rage. "You always were so smug, Julija. Anatolie thinks you can do anything. You're so powerful. What a crock. My sons are a million times more powerful than you will ever be. Anatolie just refuses to see that because he fears them. He knows that they will take all power from both of you."

"They're dead, Crina. Both of them. They came after me and I destroyed them."

There was absolute silence. Crina stared at her, for the first time looking truly shocked. She shook her head. "That can't be. You're lying to me."

"I'm not. I also removed Barnabas's little surprise bomb from the shadow cat. Your lover didn't do a very good job of securing it."

"You're lying, Julija. You could never defeat Vasile or Avram." Her voice began to swing out of control.

"They are dead," Isai said.

A peculiar noise much like the high-pitched shriek of a flock of birds or large bats moving fast through the air could be heard in the distance.

Crina smirked. "You'd better hope that you're lying, Julija, although I can't imagine that he would spare you." She lifted her hands fast into the air and tried to shout a death wave.

Isai inserted his body between Crina and Julija with lightning speed, clapping his hands to reverse the direction, sending the shock wave straight at her. Her mouth was open, and the wave rushed down her throat, turning her insides to jelly, melting everything from organs to bones. A look of horror came over her and then her face collapsed in on itself. Her body followed suit, so that she looked like a shriveled paper doll.

Julija turned her face away. "Isai."

"We have to go," he said abruptly. He didn't wait for her to shift. This was no training lesson. He caught her up and took to the sky. They needed shelter and he had marked but two places, neither of which he'd had time to examine. Inwardly cursing, he flew fast. There wasn't time to think of the cats, he could only silently send out a call to them, warning of immediate danger.

Julija didn't protest or fight him. She closed her eyes and lay quiet in his arms. She felt small, weightless but feminine cradled against his chest. Isai covered them with a concealing spell as he took her away from the lake where his brother had ended his life. There was no way to save the two hapless campers, both of whom he'd liked, not unless he got his woman to a safe place. He hadn't spent that much time with them, but they'd seemed genuinely nice people. If their bodies were found, the conclusion would be they had been attacked by wild animals.

He swore in his language. He was a Carpathian hunter first and foremost, and to leave a battleground when there was a master vampire to hunt went against everything he believed in.

He is part mage now.

Julija's voice startled him. She was merged with him and knew his thoughts. That shamed him. He didn't want her to ever think he was upset because he protected her. *Explain.*

The first crack was far too wide and easy for a vampire to spot. He couldn't secret Julija there and expect her to be safe.

He has slivers of Xavier in him. To look for the book, he has to bring those to the forefront. Sergey won't feel the book on his own.

It calls to all evil.

No, Isai, it doesn't. Xavier would like you to think that, but if that was so, my father and brothers, Barnabas and Crina would have known where the book was. They followed me thinking the book was in my possession. Remember, I went to the Carpathian Mountains and someone stole the book from the shadow cat. The shadow cat was killed. They had no way of knowing who stole the book. When I left the Carpathian Mountains, the order was sent out by the prince to find me. What would you think?

He turned that over in his mind just as he found the second crack in a large outcropping. This one was close to the ground, not up high near the top of the rock. The crack was so tight that at first, he wasn't certain it was actually an opening that led anywhere. He had to get her under cover before the bats reached them.

He took a breath and waved his hand toward the crack, murmuring to the earth to open for him. The crack widened enough that he could shift their bodies to paper-thin, so they could pass through. He had no idea what was inside, and he didn't like that with Julija there, but it was better than exposing her to the bats that Sergey had sent.

Once inside, he began to close the crack and she caught at his shirt.

"No. The cats. They'll be coming after us fast. If you shut them out, they'll be exposed to the bats."

He doubted if the bats would be able to see the cats as more than mere shadows. *Blue, I did not leave a trail.* He sent an image to all the cats of where they were. *You cannot reveal our hiding place. If it is not safe to join us, wait. Pay attention to anything moving over your head or under your feet.*

"They'll let us know when they are close," he assured and set her on her feet. He waved his hand and sconces immediately lined the chamber, illuminating the small cave. There was little room compared to many of the caves he'd used as resting places. This looked about the size of a small bedroom. Or a sitting room. He could change it at will. Right now, he just needed a place for Julija to be safe while he went after the master vampire.

"Listen to me, Isai. I know what I'm talking about. Sergey can't find the book on his own. There is no trace of it or Iulian. I didn't feel the book, that's not what brought me here. I followed Iulian. I was connected to him from that brief time when he was losing his lifemate. It was Iulian that brought me to this place, not the book. He's masked the book. I don't know for how long, but Sergey won't be able to find it, not even if it tries to call to Xavier."

"That is a huge jump, Julija." He began to weave safeguards, changing them in the way the brethren did so that no trace of Xavier's teachings showed. Sergey would not be able to get to her.

"I know it is true. Isai, you aren't really going after him by yourself, are you?"

"There are two innocent men out there. I can't just let them die." He spoke more harshly than he intended. Any fight with a master vampire was dangerous. Sergey, perhaps, the most dangerous of all.

"Stay connected to me. He will try to bring Xavier to the forefront and use his mage illusions. I can counter every one of them if you just allow me to see what he's doing and saying."

She was terrified of Barnabas, but not of Sergey. That spoke volumes to him. She watched his every move intently, so she could replicate the safeguards as needed.

"Do not leave the safety of this place, Julija." He made it a decree, uncaring if that made him a chauvinist in her modern woman eyes. "I cannot have my attention divided between your safety and destroying such a powerful being."

Julija nodded. "Just don't break our merge, even if it is getting bad, Isai."

He turned from her and started toward the opening. She caught his sleeve. "Promise me. Give me your word."

"Unless there is no other choice," he agreed. She would have to live with that. He would do his best to keep his word, but if Sergey managed to defeat him, he wouldn't allow Julija to experience his death.

Blue, Comet, if you reach the cave, you take care of her. He gave the order as he took to the sky in the shape of mist.

Sergey would find his treacherous ally, Crina, dead in her tent and he would be angry. He didn't like to lose. Julija had slipped out of his hands several times. If she was right and the vampire wasn't able to hear the book's call any longer, then it would be more important than ever to acquire Julija if he thought she could find it.

Isai had watched Crina's face carefully when Julija had accused her of being Barnabas's lover. It had been true. He had no doubt that both Barnabas and Crina could be in league with Sergey. Both wanted power. Crina had no love for her husband, Anatolie, nor apparently, he for her. Theirs had been a match all about power. When Anatolie hadn't given her what she wanted most, it seemed she had aligned herself with Barnabas.

Barnabas appeared to be everywhere. Who was he really? What was he doing in every mix? Was he more powerful than Anatolie? Isai hadn't considered that before. Now he had to answer the question of who Barnabas truly was and what kind of real threat he would be.

The sound of the bats rose to a fever pitch and a man's voice cursed. The bats had found the two campers. He doubled his speed, streaking through the night sky to try to make it to them before the vicious bats had devoured the two. They wouldn't have been afraid. Most likely, they'd even stepped out of their tent to witness the large, unusual migration.

There were seventeen species of bats in Yosemite, but these weren't any of those. These bats were servants of Sergey, mutations originally conceived of by Xavier. Xavier had used them as guardians of his caves. They were vicious and craved blood and flesh. Highly dangerous, they ate the flesh right off the bone while their prey was alive. He would have to find and kill the colony if he survived this night.

He dropped down from the sky like a bullet, throwing up a shield as he landed right in the middle of the melee. The blond, Mike had been his name, fought with a hatchet, swinging at the creatures attacking from all directions. Josh used a small machete, slicing through heads as the bats walked upright on their wings, looking macabre. More filled the air, darting in to take great chunks out of their skin.

Let me see them, Julija demanded.

Isai joined the two men, maneuvering them under the shield so it was impossible for the bats to get to them from above. They had to come at them from either direction, but there appeared to be a sea of them surrounding them.

"What kind of bats are these?" Josh demanded, wiping blood from his face and then going back to swinging the machete.

Isai didn't worry about what either man might think. He used his superior speed to fight off the bats. Even so, they were overpowering, more and more coming at them.

There are too many of them, Julija. I either have to try to fly the two men to safety or burn these creatures. I have seen these swarms before in memories given to me. They must be burned in order for us to survive. He was calm. There was a solution. If necessary, he would try to outfly the colony of mutated bats.

Are you able to burn them without aid?

He had seen it done through the memories of others. It wasn't easy. He had no device such as the one he'd seen used. It was the temperature he needed, even more than the flames. *I believe I can, sívamet. Do not try to aid me. If Sergey is near, I do not want him to find you.*

While he puzzled out what to do, the three of them went back-to-back to protect themselves from the onslaught of lethal teeth and claws.

"I am going to have to burn them. It is the only way to stop them from coming," Isai informed the two men.

"Tell me what to do," Mike said readily. He was bleeding from dozens of places, his breath coming in gasping pants.

"I'm in," Josh agreed. "These mothers are going to eat us alive."

Isai didn't waste time with explanations. He called up to the weather, stirring the clouds, sending cold air to each cloud so the top was freezing, forming small ice chunks within it. Because he kept the clouds moving, the ice pieces bumped into one another repeatedly, causing electrical charges.

"Work your way behind me and cover your eyes. You do not want to go blind on top of everything else," he cautioned.

He took the forefront, slicing through necks as the bats came at him in force. He called down the lightning, strike after strike, using the white-hot sparks as a laser, mowing down the swarm of bats. Flashes of light in the darkness lit up the sky so that it looked like a bizarre dance of dazzling whips. The air smelled of roasted meat and burnt flesh. The bats had a peculiar, putrid smell.

Wave after wave of bats kept coming, as if they had been programmed and couldn't stop flinging themselves into harm's way. *Do you have any feel for these creatures? Who might be directing them? Does it feel like Sergey? Do you have his scent?*

Every mage wielding magic had a particular scent or identifying marker. It was in the way they cast their spells. Wording, patterns, movement, stillness, all could identify a particular mage at work. Sergey wasn't mage, but with the slivers of Xavier inside him, it was very possible he could cast the way Xavier did. He had access to those memories.

Not Sergey, Julija decided after a few moments. *More like—* She broke off abruptly.

Julija?

This feels like Barnabas, but just a little different. The same but older. Much older.

Isai searched his memories for one that felt the way the flow of mutant bats did. The ranks were thinning now, but some still crawled over the dead, charred bodies of those in their colony, using their wings to do so, staring with dark beady eyes.

There had been a student of Xavier's. He'd been very close to the high mage, as close as any student could get. He was very much like Xavier, cruel and indifferent to those around him, yet brilliant and a very dedicated worker. He paid little attention to other students at the school and in truth, he seemed more of an aide than an actual student. Some thought him a companion of Xavier's and there was plenty of sly speculation, although no one dared to ask him outright.

What name had he gone by then? It was so long ago, and Isai had long given up those memories. He worked to pull it from his mind. *Barna.* The mage had gone by the name of Barna, the Hungarian version of Barnabas. Could Julija's Barnabas be the same Barna from long ago? If so, Isai couldn't believe that he would be working for Sergey or anyone else to recover the book. He would want it for himself.

Julija, do you recall Barnabas taking your blood at any time?

He lashed at the last of the bats. There were a few still moving under the burned and charred bodies they would have to kill with machetes, but he felt as if the tide was stemmed. "Josh, Mike, you can open your eyes. If you wade through them to find any alive, watch yourselves that they do not bite you."

That was his favorite thing to do. He felt her steeling herself to tell him. *He took my blood often, and at night, when we were alone, sometimes he would tie me up and cover my mouth so I couldn't call out and he would cut me and lick at the blood. He especially liked to do that when he was using my body for sex.* She stumbled over the last, but she told him the truth.

Isai found more and more respect and admiration for his woman. She didn't hold anything back, no matter the cost to her, not when she thought it might help him.

You said he was a teacher. Is he friends with Anatolie? Did you have the feeling they went way back?

They definitely knew each other very well, that's why it was so disgusting when I realized he was sleeping with Crina.

Isai thought that over. If Xavier had raised his oldest son in secret, while the rest of the world thought him dead, he would have needed help. Someone had taken care of Anatolie while he was young. Xavier would never have cared for a child. He might have used female mages, but someone had to be consistent in the child's life. Who was the dependable person in Anatolie's life, because Isai would bet it wasn't Xavier.

He kept his eye on Josh and Mike as they kicked dead carcasses aside and chopped down at the still lethal, half-burned animals as they lay dazed yet still trying to snap with teeth and tear with claws.

Can you show me their interaction?

Julija hesitated again, just for a moment, and then she opened her mind more fully to him. He realized she always kept herself a little guarded. She didn't want him to witness those years of humiliation, the times Barnabas had had her with her father's full consent. He'd always wondered why her father would allow Barnabas to keep control over his food source. Anatolie needed Julija, yet he had helped in Barnabas's cruel conspiracy.

The memory was a short one. She was called into her father's study. It was a place she wasn't invited often, and she went cautiously. The door was already partially opened, and she looked in. Barnabas was turned toward her. Isai studied the man.

He wasn't particularly tall, yet he was tall enough. He had broad shoulders, but not so much that anyone would notice. He had a muscular physique, but not with obvious muscles. He wore a suit and it sat well on him. Anyone looking at him would think he was wealthy and high up if not the president of some company. Power clung to him and confidence radiated easily. He didn't look like a man who would show off. He would allow others to do so.

He smiled at Julija and held out his hand to her. Isai's belly immediately knotted. The smile was smooth, practiced and didn't quite reach his flat, cold eyes, but when he looked at Julija, there was something there. Interest. A spark? A flair of need?

"There she is."

Anatolie stepped forward when his daughter stopped abruptly and took a step backward. "Get in here, Julija," he snarled. He glanced at the other man and when he did, he turned his head slightly.

Isai forced himself to freeze the memory right there. His woman was trembling. There was fear on her face. Clearly, Barnabas enjoyed her fear. His gaze had sharpened, and he had the look of a vicious, cruel tyrant who hurt others for his own pleasure. It was there, stamped on his face, for the world to see. Julija saw and she feared him.

What of Anatolie? Isai studied him. Julija's father at first appeared to be a man in control of everything around him. He was in his place of power. One didn't go to his study casually. He would reign there, mete out his brand of justice and dictate to family, friends and anyone who might work for him. He wore a suit that cost a fortune and he wore it well. His hair was shorter than most mages', which surprised Isai. There was power in hair, a kind of radar system. One could pick up whispers of trouble when needed.

The desk behind him was solid, made of mahogany, the color nearly a slashing red. More power symbols. A crystal decanter was half full of amber liquid and four cut crystal glasses sat on the tray surrounding it. Everywhere one looked were small signs of opulence. Anatolie indulged himself.

Isai kept coming back to that small head turn, the one where he glanced back at Barnabas. Something about it bothered him. He brought the frame of memory closer to him. What was it? What was he seeing that hadn't quite registered?

He's sweating, Julija. Do you see that? There are tiny beads of sweat trickling down his face. You weren't taking Barnabas's offered hand. He feared you would be rude.

The two campers had come back to him. Josh crouched down and then sat on the ground. "This sucks. The bodies stink." His body was bleeding in many places.

Mike sank down beside him, his head in his hands, rocking back and forth. Isai didn't have time to reassure either of them. He waved his hand to silence them. He needed to think. The two men were right, the charred bats stank horribly. Isai opened the ground, a giant, deep pit, and allowed the creatures to sink deep. Again, he waved his hand to create a breeze to drive the horrible stench away from them.

I don't know what you think that means, Isai.

She didn't want to know. Every time Barnabas came up, she shrank away from the subject. He couldn't blame her. When he looked at Barnabas, he knew he was looking at someone wholly evil.

Your father was afraid of Barnabas. I believe Barnabas trained under Xavier. He was privy to Xavier's plans. It is possible he was the only one fully privy to them. I find it interesting that he is here, not in the Carpathian Mountains. Did he follow Sergey here because Sergey has slivers of Xavier in him?

Would he remain loyal to Xavier? Would he have that capability?

Julija asked good questions. He had thought Barnabas was wholly evil and he still believed that. That didn't mean he wasn't capable of loyalty, especially if he thought there was a reward waiting for him. His loyalty would never be to Sergey. He would look upon the master vampire with contempt. He would have followed those tiny slivers of Xavier, no doubt hoping to get them transferred to his own head.

I think it is possible. He must have spent centuries with him. If he has followed Sergey here, it is because of those slivers. He is the true power, Julija, not Anatolie. I am not dismissing your father. He is a dangerous man, but if he fears Barnabas, then we should fear him as well.

I definitely am afraid of Barnabas.

Isai felt the shiver that ran through her body. He wasn't there to hold her or to comfort her, and she needed both. *You are no longer alone, sívamet. You are with me, and I stand with you against this monster.*

Monster. It was an apt word to describe a being such as Barnabas. Anyone who would trick a woman and then cruelly hurt her over and over was more than a monster. Anyone who would experiment with something so deadly as the mutated bats was a monster. There were so many in the world doing all kinds of harm to others to further their own agendas.

Barnabas thought himself unstoppable. He had gotten away with so much throughout the centuries that he'd gotten complacent. Always before he had stayed behind the scenes. Now, he was stepping out of the shadows and letting others see him. Maybe only glimpses, but those were enough for a hunter to lock on to him.

I do not think Sergey is here, Julija. I am uncertain if he hasn't gotten wind that the book is in the United States, or if he sent Barnabas thinking he would return with it.

Isai could feel Julija turning that possibility over and over in her mind. While she puzzled it out, he turned his attention to Mike and Josh. The first thing he did was remove all evidence that they'd been in any kind of battle. Their tents were in shreds, and he repaired them. Their bodies were bloody from hundreds of bites. He healed those. He took much-needed blood from both of them but was careful not to take too much since both had lost some. He laid each in his own sleeping bag and tent and removed every memory of the battle, the bats and him.

Isai, if Barnabas is hunting for the book, and he is the man you believe was in Xavier's caves centuries ago, then he would know more than any other about that book. He might be able to either bring Xavier back using the slivers of him, or take them from Sergey.

Did you feel his power, or did he mask it?

At first, he definitely masked it, she assured. *He seemed a sweet professor and kind of lonely. I never saw him with anyone in spite of his reputation with women.*

That fit. Barnabas would never trust anyone enough to spend time with them.

What about later? When he was hurting you?

Not in class. He was very steady, distant, as if nothing taking place affected him in the least. It was only when we were alone that he showed power and that he thoroughly enjoyed hurting me. He would show me videos of the things he did to me in front of everyone and he would watch my face the entire time. He didn't show those things to others and that scared me almost as much as the ways he caused me pain.

She was trembling so hard he feared she would break apart. He needed to scan the entire area for signs of the master vampire just to make certain his line of reasoning was solid. When he was fairly certain there was not a single indicator that Sergey was in the area, he searched, without much hope, for the high mage. He also needed to get back to his woman.

Do what you have to do, Isai. You have to protect any humans in the area.

And we need to know who we're dealing with. Sergey? Anatolie? Barnabas? Or all of them.

He wanted to know more about her encounters with Barnabas, but he didn't want to push her. He had the feeling he was dealing with a true dark high mage. Perhaps the most powerful since the demise of Xavier. If that was the case, the more he knew, the better. And why had he fixated on Julija? He'd taken Crina as a lover. It looked as if Anatolie knew and didn't mind, which stood to reason if Anatolie and Barnabas went way back. Anatolie would concede anything to his mentor. Why had Barnabas taken Crina as a lover if Julija was important to him?

Isai. She breathed his name softly into his mind. *Barnabas didn't love me. He didn't care about me. I was just someone he derived enjoyment from torturing.*

Isai wanted to believe that, but he didn't. He couldn't. There was something in Barnabas's expression when he'd looked at Julija in Anatolie's study that made him think Julija was important to the mage. Whatever feelings he had for her were twisted, but the emotions were there. Isai hadn't been able to feel for centuries. He couldn't see another woman now that he'd seen Julija.

Do mages lose feeling? Color? In the way Carpathian hunters lose them?

He checked the human campers one last time to ensure nothing was out of place. The event was too traumatic to be wiped completely, so Isai removed their memories, but replaced them with similar nightmares. He made certain it appeared as if Josh woke first and told Mike his nightmare and then Mike had dreamt a related scenario. To be safe, he planted the idea that both wanted to leave first thing in the morning. Once he was certain they wouldn't remember him or the bats as anything but a dream, he took to the sky.

No, but we do not live as long as Carpathians.

What of those feeding on Carpathian blood, such as your father?

That is different. He is following in Xavier's footsteps. He believes himself to be invincible, just as Xavier did.

Barnabas fed on you. The thought sickened him. *It is impossible to tell*

the age of a Carpathian. A human seeing us would think we were quite young,
when in fact we are not. Barnabas does not look a day over forty, if that.

His appearance can change. He is a master of illusion.

Isai took his time moving from one area to the next, searching for the
smallest sign that would betray a vampire. He quartered the large region
around the lake and up into the mountains. A vampire's presence could
be felt by a hunter, especially if that hunter was as old and as experienced
as Isai.

Barnabas has been feeding on Carpathian blood, Julija. You are not the
first. That is evident to me, but he did in fact look at you differently. Still, he
took Crina to his bed.

Not exactly his bed, she corrected.

What bed, then? She was his lover.

They were always in Anatolie's bed. Once, Crina came to my room and told
me they needed it and Barnabas slapped her. Hard. He told her only he decided
where or when. He pushed her away and came at me. I was terrified.

He wanted to see the memory. How could he ask her to bring it up in
vivid detail? There was just something so significant about the way Barnabas looked at Julija and he was missing it.

Can you tell me about the dates you went on with him? You said you spent
time together before he began hurting you.

Isai turned to make his way back to the cave. Back to Julija.

We just went to coffee shops, that sort of thing. We talked every night. We
laughed a lot. He didn't try to seduce me. He was very sweet.

Can you show me those memories? Again, he was hesitant to ask.

She wasn't in the least bit tentative. At once he saw Barnabas seated
across a table from Julija. All around them were humans, reading, talking
quietly or ordering coffee. Barnabas sat with his gaze fixed on Julija. He
was so focused, he didn't appear to notice anything or any other person in
the shop. Twice the waitress tried for his attention but failed. He didn't
look up. Not once.

Isai didn't think it was contrived. For the first time in his existence,
probably, Barnabas had been intrigued by his prey. And Julija had been
prey to him. The mage had set the stage and begun the biggest illusion of

all and he'd trapped her. Isai could see why. Barnabas was utterly fascinated by her. He enjoyed the conversations they had. She wasn't trying to impress him. She simply was offering a friendship with no strings. She had no idea she was being groomed by a cruel monster.

Often, you are laughing, but there are times when the conversation turns very serious and you go very still. He does most of the talking and he often touches your hand, almost as if he is reassuring you. What are you discussing?

Sadism and masochism. They were a big part of his class. At first, in class, it was a very intellectual discussion. He said they weren't even called that anymore by any of the top psychiatrists, but that because we would have a better understanding of the two terms and what they might mean to individuals, he preferred to continue using them.

Here, in the shop, when it was just the two of you, what was he telling you? He clearly is reassuring you about something.

He confessed to me that he was a sadist and that because of that, he was ultimately very lonely. No woman would ever want him for a life partner. I felt terrible for him. I told him I didn't understand how he could want to hurt someone, how that would arouse him, but that didn't make me like him any less. In all honesty, I didn't know how I felt about his admission. Mostly, I think I didn't fully comprehend what he was saying, that it could be the truth.

Isai allowed the frame to move forward, paying close attention to Barnabas's expression. He seemed to be totally wrapped up in every word Julija said, her expression. The way she parted her lips, the sweep of her lashes. The man might be the best at illusion, but he couldn't fake something like that. Not without her feeling it. Julija was too sensitive. She was far more Carpathian than any of them realized—including her.

What did he say?

He thanked me and then said he didn't know if he was born so flawed or if someone had shaped him into that being. He also said that he could teach others to enjoy pain, to crave it and that in the end they became so devoted to him that they were worthless to him. Again, I said I didn't really understand. That if he needed to inflict pain, and he found someone who liked pain, then wasn't that the perfect combination. I was a little shocked when he said no.

Isai could see by her expression that she had been shocked. She'd showed it openly. She'd also looked so compassionate that Barnabas had actually moved closer to her, taking in her sympathy, consuming her energy just as a vampire might take her blood. He'd been devouring her. And she was addictive. Isai knew. Just being in her presence gave those around her an element of whatever they needed. She had some way of providing for others and Barnabas had discovered that well. Sitting there, in that coffee shop, he'd been bathing in her aura.

It was after this particular conversation that you woke up needing sex. He made it a statement. This was the defining moment, he was certain of it. He could see that Barnabas not only wanted to seduce her but was hoping she would be the one he could keep—that she wouldn't break. She would never crave the pain he needed to give to his lover. No doubt the man went through multiple women, training them to like what he dished out, but Julija had never given in to him. No matter what he'd done to her, she hadn't broken. That had been her downfall. Had she acted as if she was enamored with him, that she had to crawl back to him, he would have left her alone. He had known, right then in that coffee shop, that Julija would be resistant to him. He had made up his mind to have her.

Isai let go of the memory and made one last pass around the lake just to ensure he was right in his estimation that Sergey was nowhere close. Barnabas was their ultimate enemy. Whether or not he called in Sergey for aid was yet to be seen, but at the moment, the master vampire was not close, nor was there evidence of any vampire in the area.

He started back to his woman. His brave woman. She had no idea just how amazing she really was.

Did that help?

The way Julija touched his mind was so feminine. Soft. Pouring into him intimately until he felt her in every part of his body. There in his mind, she stroked gentle fingers over every violent memory, every ugly one, lessening the impact of remembering the many fallen warriors, men he had respected, that he had been forced to destroy. She kept the crouching enemy from swallowing him. What could someone with her light do for Barnabas?

I know Barnabas took your blood. Did you ever take his for any reason?

Yes. There was an accident at the school. In class. I bled severely, and he was worried. He insisted I take his blood. He had a first-aid kit and we were alone. He was trying to help, and I didn't think anything about it. Why?

Did you speak telepathically to Barnabas?

Again, there was that small silence while she thought about the question, not for an answer, but to try to find where he was going with the query. She wasn't trying to keep anything from him, there would be no reason to. He found the ledge and the small crack, immediately opening it to allow moonlight into the small chamber.

Julija waited for him, pacing across the floor, her face lighting up when he came into the cave. She threw her arms around him and he pulled her in tight against him, bathing in her pure energy. He allowed himself to feel the difference she made. He had been in a battle, had fought off the bats and destroyed a mage. Ordinarily, he wouldn't have felt any emotion, or even the exhaustion of his body, but he wanted to know what Julija did to him when he was close to her. Now he knew. He instantly felt rejuvenated. There was joy and he hadn't kissed her. He'd done little more than gotten close to her.

Julija had a special light to her. It shone brightly on those around her. Barnabas had recognized that she had it and he'd bathed himself in it. He craved it. He had made up his mind to have her permanently right there in that coffee shop, for this very reason. The way she could make him feel without even trying. Imagine if she was giving him more.

16

Julija looked up at Isai's face. There was strain there. He was covered in bites from the bats. Great chunks of his flesh had been torn from his body. He had healed the wounds of the two campers but hadn't considered stopping long enough to heal his own. He'd addressed the worst of the bleeding, but his clothes were tattered and his body ripped open, in some places almost to the bone.

"Sit down, Isai. Let me take care of you." She guided him to the chair he'd left for her. He was always remembering her comfort, cognizant of her being raised in what amounted to a human environment.

"You did not answer me. Did you speak telepathically to Barnabas?"

"Yes. Now sit down." She all but pushed him into the chair. Her hands moved over him looking for more damage. "Are you hurt anywhere else?"

He waved his hand, dismissing the damage done to him. "It is nothing, little mage. I am fine. The two campers were chewed up, but I was impressed with them. Both fought valiantly in spite of the fact that the bats were particularly vicious and neither had ever encountered anything remotely close to them. I was very happy I was able to save them."

Julija was happy as well. She had felt his anxiety over the two campers regardless of his ability to feel it or not. Isai didn't acknowledge his emotions, particularly when he was going into battle. She knew that was centuries-old training and the fact that he hadn't felt emotions in those centuries. In many ways she was happy about it. She knew it would be much more difficult for him to carry fear, anger and sorrow onto the battlefield.

I call to the power of fire and water,
Combine your elements to provide me with steaming water.
As I wash through gashes, cuts and wounds,
Help me to purge contamination's doom.

She made certain she removed every bit of blood from his wounds, but she didn't like the way they looked. She frowned and touched one particularly ugly bite. "Do these things have venom in their teeth or claws?"

"Yes. I will deal with that, Julija." He made as if to stand.

She put a restraining hand on his chest. "I am your lifemate," she said as a reprimand, but her voice came out differently than she intended. She sounded sultry, sexy, a husky reminder that they were everything together—that she was his lover. "I'll take care of you." It was her right, whether he liked it or not.

Placing one hand on his chest, she closed her eyes and visualized the poison spreading through his body through the various open lacerations.

That which is poison flowing through vein,
I call to your essence, so none shall remain.
Come to my call, reversing your flow.
Exit this body so healing may grow.

At once the venom responded to her call, reversing the journey to his heart to drip from the open wounds. She immediately washed the dark liquid from his body, making certain that not one single drop remained. She visualized a second time, one hand over his heart to feel if a single vein or artery carried a drop of the venom in it. When she was sure she had managed to get it all, she closed the wounds.

Needle to thread, stitch and sew,
Mending torn flesh so none may know.
That which was damaged, return it to health
So the body gains strength to renew itself.

Next was his clothing, although she was tempted to just remove it all, especially since now he sat back and smiled at her, like a king waiting for his servants to see to his every need. In truth, she didn't mind being his servant. She liked taking care of him. "Stop smiling." She couldn't keep the teasing note out of her voice.

"I like looking at you."

"You're ridiculous. You come home all chewed up by some venomous nasty creatures and you don't think a thing about what those wounds and poison are doing to your body. If I did something like that . . ."

He reached around her and rubbed her bottom. His touch was far too intimate and sent waves of heat rushing through her veins. "I might have to warm this extraordinary part of your anatomy," he teased.

"You're obsessed."

"I am," he agreed, his expression sobering. "And addicted to you. Being with you makes me feel better. It strengthens me. Having you talk to me intimately, your mind in mine, opens up something in me that is hard to explain."

She looked down at him for a long time, her heart suddenly accelerating. He was talking about himself and yet he wasn't. She took a deep breath. "You're talking about Barnabas, too, aren't you?"

Julija couldn't help herself, she switched her attention from his amazing blue gaze to his wide chest with the heavy, defined muscles. Her palm swept down his perfect skin. She'd managed to make his body once more pure perfection. She wanted to fill her mind with that image, not think about Barnabas. She detested thinking about him. Every time she did, she felt ill.

Isai framed her face with his hands. "*Sívamet*, look at me."

His voice turned her inside out. She couldn't. She tried not to feel guilty, but to her, talking so intimately was wrapped up in her feelings for Isai. She felt as if she had betrayed him on some level by ever giving that to Barnabas. She might not have thought that way at the time, she didn't know Isai or how intense her feelings would be for him, but the guilt was there all the same.

"Julija, look at your man."

There was no denying that compelling voice. So gentle. Tender even. Her heart seemed to turn over. A million butterflies took wing in the pit of her stomach. With extreme reluctance, she raised her gaze to his.

The moment her eyes met his, the moment she saw the way he looked at her, every negative emotion melted away. Isai didn't attempt to hide his feelings for her, that stark, raw love that consumed him. She was his everything and he had no problems showing her that.

"Barnabas can never take anything from us, Julija. He simply cannot. He does not even come into our equation. Distance him so that he is nothing more than a bad memory that we are working to eradicate together. To do that, we have to get ahead of him. Figure out his moves and counter them, much like we would if we were playing chess on a board. He is nothing to worry about. Do you understand what I am saying to you? There is you. And there is me. There is us. Our family." He indicated the cats. "That is enough to worry about."

She wanted to cry. She was a crier, and that was a bit embarrassing since he was so pragmatic about everything. She was emotional. She loved him all the more because he meant every single word. He didn't view Barnabas as a threat. He was an obstacle, but not once had Isai thought in terms of insurmountable. He was an enemy that had to be dealt with.

Julija nodded, tears swimming in her eyes. "I can't believe I almost missed having you. How could I have been so careless?" She stroked the loving lines of his face. "What do you need? What are you looking for?"

"I want to know the reasons Barnabas is so obsessed with you. I think I am onto something, but the more I understand him, the better chance we have of defeating him. He has a master plan, Julija. I can feel it. If he is the same man, Barna, as the mage working under Xavier all those centuries ago, he is a mage to be reckoned with. Anatolie was afraid of him. Crina tried to curry his favor."

"Sometimes when he looked at me, I saw someone else in his eyes." She shivered and rubbed her hands back and forth on her arms for comfort. "Someone very dark and scary."

Isai didn't tell her she was crazy. Instead, he stood and wrapped his arms around her, pulling her into the shelter of his body. His chin found the top of her head and he just held her until the goose bumps receded and warmth spread through her body.

When he stepped away from her, he was fully clothed. "It is possible he has a sliver of Xavier in him. Xavier would have been working on how to possess other bodies. He used the body of his grandson ruthlessly, looking to impregnate women so he could have children of Carpathian blood. He wanted immortality. Another way to find it would have been to put pieces of himself in other bodies."

"I was always taught that weakened one. Anatolie said it was forbidden. Still, I thought he'd tried it on more than one occasion."

Isai nodded. "It does. Your father may even have a splinter of Xavier in him. Who knows how many times Xavier did such a thing before he realized it weakened him? No one had done those types of experiments before. Xavier had to learn as he went along."

"What are we going to do?"

"We need to find the book before there is a chance that Barnabas can get his hands on it. Then we need to destroy it. That is our first goal. Finding a way to destroy it. If we can, then we will chance undoing whatever Iulian has wrought. He believed the book could not be found because he'd hidden it with his blood. Unfortunately for him, I am the last of my bloodline now that he is gone. He didn't know I still lived. He had to have spilled his blood, sacrificing himself to hide it."

"If only you can find it, Isai, why can't we just leave well enough alone? If we can't find it because of Iulian's sacrifice, neither can Barnabas." She knew why. She'd argued with him over it, but now that they were here, and she knew Barnabas was so close, she wanted to run.

"You know he will never stop looking." His voice was gentle. "If we destroy him, Sergey will look for it. One after another will come until it is found. It is best if the book is gone from this earth. This is a place where many people come to view the beauty of the land. We don't want it to become the hunting ground of the vampire."

Julija's heart sank. He was right. The book had to be destroyed. She closed her eyes and when she opened them, she knew he was aware she had an inkling how to get rid of the book.

"Tell me."

She shook her head. "I don't know for certain."

"Tell me." It was a distinct order. A decree. He wasn't going to stop until she did.

"The book was sealed with the blood of every species. Iulian sacrificed his life, using his blood to hide the book. Everything Xavier has ever done has utilized blood in some way or another. He is everything dark and malevolent. So is the book. The spells it contains are ugly, vile and extremely dangerous. To destroy the book, there must be purity of heart and soul."

Isai frowned. "I do not understand. The only creature on this earth that has purity of heart and soul is an infant. Are you suggesting we need the blood of an infant to destroy this monstrous thing?" Everything in Isai rejected the idea. It was wholly repugnant to him.

Despite his being a man who went without expression, Julija had no problem reading his complete refusal of that conclusion. She smiled up at him, she couldn't help it. She loved him all the more for his reaction. Anatolie or Barnabas would have just nodded at the idea of killing an infant for something they wanted, and then immediately gone off to acquire one. Her brothers and Crina would have no problem with the idea of sacrificing an infant. But her man . . . She shaped his face with her palm.

"If we sacrificed an infant, Isai, we would be adding to the bloodthirsty monster the book has become. Of course that is not the way to destroy it."

Relief made him breathe and she realized he had been holding his breath. "I do not know why such a thing even crept into my mind," he said. He tugged at her hair. "Tell me what you think."

"I think we need to decide if we really want to do this thing. Find the book and destroy it. We would have to have it in our hands. It is powerful, Isai, and it will call to the mage in me. I am Xavier's blood. I bear the high mage mark. The moment that book is anywhere near me, the mark will fight to own what is his. We have exchanged blood numerous times. We will exchange more before it is found. I have to give you blood now before we leave this place. In doing so, I give you mage blood as well as Carpathian. Who is to say how that will affect you?"

In a way she was pleading with him. The Carpathian was strong in her. She knew it was. She felt it now in everything she did. But the mage was equally as strong whether he wanted to believe it or not. She held his light. She hoped that light was strong because she knew the call of the book would be extremely powerful, almost irresistible to a member of Xavier's bloodline.

Isai paced away from her, then turned back. "Barnabas knows that you bear the mage mark. He's seen it. Is he aware you also bear the mark of the Dragonseeker? The little dragon that is positioned over your left ovary?"

Julija shook her head, frowning. "No. The dragon fades at times."

"To protect itself. To protect you. Do you realize that throughout the history of Carpathians, no matter the lineage and how strong it is, including that of the prince and his guardians, every bloodline save one has had those turning vampire or succumbing to the madness strain? Only one has been pure. That of the Dragonseeker. The Dragonseeker represents honor and purity, Julija. The dragon warns you when vampires are near. It also protects your greatest treasure. It guards other Dragonseekers, the eggs you carry in your body. *You* are purity, Julija. You are Dragonseeker."

"I cannot possibly have purity of heart and soul, Isai. I am mage and I have all kinds of negative thoughts. I can be petty and want revenge. I would have taken Crina's life had she in any way threatened you when you could not defend yourself."

He stepped close to her, cupping her face with gentle hands, his thumb stroking down the curve of her cheek. "My beloved. You are *hän ku vigyáz sívamet és sielamet.* The actual translation is 'keeper of my heart and soul.' I live in darkness. You live in the light. You always will. There is no way that your mage mark will overcome the mark of the Dragonseeker. It cannot happen. It cannot. The mark of the high mage is not a mark against you. Not every high mage throughout history was like Xavier. His father was not. You are purity and honor, Julija."

She looked up at his face. He believed what he was saying. She wished she could believe it as well, but she knew herself. She'd made so many mistakes. Growing up, when Crina was so mean to her, she'd often taken petty revenge.

When Julija was around the age of ten, after Crina had been particularly mean, beating Julija until she couldn't stand up straight, her stepmother had come out of her own bedroom, that sacred place no one was allowed to go, and when she'd emerged, every inch of her skin had been covered in an ugly yellowish-gray color. Her face had been lined and aged with deep wrinkles. Her hair was thin, white and stringy with bald spots showing through on her bumpy scalp. Julija had cast a spell on the room, asking it to show Crina in her true form, what she should look like if she wasn't greedily gulping Carpathian blood from Julija's wrist continually.

Crina had been hysterical. Completely hysterical. She'd rushed to Anatolie, furious, but no one thought the ten-year-old they didn't believe had much mage in her could possibly have cast such a complicated spell. They hadn't realized at first that the spell was on the bedroom, not on Crina. She would fix herself, and then each time she went to her room, the phenomenon would happen again.

Julija showed her retaliation to Isai, who burst out laughing. He actually leaned down and kissed her.

"You are perfection."

"It wasn't in the least bit nice, Isai," she scolded, trying not to laugh. "I've never felt one iota of remorse." She bit her lip. "Okay, that isn't exactly the truth. Crina cried and cried and I did feel bad, but then she slapped me for looking at her when she looked so horrible and I forgot about feeling sorry for her."

He rubbed his thumb over her cheek. "Purity of heart and soul does not mean you cannot ever feel anger or the need for revenge. You did not consider killing her. Or permanently damaging her."

"Of course not." She frowned at him. "That's not normal, Isai. People don't think about killing others they don't like. It isn't done."

"Anatolie no doubt killed often if someone was in his way. I imagine your brothers did as well."

"I come from a murderous brew, but *most* people do not think of killing. Mages are, I think, for the most part, good people. They stayed away from Anatolie and Crina, and they kept their children from Vasile, Avram and me."

"That must have hurt." He walked her to the entrance. He had widened the crack enough for her to look out and see the night sky. It was scattered with stars and very beautiful.

"It did . . . at first. I learned to accept it and later, when I got older, I realized it was a good thing. Anatolie was a lot like Xavier. He was very driven to experiment and he was always looking for power. He still is. It doesn't matter that the modern world has caught up with us and he lives in it now, even comfortably. He still craves power and is determined to get it."

"Merge with me."

She knew he wanted her to learn from him. To use her Carpathian skills rather than her mage gifts. She did as he asked. He was so fast at everything, visualizing exactly what he wanted and moving almost before it had a chance to happen. In his mind the crack widened to accommodate them and as he pictured it, the fracture in the rock obeyed. The actual operation was so smooth she was shocked at how quickly it was accomplished. She could have done the same thing, but it would have been much slower.

"Both talents have their uses, Julija," he assured. "I love the mage in you. I want you to love that part of you as well, but you need to work on your Carpathian skills and bring them up to the level of your mage abilities."

"I've had a tremendous amount of time to practice my mage skills. I don't think in Carpathian the way you do, Isai."

"Exactly, *sívamet*. In battle, most likely, you will need to think and act

as Carpathian. Had you tried to come up with a spell to give you the ability to fly when you were falling, you would have hit the ground before you
recited it, even in your mind. Visualizing what you need and having it
take place immediately is an asset, *odam wäke emni*."

"What are you calling me now?" she demanded, hands on hips, but
she was looking at the peaceful scene below her. The blue lake, the mountains rising around it. The meadow with the wind creating waves in the
tall, green grass.

"Mistress of illusions," he interpreted immediately. "You knew the
answer. You are learning more and more, taking what you need from my
memories. The more you do that, Julija, those things you see in my experiences will aid you when you need them."

"It feels a little like invading and stealing."

He turned his head to look away from the scenery to meet her gaze.
"That is why, right there, you are Dragonseeker. I am your lifemate. We
share every memory—every experience, good or bad. I have opened my
mind to you because there is no one in this world I trust more than I
do you."

She put her hand on his arm, needing to touch him, to feel close
to him while she expressed her one concern. "You know that Barnabas
and I exchanged blood. I didn't look at it in those terms, but that's what
actually occurred. It was that exchange that allowed us to speak to each
other telepathically. Can he still reach out to me and find me? Speak
to me?"

"Before you went to ground with me, you said you had nightmares.
Those nightmares were of Barnabas."

Julija closed her eyes and leaned into him for comfort. Immediately
his arm swept around her, locking her tight to his tall, powerful frame.
He felt invincible and right then, when she was feeling fragile, she needed
invincible.

"Yes. He was hurting me. Smiling while he did it. Happy to see my
tears and very aroused. It made me sick. I would force myself to wake up."

"He spoke to you."

She heard the grimness in his voice. It was very rare for Isai to take that tone around her. He was always gentle, his voice like velvet stroking her skin.

"Yes," she whispered as realization came to her. "He was reaching out to me, deliberately putting those things in my head, wasn't he? It wasn't so much a nightmare as Barnabas talking to me."

"That is so. He cannot reach you in Carpathian sleep. He will eventually become angry, Julija, and you have to be prepared for that. As soon as he contacts you, and he will, if I am not with you, you must reach for me. We will share the burden whatever he says."

Automatically, she shook her head, rejecting the idea before she could stop herself. "The things he proposes, the things he has done to me are too foul for you to know, to see."

"I have seen them, my little mage. There is no need to try to hide these things. He made them public in his class. He did that to humiliate you, and in that he succeeded. He made you ashamed. He thought that would bring out the darkness in you, but there is no darkness. That was what he never understood. You had no recourse but to attempt to take your life."

"He found me. There was so much blood. I thought it was an offering as I watched it flow out of me. I never had seen him like that before. He was frantic. Shocked. Almost beside himself. He stopped the flow instantly and forced his blood into me. He called for Anatolie and demanded he give me blood. Then my brothers. He held me."

"Julija. It is enough."

He wiped at her face with his thumb, little brushstrokes. She hadn't realized she was crying again. "I'm sorry. I don't know why I'm so emotional. If I watch sad movies I cry." She looked around for the cats. The animals always made her feel better. "They can't kill off an animal in a movie or I completely fall apart."

He laughed softly. "Naturally. You are very softhearted. Something I am not. I can deal with this dark mage, Julija. I know the things he did to you. He should feel shame, never you. He had to tie you to control you. Tie you not only with actual physical chains, but with his mage spells. He didn't ever get you to cooperate. That is your triumph. As I have said, you are Dragonseeker. He cannot steal your light, and that is what he craves, just as Sergey craves the light in Elisabeta."

Her heart jumped. "I never once considered that idea. I hadn't really understood exactly what it was that Sergey wanted from her. I know that he held her prisoner for centuries, but I didn't truly understand the point."

"Sergey had vision. Actually, all the Malinov brothers did, but he thought ahead to those long, empty years and planned for them. Elisabeta was his plan. He took her knowing as long as he could merge with her, he would have access to her light. To her emotions. She would never lose them even when his were long gone. That allowed him to feel. In some ways, she saved him from the worst of being a vampire."

The wind touched her face and she raised it to feel more. It was a cold bite, crisp with the feel of snow on it. "And you think that's what Barnabas saw in me? He feels emotion. When he walked into that room and saw all the blood, he actually went pale, Isai."

"Barnabas no doubt feels emotion. He is mage, not vampire. But he is dark inside. All darkness is a tremendous burden to bear. You took that from him. It appears no one else ever has, and once he found you, he did not want to lose you. How could he? Just as Sergey desperately needs to reacquire Elisabeta to stay sane, Barnabas needs you back as well."

"If they needed us so desperately, why didn't they treat us better?" The cold air helped to clear the sick feeling just talking about Barnabas gave her. She let herself see the beauty again. The depth of that blue, blue lake. The rise of the mountain with the rocks jutting out and the scattering of brush and trees. The meadow with the sea of waving grass, beckoning her to take a walk. To just put down the burden of the dark world that surrounded her and drink in the true beauty of the sights.

"They both believe that fear controls everyone. It would never occur to them that loving can bring loyalty."

She wrapped her arm around his waist. "What do we need to do now?"

"I need to know what you were thinking when you said to destroy the book we need purity of heart and soul. Once we figure out how to destroy it, we will find it and do so. Then we will leave this place and hope Barnabas follows us back to the compound the brethren guard."

She rubbed her palm over the Dragonseeker mark on her left side. Low. Exactly where Isai had said it was. The mark never hid from him. It guarded her eggs, the Dragonseeker eggs, just as he'd said.

"You were reluctant to tell me when it came to your idea for destroying the book. Surely you do not think we would have to have a true blood sacrifice. There would be nothing pure about that, Julija."

She frowned. "No, but there wouldn't be cutting into a child's arm and dripping blood over it, either. And I'm not certain that would be strong enough to destroy the spell Xavier wove around the book."

"You are no child. You are the one. I am certain of it. Everything led you to this point as often happens when there is a call. This is your call."

Julija shook her head, rejecting the idea, but she couldn't quite get what he was saying to leave her mind. It did seem a big coincidence that she had become aware of Anatolie's plan to continue Xavier's work in destroying the Carpathians. She didn't consider herself adventuresome, but she had lain awake for several days, considering what to do, how to warn the prince of the Carpathian people. She was mage. She also carried the birthmark of the high mage on her arm, in plain sight where anyone could see. She was fairly certain she wouldn't be welcomed by the Carpathian prince, but she'd gone anyway.

She sighed and rubbed her lower lip with her thumb. What were the odds that she would connect with a Carpathian male losing his lifemate? That she would gain so much sympathy for him that she was pulled into his life and knew what he was doing? That had never happened before.

If she hadn't left precisely when she had and traveled across the ocean to Romania and then hiked alone into the Carpathian Mountains, she never would have been in the right place at the exact time that Iulian was also traveling to the mountains. What were the odds that they would be so connected that they were traveling to the same place? He was taking his beloved to be buried in what he considered sacred ground. She was trying to warn another species that they weren't safe.

Then there were the shadow cats. She had spotted blood, spots of dark crimson, and she followed those spots back to a small property just on the edge of the hills behind their home. A shed was there, and as she approached it, she recognized a very strong spell that kept everyone away. This was definitely Vasile's work and she unraveled the spell within minutes. She had found the dead, dying and severely injured cats. Immediately her heart went out to them and she came each night to try to heal them. In doing so, she developed an affinity for them and knew when they were on the move.

Once in the Carpathian Mountains, she had known the exact moment when Iulian hadn't followed his lifemate to meet the dawn. She knew when the shadow cat stole the book and Iulian killed the cat and took the book, racing to get out of the Carpathian stronghold. Could all of that really have been complete coincidence, or, like Isai thought, had destiny placed her in the right place with all the knowledge she needed at the right time?

She looked toward the lake. The beautiful shimmering blue water held the most dangerous item in the entire world. Xavier's book of spells. She didn't want Isai to be right. She didn't want to think that the fate of the Carpathian people might rest on her shoulders. She wasn't a heroine by any means. She was terrified, *terrified* of Barnabas. She was afraid of Anatolie, but Barnabas was in another league.

"Where did he come from? Barnabas? The man you think worked with Xavier?"

Isai hesitated, and for the first time she realized they weren't merged together. He also was looking at the lake.

"Isai, no matter how bad something is, if I have to be a part of this, I need to know the worst. I need to know what or who we're facing. I already am very aware Barnabas isn't the professor everyone sees. No one knows that better than me at this point."

"It turns out Xavier was a triplet. He had two brothers, equally as corrupt and dangerous as he was. Not long ago, it came to light that one worked at wiping out the Jaguar species and has all but succeeded. The other worked to wipe out the Lycans. He tried to start a war between Lycans and Carpathians. His name was Xaviero. He was defeated and killed by Dragonseeker women. There seems to be a theme going on here with the Dragonseeker lineage. I think it is very possible that Barnabas is Xaviero's son."

Of course she knew that Xavier had two brothers. She thought them long dead. The rumor had been that Xavier had murdered them, until Xaviero had surfaced and made his try to start that war. Anatolie was furious when it hadn't succeeded. No one had mentioned that either brother had children, but it made sense. For a long time, she had considered that she had been a child of one of the brothers and that was why Anatolie hated her so much. It would make sense that the brothers would want to do what Xavier had done.

She shook her head and looked up at him. He always appeared so confident. So completely at ease with himself and his environment. It didn't matter that they were discussing a very powerful mage who very well could annihilate them and Isai's entire species of people. Isai just looked as if he could take all that on his shoulders. She wasn't like that. The thought of facing Barnabas made her want to curl up in a little hole and cover it so no one would find her.

"I'm not brave like you are, Isai." He might as well know.

He burst out laughing. "I know no one braver. I do not want you to try to take on Barnabas. We just have to find the book. I think we can do that. You know Iulian better than I do, although my blood will call to his. Once you figure out exactly what he did, we can raise that book. Before we do, we just need to figure out how to destroy it." He framed her face with both hands. "Give me your ideas. The first thing that comes into your head."

She forced air into her lungs while she looked into his eyes. Those amazing sapphire eyes. Who had eyes that blue? She turned in his arms and leaned her back against him while she studied the lake. In the night, with the brilliant moon shining down each time the clouds moved, she caught glimpses of that same blue. Deep. A color almost never seen. She was seeing it through Carpathian eyes, giving it the colors she believed it was.

"If you are right about me, and I'm not saying you are, but if so, I think I can't do it by myself. I'm strong, Isai, I know that I am. I've always been aware that I had untapped power in me; no matter how much my family put me down, they couldn't take that away. I even became aware that Crina was afraid of me. That Vasile and Avram became afraid of me over time. The more they feared me, the meaner they got. The more they were ugly to me, the harder I practiced."

"Julija, if you know they feared you, how is it you do not believe in yourself?"

There might have been a gentle reprimand in his voice. How could she explain the wearing down of all self-confidence in spite of trying to understand why they would be afraid if they truly believed she was nothing. Over time, over years, their evaluations had taken their toll and there was no way to explain that to him.

"I will admit that not once did I believe in myself, but I found a strength I didn't know I had, living the way I believed was right in spite of my family tearing me down. I am not, however, good enough to take on Barnabas, especially if he is a high mage's son."

"Again, you will not have to. We just have to concentrate on destroying the book. But, Julija, know this, he may be Xaviero's son and a high mage, but you also carry that mark. It is your birthright. You do not consider yourself a high mage, because your family has made it very clear to you that you are nothing. There are many high mages throughout history that were good, decent people. They tried to use their gifts to better the world, not tear others down. They didn't look at other species with contempt or envy. You fit into that category."

She shook her head, rejecting what he was telling her. She didn't want the title of high mage in spite of carrying the birthmark. She had studied for years, and she was adept, but . . .

"Think about it, *sívamet*. You stole Vasile's magic right out from under his nose. Who else could have done such a thing? Could Avram?"

She remained silent. She doubted if Avram could have done it. Maybe Anatolie, although he had a heavy hand. He wouldn't have worked at removing the layers of magic her brother had so carefully constructed.

"If, and I still am not convinced I am the person you think I am, but if I were capable of destroying the book, I believe we would have to do it together. Your brother used his blood for a good purpose. He sacrificed his life to hide the book. I will know if his intentions were pure when I find the exact location where he took his life, but if that was so, then it is your blood as well as mine that is needed to overcome the dark spells, as well as your brother's. We have to do both."

"I am not willing for you to sacrifice your life," he warned.

"Killing a living, breathing soul would invoke dark magic, Isai, and that is not what we want to do. If we wanted to open the book, we would need a blood sacrifice of each species, but we want to destroy it. I think together we have to give our blood to the book. I honestly don't know how much, but I am going to give this a lot of thought and work out how it can be done. If you're correct and I have purity of soul, and your blood is the same as that of Iulian, who gave the ultimate sacrifice to seal the book in the ground, our combined blood should burn the book. If not, I am out of ideas."

Julija continued to look out over the beautiful scenery, wishing she was walking with him around that lake. She had learned—somewhat—to control her body temperature. It wouldn't matter that it was cold, only that they were together and doing something other than fighting the mages. She just wanted things to be normal. Even if it was only for a few minutes. She didn't want to think about dark spells and evil books and monsters. She just wanted normal, so she could breathe.

"I often think of Elisabeta and wonder how she managed to live all those years without going insane. She has to be so strong."

Isai turned her back into his arms, holding her close to his body. His chin rubbed along the top of her head, so that her hair was caught in the bristles along his jaw, weaving them together. "You are just as strong, Julija. Never think that you're not. You have endured the murderous relatives you have and yet you have come to me pure of heart and soul. That, in itself, is a miracle."

She wasn't going to argue with him. She knew how close she'd been on more than one occasion, wanting to end what appeared to be a hopeless situation. More than once, she'd left and always, Anatolie had found her and brought her back.

She frowned, pushing against his chest with both palms to create space so she could look up at him. "The times I left home to get away from them all, no matter where I went, Anatolie could find me. Blood calls to blood. He knows where I am. He's waiting for me to find the book."

"Julija." His voice was calm. Steady. As soft as velvet stroking over her skin. Her senses. Soothing her. "We knew he was following you. Your brothers made their move too fast. They conspired to get the book for themselves and wanted control of you. Crina made her move, most likely because Barnabas threw her out. She was nothing to him and she had to have known that. Anatolie is wiser. He believes you can find the book. Once you do, he intends to take it from you."

There was no change of expression on his face. Nothing to indicate that he was worried about the outcome of doing battle with her father. He was a strong, ancient warrior and he'd seen countless battles against any number of foes. This, to him, was just one more.

"I'm glad I have you with me," she whispered, and went up on her toes to kiss him.

17

I sai had time to find the perfect place to go to ground. It was beautiful beyond comprehension, a lost world. When the earth had exploded, and lava had run in rivers and then earthquakes had followed, the phenomenon had created a deep crater inside one of the tallest mountains. The hole that allowed one to peek into the world was very small, one that could easily be overlooked and so far, no climbers or hikers had discovered the eye that would have shown them the entire little ecosystem existing in that rocky bluff.

The rock itself was quite thick, covered with larger boulders and strange jagged-shaped protrusions, as if the rock were rising toward the skies with fingers. If one looked closely, the outcropping looked like a giant hand. Most tourists took pictures of that and ignored the ground that was under their feet. That ground was riddled with a dozen holes, tiny pinpoints that allowed light to shine into the empty space below.

Over time dirt and seed had fallen into the cavern below. Water trickled in from the southern wall. There was no crack to give the cavern away. Isai wouldn't have found it if not for Blue and his avid curiosity. The cat kept pawing at the dirt and uncovered one of the larger peepholes. The crack was there, running on top of the rock, rather than on the side. That was unusual. Isai had instantly investigated and discovered the small little paradise beneath.

It wasn't unusual to find trees and brush in some of the larger caverns, especially the ones with plenty of water and a way to get sun. This was very small on the scale of the ones he'd seen in his lifetime, but he'd take it. Julija needed to feel safe. For just a few hours she needed to have a place to sleep and relax. He wanted time with the cats, so all of them could build a stronger bond. It was also necessary for the cats to practice adhering to skin without tearing them up. He didn't want a single scratch on Julija, but if she had the cats on her the way Ivory Malinov and her lifemate, Razvan, wore their wolves, they would watch her back and be an asset in any situation.

Carpathians shared information. Ivory and Razvan were notoriously private, but most Carpathians were aware they had a wolf pack that rode on them as tattoos or a fur coat. He doubted if he would do the same—make a coat of panther fur—but the tattoos would be an advantage.

The cavern opened up to three rooms, each going deeper into the mountain. A small stream ran from where the water poured down the wall to the first basin and then over the sides of the rock into the brook. Rocks lined the sides and bottom, so the water tumbled over them, smoothing and rounding them into shiny pebbles.

"This is really pretty, Isai."

He watched her as she made a little circuit of the sanctuary he'd found for them. There was a note of happiness in her voice. He liked that. He even needed it. She'd been broadcasting fear ever since they'd talked about Barnabas and the possibility that he might be Xaviero's son. No, she'd been fearful every time the man's name was mentioned. More fearful even than when talking about Anatolie. She seemed to take Anatolie's cruelty in stride, which gave him pause. If she was that afraid of Barnabas, he had to be a force to be reckoned with.

"It is, isn't it? Blue scratched at the dirt and uncovered a small hole. Above us, the rock has formed a very thick roof. The holes are tiny. I doubt anyone would have realized they go all the way through the rock. The crack was faint, but it was there."

She touched a very green and healthy bush, rubbing the leaves between her finger and thumb in a kind of fascination. The foliage was lush, very dense, and all kinds of wildflowers grew along the slopes. Vines wound their way up the tree trunks. There were nettles with delicate pink and blue flowers.

Isai watched his woman through half-closed eyes, absorbing her. Feeling her. She was beautiful to him. Every movement. He noticed what she touched, the way she smiled down at the two females pacing along beside her. Phaedra and Belle moved with her every step. She could have found them annoying. They were big cats, and they kept getting in her way, but rather than pushing at them or snapping, she laughed softly and ruffled their ears.

"What do you think, girls? Did the boys do us proud?" She swung around to look at him and then flung her arms wide to encompass their little paradise. "I love this, Isai. We could live here."

He found himself smiling just because there was joy on her face. She was living in the moment, something she had probably learned to do for survival. "Yes, we could."

"No neighbors. No family to bug us," she went on. "When we decide to come up for air, we have a beautiful backyard. The Sierras are amazing. So much to explore." She looked around the cave. "I could do a lot with this. Make it a home."

He folded his arms across his chest. She was already turning away again, following the stream into the next chamber.

"*Isai*. Have you seen this? The soil is so rich with minerals. It's a gold mine for Carpathians." She flung herself down into the soft earth, uncaring that she was wearing clothes and getting them dirty. Stretching out her arms and legs, she made an earth angel, instead of a snow angel. He thought it was very appropriate.

"What are you doing?" Amusement crept into his voice.

He leaned one hip against the curving rock wall and watched her. Belle rolled around beside her like a kitten. Phaedra took a few minutes to join her and then, at last, Sable made her way stealthily to them. She stood on the edge of the expanse of soil that was centuries old and had never been touched. The nutrients were still intact, as powerful and potent as possible.

"Don't be such a stodgy old man. I know you're like a million years or something and think you have to be dignified, but no one can see you but me. This is the greatest feeling. Even the cats know." Her eyes were on the cathedral-like ceiling.

On the walls were narrow ledges running around the room like stepping-stones—or bookcases—from the floor to that massive ceiling. Already, Blue had found his way to the top where he could oversee the space and still peer into the first chamber through the open archway.

Isai took a few minutes to pull the designs from Julija's head he'd noticed when he was merged with her. Each time he put a bed or a chair in a room for her, there would be the briefest flash of a memory. That memory seemed to soothe her and yet she never brought it up. He copied the chairs and rug, placing the furniture exactly as he noticed in her memories. The room always appeared to be a sitting room, one that she thought of often.

"You do know you are supposed to have your clothes off. The earth heals and rejuvenates you through your skin." He positioned a third chair, so he could watch her antics with the cats. He sprawled out, legs in front of him, ankles crossed, his arms folded as he watched his woman making her ridiculous shapes in the soil. She made him want to smile every time he looked at her.

"Seriously, Isai? Are you just a little crazy right now? If I was completely naked, I would get dirt in places ladies prefer not to have dirt."

Her snippy tone sent fingers of desire dancing up his thighs. She had lifted her head just inches, her dark eyes meeting his. There was laughter in her dark chocolate gaze—an invitation for him to join in her silly fun. He would have, but just watching her gave him a feeling he'd never had. It was sharp and terrible and wonderful all at the same time. The intensity of his joy—and he identified the emotion as that, even though he'd never known it—was nearly overwhelming. He could sit there forever and just watch her play.

"If you were naked, as you should be, the soil would take away your exhaustion."

"You just want me naked rolling around in the dirt. You're probably one of those weird men who would enjoy mud wrestling."

He raised an eyebrow. "Mud wrestling?"

He couldn't help joining in the fun his own way. He lifted one finger and gently directed air toward her. Just the lightest of touches, unfelt by her. She had exchanged tees for a pale mint green blouse with tiny pearl buttons. It was impractical for where they were, but he hadn't said a word to her because she looked beautiful in it, and she could control the temperature of her body.

She raised up on her elbows. The action emphasized her breasts beneath the mint green fabric. "You don't know what mud wrestling is?" She gave a little pretend shudder. "It is something I would never do."

"And yet you make snow angels in the soil."

The little puffs of wind had done their job. Her blouse slid open, exposing soft skin. She wore a lacy green bra, a little darker than the mint. His body stirred.

"It's *way* different."

There was that snippy tone that kept those fingers dancing over his body, stroking his cock and making him think all kinds of impure thoughts that had nothing whatsoever to do with mud wrestling.

He lifted another finger as Phaedra distracted her, rolling close and pawing at her hair. Julija laughed and rubbed her belly. Her jeans slid open. Julija caught the band with one hand. "What are you doing?" Suspicion edged her voice.

"I am merely watching my woman lose her mind a little bit." He sounded as innocent as possible.

As she sat up, her blouse slid off her shoulders. When she let go of her jeans to catch at the two sides of her blouse, the denim began to slip off her hips. Even the soil beneath her cooperated with him, scooping out just enough room so the material could slide out from under her bottom. Her eyes widened, and she made a desperate grab for her jeans, trying not to laugh as her blouse once more began to slide from her body.

"You can't get the blouse off my arms, silly. Stop being such a guy."

Isai didn't respond. He simply flicked his finger at the blouse as she tried to lift herself to pull the jeans back over her bottom. She paused, noticing his finger flicks, trying to determine what he was doing. Her blouse fell apart at each seam, the separate pieces of material floating off her, dancing to an unfelt breeze. Once off her completely, the blouse mended itself, the pieces going back together, but then the entire thing floated into the other chamber. She watched it go.

"You are totally crazy," she accused.

She lay on the ground, two huge panthers stretched out beside her, in her dark green bra with her jeans halfway to her knees. She looked a completely sensual creature. His entire focus was on her, noting everything about her. The least little detail. The way she continually shoved at her hair told him she was a little nervous. She wasn't afraid of him. He knew his little mage wasn't afraid too much, but it was enough that her emotional reaction to sexual play would heighten her pleasure in the end.

Her laughter was musical. He could only look at her as she threw herself backward in the rich soil, shaking her head and clutching her stomach as if just laughing that much could hurt. His cock hardened more, a savage, relentless ache demanding relief. He was going to have his woman do something about that very soon, but playing was what she needed. Not to think. Not to worry. Just this, a place where she was safe and she could just be her.

Deliberately, to draw her attention, he lifted his hand slightly, just enough so she would see he was still in command and up to something. He flicked at the hooks on her bra; one at a time they opened for him.

She gasped and caught the material, holding it over her breasts, trying to glare accusingly. "What are you doing? You'd better stop, Isai. I'm warning you."

It was going to take some doing to remove her jeans. She had a death grip on the waist band, although they were off her hips now and had settled around her thighs. She kept trying to tug them up with one hand while she held the bra to her with the other.

He flicked wind at her and one side of the bra lifted so that her breast peeked out at him. Full. Round. Her nipple erect and pink. The sight took his breath. He hadn't expected to react to the sight of her body, all that bare skin. His. He loved that she was his.

"Isai!" she wailed, somewhere between laughter and feigned anger. "You'd better stop."

The moment she tried to stop the bra from lifting up, he tugged the jeans down below her knees. For one second, she threw her arms into the air in exasperation. Instantly, the bra floated away, following the blouse into the first chamber. The jeans slipped down to her ankles, one leg sliding off completely.

"Oh no you don't." She sat up again, catching the jeans in a death grip. She tried to pull them back up, but the material wouldn't budge. She looked up until her eyes met his. "What have you done?"

Deliberately, he smirked at her, her breasts drawing his attention as they bounced a little, two perfect spheres that made him all the hungrier for her. His cock screamed for attention, throbbing painfully.

She wore only a pair of lacy dark-green panties. Abandoning the jeans, she put both hands over the underwear, silently daring him to try to take them from her. He first took the jeans, sending the denim into the other chamber, leaving her beautiful legs bare. He loved looking at her and he loved that she liked to play.

Julija shrugged, holding her panties tight. "Fine, you've got the others, but there is no way you'll manage to get these from me."

The way she positioned her arms, pushed her breasts together, it looked almost as though she was offering herself to him. He dropped both hands to his lap and she followed that downward motion suspiciously with her gaze.

He heard the swift intake of her breath and that made him want to smile, but he didn't. Very slowly he unbuttoned the jeans, each movement measured and precise. She didn't take her eyes off him and very slowly she loosened her hold on her underwear. He slipped them down her body and had them to her ankles before she stopped staring at his hands and realized she was going to be entirely naked.

She started laughing again. This time the sound was low and sultry. Sexy. "You can have them."

"Do you surrender to me?"

She regarded him suspiciously, reaching down to try to get the panties off her calves. "I don't know, what does that entail?"

Her panties stayed right where they were. She let go of them and turned her complete attention back to him.

"Everything. You give everything to me. Complete surrender." He used his nonnegotiable voice. He wanted her to concentrate entirely on him—everything else in the world to fall away so she was totally free from worry and fear.

Her lashes fluttered. She swallowed hard and her gaze dropped to the thick shaft he drew out into the open air. His heavy erection pulsed with life. With need. He knew he looked intimidating sitting there. He had pushed the jeans down just enough to release his cock and overheated sac.

"What is total surrender?"

Her voice was soft, trembling. The idea appealed to her, he could see it in her eyes, but she still had trust issues as much as she didn't want them.

"Give yourself to me, Julija. Let yourself go. Think only of me. Of my pleasure. Serve me. Trust that if you do that, I will give you everything." If she did focus so completely on him there would be no room for doubt. For fear. There would be nothing of the outside world in their little new-found paradise.

The tip of her tongue touched her upper lip. "You want me to think only of your pleasure?"

She was a little minx. He could hear speculation in her voice. She wanted it as much as he did, but there was a part of her that feared letting go.

"Julija. This is Isai. Your lifemate. Do you really think I could hurt you?" He brushed his voice with velvet, stroking at the insides of her mind. Shamelessly he did the same to her nipples, teasing them with his mind, nothing else. Concentrating on bringing her the most pleasure possible when he wasn't touching her with hands or mouth.

She gasped, arched her back and brought both hands up to cup her breasts. "Yes then. I surrender."

The moment she agreed, her panties slid completely off her legs, leaving her totally bare. He sent her underwear sailing into the next room. The moment she'd whispered her agreement, every cell in his body had tuned to her.

He closed his fist around his shaft, his thumb smearing the seed dripping in anticipation. "Come here, little mage." His fist squeezed down on his cock, slowly pumping, his eyes on hers, compelling her to obey.

Her gaze jumped to his face then dropped once more to his cock. She looked mesmerized. She was only a few feet away from him, and rather than stand, she knelt up, threw back her hair, waving her hand down her body to ensure she was totally free of all particles of the soil from her hair to her feet.

Isai couldn't take his eyes off her. She looked a dangerous, sensual creature, as wild as any of the shadow cats. Her eyes seemed to burn over him, her breasts swaying temptingly, her sex glistening as she came to him, moving every bit as gracefully as a leopard in the wild. Her body had reacted to his teasing. He could smell her arousal, her spicy call to him.

He spread his legs to allow her to crawl right between his thighs. The chair was at a slightly higher elevation, so when she knelt up, she was at the perfect height. He reached out and tilted her head up, one finger under her chin. "I dream of your lips stretched wide around me. Your hands on my thighs while you suck me off. Draining me while you look at me. When I am supposed to sleep in silence, no thought whatsoever, you are there."

He kept his voice low, watching her face. Watching her elevated breathing, the rise and fall of her breasts. He kept stroking his cock, but this time, he smeared the leaking droplets using his thumb. "Are you hungry for me, little mage? For my seed? My blood? Do you crave me the way I crave you?"

He brought his thumb to her mouth and she automatically opened for him, leaning almost eagerly toward him. He made her reach. Her lips closed around his thumb, tongue stroking slowly, as if she was really savoring his taste. Her eyelids fell to half-mast, a slumberous, sexy look that poured more hot blood into his cock. She was a sensual creature and it showed in every line of her body, every move she made.

This would be her hardest moment. The most difficult thing of all to give was trust. Real trust between two people, especially when one had been so brutally deceived, was always difficult. They had to know absolutely they could depend on each other for anything and through anything.

"I want to chain your breasts." He flicked her left nipple and then rubbed and tugged at her right one. "Put a rein on you to draw you to me when I desire."

Her gaze jumped to his face and her breath hitched. Automatically she shook her head, but he was already stroking her breasts gently, adding the sensation of his mouth on her. She arched a little, her breasts swaying invitingly.

"So beautiful, Julija. So mine. All of you. I can barely comprehend some risings that you really exist." He continued pumping his cock, using a slow, mesmerizing motion.

"What would you do?" Her gaze was back to his cock.

"My desire, remember, *sívamet*. Total surrender. *My* pleasure." More than anything he wanted to give her this freedom. She tried. She wanted it, but it eluded her. She had to take the step. He could only offer. He could only set up the scene for her, but she had to take the necessary step to get there.

"You like me to tease your nipples, don't you?" He whispered the temptation. "Each time I tug like this, or pinch like this, you get wetter. Don't you, Julija? Between your legs. You are hot. So hot. For me. That's all mine. All that hot liquid spice I want pouring down my throat." He took her nipple between his thumb and forefinger, pinching, his mind fully merged with hers, in order to feel when the pleasure rode that fine line before pain. When he found it, he stopped and simply tugged so that she gasped, her face flushing with need.

"I asked you a question, *kessake*." He didn't repeat the question. She'd heard him. She could blush all she wanted, turning her entire body that soft rose. He didn't mind, but he waited for her answer.

She licked her lips, her breath coming in soft, ragged pants. "Yes. I do like you to tease my nipples." Her face flushed that soft rose that he loved.

"And it makes you wet?"

She nodded. "Very."

He smiled at her. "And you will allow me to do whatever pleases me?"

"Yes," she said firmly.

He wanted her to be firm in her answer. In her desires. In the things she wanted for herself. Mostly, he wanted the world to fall away for her so she could have just a few hours, perhaps the entire rest of the night before she gave one more thought to challenging a high mage—one who terrified her.

He shaped what he needed in his mind, and then with one hand, he waved, spreading the jewelry out across his thighs. Each gem sparkled, the sconces he'd lit dancing light over them. The chain was a fine gold, twisted braids, the links so delicate they looked fragile, yet he knew, because he had forged them the way he wanted, that they were strong, just like Julija. Deliberately, he'd made the chain long, so when she wore it, it would loop low, halfway to her belly button.

"It's beautiful," she admitted.

He didn't want to wait, to give her time to be afraid. This was play, not torture. This was to make her feel pleasure, not pain. This was beautiful between the two of them, not something corrupt and ugly that would hurt her in the end. He leaned forward and took her left breast into his mouth. He knew his mouth was scalding hot, and she gasped, confirming it. He suckled, kneading gently, using his tongue. Using the edge of his teeth to tease her.

He brought the clamp to either side of her nipple and adjusted it to the exact pressure he'd used with his finger and thumb. No more. Only pleasure. Again, she gasped and then she was back to her ragged breathing. He repeated the action with the second clamp. The chain swung delicately against her skin, glittering each time the flickering lights reached it.

She looked beautiful kneeling between his thighs, looking up at him, her hair tumbling around her shoulders, wearing nothing but his chain. He thought of it as a chain of love. He loved her so much and he never wanted her to be afraid of anything at all. He wanted her to know he would always take care of her.

"How does that feel, *sívamet*? And be honest with me."

She nodded. Swallowed. "I like it. It feels like your fingers."

It was designed to feel like his fingers. He wanted only pleasure for her. He reached for the chain and tugged gently. She gasped.

"And that?"

"Like fire. So good."

"I need your mouth on me." He did. Right away. If his cock got any harder, he was going to shatter like glass. Just looking at her was sexy. This night was designed for her, but having his woman surrendering everything to him was as erotic as it could get. He hadn't realized he would feel this way.

She cupped his sac, her fingers rolling and tugging gently. She leaned down and licked and then sucked. His fist automatically tightened as his head nearly exploded with sheer pleasure. She spent time lavishing attention on his balls, so that they grew hotter and the seed inside boiled and churned in expectation.

Julija licked up his shaft, from base to crown, her tongue lingering for a minute in that little vee just under the flared head. Without warning her lips stretched over him and she engulfed his cock, taking him into the hot cavern of her mouth. At once her mouth was tight and her tongue danced, driving him wild.

Her hands went to his thighs, just as he'd said he'd dreamt of, leaving him to control how deep and how hard he took her mouth. He'd said this was about her giving him pleasure, but for him, it was about showing her that her trust was well placed. He moved in gently, very carefully. When he took the chain and tugged, he did so with the same care. Wanting her to see that this was love, too. That anytime they came together, it was love.

He found that her mouth could make him lose control if he allowed it. It was wet and hot and tight. She was good at what she was doing, too good, driving him right out of his mind, because for him, she wanted to be good. His pleasure mattered to her. Love rose up. She could have refused. He'd half expected her to. Instead, she knelt at his feet, sexy as all get-out, wearing his jewelry when it had to have scared her to death.

He tugged again to give her that bite of fire, and then he waved the chain away, soothing her nipples at the same time. He bunched her hair in his fist and pulled to get her mouth to release him. If she didn't, he would be sending his seed right down her throat.

"Another minute and it will be too late. I want to be inside you."

Reluctantly, Julija's mouth freed him, but her tongue chased after his cock. With one wave of his hand as he rose, his clothes were gone. He took her to the cool earth right there on her hands and knees, his hand checking to make certain she was ready for him.

She felt hot. Needy. Pushing back against his palm. Hungry for him. He caught his cock and guided it into her, not waiting, just surging inside. Hard. Streaks of fire raced over both of them. He felt it in her mind. She felt it in his. His hands went to her hips, and then he was losing himself in her. In paradise. Taking her to that place with him.

He wrapped her in love. In him. Showing her what she did to him. What she gave him, even as his body declared over and over that he worshiped her.

"More." She'd said it softly enough, but it was a demand. "I'm not fragile, Isai, not with you. Let yourself lose control."

He loved that tone. More, he loved her command. He savored looking at her, that body that was all his. He ran his hand lovingly down her spine, from nape to buttocks. He caught her hips, digging his fingers deep, and did exactly as she asked—he let go. Burying himself in her over and over, a hard, deep driving that was endless.

Her body jolted with every stroke, her breasts swaying. She went down on her elbows, but that just allowed him to get an even better angle. He used his body like a piston, pounding deep, letting the fiery sensations take him. Her breath became ragged and she made little musical noises that bound his heart up in wonder.

"I'm so close," she gasped. "Hurry, Isai, I'm not going to be able to hold on."

"Let go, *sívamet*. Fly for me."

He felt that first ripple running through her and he slid one hand to her belly, wanting to feel as the tsunami overtook her. He kept his mind firmly merged with hers, sharing his own reaction, the way fire began spreading up his legs, gathering force. The magma burning in his balls, churning like a massive storm ready to throw out a comet streaking across the sky.

He let it happen. Welcomed it. His balls tightened as the firestorm took him, spreading through his groin to center in his cock. He thought he couldn't stretch any further, grow any thicker, but her tight channel was scorching hot and squeezing down on him with a silken fist that was stronger than he could have conceived of. Hotter as well.

Isai heard himself call her name as he emptied himself in her, sharing the ecstasy with her. *You did this. You gave this to me, Julija. Your surrender, your selflessness. Thank you for loving and trusting me enough.*

Her body surrounded his, her orgasm biting deep, clamping down on his cock, wringing every last drop from him. He collapsed over her as she went all the way to the floor of the chamber. At the last moment, he managed to place a thick mat of grass beneath her. They lay together, their hearts pounding. He felt that same out-of-control rhythm in his cock, as it jerked and throbbed to the beat of their hearts.

It took minutes, or maybe hours, who knew the passing of time, before he had the energy to lift his head and spread kisses down her back. "You are so brave," he murmured, meaning it. "So very brave."

"If I could breathe, I'd tell you I love you."

He smiled against her back. She always managed to make him want to laugh. His woman. He rubbed his face along the sweet curve of her lower back, seeing the way her fair skin reddened when his bristles came into close contact.

"We could just lie right here, Isai. Not move. If the sun comes, we'll just fry together."

He frowned and rolled off her. "But you do not actually burn, Julija, and you have been Carpathian all along. You did not have to go through the conversion."

"I burn." She rolled over onto her back and regarded him steadily. He sat facing her, trying to figure out the puzzle that was Julija. "I've always burned. I learned to wear long sleeves all the time and a hat to shade my face. I wear sunglasses all the time and heavy-duty sunscreen. You won't ever see me tanning on the beach."

"Getting a sunburn and actually burning in the sun are two different things, *kessake*." He called her a cat—she reminded him of one with her lazy way of stretching and then curling back in on herself. "If I were to stay in the sun, it would kill me. I am an ancient and it has become much more difficult to wake early or go to ground late."

Julija glanced around the chamber. "You thought we would both sleep in the ground." She made it a statement.

"We did the other night."

"No, I lay in the soil because it felt good, but I didn't bury myself deep. I didn't cover my face. I wouldn't like that at all, and I don't need to do it."

He reached out and gently shackled her ankle, his thumb sliding up and down her skin. "Uh-oh. I believe we are about to have our first real fight," he said gently. Sadly. Watching her closely.

She sat up as well, but she didn't pull her leg away. "There's no need to have a fight. We can do what we did together the other night. We were close, but I didn't have to feel as if I was being buried alive."

She put one hand to her throat and then, noticing that he was watching her carefully, stroked it as if that had been her intention all along. He wasn't buying it.

"Julija, were you ever buried alive? Did someone do that to you?"

He expected her to say Barnabas. He already had the man so entrenched in his mind, he was so absolutely certain, that when she replied, he at first didn't comprehend.

"My father. Anatolie. He buried me several times." Her voice was very low, and she looked around the chamber as if she expected him to leap out at her from behind a rock.

Isai sat in silence trying to digest that. What father would be so cruel to his daughter? "Was it a punishment? What crime did you commit that your father would do such a terrible thing?"

She shook her head. Shivering. Wrapping her arms around herself for comfort. Immediately, Isai waved his hand to clothe her in a warm robe.

Gathering her into his arms, he sat in the chair again, this time with his woman cuddled on his lap.

"When I was very young, he wanted to see how much Carpathian I had in me. I remember her crying. Trying to tell him not to do it. She whispered to me all night. Told me to be brave, that she was proud of me."

"She?" he prompted.

"My birth mother. Francise. I don't remember much about her, although I try to hold on to her, but I was so young when she died."

"You said more than once?" He had to know. How could any man do such a thing to a child? He didn't ask how old she'd been, but he knew, from what she'd told him, that her mother had died when she was very young.

"The second time I was twelve and had gotten my period. Carpathian women don't have periods. Not like we do."

"We? Julija, you are Carpathian."

"I'm both. And mage women have periods, so when mine showed up, Anatolie was furious." She pushed deeper into his chest, nuzzling with her cheek. "He talked to Crina and she convinced him he needed to be sure."

Isai wanted to swear, but what was the use? That time she'd had no mother to whisper to her as she'd lain beneath the earth.

"It was the most terrifying night of my life. I thought a million times that I was going to suffocate. I could feel my air closing off, and I just don't think I can do that again."

"The third time? Was Barnabas involved?" He was just so certain. The man was cruel. He liked hurting things. Xaviero had been crueler than any other mage ever recorded. If Barnabas was his son, trained in his ways from childhood, there was a good chance that he was equally as cruel.

"He objected strenuously when Anatolie told him he was going to test me again. I don't remember how old I was at that point, but years had gone by. Barnabas left angry and threatened retaliation if I was harmed. It felt strange to have him stand up for me and, more, to threaten revenge. In any case, I was able to get through the night, but I didn't like it."

He heard in her voice the struggle she'd had with sanity, but he didn't question her further, wondering why Barnabas had passed up his chance to be cruel. "Was that before you knew he was involved in a cruel hoax on you?"

"Yes. When I first started attending his classes. Anatolie told him I was Carpathian but when he fed, he said he didn't believe it. My blood wasn't . . . intoxicating or powerful enough."

There it was. Barnabas had deliberately sneered at blood that was both those things as well as compelling. There had never been a doubt in his mind that Julija was Carpathian, but he'd wanted to appear to her as a man who would stand up to her father. She still didn't get that he had been the instigator, deliberately questioning so Anatolie would put her in the ground.

Isai didn't enlighten her. It was over with. Barnabas hadn't been showing her kindness at all. He kissed her upturned lips. "Let's get you in the soil, but just like the other night. You will not be buried, Julija."

He opened the earth right over the spot she'd been playing in earlier. Calling the cats to them, he slid down into the cool soil, removing her robe as he did so. Holding her close to him, he waited until all the cats were with them before he covered them with a thick blanket of dirt. All the cats wanted to be pressed close and under the soil. In the end he lay with his head out of the bed of dirt with his woman curled right into him. Only when she fell asleep did he cover himself completely.

18

The wind howled across the lake, carrying the promise of snow. Every gust sent a bitter cold, chasing the needles off the trees. At times the howl turned to shrieks of fury, as if winter herself was angry with waiting. Above, the clouds were heavy and growing darker with each passing hour. Although the moon was full, shining her light was difficult through the gray shadows crossing the night sky.

Julija shivered and moved closer to Isai. "I don't like this weather. It came on too fast."

"It is real, little mage," he assured, curving his arm around her waist. "If it were not, I would have stashed you somewhere safe, even had I been forced to send you to sleep."

She widened her eyes at him, a little shocked, but anger stirred beneath the astonishment. "You can really do that?"

"Yes." He sounded distant, matter-of-fact. Not paying attention to their conversation.

Isai wasn't looking down at her, but out, over the lake. They had to walk around it, circling the entire lake. Finding the exact spot where Iulian had sacrificed his life in order to seal the book to the lake wouldn't be easy. They were counting on the fact that she had a connection with Iulian and would pick up his trail when they came across it, and that Iulian's blood would call to Isai's. If they were wrong, and this hadn't been the last place he'd come, she had no idea what they were going to do. The Sierras were a huge mountain range and finding Iulian's resting place would be impossible.

"I can do that, too," she said.

Isai scanned the rocks around the lake, and then the meadow, his senses and attention on making certain they were safe. That was his job, while hers was to pick up any psychic footprint Iulian had left behind. He was doing a better job than she was, and for some reason, she'd woken up annoyed. She sighed. Not annoyed. That wasn't the truth. She rubbed her palm over the mark of the dragon. She should have told him everything she believed. It sounded ridiculous, even to her, but the thoughts kept coming into her head and she couldn't keep them out. It was a good thing she didn't have his full attention.

"You have my full attention," Isai said, still not looking at her. He slid his hand down her hip to cover the hand over the mark of the Dragon-seeker on her body. "And you cannot put me to sleep, even with your mage spells, *sívamet*. Not unless I give my consent."

"Why would you think that?" she challenged, more because she didn't want to think too much about why she was so disgruntled and out of sorts.

He pressed his hand over hers and then moved it up to cover her womb. Her heart jumped, and she looked up at him. His eyes met hers, sapphire blue, deeper than any color she'd ever seen. His eyes held knowledge, too much. She had to look away, feeling the inevitable burn of tears. She wasn't going to cry in front of him. Not again. Not when it seemed to her that in every crisis, that was her first reaction.

"This is not a crisis," he murmured. He curled his fingers around hers, took her hand off her dragon and brought her fingertips to his lips.

She snuck another quick peek at him, her heart pounding so hard it hurt. Once again, he was scanning the entire area around them. Their six shadow cats had spread out under orders from Isai. He was certain they would be attacked the moment they found the book. She didn't feel eyes on them, but that didn't mean there wasn't anyone or anything watching them. She supposed the smart thing to do would be to hang back, let them find the book and then attack.

"Are we going to talk about it?"

"No." Her voice was tight. She couldn't help it. She was turning into one of *those* girls. Needy. Leaning on him. And now she'd trapped him.

"Do you remember how it felt when I put you over my knees and spanked your rather superb bottom?"

There was something in his voice, an equal tightness. She glanced up warily, but he was looking over the lake again.

"Yes." She bit her lip and kept her head down, staring at the icy ground. The blades of grass looked as if they were lined with frost, lending them a silvery appearance. Even though it was cold, and the wind was really kicking up a fuss, it was a beautiful world to be sharing with a man she was falling in love with. Or maybe she was already gone. Completely. Maybe she loved him so much she was afraid they would lose their chance at a life together, because he would never stop doing what he thought was right.

"I suggest that you bring that memory up and revisit it. Let yourself feel it all over again."

"Why would I want to do that?"

"We can re-create it if you would rather."

His voice was so mild she looked up at him sharply. There was nothing mild about his expression. He wore his stone-face. Implacable. Filled with resolve.

"Isai . . ." She started hesitantly. He was upset with her. Isai didn't get upset.

"Trapped me? You do not want to talk about it? You are my lifemate. You were born with the other half of my soul. We are destined to be together. You may not have wanted that fate, but you accepted it. We are tied together and there is no way to break that bond. I knew the first time I made love to you. Not the first time we had sex, but that very first time, when we came together, and I was loving you. You know when. I knew it happened then and I waited for you to say something. Your dragon grew bright and hot. Glowing. I saw him. I felt him. He didn't hide from me because he knew I was your other half. He would never have allowed such a thing to happen with another man."

There was a bite to his voice that made her wince. They walked for a few steps, the pace slow, as if they were two lovers strolling around the lake together. She wore a warm coat, long, with weapons hidden in the inside lining where there were loops to hold them. The hood was warm and covered the back of her neck, the lining made of some material Isai had come up with to shield her from any weapon should they be attacked. She had reinforced that armor with a protection spell.

"Why do you insist on casting me in the worst possible light, Julija?"

Her heart twisted and squeezed down hard. Was there hurt in his voice? "Isai, I don't do that. My insecurities have nothing to do with you. You're like this larger-than-life hero who has come into my life and swept me off my feet. You're perfect, other than that spanking thing." She tried to insert a little humor, but it fell flat. She wasn't feeling humorous. She wanted to cry for herself. For him. For the knowledge that they weren't going to survive this deadly task.

"Everything seems so fated. Like we have no choices. I knew when we talked purity that innocence was involved and, low and behold, I believe absolutely that I'm pregnant. There is an innocent life growing inside me. It hasn't had time to even develop and yet I'm taking it into a conflict that we have little chance of living through. More, I will use my blood, *our* blood, the blood of my unborn child in an attempt to destroy a book that is so vile that I would never want my child on the same continent with it." She had known the moment she realized she was pregnant that it would be a combination of their blood, the child's, hers and Isai's. It was fated. None of them had a way out.

"This is not so. We could turn our backs on our duty."

"You would never do that." She tried not to sound bitter.

"Neither would you."

He turned her to face him, to stand directly in front of him. She realized that tears were running down her face when he brushed at them with his hands.

"Julija, why wouldn't you tell me of your fears instead of jealously guarding them, keeping them from your lifemate? I am your partner. When you are afraid, when you have these kinds of worries, who better to share them with?"

She'd been alone so long, holding things to herself, she almost didn't know how to reach out and share with him. This? This was huge. She wrapped both arms around her body, trying to shield her child. "I don't want this for our child. I don't want either of us to die here. We haven't had a chance at a life together. We have to do this and even if we didn't, Barnabas and Anatolie won't ever let me leave."

"Anatolie might, but you are correct: Barnabas is not going to leave you alone. I know you fear his power, Julija, and you have every reason to do so. I believe you are a match for Anatolie. Barnabas, no. But together, you and me, I believe we are. I feel very strongly about that. Now we have a third. A triangle of power."

"I don't want our child to have been conceived because we need him or her to complete this task. It feels like I did that. Worse, we haven't been together five minutes and already there's a baby coming. Who wants that?" She pressed her fingers to her mouth and to her horror, they were trembling.

"*I* want that, Julija. I hope you want it as well. Neither of us planned for it . . ."

"But we didn't do anything to not make it happen. That was irresponsible of me. Of both of us. I knew I wasn't on birth control. I had been, but the shot wore off and I didn't get back in because . . . well . . . for reasons." She hadn't wanted the doctor to see her with bruises and lacerations from the shadow cats. They hadn't accepted her help easily. If the doctor had told her father, they all would have found out. "That doesn't matter. I should have been careful."

He shook his head. "It would not have mattered how careful you were. You are Carpathian. Your birth control did not prevent you from getting pregnant. In your case, your dragon did. Or maybe both, your Carpathian nature and your dragon. We do not have the exact same concerns as humans. Perhaps mages do, but we do not. A Carpathian's body releases the egg only when it believes it is the right time for that being to come into the world. Sometimes it is only one every fifty years or so. Sometimes longer. A few lucky ones are close together and raised that way. You do not have the control."

She shook her head. No matter what he said, it didn't take away from the fact that their child was barely a thought and yet already he or she would be going into a very dangerous situation. If Anatolie or Barnabas found out she carried a Carpathian child, one fathered by a powerful ancient, they would move heaven and earth to get her back. She knew both would abandon their quest for the book, at least for the moment, in order to secure her. Like Elisabeta, she would become a prisoner.

Isai framed her face with both hands and gently ran his thumbs over her cheeks. "Like Elisabeta, you have been a prisoner your entire life. You tried not to look at it that way because you had some freedoms, but that was what it amounted to. It will not happen again. They cannot have you. You are free now, Julija. You can soar through the sky or lie with your feet up in a house of your choosing. You will meet many men and women back at Tariq's compound. They will offer you sincere friendships and you will be able to wreak havoc with the other women and laugh about it. Our child will play with their children in a safe environment, well protected from vampires, mages or any other danger. As for me, I want you with every breath I take. Not just your body, but your heart and mind. You bring me joy. This child, *our* child, how could it not bring the same to me? To us?"

"This book . . ." She tried to hold on to fear and distress when he was so matter-of-fact.

"We have a plan to destroy this book. The very fact that you are pregnant only reinforces that we are on the right path. I have absolute confidence that we can destroy it."

"I'm so afraid," she admitted, trying not to let her teeth chatter.

"You should have told me. Come to me when you have these fears. We are meant to face them together."

"If we're wrong about Iulian and this isn't where he was last?"

He shrugged. "Then all along we were not meant to destroy it. We leave fate to find another couple and we return to the compound. Ferro will not wait much longer for Elisabeta, and you need to be there to help her through her transition. It will be very hard on her."

Julija appreciated him understanding about Elisabeta. She had never had such a friend. They hadn't really spent any time in physical form together, it had almost always been telepathically, but the conversations were meaningful, and they told each other almost everything. Elisabeta meant quite a lot to her and Julija had given her word that she would be there to help her when she rose. Of course, at the time, neither knew of the complication that her lifemate would be right there in the same place where they had put her to ground.

Isai brought her in close to him, his arms around her. "You have to get to a place, Julija, where you fully trust me. I think we are there and then you retreat."

She opened her mouth to deny it, but then she snapped it closed. He was right. Her ear was over his heart and she listened to that steady beat. "They wanted a baby from me. A baby whose father was Carpathian. They discussed ways to achieve that goal. I overheard them talking. One of the ways was to deceive me into thinking that any Carpathian male was my lifemate."

Isai rarely reacted to anything, but she felt the difference in him immediately. A kind of raw fury burst through him. He shook with it. Not overtly, but rather beneath his skin where no one would see, but she felt it. That fury ran like a river, very deep in him and anything or anyone caught in it was risking their life.

"I assure you, woman, I am your lifemate. There is no other and there will never be any other. There is no hoax. You are free to examine my mind at any time. I will hold nothing back from you, not even the things I have seen in this life that you should never see. If that is what it takes to convince you I am real, and you belong to me, then that is what we will do."

Julija bit down hard on her lip. She had never seen Isai's cool demeanor so intense, or electric. He meant every word. The sapphire eyes burned into her. Burned deep. She held her breath, thinking flames burned behind that blue.

"We have to be totally in sync, Julija. This entire lake could be a trap. The moment we bring that book to the surface, we will be attacked. We do not know who or how many enemies we will have coming at us. If we are not totally together, if you do not trust me implicitly, we are not going to survive."

Julija looked up at his face. He looked a warrior of old, honed in violence, invincible. She couldn't imagine anything or anyone defeating him—not even Barnabas. Her breath caught in her throat. For a moment she couldn't breathe. Her hand went up defensively, as if she had just committed blasphemy of some sort. She forced her mind away from panic. She'd been having panic attacks far too often and she was letting them get the better of her. Where was this coming from? She refused to think about the lack of air. She was Carpathian and didn't need it. Instead, she turned her attention to her throat. Was there something there? A tendril of something elusive? A wisp weaving in and out of her throat.

She stroked her finger along her pulse thoughtfully, pulling the air from her lungs and forcing it through her mouth and nose.

"Do you think my 'lesson in love' started out in order to make certain if I did, by chance, ever meet you, I would be so afraid I wouldn't accept your claim on me? If Anatolie went to Barnabas first and asked for his help, I think Barnabas would have agreed, maybe for a price, but he would have agreed."

"That is possible, Julija. What are you thinking?"

"When you looked at me just now, I thought that you looked invincible, as if no one could defeat you. The moment I did, my throat started to close, and I recognized the touch of a spell. I think my panic attacks and my belief that Barnabas can't be defeated have been spell-cast. I don't know how or when it happened, or even if it was my father or Barnabas, but it's there."

"How do we remove it?"

That was Isai, back to his pragmatic, logical self. She wanted to throw herself into his arms and hug him. She was already counting on that reasonable, rational, no-nonsense, sometimes annoying attribute in him. Instead she smiled up at him.

"We're in sync, Isai. I may be under some ridiculous spell, but my feelings for you, apparently, are so strong that I am able to catch glimpses of how I really view you—and us—together. I feel so silly for allowing someone else to interfere with what I know is truth about you. Even with a spell on me, there is no excuse. Even though I overheard the ideas about trying to get me pregnant so they had another body with Carpathian blood to use, I know who you are in your heart. I know your mind. I do have enough confidence in myself to know that no one can hide from me forever. I would know Barnabas's taint anywhere now. As many times as we have merged, he could not hide that from me."

"We need to get rid of the spell and make certain there are no others lurking to harm you. Once the book is brought to the surface, we will have to either go to ground with it in a safe location, or destroy it, depending on how much of the night we have."

"Vampires sleep during the day," Julija reminded. "Mages do not."

"Even should they find our resting place, they would not be able to enter. We will have the time we need if we can make it back there."

Julija wasn't going to think that maybe that was far too big of an "if." "If I cast a revealing spell, would you be able to describe to me what you see from inside my throat?"

"Of course."

The wind shifted just the slightest, and Isai stiffened. His blue eyes stared down into hers. "Look only at me, Julija. We have someone watching us. We knew this would happen. I want you to keep looking at me. I'm going to put my arms around you. You are very small in comparison to me and my body will shield you. Reach out very cautiously, masking your energy, and let me know if you recognize our enemy."

Julija went gladly into his arms. She knew she was trembling, remembering that her brothers had come with other mages and those mages carried weapons. Rifles. Bullets that could reach them from great distances.

"They want the book and they cannot find it without us. Keep that in mind. We will learn who our enemy is and then we will rid you of all spells. When you cast the revealing spell, make certain it encompasses your entire body."

He pressed a kiss on her forehead, his arms enfolding her gently. She took a deep breath and let her mind expand. She sent herself seeking into the cold, crisp air. It took a moment to find the trail. It led back toward the campsite where Crina had set up her tent. All along Julija had been so certain Crina and Barnabas had come looking for her, Crina bent on killing Isai for him, but this wasn't Barnabas.

Julija wasn't that surprised. He wasn't going to be that easy for them to find. He had a way of blending in with the surroundings, spreading his energy so he was extremely difficult to find. She wasn't easy to hide from, yet on more than one occasion, Barnabas had come to her without her knowledge.

"It is Anatolie. He is the one who deserted Crina, when we confronted her, not Barnabas. I don't understand any of them, Isai. Why would he encourage her to come and then not protect her? There was no protection spell. Nothing."

"Had there been you would have known."

"They weren't in love, I know that, but she gave him two sons. They lived together for centuries."

"But she was not loyal to him. You said she conspired with her sons to get rid of him."

"She did."

"He had to have known. Anatolie may not have the need for cruelty in the way Barnabas does, but he can be extremely cruel when he does not get his way. Or he wants to punish someone. Anatolie is Xavier's son, and Xavier was very much that way. Cruelty was in his blood, but he did not, for want of a better way to put it, derive sexual pleasure from it. Seeing others suffer might make him happy, especially if he considered them an enemy, but mostly Xavier used torture for information and experiments. His brother, Xaviero, needed to be cruel. By all accounts, he did derive sexual pleasure from watching others suffer. Clearly, his son Barnabas is the same."

She sighed and shook her head. "They have these amazing long lives and yet what do they have to show for them?"

"Anatolie left Crina by herself because he knew you would defeat her or I would. She was of no more use to him and he was not going to take a chance on her getting her hands on the book. It was that simple. Now, he has to wait for you to bring the book out into the open." He caught her face between his hands. "You remember that, my little mage. *You* can do what he cannot. You have always been able to. You were just far younger, and he made certain you had no idea what a little powerhouse you really are."

She found herself smiling. She didn't understand how that could be possible, not under the circumstances, when they were in the midst of unseen enemies, but Isai had a way of making her feel confident in herself. In him. In anything they did.

"Get rid of this pesky spell and any other hold Barnabas may have put on you. Then we can find this book. I am ready to destroy it and take you back to the compound to meet the others. If we are very lucky, my brethren have heeded my call."

"Your call?"

"I sent for them last rising. They are a great distance from here, but I believe one or two will come. I did not tell you because we must count only on each other."

"One or two?" she echoed. "I was thinking an army."

"That is an army."

She laughed and reached up for him. He obliged immediately, leaning down to kiss her. The moment he did, the world was right. He could kiss like sin, but it felt like heaven. There was something so perfect about the way he held her. About the way his mouth moved over hers. It didn't matter if he was gentle or demanding, she felt love. She *felt* it. When he lifted his head and smiled down at her, her heart did a little curious shift.

"You ready to get this done?"

She nodded.

"Stay facing me as if we are still talking. Discussing what to do. Every now and then look toward the lake. I will be doing the same, following your lead. At the same time, I will be able to tell you what your throat looks like and if there are any other places Barnabas has left a command for you."

Julija took a deep cleansing breath and murmured the revealing spell.

Light of life, help me to see,
That which was left behind to do harm to me.

She waited, her heart beating a little too fast. It was never a good thing to have a spell left behind by a high mage. Once entrenched, they could be difficult to remove. She'd been having panic attacks for quite some time.

"I can see small trails of what looks like blue running in tiny streams down your throat. Almost wispy, but definitely blue. The threads are so thin they are barely there, but there are several."

Julija frowned. "Blue? That's odd. What the heck did he use?" She thought about it for a moment. Isai didn't hurry her in the least. She loved him for that. It took a moment to remember to look toward the lake and gesture.

Immediately Isai followed her lead, looking in the direction she indicated, shaking his head and murmuring nonsense to her. "If the lake was not so cold and we did not have such an audience, I would suggest we swim there together. You naked of course."

She burst out laughing. He was wonderful. He had a way of freeing the lock on her brain, allowing her to think. Blue.

Time to remember that which has been forgot,
Show me the way to that which was lost.

It took a moment before she remembered the drink composed of blue flowers. She was certain the poisonous effect was what was blocking her fifth chakra.

Vishhuddha, center of communication, element of Aether, color
    of blue,

Deadly wolfsbane, I call to you.
I seek to reopen that which lies in repose,
Establishing balance to that which can close.
Power of Akasha, remove this blight,
Replacing it with healing light.

"Perfect. No more blue." Isai sounded admiring.

Julija felt much better having removed the high mage's spell. She should have suspected. "Any others?"

"Only the one on your sex."

"Are you going to describe what you see?"

"I am giving that a lot of thought. This particular spell benefits me."

She glared up at him. "I would have thought a man such as yourself would never need such a thing as a spell. In any case, if we really needed one, I could provide it for you."

"You think I need a spell to keep up?"

She pretended to think it over and then nodded slowly. "I fight this particular spell and have gotten rather good at it, but I'm afraid I won't be able to fight my natural attraction to you and you would have no choice but to try to keep up. You'd beg me to put a spell on you."

This time it was Isai who laughed. She loved the sound of it. He sounded as if he didn't have a care in the world.

"There is a continuous circle that runs around your clitoral network. The stream goes from smooth to bumpy—presumably the bumps are what keep stimulating you."

"Is there color?" She held on to his loose jacket, uncaring that she was supposed to be conversing with him.

"Red. Very, very red. Fire-engine red."

"Can you detect any runes running in the stream? They might be disguised as something else, some small movement within the stream of red."

"Yes. They look almost like the stream runs over rocks."

"That bastard actually added in a protection spell. That's why I haven't been able to get rid of it or figure it out. It was hidden, protected and—"

"Julija, beloved, we have an audience. I love to hear you call that man names, but I would much rather remove these spells from your body. The more time we have to find and destroy the book all in one go, the better off we are."

She took another deep cleansing breath.

That which was hidden so long in dark to conceal,
I now seek to reopen, reverse and reveal.
I call to the spirit of fire to trace,
Tracking each root of this evil's embrace.
I command fire to burn each line of this dark,
Removing all traces of evil to charm.
Light to dark, dark to light,
I bring forth that which has been hidden from sight.

"Do you see any more runes? Any little waves like before? We can't miss a single one."

"No, they appear to be gone." His tone dripped with disappointment.

She hid a smile, but she thumped his chest with her fist. She didn't want to get overconfident, but if she could really break Barnabas's spell after all this time, she would be overjoyed. The relief would be tremendous.

Lust, desire, sexual need,
That which runs through my body without thought or heed.
I call to my soul child to help me undo,
These thoughts that were planted to harm and abuse.
I call to the moon mother to join with my spell,
Following the bloodstream, I now cast out and dispel.
Remove from my body this continual need,
So that which remains is only heartfelt needs.

She waited a moment, holding her breath, sending up a silent prayer that it worked. For the first time in as long as she could remember, that terrible need was gone. Really gone. She wanted to dance. Instead, she looked up at him, beaming.

"We did it. Do you know how incredible it is to have actually destroyed a spell that a high mage put on me? I can't believe that we could do that."

"We can do anything. I told you, Julija, you are extraordinary. You should have all the confidence in the world." He stepped back away from her and took her hand, once more gesturing that they continue their loop around the lake. "Hopefully, we find Iulian's psychic print sooner rather than later."

"I was kind of hoping we didn't find it at all," she said truthfully.

He smiled down at the top of her head. "We would leave this place and you know what would happen? You would say to me that we had to return."

She started to protest, but she knew he was right. As much as she didn't want to face Anatolie or Barnabas, she knew the dangers of that book. "When you think about it in terms of being just a book, it seems so ridiculous that it could cause this much worry."

"I had little to do with mages, other than the obligatory training period of spells. Most of what I learned throughout the centuries, I took from those I met along the way. Most of those born mage that I came across were good people as far as I could discern. Later, when they were scattered after it came to light what Xavier was doing, most I heard of were ashamed."

"How did you hear of them?"

"Carpathians shared mage knowledge with me." He shrugged. "Even in the monastery, Fane would come across Carpathians, get all the news and bring it back to us. Other times, a few would come to the monastery looking for a little respite and they would bring news and more information."

"You have a good network."

"We have to. There are not many of us left in this world."

As they neared the lake and once again began to circle it, Julija picked up various energies of campers and hikers, even those on horseback who'd visited the lake. The temperature dropped even more, so that the wind coming off the surface of the lake seemed to bite at their faces.

"I don't think he would have been this close to the road where humans travel. He would have wanted privacy. He was suffering. His grief was so strong, I could barely breathe with it." Julija turned her head to look up at Isai's face. "I find it so strange that Carpathians without their lifemates can't feel, yet I could feel your emotions and his as well."

"I have heard that from some of the other women. I thought, when I first heard it, that those women were gifted in some way, but perhaps we broadcast what we do not feel ourselves."

She kicked at a small pebble. It rolled away from the lake, spun around and came back toward her as if she was a magnet. Her heart took another plunge and a thousand knots seemed to form in her stomach. She pressed her free hand there and tightened her fingers through his.

"Isai." She kept her gaze fixed on the small, rounded rocks lining the path they were taking around the lake. "He's here."

"Of course he is." Isai didn't ask who "he" was. His voice was the same. Steady. Matter-of-fact. Unemotional. "We knew he would come. Anatolie is a very powerful mage and we cannot discount him, but never for one moment forget who our true enemy is. Barnabas is far more dangerous. Because Xavier was the mage before everyone's eyes, he became the greatest enemy of the Carpathian people. Everyone thought he was more dangerous than anything they had faced."

"You don't think he was?"

"How much do you know about the battle that took place quite recently between the Carpathians—specifically four women, three born Dragonseeker and one mated to one—and Xaviero? He tried to start a war between Lycans and Carpathians. His intention was to bring Xavier back. He would have succeeded if those women hadn't been able to stop him. The brethren analyzed all the data, as we often do, and we concluded that it was not Xavier who was the most dangerous. We do not even think it was Xaviero. There is a third brother, Xayvion."

"Yes, of course. Anatolie mentioned him several times."

"He showed himself briefly but disappeared. He was heard calling to

Xaviero, advising him to leave while he could, but Xaviero refused his advice."

"Why do you think Xayvion is the most dangerous?"

"He had nothing to prove. He read the situation and left a battle he could not win. He succeeded in wiping out the Jaguar shifters. Yes, a few remain, but they cannot possibly rebuild their species. He remained in the background, allowing his brothers always to take the forefront, allowing them to think themselves superior. His ego is not what theirs was. He will not be taken down easily."

She was silent for a long time as they continued around the cold, glacier-blue water. "Why do so many people crave power, Isai? Why don't they want families and people to love them?"

"I do not know the answer to that."

She wanted to weep endlessly. Her heart hurt it was so heavy. She pressed a hand to it and took a few more steps, feeling as if she waded through quicksand, and her grief for the world was so severe, so deep, she could hardly go on. She forced herself to put one foot in front of the other when all she wanted to do was sink down and just rest. She needed rest desperately.

"Julija." Isai's voice was extremely gentle. He cupped the side of her face. "You are feeling Iulian. We have found his psychic footprints. Can you manage to follow them?"

She honestly didn't know. His sorrow was overwhelming. Terrible to endure, to feel. She also felt like a voyeur. This was Iulian's private grief and she didn't belong there. In a way, it was his tribute to his lifemate.

Sívamet, he cannot feel as you can. This grief was buried so deep he was unable to tap into it and that was a good thing. He went to her. He told her he would find her in the next realm. I do not know if he bound them together, which is a possibility even without his taking her blood or she his. Once the ritual binding words are said, their souls are tied. You said she couldn't speak. If that is so, he felt no emotion, he saw no colors, but he could find her, and clearly, he always meant to follow her.

She swallowed hard, fighting not to go down to her knees under the weight of Iulian's sorrow and the long centuries of nothingness. Too many when, in the end, he hadn't reached his lifemate in time. She knew the moment Isai intervened, taking the burden from her, but he couldn't shoulder it all, not when she needed to follow Iulian's psychic trail.

He put his arm around her when she stumbled. She had been with Isai long enough to know she couldn't leave him, their connection was too strong, but she hadn't realized until that moment just what he had gone through. He was far older than Iulian and had endured so much longer and so much more. For her. Waiting for her. She turned her face up to his, love for him overwhelming her.

He slipped his arm around her waist. "You are worth every moment of being alone, Julija."

That was humbling beyond words. She gave him a watery smile and forced her attention back to Iulian. "I'm glad he at least saw her before she died. He had that and knew who she was."

"If he bound them together, soul to soul, he will find her," Isai said with great confidence.

That made her feel better. They rounded the next little curve of the lake and she stopped abruptly. They were on a small rise and could see far out onto the lake. The surface rippled madly with the wind, but it didn't matter. She could see Iulian clearly now.

"He stood for a long time, right here, right in this spot, thinking of her. For a few minutes he paced, but he had already made up his mind. He knew what he was going to do and had no hesitation whatsoever about it." She turned her face up to Isai's again. "He had no interest in the book other than to protect Mikhail from attacks and the Carpathian people from the book falling into the wrong hands."

He smiled at her reassurance. "Once I knew he'd found his lifemate, I was certain he would not have wanted the book for his own gain."

"Well, we know for certain."

"We have to have a plan for destroying it as soon as it is in our hands. We will be attacked the moment you bring the book to the surface. It is in the lake, isn't it?"

She looked out over the expanse of water, the wind ruffling the surface, causing choppy waves. "It isn't there, Isai. He considered it. That was his intention, but the lake was too beautiful, and he didn't want to mar it with the ugliness of the book."

He sighed. "I suppose it was never going to be that easy."

"It is close. He chose to end his life here. He sliced his wrist and sat here, allowing his blood to coat the book completely. He had no idea you were alive, or that I could track him through our earlier connection. With his blood sacrifice, that of a good man of honor, he was certain no other could find the book."

"If the book is not in the lake, where did he hide it? Perhaps we could leave it alone."

She shook her head. "Sooner or later, someone would stumble across it. Even if he buried it deep." Isai had told her the exact same thing earlier, and he was right, no matter how much she wanted to walk away from the task. She took a look around her.

"Iulian would be weak from blood loss. He had to have had a plan." Isai looked around as well. What would his brother have devised at the last minute? He wouldn't allow anyone to find his body or the book. The only way to get rid of a body without moving it far was bury it or burn it. He couldn't burn it after he was gone, and the book didn't burn anyway. So what?

"He buried it," both said simultaneously. They looked at each other in agreement.

"He opened the earth and moved down inside, taking the book with him," Isai guessed.

"Deep then," Julija said. "He had to have gone very deep if he thought the wind and rain wouldn't eventually uncover the book." She began to walk in an ever-widening circle around the spot where she knew Iulian had rested and then cut his wrist. There was no trace of his blood anywhere. She knew because his blood would have called to his brother. He had done so in the open earth.

"Do you feel him?" Isai asked.

She stepped right and then left on a narrow track, trying to feel, trying to puzzle out Iulian's way of ridding the world of the book. Then she stepped right on the exact spot. She knew because it was overwhelming as the hunter's last thoughts were of his woman.

She looked up at her man. "Here. He is buried right here."

19

You have to be ready for an all-out war, Julija," Isai warned. "We are very exposed standing here out in the open." He knew what was coming even more than she did. This book had been the thing of controversy for hundreds of years. If they were right, and he feared they were, the mages—particularly Anatolie, Xavier's son, and Barnabas, Xaviero's son—would come at them with everything they had to get possession of the book. Once it was destroyed, they would be furious.

"We have to stand over the exact location in order for me to counter what Iulian did to hide the book," Julija protested. "You have to be here so your blood calls to his."

His heart sank. He had to be prepared for either event. If they were wrong and they couldn't destroy the book, they would have to flee with it. "The moment the book is destroyed, we take to the air in the form of mist." He poured confidence into his voice. "Owls can be shot down. I want you to do what you have to do and then immediately, *immediately*, become mist. I'll blanket the entire area with heavy snow to slow them down. I want you to head back to our sanctuary and wait for me there."

"You can't deal with these mages on your own. Both, *both* are high mage. That means very few could defeat them in a battle. It took four of your most powerful women to defeat Xaviero. They were Dragonseeker and they knew all the mage spells."

Isai knew she was right, but he didn't want her exposed to their enemy. She wasn't the type of woman to obey when there was danger. He could force her obedience . . .

"Don't you dare. Don't you even think about doing that," Julija snapped. "I would never forgive you. It's my right. My choice. You're mine, Isai, and I have the right to fight for you if that is what I choose to do and it is. I will not leave you here alone."

He kept his hand low by his side but sent a command to the clouds by murmuring under his breath and twisting his fingers. The wind picked up just a little, enough to blow leaves and twigs in small little eddies, tiny twisters that danced over the ground around them. Any other time it would have been a beautiful heralding of winter, but tension was growing.

"I have a small knife. I carry it on me just in case. It's a ceremonial knife. I've cleansed and blessed it. No one has ever touched it but me."

He almost asked her why she carried it with her, but something in her voice warned him not to.

"I'll bring the book up and immediately, before either of the two mages realize what we're doing, I'll cut myself and you cut yourself. I can't do it to you, so you're going to have to. I'll say the ritual release words to release the souls from the book. Once they are gone, we should be able to drive the book from this world with our blood."

"How long will it take, Julija?"

Impatience crossed her face, and he realized she was holding it together by a thread. He was used to switching to his hunting mode. He pushed all emotion aside and just got the job done. She felt everything, including terror, knowing her two worst enemies were on standby to kill them.

"You have to be prepared for me to be wrong, Isai. The book can't fall into their hands. That has to be the first priority. If we don't destroy it, you take possession of it."

She was of the high mage's bloodline. The power of the book could be overwhelming to her. "You have the better chance of getting it out of here safely. I can slow them down. Don't shake your head, Isai, I can do that far better than you. I can counter their every spell."

"You cannot just counter, Julija. You are going to have to get aggressive if we are going to get out of here alive."

He could fight them off and give her time to get away, but if she had to defend the book, she was going to have to come into her own and recognize that she was every bit as powerful as either of their enemies. Anatolie and Barnabas were far more experienced, but her blood was both Carpathian and mage, and she had the best of both species. He was ancient and had no doubt that he would kill one or both of them, but it would take time and they would throw everything they had at him. If they were very, very lucky, his brethren would come.

"I understand," she said. She tilted her head and looked him in the eye. "I can do this, Isai. I'm with you all the way. I knew it would come down to this someday. I have always been afraid Barnabas would convince Anatolie to let him have me again. If that happened, I promised myself I would never make that descent into hell again."

He cupped her face in his hands. "You do know that I can find you anywhere. *Anywhere.* I would follow you straight into hell if that was where you were. I'd come for you, Julija, never doubt that."

He kissed her with exquisite tenderness. "My beloved. My little mage. I love you more than I can ever express."

"I love you the same way."

She had stars in her eyes. They were surrounded by her worst enemies and she looked at him as if he was everything. He brushed her lips again. "Are you ready?"

She nodded. "Let's do this."

Facing the lake, Julija took a deep, cleansing breath and closed her eyes to remove one of her senses, better to feel what she needed. The moment she did, Isai kicked the wind up a notch and the clouds above them swirled and groaned with the heavy burden of so much snow. Flakes fell in little flurries, were caught in the wind and carried out over the water.

She lifted her hands toward the lake. Isai knew the two high mages were expecting the book to be buried in the depths of the water, just as they had been. Both men would be concentrating their energies on the lake. He increased the snowfall so that their world turned white as the clouds, burgeoning with snow, finally burst open. He made certain the snow felt entirely natural. It was already there, he just added to the intensity of it.

Blood calls to blood, to that which is unseen.
Syphoning away darkness, so clarity is seen.
I call to the power of the earth below.
Open your arms that I may see what is hidden beneath and
　　　now know.

Isai wrapped Julija in his arms, pulling her back from the earth where it fell in on itself. He hoped that they could only be seen as shadowy figures walking closer to the lake.

The moment the deep grave was open, something stirred at the very bottom of the hole. It appeared indistinct, transparent, shimmering one moment black and the next gray, insubstantial in the ever-moving smoke. The thing tilted its head and looked up at them. The pits that had been eyes took on a fiery glow.

Isai's breath caught in his lungs. "Shadow warrior," he identified softly. Now he knew why his brother's burden had been so intolerable, so heavy. He hadn't just buried the book and chanced that no one would come upon it. He had left himself behind as a guardian. It was a terrible—and wonderful—sacrifice.

"*Stop* admiring him." Already the apparition was standing upright, looking up at them, his body beginning to take form. She patted her thigh hard to clear her mind. "Vapor. Particles. Dust, dirt, whatever is available. Small molecules." She murmured aloud what the shadow warrior was made of. She swallowed hard.

"Hear me now, Iulian. You deserve to rest in peace after all your years of service. Your blood-kin Isai will take over to allow you to go to your lifemate. I am Julija, his lifemate, and I bear the mark of the high mage and the Dragonseeker."

I call on the wind to take this warrior home.
I call on earth and fire to carry him to rest.
I call to the powers of air, circle and clear that which has been shadow
  so long.
I call to the powers of earth, open and provide a resting place for this
  warrior.
I call to the powers of fire, bring back his heart so he may find his
  true love.
I call to the powers of water, may this warrior find peace and balance
  within you.
Air, Earth, Fire, Water, hear me.
Surround this warrior, take him home, give him rest.

The shadow warrior moved between insubstantial gray smoke and what appeared to be a living, breathing Carpathian. His eyes went from a fiery glow to blazing blue, meeting Isai's. Something passed between the brothers and then those eyes went to empty sockets. The wind picked up and blew him apart so that great, long strands of smoke twined with the snow and lay on the ground around them.

Julija staggered and Isai immediately caught her, his gaze on the snow falling in the meadow to their left. The meadow was flat, and already the blades of grass and small bushes were covered with snow. The skies were heavy with flakes, but he could see movement in the distance, completely across the meadow. It was slow, but it was coming steadily toward them.

"Hurry, *sívamet*," he whispered into her ear. "I know you are getting tired, but you must keep going. The moment the book is gone, we can leave this place." He reached for the shadow cats. *Can you see what is coming at us?*

It was always best to keep the images as easy as possible for the creatures, although, he had to admit, they were getting very adept at reading his words and images. Blue especially was adapting fast.

Below them was the book. It sat looking very innocent, deep in the hole. Julija closed her eyes and leaned into Isai for strength. "The pull is tremendous. The call of the book on me." She showed him her arm where the snake coiled around the scorpion hissing, mouth wide and tongue out seeking the powerful energy. The scorpion rattled its claws and the stinger was up and ready.

"They're coming for us," Isai warned, hating to hurry her, not when she needed to gather strength to fight the pull of her mage bloodline.

She nodded. "Be ready. We'll have to do this very fast. I don't know how long I'll be able to fight the need to open it. It's incredibly powerful."

Isai could see tiny blood droplets beading on her forehead. Already her Carpathian blood was at war with her mage blood. "Do it, *beloved*. Rid the world of that thing."

He slipped one arm around her waist, pulling her into him so she had a place to rest, so she knew she wasn't alone in this. All the while his gaze was fixed on the blizzard of swirling white flakes. He added to the whiteout, diminishing his own view, but slowing their enemy more.

He constructed warriors of old, an army of them, and sent them into the night to battle with the entities coming at them. Occasionally, from the outside edges of the oncoming army, bloodcurdling cries could be heard.

He knew the two mages had thrown in together. He could feel both of them in the storm. Their touches were quite different. Anatolie was sophisticated, almost light, constructing a multitude of monsters to come at them. He hadn't differentiated between Isai and Julija. Every one of those creatures shuffling toward them were ordered to kill. He knew because he could feel the powerful need radiating off of them.

Barnabas was completely different. The beasts coming at them held great purpose and were mythical demons from hell. Hellhounds. Why they weren't running toward them, Isai didn't understand. Hellhounds were fast and difficult to kill. He would need arrows and hyssop oil, and a lot of luck. Barnabas was precise, methodical and focused. He had a purpose for his hellhounds and they were totally under his power.

Hellhounds, once unleashed, were ferocious, demonic creatures, difficult to control. Set on a target, they rarely were capable of being pulled back. These hellhounds showed almost frightening restraint.

Julija took a deep breath, drawing his attention. He glanced down at her. She lifted her hands and began to invoke protections.

Fire surround us with a tower of flames,
Holding back that which would do harm or maim.
Water wash clean of all dark magic cast.
Air bring forth your breath with a mighty blast,
Holding back powers from below and the past.
Earth protect us from that which is unseen,
Lying within your realm yet to be redeemed.

"Are you ready, Isai? I've made certain we're as protected as possible, but if something goes wrong and I can't resist its power, you have to take control. Take the book. Leave me if you have to. Get away and hide it."

"You are going to destroy it," he assured. Absolute conviction was in his voice because he believed it. Julija was far stronger than she gave herself credit for.

"We," she corrected. She closed her eyes for a moment and then once again lifted her hands, weaving a complicated pattern.

That which is bound, deep within the earth,
I place forth my hand to you.
I now release your bonds,
Arise and come to me.

At once the book began to float upward toward them. As it did, the snake and scorpion on her arm shook in excitement. "I don't want to touch it, Isai," she cautioned. "You were just thinking of hyssop oil. Coat your hands in it so they don't touch the book. I can hear the wailing of the dead. They might try to retaliate against anyone attempting to wield the book."

He glanced at her sharply. He couldn't hear the cries of those murdered, but she was so sensitive. He could see the little dots of blood on her forehead beginning to trickle down her face. He did as she said, and the moment the book cleared the deep hole and rose into the air, there was a sudden silence. It was brief—too brief. The creatures in the snow coming at them went wild, picking up their pace to run at them.

The air filled with power, clashes of it, whiplike attacks coming from two different directions seeking the book. The book tried to go toward the stream of energy coming from the east. Isai recognized that malevolence as Barnabas. Before the book could be taken, he grabbed it, remembering at the last moment to coat his hands in oil.

Julija didn't hesitate. Her hands went into the air and she once again wove a complicated pattern. The moment she did, the snake hissed its displeasure and sank its teeth into her arm repeatedly. Strike after strike. Bite after bite. The scorpion plunged its stinger viciously into her arm.

Isai wanted to knock the snake and scorpion from her arm, but it was a birthmark, and there was no way to stop its reaction when it knew what she planned.

Julija pulled out the little ceremonial knife. Curling her fingers around the hilt, she cut into her wrist and then she offered the knife to him and he did the same. They immediately allowed the blood to splatter across the book, the two streams mingling together. Julija began to invoke the spell.

Those whose lives were ended by blood, hear my voice.
Be at peace. Return to your resting places.
There are no more fights to fight.
No more fears to face.
Be at peace with yourself.
Now lie at rest.

Now, Isai could hear the wailing of the dead—one from each species sealing the book closed against any unworthy intruders. Only someone of the high mage's line could open the book and only with the blood sacrifices of each of the species.

The head of a large wolf rushed off the cover, teeth filling its jaws, eyes that of a man. He looked around him and then, as if satisfied, the Lycan was gone in the same way the shadow warrior had dissolved. Next was a human. A man of good physical strength, his intelligence showing in his eyes. He nodded to Isai and bowed toward Julija before the shadows tore him apart.

The moment the mage appeared, Isai felt the difference. This being was filled with rage and immediately flew at Julija. He was an insubstantial mass of roiling shadows, spinning and churning, gathering strength. He fastened his hands on her neck and sank his teeth into her to anchor himself.

Isai couldn't let go of the book. Swearing, he tried with one hand to remove the apparition, but his hand just went through it.

Julija surprised him. There was no panicking. "I've got this." Clearly, she had been expecting something like it, although he didn't see how. Mage magic was always complicated because of the twists and turns.

That which is born of darkness, anger and hate,
May the fires of darkness forever seek to purge you.
May your soul seek rest among the lost.
May you forever be judged for the sins you have committed.
I send you back from whence you have come.
May you never walk this plane again.

With a shriek, the mage was torn apart by the wind, spinning away from them until he was nothing but small threads of gray. Those, too, disappeared.

"He volunteered to guard the book. Xavier gave him permission to study all the spells so when Xavier once more brought him from hell, he would be a powerful mage."

"Xavier was never going to do that, was he?" Isai asked.

"Of course not, and he should have known." She turned her attention to the jaguar emerging. He was roped with muscle and had thick dark hair. Faint dark rosettes appeared in his skin. He regarded them suspiciously.

She waved her hand to dismiss him; the jaguar hesitated and then the shadows pulled him apart.

Isai's attention was on the approaching army of creatures coming toward them. They were so close he could feel the heat from the mass. The ground trembled, not liking the unnatural beasts treading over the miles of meadow. He sent a wave through the earth, so that the floor rippled violently, sending anyone in its path to the ground. A roar of rage went up, and then Isai's army of shadow soldiers were clashing with the horrific beasts. It would delay them, but not stop them.

The last guardian of the book was clearly Carpathian. Isai winced inwardly when he saw a boyhood friend. This was a powerful Carpathian and yet he'd been trapped by the mage. That gave Isai warning that he couldn't get arrogant or smug. He thought mages tricksters, using illusion to get their way. Seeing an ancient warrior trapped on the cover of a book was not only shocking but alerted him to the real danger they were facing—two high mages—both from the most powerful bloodline the mages had.

The Carpathian warrior looked Isai over for what seemed forever, those eyes piercing through him, judging him. Then he turned his attention to Julija. She bore his scrutiny, not bowing her head under that intense inspection. Lastly, he looked at the mark on her arm, the vicious stinging and biting taking place. Julija's arm had blood trickling down it and droplets hitting the open grave.

Without warning the warrior leaned down and tasted the blood leaking from her arm. He pulled his head back before the scorpion and snake could attack him. Once more his gaze shifted, so that he was looking out into the night, into the blinding snow. He looked at Isai. *I would help if you have need.*

Julija shook her head. *We cannot accept his offer. That would be selfish. He needs and deserves rest.*

They needed and deserved help, but Isai wasn't going to tell her that. He looked the warrior in the eye. *"Ainaakfél.* Old friend"—Isai's voice was filled with admiration and respect—"you fought a long battle and held on to your honor against all odds. You deserve to rest. *Jonesz arwa-arvoval.* Return with honor."

The Carpathian warrior inclined his head and then was gone. The moment the last of his shadow had been swallowed up by the night, Julija caught Isai's wrist and mingled the stream of his blood with her own once more, sending it over the entire top of the book, using a grid pattern to make certain she dripped their blood from corner to corner.

The scorpion on her arm went into a frenzy, plunging its stinger into her viciously. The snake tried to slide down her arm in an effort to get to her heart, but it was caught by the coils wrapped around the belly of the scorpion and couldn't get loose. It had to be content with feverishly striking at her with its fangs.

In the midst of the hordes coming at them, shrieks of protest, wild wails of rage rose into the air, the sound so ugly it hurt their ears.

Julija ignored all of it. She lifted her hands and once again sketched patterns in the air. She invoked the spell of protection for the two of them, asking for aid to accomplish this difficult task.

I call to light, surround us.
Bring forth your shield, encircle us with your light.
Keeping us safe from that which would do harm.
Provide us with your strength and ability to accomplish our task.
As is above, is below, so mote it be.

She continued, her blood dripping steadily over the book, mingling with Isai's. *It's now or never, Isai. I love you. No matter what, know that you were loved.* Before he could answer, she began her spell.

That which is aged. Old.
Bearing the burden of power untold.
Bound by years of destruction.
I now undo you. May your bindings rot.
May your pages crumble.
May you become dust in the wind.
Forever gone.

Holes began to appear in the cover of the book. At first the cover was dotted with tiny pinpricks, but little by little they began to enlarge. It seemed the process was too slow. The army had nearly reached them. The book shrieked, adding hideous voices of protest to those rushing to stop them from their task.

"When is it safe to go?" he demanded.

"The book has to dissolve."

"Can you touch it now?" She'd managed to put up with her own birthmark attacking her; he figured she was strong enough to endure the pull of the book.

She swallowed hard but nodded, holding out her hands for it. The tome was heavy. He coated both of her trembling hands in hyssop oil and then carefully placed Xavier's spell book into her open palms. As he turned toward the approaching enemy, he saw the holes in the book grow into gaping wounds. Blood poured from the pages. Insects rushed up Julija's arms.

"Sun scorch that book from hell," he snapped and tried to take it from her.

"Just go," she hissed. "Hurry. Keep them off of me until this book has disappeared."

She had no idea tears were running down her face. She looked exhausted. Her arm was chewed up and bloody. Her wrist still dripped blood. She tried to keep her wrist over the book, holding the spine of the book with one hand, but she looked as if she could collapse at any moment.

It was one of the hardest things he'd ever had to do, but he turned back to face their enemy. *Just know, Julija, that you are very loved. You are everything to me. My heart. My soul. And I am prouder of you than I can say.* He poured the truth into her mind, sending her as much strength as he could spare.

She sent him a watery smile and immediately switched her attention back to Xavier's spell book. As he was turning to go, he caught a glimpse of the hand beneath the book, only because the wind had blown the snow onto the ground, covering it completely. Great drops of bright crimson blood fell in globs onto the snow. Her hand was welded to the spine of the book with several sharp hooks that had pierced right through her skin.

"Just keep them off me," she hissed, concentrating on spreading the blood over the cover of the book. She began to whisper softly, as if talking to her birthmark.

I call to snake, you who are of my blood.
Through you I am reborn, transformed.
Heal me. Renew me.
I call to scorpion, whose wisdom runs through my mind, my body.
Rid me of all poisons, protect me from unseen attack.
Guide me as I fight.
Three now become one together. We are whole.

The gaps in the book widened. With every minute growth, more mutant bugs and vile wormlike creatures that snapped sharpened teeth at her as they crawled up her arm emerged. Isai couldn't take it. He turned back to help her. As he did, the scorpion switched allegiances, ceasing to fight Julija's will and suddenly joining with her. The arachnid attacked the worm creatures, stinging them repeatedly. The snake joined in, devouring the insects as they raced up her arm.

"Go," Julija insisted. "They can't reach the book before it is fully destroyed." She couldn't let it go. It had wrapped roots into her hand and wrist, trying to feed off her blood, fighting to stay alive. The fate of his mage and the book were tied together.

Fetid smoke rose in the air as the book tried to fight back. He gave it one last shot of his blood, snared the nape of her neck and kissed her, and then loped off, whistling softly.

Blue. Give me a report. He shared the request with all the cats.

Hellhounds are held in check. Anatolie has sent the shadow warriors to you. We have surrounded them, but there is no way to kill them. There are others mixed in, mage followers he has sent to bring Julija back to him.

The images the cat sent back at first were difficult to decipher. He was getting better at it the more the cats communicated with him.

We are picking the mage followers off one by one.

That explained the occasional bloodcurdling shriek he'd heard. He knew the moment his warriors engaged with the shadow warriors. The night erupted with the sound of metal clashing as swords struck swords or shields.

Do not take any chances. Any of you. Whatever you do, do not get close to the hellhounds or the mages.

All six cats gave a little sniff of disdain, as if his order was ridiculous. Who knew shadow cats could be rebellious? He couldn't think about anything right now but slowing down the approach to Julija.

He moved into the swirling snow, coming up on the first of the combatants. Anatolie had forced the shadow warriors to rise. They were decent men who had been ripped from their resting places and forced to serve the high mage. He had come across them at various times. Fighting them did no good. Nothing stopped them from their appointed task. They could be duped, but not killed.

He had escaped such as these on occasion by tricking them, but their ultimate goal was the recovery of Xavier's book and he couldn't allow them to get the unholy tome. He had been sharing Julija's blood often. If he merged his mind with hers and spoke from that place, was it possible to mislead them again?

As they came close to him, still fighting his mythical warriors, he held up his hand. "Be at peace, shadow warriors."

The moment he spoke, the moment he moved, all eyes found him. Red. Glowing. They looked like snow monsters, yet various shades of gray shadows swirled around them, giving their position away in the world of white as nothing else could. They were silent, but they moved quickly and purposefully, always driving forward toward Julija and the book no matter how many times Isai's warriors sliced through them, trying to slow them down in vain.

Now he had their attention. He knew better than to physically fight them. He had to gain control of them. They came toward him, fighting through his warriors. They were struck down over and over, but always, they reformed and continued forward.

He held up his hand to check them. "Brothers. I am both mage and Carpathian. My blood calls to you." He hoped that Julija and he had exchanged enough blood that they would feel the pull of mage blood. He knew their creator, Anatolie, had used a blood sacrifice to enslave them. Julija had her father's blood in her veins. Isai had hers.

Most stopped moving, as if confused. A few shuffled forward a few steps and then halted. He sent a silent command to his shadow warriors to cease and they, too, went still.

Hear me now, great shadow warriors,
Torn from your resting place without your permission.
I call on earth, fire, water, wind and spirit and bind them to me.
I invoke the law of the shadow.
I invoke the law of all true warriors.
I ask for release for these men who fought with honor.
Spirit, wrest them from the dark mage's bindings.

As he spoke the snow rose around the warriors in columns of white mixed with gray and black and now purple.

Water, cleanse them from the dark blood of sacrifice.

Blue joined the colors swirling around each of the shadow warriors. They stood very still, holding their weapons in front of them as if they might need them at any moment.

Fire, burn the dark mage's unholy spell back into his soul and release
these honorable shadow warriors wholly from his claim that he
may never call them again.

A high-pitched shriek echoed across the battlefield and in the distance, across the meadow near a high bluff, a column of dark red burst into the sky. The warriors were ringed now in colors, and orange-red flames joined the various shades spinning through the shadows.

Wind, carry these men home to their resting place.
Earth, open your arms that you may accept and protect them.

Deliberately, Isai stepped toward the shadow warriors to salute them respectfully.

He felt for them, these men who had lived with honor, fought bravely and yet weren't allowed their rest.

Dust to dust. Ashes to ashes.
Warriors return, breathe your last.
Air, earth, fire, water, hear my voice, obey my order.
Thrice around your grave do bound, evil sink into the ground.

As he spoke the words to return and protect the shadow warriors, a thunderous clap rent the air. In the distance, across the meadow, rocks slid from the bluff as the earth shook. The bluff collapsed into a pile of boulders, rocks and pebbles as Anatolie sank into the ground.

I now invoke the law of the three, this is my will, so mote it be.

Isai knew Anatolie would try to retaliate, either that, or he would realize the book was already lost to them and he'd slink off. Either way, Isai knew he had to get the shadow warriors free before the dark mage did something to wrest them away from him.

The shadow warriors, almost as one, saluted him and then the wind came through, howling like a banshee, tearing at their indistinct bodies, ripping through the faint streaks of black and gray, tearing them apart and carrying them off into the night to return them to their resting places.

"May you find eternal peace," he murmured softly and for a moment let himself feel the fatigue that came with combating a mage spell as dark as the one Anatolie had used to seize the warriors from their graves. His woman had been doing just that for what seemed like hours.

He sent his shadow warriors forward to meet the next line of evil coming at them. He suspected it would be Barnabas's hellhounds. He had no idea what they might do, and he wanted Julija out of there. He hurried back to her.

The book had wrapped long, disturbing-looking roots of black and ash wood-like vines around her arm and through her hand. The book was pierced with holes through and through, but still it fought back, desperate to survive. It had changed tactics, bringing forth those who had been sacrificed for each of those dark spells preserved inside the pages of the book. Julija was forced to relive each life taken.

Bloodred tears ran down her face and dripped onto the book. With each tear, more small holes burned through the papyrus pages. For once, the safeguards Xavier had so cleverly woven into the spell book had backfired on him. For all that, no lifemate could bear to see his woman suffering. Even as he hurried toward her, the book changed strategies again. Dark vines grew from the papyrus, coming directly from the piercing of her hand, moving down her belly in a twisting snakelike movement in a very threatening manner.

A look of horror crossed Julija's face. "The baby, Isai. It's after the baby. It knows it is our combined blood, all three of us, that is destroying it."

Isai hacked at the growth nearest her stomach with a knife. Even as he did so, a bright light burst from beneath her clothing and the dragon was there. The scales were a shiny black obsidian. Although small in stature, it didn't need to be anything else. The fire was just as effective as if it had been a full-sized dragon.

The little fierce dragon sprayed fire all up and down the roots, so that they withered and turned completely to particles of black ash, dropping to the snow, covering the blood Julija's hand had shed.

Without hesitation, Isai tore open his wrist again and added the power of his blood to Julija's. At once he could see the difference, the tears in the book gaping wide so that there were only the outer edges and a few troubling places where the safeguards stubbornly held.

A dread, so dark, so malicious and all encompassing, overtook both of them. They looked at each other. It felt for a moment as if time had stopped. The wind rushed toward them, carrying a sulfuric stench, much like rotting eggs.

Julija pulled her gaze from Isai's. "Brimstone," she whispered. "Hell-hounds, Isai. *His* hellhounds."

"You get rid of that book, woman. You are very close. You can do it," Isai instructed.

"You can't take on all of them. He'll have impossible numbers coming at you."

Isai called to the cats. *To me now. All of you.* "Just as you have to destroy that book, I have to destroy his hellhounds."

The cats came out of the night, great slinking shadows, huge panthers. He held out his arms and one by one, they leapt onto him, merging with his skin. He noted that they were getting better at it, not using their claws as much. If they all survived this night, they would soon be able to fuse with Julija as well.

Once more he leaned over to brush her mouth with his. "Get it done, little mage. You were born to stop them." He'd infused confidence in his voice and left her, striding into the snowstorm to stand between his woman and the monstrous animals coming for them. He covered himself in hyssop oil as well as every arrow for his crossbows. He needed mobility. There was only one way to kill them. He had to shoot an arrow in each eye and then sever the head. Unfortunately, they often had more than one head. They were fast and vicious, and once set on their purpose, they didn't ever stop.

Hellhounds were not unknown to him. Isai had fought them more than once in the past. They were faster than anyone could possibly imagine, and even calling up the memories didn't always prepare him for that first encounter again. A throat shot could slow them down if it was needed. He didn't want one to slip past him while he was dealing with others coming straight at him.

He waited, breathing easily, listening for the first of the pack to arrive. Strangely, other than the powerful stench, the lead hellhound broke silently out of the snow, coming straight at him. He was massive, much like a giant buffalo, running at full speed, eyes glowing like two fiery coals. His massive claws left few tracks in the snow. His fangs dripped with venom. Behind him came the rest, all rushing toward him like one enormous freight train.

Isai moved then, using his preternatural speed and the experience he'd earned over centuries of battle. He fired arrow after arrow, hitting the eyes of the creatures as they came close, some a breath away. As he fired, he ran toward them, slicing down with his sword as often as possible. There were so many, and they kept coming. He knew they were being used to distract him. Julija was going to be in trouble very soon if he couldn't halt the hellhounds.

The animals were trying to circle around him, to cut Julija off from him. He tried backtracking and they became fiercer, a galloping horde of ferocious beasts, canines like those of a saber-tooth tiger, razor-sharp, their attention completely centered on him. The closest one to him received two arrows straight into his burning eyes. It skidded to a halt and tumbled, headfirst, rolling. Two behind it couldn't slow down and tried to run over the top of the downed hellhound.

He's coming.

She never used Barnabas's name if she could help it. He knew it was Barnabas, not Anatolie using the hellhounds to keep Isai apart from her.

How close are you? He fired four arrows with blurring speed.

It's dissolving now at a rapid rate.

He could hear the pain in her voice. *What is wrong?* He fired off four more arrows and followed up with the sword. One hellhound grazed him. The fur was venomous, but he was covered in hyssop oil and the creature screamed as the substance burned through it.

The dragon, scorpion and snake are attempting to free me from the last of its tethers. I am unsure if it is possible.

Isai swore and sliced through the head of the beast turning on him. So close. Everywhere he looked they were too close. He needed to dissolve. To take to the air, but where would that leave her? He was all that kept Barnabas from having a free path straight to her. He needed his brethren. He needed a miracle.

You are high mage, Julija, every bit as powerful as he is. He is dead. In another realm. Take that vile book off you as if it is no more than garbage. He was asking a lot of her, but he knew she was capable.

Isai shot three more beasts with arrows, but he couldn't get to them to chop off their heads. Another came at him from his right, a huge monster of a hellhound, and he quickly ran backward, leapt up and over its back, shooting arrows into its eyes.

One particularly large hellhound shook its head, the arrow dropping from it. It pawed the ground, looking at Isai with hatred and purpose. Its eye ran with blood, and it was fixed on him. Around him dozens more charged.

20

The pain in Julija's hand and arm was excruciating, but the little dragon was valiant and refused to give up, breathing fire steadily at the roots protruding from her palm. She felt a second stem drop away. The snow hissed a complaint and melted right through to bare dirt. She was growing weak and the book sensed it, holding on, wrapping the last root around her wrist and trying to stab through her skin to get to her artery.

The snake and scorpion moved together as one unit, rushing down her arm so the snake could slip between the wood and her wrist and the scorpion could use its claws to pry it off her. The pages of the book were gone, but the binding stubbornly held on, desperate to carry out its maker's wishes. She dripped her blood up and down the spine in the same pattern as she had over the pages.

She heard the fierce battle Isai waged against the hellhounds, trying to give her the time she needed to destroy the book once and for all. There was a sudden hush over the battlefield, as if the very world around her in the midst of the thick storm held its breath. Nature, even the wild snow-storm, seemed to pause.

Her heart accelerated. Pounded. Threatened to burst through her chest. There was no time to waste. He was coming. She knew it was Barnabas. She felt his power as she'd never felt it before. She'd had glimpses of it, but she'd been too cowed by him, too humiliated, to recognize anything but his cruelty.

Deliberately, she brought her wrist to her mouth, allowed her teeth to lengthen and tore a larger hole in her own flesh. Blood poured over the spine, so much that for a moment it scared her, but the terror of Barnabas coming anywhere near her again overcame the sight of her blood consuming the spine of the book. Now, there was only the wood to get off her and the book would be done with.

I can't become vapor and he's coming. He's coming, Isai.

She needed him. Isai. Her savior. Her talisman. She needed him to get to her before Barnabas. She knew there was utter panic in her voice, that chaos reigned in her mind, and that her body was trying to shut down on her. Her legs and arms tingled, pins and needles striking throughout. Her lungs refused to work, desperate for air. Her head spun. She felt so faint she knew she would crash to the ground if she didn't sit, but it was as if she'd forgotten how to move.

He's coming now. Can you feel him? She didn't bother to try to keep the sob from her voice.

I am on my way to you, little mage. Isai's voice was as always—calm, matter-of-fact. Peaceful even, as if he wasn't fighting a terrible, impossible battle with the hounds from hell, or that one of the most dangerous mages wasn't striding across the battlefield toward them right that moment.

You are as powerful as he is. Remember that. He has experience, but you are both high mage and Carpathian. The moment you are able, dissolve into vapor. He can do a lot of things, but that he cannot do. He will not be able to find you within the storm. Close off every wound. That is important. One drop of blood can give you away.

She took a deep steadying breath. Of course. She was letting herself panic when she'd known this moment would come. Barnabas. It was just that no one else saw him as she did. They thought she was terrified of him because of the things he'd done to her. She knew better. There were many moments when she'd caught glimpses past the cruel mage into something deeper, something far more sinister than even she could conceive. That was what shook her. He might have long surpassed his masters in his ability to weave and bind with magic.

She sank slowly into the bloodstained snow. The scorpion and snake were doing their best to remove the last of the roots that had driven through her hand and twined around her wrist. She would help them in a moment, but she was weak from loss of blood and that ever-present fear she couldn't quite let go of. Isai had to come. He would. He said he would. He just had to get there before the dark mage did.

Isai fell back, making his retreat as unnoticeable as possible. He realized when he made any move to go back toward Julija, the hellhounds adjusted their positions in order to cut him off. This was no battle where the massive creatures were just flung at him or put in place to kill everything in their path. They didn't go around him to get to Julija. These demonic creatures from hell were being directed with purpose.

There was a general on the battlefield and he was ensuring his soldiers did exactly as he wanted. Each strategic move was designed to keep him separated from Julija. As he turned to face the threat coming in from the south, a stampeding group of four, an extremely aggressive attack came from directly in front of him. The beast was on him just as he let loose three arrows at the ones coming in from the south. He felt the hot bite of the demon's breath as the jaws just missed his leg and then he was on the ground, the last place any warrior wanted to be, not when hellhounds continued to multiply no matter how many he managed to kill.

He slashed open the hellhound's belly, rolling to keep the burning intestines from reaching him. As he rolled he leapt into the air, shooting off half a dozen arrows. All but one hit their mark, penetrating eyes. He pushed forward, using his sword to sever heads as he went. One arrow hit just to the right of the eye of the lead hound coming in from the south and bounced off. The second penetrated deeply so the animal skidded, shook its head and stumbled into the hound next to it, forcing it to veer off course.

Instantly, Isai could see the black, turbulent cloud churning behind the five hellhounds. The beasts were massive. Venom dripped in long strings of saliva from their mouths. Their eyes glowed fiery red, like hot coals pressed deep into their skulls. Nostrils flared as they breathed, smoke coming from noses. The one with the arrow in its eye shook its head over and over, trying to dislodge it. The eye dripped with blood, adding to the hideous effect.

Isai had intended to shift into vapor and get ahead of the hellhounds, making his way back to Julija. But now he was aware these hellhounds weren't after Julija; they were programmed to kill him. Somewhere hidden in that black cloud was the mage. Along with fighting for his life with the hellhounds, he knew the worst was coming. He was certain of it. Isai took his time with his shot, ignoring the pawing, snorting and galloping of the rest of the herd of hellhounds coming at him.

He dropped back another two feet and then, as the hellhounds went into a frenzy, determined to stop him, to cut him off from Julija, they opened ranks just enough for him to see the churning black cloud. He let the arrow fly.

The hellhounds were on top of him so he did the only thing left open to him, he leapt into the air, over their backs, letting four arrows fly before he landed on the ground, just a few feet from the cloud. The hellhounds snarled and snapped at him and at one another. They had to change direction in order to keep him in their field of vision. Swinging around wasn't easy for them. They were massive beasts and running full out.

Isai scored a hit in the direct center and the roiling, agitated murky veil lifted, enabling him to see the mage lying in wait for him to make a mistake. Shockingly, it was Anatolie who lifted his hands instantly, not Barnabas. Barnabas still commanded the hellhounds, his hand was everywhere, but Anatolie was the mage he faced. One hand held a staff with an amber ball at the top of it. He pointed that globe at Isai. Lightning slashed over the backs of the hellhounds, singeing their fur, so blackened smoke rose while the beasts howled, the sound grating on ears, sending nerves into a jangle so it was difficult to move quickly.

Whips of lightning struck the ground all around Isai, snapping and crackling, sizzling with electric life. The animals, programmed to continue forward after Isai, were confused, running into one another, slashing with razor-sharp teeth, opening the motley fur so blood ran like rivers into the pristine snow.

Isai concentrated on the lightning. The weather was his forte. He'd been managing lightning since he was no more than a child. He timed the strikes. Each one was getting closer and more severe. Anatolie clearly had wielded the lightning on more than one occasion, but Isai had complete confidence in his abilities. He waited until a whip slammed into the ground just feet from him and then he called his own whip down and struck hard right at Anatolie, slamming the full force of the electrical storm down on him.

Anatolie moved at the last possible moment, as if he had been waiting for the retaliation. The staff had gone up and swung toward Isai, redirecting the streaks and whips right back at the Carpathian. Each time Isai tried to get into the air, Anatolie took the route from him. Each time he stepped back in order to close the distance between him and Julija, Anatolie slashed at him with the lightning strikes.

It was difficult to see in the whiteout of the blizzard. The sizzling and crackling added to the chaotic scene. The light flashed, ultrabright, illuminating the snow, but causing a terrible glare. Anatolie appeared to be in the middle of that spinning, churning web of smoke and deceit.

Then he was hovering above the hellhounds, and they snapped at him, spinning in circles trying to see him. Next, he was a few feet away. Isai could see him easily, his dark eyes spitting hatred at him, that staff directing the lightning.

Isai directed his own electrical whips straight at Anatolie. The lightning forked in the air and wrapped around the columns Anatolie had sent at him. A shower of sparks rained down on all of them, hellhounds, Carpathian and mage alike.

Where are you?

Julija sounded scared. Forlorn. Terrified he had abandoned her. Isai turned toward her, deciding to get to her and fight from that position. Just as he chose to streak away, a loop caught his ankle and yanked him down.

At once the hellhounds went into a frenzy as their quarry went from the air to the ground in seconds.

———

Desperately Julija fought to get the root off her hand and arm so she could shift. The ground moved under her. Rising. Falling. As if it was breathing. Her own breath caught in her throat. She could see the battle of lightning taking place a distance from her and knew something had prevented Isai from getting to her. Tears burned behind her eyes and her throat closed. She felt helpless. Without hope.

It is a snare. You know better, Julija. Take one step at a time. Close the wounds and rid yourself of the last of the book. I will join you as soon as I am able to do so.

There it was again—that complete calm. She had touched Isai's mind on several occasions and never once had he closed it to her. She could see his every intention was to get to her. Anatolie had confronted him. *He is a master of illusion, Isai.*

She needed to hold up her end. Isai was battling so many things. Hellhounds were demonic. They had been programmed so they would obey Barnabas's dictates, but his orders slowed them down and confused them. They were demons and wanted to feast on the flesh of the Carpathian, not be dictated to and forced to obey.

She took a deep breath and forced air through her closed lungs. Barnabas had more than once sent ahead such a spell, one to make her feel helpless, small and as if she couldn't do anything but obey his every command.

> *That which is cloaked in shadow,*
> *Bring clearness to my sight.*
> *Taking on none of the illusion,*
> *I surround myself with light.*
> *Send back that which came along this path,*
> *Tracking from whence it came.*
> *Let the helplessness and shadow*
> *No longer in my heart and mind remain.*

Julija hurriedly began closing the numerous wounds on her body. She worked fast, but was meticulous, all the while trying various ways to rid herself of that last, stubborn root. As it fell away from her arm, she used several healing techniques to ensure not one bit of wood was left. She dripped blood on the scattered splinters so that they withered into black, crispy curls of ash there in the snow.

The scorpion and snake rushed back up her arm, clearly alarmed as she got shakily to her feet. She still felt faint and dizzy from lack of blood. When she tried to dissolve into mist, nothing happened. Nothing. She was left there, standing out in the open, once again caught by the foulest and most dangerous of all the mages she knew.

Barnabas stepped out of the blizzard of white. He looked—invincible. Cruelly handsome. He wore a suit, unlike Anatolie, who enjoyed wrapping himself in robes. He smiled at her, satisfaction gleaming in his eyes.

"Julija. You look worn. Exhausted. I don't think your Carpathian lover is taking such good care of you. You need your master." He sounded benevolent. "I have never been one to forgive grave sins such as yours, my pet, but I will admit I have missed our delicious games."

Her entire body shuddered. Intellectually, she knew his voice was part of his spell. He enthralled the listener, hypnotized and mesmerized, much like a cobra. That's how she thought of him now. A cobra, ready to strike when she exposed any weakness.

It is true that you are worn and exhausted, my love, Isai said softly, brushing love into the walls of her mind. *You have lost far too much blood. Those things are very true, but you belong to no one but who you choose to give yourself freely to, Julija. You are strong. You destroyed the high mage's book when no one else could do so. Every wound you've suffered, every scar you've gotten, is a badge of courage and shows me the strength of the woman you are.*

Isai's voice was filled with admiration and respect, everything Barnabas had never given her. Her warrior championed her in all things. Even now, he was fighting against impossible odds to get to her.

Julija lifted her chin and looked Barnabas right in the eye, something he'd trained her never to do. "I have no master. I'm no one's pet. And your games are anything but delicious, Barnabas. I find them cruel and vile."

He smiled at her, his white teeth gleaming. There was no hint of amusement in his eyes. "I can see our lessons will have to begin all over again right from the very start."

He glanced at the ground around her feet. It was bare of snow and still smoking in places. It was also stained red with her blood. "You destroyed Xavier's book."

"I did."

He sighed. "You amaze me with your continual poor choices, Julija. That book was invaluable, although it is not necessary to me, just a mere shortcut." He glanced uneasily over his shoulder, looking not toward the hellhounds, lightning and battle between Anatolie and Isai, but west. "We must go now." He snapped his fingers at her and pointed to his side, expecting her to obey his command to come to him.

At once she felt humiliation. That moment when he had forced her to her knees and made her crawl, begging for scraps of food, begging for water. He made her pay dearly for every concession. She shook her head. "Go, Barnabas. Go before Isai comes for you."

"Isai is nothing. I have no need to worry over him. The longer you resist, the more I will punish you. Do you remember how the lash feels tearing through your flesh? The pain of it?" He paused and let his gaze drift over her. Claiming her. "The pleasure?"

He was making her feel those things just with his words. With his breath. She countered, knowing she was feeling a little desperate, but trying not to show him.

Circle of light become a pillar.
Wrap around me as if a cocoon.
Holding back both words and sound,
That would seek to harm and wound.

"I see you think you have learned to protect yourself from me. Do you think your childish spells can possibly counter mine? You are a child next to me. I learned from my uncle Xavier, no more than a child working by his side. My father, Xaviero, also taught me many things, things Xavier had never learned. I also had the advantage of training under my other uncle, Xayvion, and, although he preferred to stay behind the scenes, in the background, he undoubtedly was the most powerful. I have the advantage of all three."

As he spoke, his tone casual, almost conversational, his hands moved gracefully by his side, fingers tapping a rhythm on his thigh. He never spoke casually or conversed with her, not since he had revealed himself to be dark and cruel. She wasn't in the least deceived. She knew it was an attack on her, she just was uncertain where it was coming from. She had protected herself against his voice—

The ground opened up, dropping her straight down. He smiled at her as she fell into the dark hole, the one he would bury her in and leave her in for indeterminate days and nights with only a small straw to breathe through. Dirt filled in all around her. His hands were up now, weaving a pattern, as he murmured his command. She kept her gaze fixed on that pattern as well as his lips as the soil consumed her.

As the dirt filled in around her, Isai's voice poured into her mind. *You are Carpathian, my love. The earth welcomes you. You have no need to breathe air if it is your desire not to. He cannot harm you by putting you in the very place that rejuvenates you.*

Julija hadn't considered the soil would revitalize her. It would regenerate her torn flesh and restore her. It took a few minutes to overcome her need for oxygen. She had to fight not to panic, but she was able to follow Isai's steady breathing. Once she realized she could do it, she took her time thinking how best to counter Barnabas as she rose from the soil. Something to put him down hard. Very hard. She still had the little ritual dagger. It was small, but it carried a tremendous amount of power.

Her heart began to pound. If he was listening, he would feel triumphant, as if he had gained what he wanted—her terror so she would cooperate. It wasn't that. She knew the moment she struck at him, he would retaliate just as hard, just as fast, or even harder and faster. She was *so* afraid of him.

Steeling herself, she burst through the soil, practically right at his feet, giving her command.

Earth surround me. Air encircle me.
Thunder sound loudly. Lightning strike.
Bring this evil down as I rise.
Fire surround him.
Earth help bind him.
Vines entwining so he may not rise.

Barnabas fell to the ground, slamming his head hard as he went down; his arms went limp like those of a rag doll, unable to cushion his fall. She lifted her hands to give him a second command and found herself on the ground, a rag doll beside him. He had simply used her own spell against her, so that neither could move.

I am in your head, Julija. I know what you think to do with that dagger.

The dagger began to slip from her pocket and move into the air above her throat. She countered quickly.

That which is made of finest steel,
I know your maker, I control your will.
Steel that would cut and harm,
I command your movement and order your return.

She reached for Isai, knowing she had only seconds before Barnabas would counter the simple spell she used. She was already doing so, which would help him do the same.

Your Carpathian lover has abandoned you, left the battlefield like the cur he is. He will not save you from me.

She was on her feet first and she exploded into action, catching at the dagger, stepping into him as he rose to plunge the blade into his heart. She'd forgotten her own blood was on the blade and the moment it entered him, those fresh drops gave him the advantage. He caught her hand with both of his, preventing her from shoving it all the way in. Looking straight into her eyes, using a blood sacrificial spell, one of the strongest, he commanded her body to come under his complete authority.

She fell into his arms. He held her, shaking his head, and then he took the knife and plunged it into her abdomen just above her baby. Not deep, but it hurt like hell and scared her, wondering if he knew about the child. When he pulled out the blade he licked at the drops of blood. "I had forgotten how good you taste, Julija. I dream of your taste and yet when I actually have the blood in front of me, it is even better. We will leave this place. I have no doubt the Carpathians will succeed on the battlefield, defeat Anatolie and the hellhounds, but in the end, they lost the war, didn't they? I have the prize."

He was locked out of Julija's mind. Isai couldn't reach her and had no idea what was happening to her. He knew the moment she had fallen to the ground beside Barnabas, and that her intent had been to use the dagger on him, then he was completely closed off from her. Barnabas had constructed some kind of spell. Isai wasn't mage, but he had mage blood running through his veins. He had no doubt he could find a way to reach her. It was imperative since he couldn't tell what was happening to her.

Dividing his attention could get him killed. He was dragged along the ground right through the thick of the hellhounds. They went after him as if he was a fox and they had been let loose to exterminate him. Better Anatolie had killed him outright. He had all of his weapons and even as he was dragged, he continued to shoot arrows dipped in hyssop oil straight into the eyes of the hellhounds.

His mind raced. He needed to open communication with Julija. He didn't fight the whip. Anatolie's attention was riveted to the wild ride he was forcing the Carpathian on. His sense of power was growing the longer he wielded the lightning, something only Carpathians did. Isai gave him that. Anatolie was a powerful mage, dark and dangerous. As long as he was concentrating on keeping the whip under his control, he couldn't think of other, much more perilous spells.

Anatolie's wild laughter echoed through the battlefield. Around them, the snow thickened. The wind howled, spinning great funnels of snow into columns. Isai felt them at once. The brethren had arrived. His brothers from the monastery. They were already wading into battle with the hellhounds.

You should have called earlier, brother, Ferro reprimanded. *Why save all the fun for yourself?*

All of the brethren were large and muscular with ropes of defined muscle. They each had long, salt-and-pepper hair flowing down their backs, the result of all the centuries spent battling. All had scars to prove they had been wounded mortally on more than one occasion and yet had survived. Each had the tattoo of their creed flowing down their backs, but that was where the similarities ended.

Ferro was the most intimidating of the brethren. He had unusual eyes the color of iron complete with rust running through them. It gave him a stare that was mesmerizing. He was quiet in most situations, but of all the brethren, Isai considered him the most dangerous.

I am grateful you are here. The high mage put a spell on the hellhounds. They want to kill me and as many as I kill, more arrive, Isai explained.

With the snow thickening and throwing itself in every direction seemingly at a capricious whim, Anatolie's vision was completely cut off. He could no longer delight in his prisoner being eaten alive by the demonic hellhounds.

I have come to save you, brother, Sandu weighed in. *It seems this is to be my lot in life.*

Sandu had eyes as black as night yet a red flame burned deep in their depths, giving one a glimpse into the fiery volcano inside of him.

Someone has to give you a little work. You were becoming lazy.

Isai shot two more of the hellhounds, and this time, Petru, with slashing eyes of mercury, sliced off their heads.

Do you plan on riding that hellhound back to hell or are you going to get off your butt and help out? Petru inquired.

Isai placed his exact weight in the noose of lightning and freed himself, allowing Anatolie to think he still had his prisoner. It appeared to be so when Anatolie managed to glimpse the Carpathian warrior being dragged over the ground. Carpathians could produce illusions as easily as a mage.

Benedek, with his unusual dark eyes and long flowing hair, came out of the blizzard and signaled to him to go east. He circled around to the west to get behind the high mage. Anatolie would know in a few moments that Isai had tricked him and that others had joined the battle. He didn't want to fight toe to toe with a high mage. If the man chose to cast spells and then run, which Isai was certain he would do, he might succeed. However, if Isai could catch him unawares, he had a chance to kill him. The last thing any of them wanted was a powerful mage coming at them from behind when they went after Barnabas.

Anatolie had done what Isai would have predicted, given that his son Vasile had chosen the same method to protect himself. He was in a sheltered alcove of rock, a small fortress surrounded, Isai was certain, by a powerful grid that, moving through, would trigger the same types of traps Vasile's defense system had. Isai didn't have the time to take them all down.

Rising as vapor, he streamed over the defense grid, warning Benedek. He felt his way carefully, knowing the air could be protected as well, although Anatolie didn't have a lot of time to spend on his own defense, not when he'd gone right away on the attack.

The high mage had to step outside the grotto-like fortress in order to wield the lightning, but as long as he had his enemy on the end of his whip, he wasn't worried. Isai came in from his left side, dropping low. As he did so, the shadow cats leapt from his back. The six cats distracted Anatolie as they emerged from the snow, coming straight at him.

When he looked up, Isai was in front of him, his face set in an expressionless mask. Benedek was at his back, just as stone-faced. Isai plunged his hand through the chest wall and got the heart while Benedek took the mage's head with one slice of his sword. It was Isai who called down the lightning to burn the body.

"I will make certain that Julija removes the spell to replenish the hellhounds once I find her. Thank you for coming."

"The others are guarding the compound in case there is trouble there. Elisabeta was very uncomfortable. All of us felt your need."

Isai nodded. They had been together so long, when one was in trouble, often the others knew and immediately set out to find them. "Good hunting, my brother."

Benedek nodded. "Same to you, *ekäm*."

Isai took to the skies, allowing his brethren to fight the hellhounds. In the many centuries each had lived, they had encountered the demonic beasts and learned the best ways to kill them. Unfortunately, as he had learned, these creatures were spellbound and replenished when one went down. They would try to follow him because they were programmed to kill him, no one else. Barnabas hadn't counted on the brethren coming when they felt his need.

Isai took the form of a snow flurry as he neared the place where he had left Julija destroying the book. Occasionally, he caught a glimpse of one of his cats, but mostly their bodies were transparent now, as they were hunting, just as he was. He spotted Barnabas bending over Julija's limp body and plunging a dagger into her. Each time he did, he made shallow cuts and licked at the crimson drops.

Isai pushed fury away. He couldn't allow anything of himself to get in the way of getting his lifemate back. Before he could decide what to do, he saw Julija's gaze shift to one of the cats. She was not only alive but thinking. Gathering her strength. Deciding what to do. She had a plan. More than anything he wanted her to throw Barnabas out of her mind, but that wasn't the most critical thing for her to do.

"You didn't take my voice, Barnabas."

"Your screams are delightful, my pet." Deliberately Barnabas bent his head to kiss her eyes and cheeks and then down her throat, the dagger poised in his fist.

Earth unbind me. Air set me free.
Thunder away. Lightning may I see no more.
Fire now burn, releasing this spell.
Water I command you to become a wall.
As water's wall is built, I bring forth fire for steam,
Separating all so none may be seen.

Julija whipped up both hands and stabbed her fingers into Barnabas's eyes, immediately rolling out of his hands to land on her hands and knees in the bloodstained snow. Barnabas swore repeatedly, his hands coming up to his face where his eyes were streaming. He murmured a quick spell to relieve the pain and damage.

Harm sent to me by sacred steel.
I now reverse your direction seeking only the evil that yields.

Julija staggered a few feet from Barnabas, and instantly Blue leapt out of the shadows and sank his teeth into Barnabas's neck. Belle attacked from behind him. Comet and Phaedra assisted in pulling him down. Even as they did, he shouted out a spell and the cats fell to the ground panting. Before he could retaliate against them, Isai was there, driving Barnabas away from them—and Julija.

She tried to reach out to him, to merge mind to mind, but Barnabas's spell had forced a separation. Immediately she countered it.

That which dwells in darkness,
I banish you from my mind.
Allowing only that which is tied by love,
To merge within my mind.

As Isai slammed his fist deep into Barnabas's chest, the dark mage struck hard, using a spell to splinter the ancient Carpathian. Isai's body separated into what appeared to be numerous life-sized paper dolls. Barnabas smiled his most charming smile and blew on the one closest to him so they fell like dominos almost at Julija's feet.

"You shouldn't have made me angry, pet," he advised. He turned his right hand palm up and began to make a circle with his left over his palm. As he did so he began a little singsong chant. Orange and red flames licked at his palms, forming a ball that grew and grew.

Julija's heart pounded so hard it hurt. She took a deep breath, not daring to look away. As Barnabas casually tossed the ball toward Isai's splintered body, she whispered her counterspell.

> *I call the clouds above,*
> *Bring forth your waters, stopping fires hold.*
> *Let droplets of water dissipate and drown that which would burn,*
> *Returning it all to ground.*

Isai rolled, the splinters bonding together as he came to his feet. Both Barnabas and Julija stared at him in shock as he faced the dark mage, his body slightly in front of hers. He bowed toward Barnabas.

"Surely you did not think you were the first to ever use a splinter spell."

Isai touched Julija's mind. She felt him come into her and she nearly lost it, wanting to cry with relief. He sounded the way he always did. Confident. He looked invincible.

"Very few know it," Barnabas conceded. He glanced toward the blizzard of snow. He couldn't see the battle taking place, but he could hear it. No hellhounds had come to kill Isai, their primary target.

Behind Barnabas, Julija caught a glimpse of the cats moving in the shadows behind and to the right of the high mage. They waited for Isai's signal to attack. Having Isai there and knowing the cats were close and willing to aid them gave her the necessary strength to face her worst nightmare.

"Very few *alive* know it," Isai qualified. "Your hounds are occupied at the moment. Julija, I need you to counter the spell that replenishes them. The brethren are having fun, but it will grow tiresome over time."

Julija immediately responded.

> *Those who have arisen from earth's deepest core,*
> *When one is banished, you may reproduce no more.*
> *Though your mind is as one,*
> *May your memory be lost,*
> *Banishing all thoughts of your targeted host.*

"Who are you?" Barnabas asked. "Do I know you?"

"I knew you when you used a different name. You were called Barna all those centuries ago, son of Xaviero. You were chosen over Anatolie, son of Xavier. Why?"

Barnabas shrugged. "You saw him. His ego grew faster than his skills." He indicated Julija. "He had exactly what he needed, but he didn't recognize it. He used her as fodder, when she is the main prize. I cared nothing for the book. I saw every spell my uncle chose to include, I learned them and put them aside. Anatolie wanted to destroy your species. I would much rather keep all of you alive." Again, he flashed a smile, his white teeth mocking them.

Julija's stomach tangled into a thousand knots. Barnabas was unfazed that he faced her, Isai and the shadow cats. He didn't care that Ioni's brethren fought the hellhounds and were at that moment destroying them. She wanted to shove Isai behind her, to caution him to be careful. Barnabas was up to something.

"You wanted Julija." Isai made it a statement.

"I *want* my little pet back. She belongs to me. She knows she does." He held out his hand toward her. "If you come with me now, I will spare your lover."

The way he said the last two words told her everything. Barnabas planned to kill Isai no matter what she did. Beneath his calm exterior, he seethed with rage. Whatever he was planning was going to be spectacular. She began to form a defensive grid in her mind, building it up. To her astonishment, Isai joined her, taking it over, meticulously building the barrier against the dark mage from the ground up. Soon it surrounded them like an invisible fortress.

Isai called to the cats with a silent command, stretching his arms wide indicating for them to become part of his skin immediately. One by one, the cats obeyed. Blue was last and he appeared reluctant, but in the end he did as Isai demanded.

"Very clever of you to turn the shadow cats," Barnabas praised and slowly allowed his hand to drop by his side.

Julija kept watch on his hands. He could murmur a spell under his breath and she might not see, but if those fingers began to move against his thigh, or he sent a blast of air at them, she would know.

You are Carpathian. You are mage. Your power is equal or more than his. Why do you think he wants you back? This is not about a sex slave escaping him. He could enslave any number of women. This is about your power, Julija. You can defeat him.

Just as they had merged their blood to destroy the book, she thought their strength was in the way they were together.

Barnabas's hands moved fast, too fast for her to follow the patterns, but she heard the roar go up and the ground shook. Giant paws thundered as they pounded into the earth. The sky opened up and rained insects.

I call to alloy, carbon and steel,
Build us a dome to withhold and repel.

The moment they were safe from the thousands of insects, Julija sent up a small prayer for forgiveness. She'd never used her magic for anything but good.

The hellhounds came at them, a good dozen, trampling every bush or tree in sight, flattening the grass the snow hadn't already covered. Barnabas whirled into their midst, his hands clapping like thunder, shaking the earth so that it was impossible to stand. Isai simply floated up, gripping Julija's arm as he did so. The moment she was safe, he left the shelter they had constructed together. Julija couldn't wait to see what he did. She hurtled the spell at Barnabas, hoping to ensnare him in his own dark magic.

By the power of three times three,
May all you have done return back to thee.
Let all harm and hate be returned tenfold,
So that you may suffer pain both new and old.

She cried out Isai's name, reaching for him, uncertain whether or not her spell had been enough to turn the tables on a high mage. The hellhounds were horrific, great, lumbering demonic beasts. Ordinarily she felt sorry for creatures twisted by the mages, but these were killing machines, eagerly looking for flesh to devour.

Barnabas went under what appeared to be four or five ravenous beasts. Their red glowing eyes looked like hot coals. She saw the mage's coat torn and striped with blood, but it seemed impossible that his own hellhounds could have killed him that quickly. He was too powerful. Too good at what he did.

She looked around in alarm, checking every direction. The storm had let up, although it was still snowing, blanketing the world in pristine white when blood flowed so fast there on the meadow floor.

She'd never seen anyone move as fast as Isai. Arrows flew, and she could see the flash of swords. His brethren joined him, occasionally tossing a sword through the air for another one to slice off a head.

Very slowly she put her feet back on the ground, testing it, making certain there was no sign of the high mage. If he was dead, would the hounds have left a body? They didn't have time to consume him before the brethren were there, killing them one by one. They were machines, mowing down the slavering beasts.

Then, without warning, there was absolute silence. Not a single hellhound still lived. Isai slowly straightened up and looked at his brothers. They saluted him and turned their attention to the battlefield, to mop up.

"Is he there? Barnabas? Is he there, Isai?" It was more than she could have hoped for, but still, it might have happened.

"His coat, nothing else. No body."

She closed her eyes. Of course he'd escaped. She could destroy a hideous book that should never have been in the first place, but she had no idea how to kill a mage like Barnabas. Maybe no one did. "I'm sorry, Isai. I stopped him for the moment, but he'll come back."

"Carpathians have lived with enemies for centuries, Julija, and we will live with them for centuries more." He was pragmatic about it, just as he was about everything else. "I want to take you home. We have to clean up here and then we will have to go to ground. The sun is coming up and none among us can take the sunshine."

"I can guard all of you," she offered.

"There is no need." He took her hand, his thumb sliding over the back of it, making her shiver. "Come meet my friends."

His friends were calling down the lightning, sending the hellhounds back to their resting place with a fiery inferno. She thought the send-off was very appropriate.

21

The house Isai took Julija to was small and set well back from the main house of Tariq Asenguard's compound. He had explained to her that the ancients were looking into purchasing a large tract of land with several homes on it, just along the lakefront and bordering Tariq's land on one side. In the meantime, they could use the little house that was on his friend's property.

They spent a week there, alone with each other and the shadow cats. She loved it. Every minute of the day with Isai seemed a miracle. She laughed a lot when she never had. She often didn't recognize herself, teasing Isai and being completely relaxed with him. And the cats . . . She loved spending time with them and watching them pounce on Isai. They were big and strong, their health much improved in that one week. They would ambush Isai whenever he came through a doorway.

Julija loved watching her lifemate with the cats. He never seemed to tire of their antics. No matter how many times they knocked him over, he would laugh and wrestle with them. The two youngest, Phantom and Sable, had been won over that last battle, when Isai had been so careful not to send them out to fight. He had left the decision up to them completely, in fact, had tried to protect the cats. That had been enough to convince the two that he was nothing like the men who had created them.

Julija wanted to stay cocooned in her little world. She knew Isai wanted her to meet the others living close to them, but that meant once again stepping out of her comfort zone and trusting others. He had been patient with her, but she could tell that was coming to an end.

Each evening she reached out to Elisabeta in hope of encouraging her to surface. Part of her was doing so for selfish reasons. She thought if Elisabeta needed her while she was being introduced to everyone, it would make it much easier for Julija to be introduced. Cowardly, she knew, but there it was.

"You are not a coward," Isai whispered, wrapping his arms around her and pulling her onto his lap as he often did. He seemed to prefer her sitting on him whenever there were chairs close by.

"I am," she refuted, being honest. "A total coward. I'm supposed to be Elisabeta's friend, but I'm thinking of using her to make it easier for me to meet all of your friends. That is cowardly."

"I suppose you could look at it that way." He nuzzled the top of her head with his chin. Immediately her hair got caught in the bristles on his jaw. "Another way might be the two of you help each other out." He pressed little kisses over the top of her head. "I do prefer that you depend on me, but if you need Elisabeta to help you overcome your fears of meeting my friends, then I want that for you. Whatever makes it easier."

"I'm sorry, Isai. I do want to meet them. It's just that, over the years, I learned never to make friends. It didn't end well. And learning to trust others will be difficult. I'll do it, but it won't be easy," she warned. She didn't want him thinking she could so easily fit in. She could pretend, but that wasn't what she wanted. She didn't think he would want that, either.

"I will not allow anything to happen to you, Julija, nor do I want you unhappy."

She turned her face up to his throat. She loved the way he smelled. Like home. Like her man. He made her feel safe even though she knew the world around her wasn't.

"I know, Isai. I want to be friends with them and I will. I just really have enjoyed this week with you without having anyone try to kill us." She tried to make a joke of it, but instead, knew she was stalling. "Let me just talk to Elisabeta and see if I can coax her to come to the surface. She'll want to meet everyone, too." That was just ridiculous. She knew it. He knew it.

Isai didn't call her on it. He hugged her closer. "If that makes you feel better, Julija, by all means do so. I would love to be introduced. She is a good friend to you."

Julija knew Elisabeta was a very good friend, but she wasn't going to abandon her resting place anytime soon. This was another delaying tactic. She circled Isai's neck with her arms and laid her head against his chest, her ear over his heart, so she could listen to the steady beat while she reached out to Elisabeta.

As always it took a few minutes for Elisabeta to fully awaken. There was a part of her that worried it was taking just a little longer each time. What if she refused to surface? Had anyone ever done such a thing? For a moment there was panic.

Isai kissed her ear. "She has a lifemate, Julija. He would never allow such a thing."

"Then why hasn't he insisted she rise?"

"I do not know, but he will do what is best for her."

She closed her eyes and pressed her forehead against his shoulder. How many times was he going to say that to her?

"As many as it takes," Isai said with confidence and a little amusement.

She took a deep breath and reached out again to her friend. Aside from Isai, Elisabeta was her only friend.

I have so much to tell you. My lifemate has made me incredibly happy. He is here with me now, eager to meet you. Remember when I was so afraid, and you reassured me that he would find a way to make me happy? You were right. Deliberately she used the term *lifemate* in order to remind Elisabeta that she had a partner and he would do the same for her.

Are you happy, Julija? Really happy?

Elisabeta's voice was a sweet relief, removing the last of Barnabas, pushing him from Julija's mind. There was just something about listening to Elisabeta, hearing that soft voice, her tone, that brought peace and comfort. Hers was a rare gift.

I cannot wait to see you in person again. It feels like a lifetime. Do you feel strong enough to come to the surface soon?

There was a small hesitation. That hesitation had been there for the last week. Julija had the feeling Elisabeta had made up her mind to stay in the comfort of the ground.

My dear friend, you can't stay there forever. Come to the surface and be my friend.

Again, there was the slightest hesitation. *I must wait.*

Julija frowned and turned her head to look at her lifemate. She had wanted to introduce him to Elisabeta, but this was new. Each rising Julija asked Elisabeta to come to the surface and she'd always refused. This was the first indication that she was waiting for a reason. *Wait for what? I don't understand.*

I must wait, Elisabeta repeated. *Soon, I think. I wish to see you, Julija.*

I have Isai with me, she repeated, wanting Elisabeta to realize she meant he was right there listening. *I want you to meet him. He's a wonderful man. My man. Everything I could have ever wished or hoped for.*

Isai wrapped his arm around Julija and settled her more comfortably in his lap. *It is good to finally meet you, Elisabeta. Thank you for being such a good friend to my Julija.*

There was a long silence. *May I speak?* Elisabeta's voice shook. *I don't know what to do in these circumstances. He hasn't told me.*

Julija felt Isai stiffen. His eyes went from warm to cold in seconds.

Elisabeta, you may speak, Isai confirmed. *Who tells you? Who needs to give his permission for you to speak?*

Julija put her hand very gently on his arm to restrain him. The last thing she wanted was for Elisabeta to shut down. She was deep beneath the earth, safe, where nothing could happen to her. She was fed and then allowed to go back to the healing soil. Julija wanted to coax her to the surface, not scare her into staying underground. She was very aware Isai's first thought was that Sergey, the Carpathian who'd kidnapped her then turned vampire, was spying through her. Julija was certain many of the Carpathians feared that very thing.

Elisabeta. Honey? It's all right. You haven't done anything wrong, Julija insisted.

I don't understand the rules, Elisabeta whispered. *No one will tell me the rules.*

Julija took a deep breath and turned a little helplessly to Isai. He kissed her fingertips in reassurance.

Have no worries, Elisabeta. Your lifemate will tell you the rules, Isai assured.

There was silence again. *May I speak plainly?*

Yes, of course, Julija said immediately.

I will leave and allow you your privacy, Isai said. *I enjoyed our brief encounter and look forward to meeting you in person, Elisabeta.*

Thank you, sir.

Julija closed her eyes again and let Isai cuddle her closer to him. He always seemed to know when she was upset, and she appreciated his immediate response. He knew her reasons for identifying so much with Elisabeta. In retrospect, her time with Barnabas didn't seem as if it could possibly reflect the time Elisabeta had spent with Sergey, because Elisabeta had been held captive for so long. Sergey hadn't enjoyed torturing his captive. He wanted her to obey him and as long as she did, he was somewhat pleasant to her. Still, Julija would never think that she'd had anywhere near the difficult time Elisabeta had endured.

She didn't like that Elisabeta felt subservient to all of them. *I am your friend, right?*

My only friend.

You talk openly to me.

You gave me your permission when we first met, and you said you were going to find a way to unlock the cage he kept me in.

Isai is my lifemate. He will be your friend and neither of us wants you ever to feel as if you need permission for anything around us. She was fierce about it because she felt fierce.

Thank you for sticking up for me. As always, Elisabeta sounded gentle and sweet.

That is what friends do. I have something really important to tell you. Only Isai knows and for me, it's a little scary. I am carrying a baby. What do you think about that?

There was a stunned silence. Julija took the opportunity to nibble up the side of Isai's neck to his ear while her heart beat rapidly. He always tasted so good and hopefully could distract her from the panic she always felt when she acknowledged her pregnancy.

That is amazing news. I'm so happy for you.

Elisabeta was. Julija not only could hear it in her voice. Her friend spread waves of warmth and love easily, without trying.

I think I'm becoming happy as well.

Right away Elisabeta wanted to know why she was *becoming* happy instead of being happy. Julija told her about the mage and Barnabas in particular and how he so easily got away. *I know he will find a way to return. If not for me, then for a daughter of mine. He is patient. And he will not forget.*

There was a small silence. *I have the same fear of Sergey, so I will not dismiss your fears as invalid. Do not allow him to mar your happiness. Live your life as fully and as happily as possible, Julija. You do not know when it might be taken from you.*

It was good advice, especially coming from someone whose life had been yanked away from them. *I will do that.*

I am tired, Julija.

Julija didn't like that. Elisabeta was making herself tired by staying in the ground. She wanted to go to Elisabeta's lifemate and shake him. He was too big. Too intimidating. When she tried talking to Isai he shrugged and said no one interfered with lifemates.

Good night, Elisabeta, I will talk with you soon.

She broke the contact and was silent, just absorbing Isai's strength. They sat in silence and then she looked up at him. "What do you think?"

"I do not know. I did not feel any taint in her. Or a feeling of evil. Just the opposite. She radiates peace. I love that you worry so much about your friend, Julija, but she is Ferro's responsibility. He will deal with whatever it is or whoever it is that you think may be talking to her. In the meantime, I want to introduce you to my friends. We have been here a week and you have not met a single person."

She hadn't wanted to meet anyone, but she didn't want to admit that. In any case, he was merged with her most of the time and probably already knew. She was being a coward. She could hear laughter and the sound of children calling to one another as they played. Normal sounds. She didn't know normal. She'd been guarded her entire life.

Coming into Tariq Asenguard's compound meant she would have to learn to live differently. She would have to accept people into her life and let them in. She didn't know how to do that.

Isai leaned down and gently nipped her chin. "You are more frightened of meeting my friends than you were of facing the dark mage."

"I don't know that I would say that."

"In any case, *sívamet*, Tariq has been more than patient. The prince needs to hear an account of the destruction of the book. That will involve an actual accessing of our memories to give him a true account."

Julija heard the warning in his voice. She frowned at him. "What does that mean?"

"One of the men, most likely Tariq's second-in-command, Gary Daratrazanoff, will conduct the inquiry. He will access our memories and send those to the prince."

"We can't just write down what happened like normal people?"

"There was nothing normal about our battle with that book," Isai pointed out, amusement coloring his voice.

She shook her head. "What other memories can he see? I don't want him to have access to anything to do with Barnabas. I won't do this, Isai." She tried to move away from him, but he was fast, tightening his arms like shackles. She held herself stiffly, refusing to give in.

"I will tell him he is only to access your memories of these last few weeks, since the moment you started your journey to warn the prince of the conspiracy your family was involved in." When she didn't relax into him he leaned forward and bit down gently on her earlobe. "I would not allow anything to hurt you. Those memories are not anyone's but yours."

She was silent a moment, turning over and over what he'd said, trying to come to terms with the fact that she now lived in a society where the members all worked with one another in order for their species to survive. She was part of that now. She lifted her face to look up at the man she loved. She was part of him.

"Fine, but do we have to do it now?"

"Tariq has put off Mikhail, our prince, to give us a chance to be together and heal should we need it. He has asked that we attend a meeting tonight with everyone there."

She made a face. "Lovely." Her hand slid down his chest. Lower. Hoping to distract him.

He laughed softly and shifted her slightly to give her better access. "I can see you are determined to get your way."

Her hand stroked. Caressed. She turned her face up for his kiss. "Absolutely." There was triumph in her laughter.

He didn't tell her until much, much later that the meeting hadn't been scheduled until very late in the night.

APPENDIX I
Carpathian Healing Chants

To rightly understand Carpathian healing chants, background is required in several areas:

1. The Carpathian view on healing
2. The Lesser Healing Chant of the Carpathians
3. The Great Healing Chant of the Carpathians
4. Carpathian musical aesthetics
5. Lullaby
6. Song to Heal the Earth
7. Carpathian chanting technique

1. THE CARPATHIAN VIEW ON HEALING

The Carpathians are a nomadic people whose geographic origins can be traced at least as far as the Southern Ural Mountains (near the steppes of modern-day Kazakhstan), on the border between Europe and Asia. (For this reason, modern-day linguists call their language "proto-Uralic," without knowing that this is the language of the Carpathians.) Unlike most nomadic peoples, the Carpathians did not wander due to the need to find new grazing lands as the seasons and climate shifted, or to search for better trade. Instead, the Carpathians' movements were driven by a great purpose: to find a land that would have the right earth, a soil with the kind of richness that would greatly enhance their rejuvenative powers.

Over the centuries, they migrated westward (some six thousand years ago), until they at last found their perfect homeland—their *susu*—in the Carpathian Mountains, whose long arc cradled the lush plains of the kingdom of Hungary. (The kingdom of Hungary flourished for over a millennium—making Hungarian the dominant language of the Carpathian Basin—until the kingdom's lands were split among several countries after World War I: Austria, Czechoslovakia, Romania, Yugoslavia and modern Hungary.)

Other peoples from the Southern Urals (who shared the Carpathian language, but were not Carpathians) migrated in different directions. Some ended up in Finland, which explains why the modern Hungarian and Finnish languages are among the contemporary descendants of the ancient Carpathian language. Even though they are tied forever to their chosen Carpathian homeland, the Carpathians continue to wander as they search

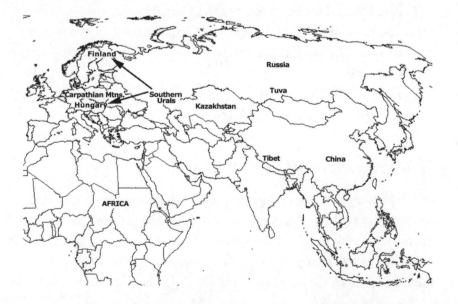

the world for the answers that will enable them to bear and raise their offspring without difficulty.

Because of their geographic origins, the Carpathian views on healing share much with the larger Eurasian shamanistic tradition. Probably the closest modern representative of that tradition is based in Tuva (and is referred to as "Tuvinian Shamanism")—see the map on the previous page.

The Eurasian shamanistic tradition—from the Carpathians to the Siberian shamans—held that illness originated in the human soul, and only later manifested as various physical conditions. Therefore, shamanistic healing, while not neglecting the body, focused on the soul and its healing. The most profound illnesses were understood to be caused by "soul departure," where all or some part of the sick person's soul has wandered away from the body (into the nether realms), or has been captured or possessed by an evil spirit, or both.

The Carpathians belong to this greater Eurasian shamanistic tradition and share its viewpoints. While the Carpathians themselves did not succumb to illness, Carpathian healers understood that the most profound wounds were also accompanied by a similar "soul departure."

Upon reaching the diagnosis of "soul departure," the healer-shaman is then required to make a spiritual journey into the netherworlds to recover the soul. The shaman may have to overcome tremendous challenges along the way, particularly fighting the demon or vampire who has possessed his friend's soul.

"Soul departure" doesn't require a person to be unconscious (although that certainly can be the case as well). It was understood that a person could still appear to be conscious, even talk and interact with others, and yet be missing a part of their soul. The experienced healer or shaman would instantly see the problem nonetheless, in subtle signs that others might miss: the person's attention wandering every now and then, a lessening in their enthusiasm about life, chronic depression, a diminishment in the brightness of their "aura" and the like.

2. THE LESSER HEALING CHANT OF THE CARPATHIANS

Kepä Sarna Pus (**The Lesser Healing Chant**) is used for wounds that are merely physical in nature. The Carpathian healer leaves his body and enters the wounded Carpathian's body to heal great mortal wounds from the inside out using pure energy. He proclaims, "I offer freely my life for your life," as he gives his blood to the injured Carpathian. Because the Carpathians are of the earth and bound to the soil, they are healed by the soil of their homeland. Their saliva is also often used for its rejuvenative powers.

It is also very common for the Carpathian chants (both the Lesser and the Great) to be accompanied by the use of healing herbs, aromas from Carpathian candles and crystals. The crystals (when combined with the Carpathians' empathic, psychic connection to the entire universe) are used to gather positive energy from their surroundings, which then is used to accelerate the healing. Caves are sometimes used as the setting for the healing.

The Lesser Healing Chant was used by Vikirnoff Von Shrieder and Colby Jansen to heal Rafael De La Cruz, whose heart had been ripped out by a vampire as described in *Dark Secret*.

Kepä Sarna Pus (The Lesser Healing Chant)
The same chant is used for all physical wounds. "Sívadaba" ("into your heart") would be changed to refer to whatever part of the body is wounded.

Kuńasz, nélkül sívdobbanás, nélkül fesztelen löyly.
You lie as if asleep, without beat of heart, without airy breath.

Ot élidamet andam szabadon élidadért.
I offer freely my life for your life.

O jelä sielam jörem ot ainamet és soŋe ot élidadet.
My spirit of light forgets my body and enters your body.

O jelä sielam pukta kinn minden szelemeket belső.
My spirit of light sends all the dark spirits within fleeing without.

Pajñak o susu hanyet és o nyelv nyálamet sívadaba.
I press the earth of our homeland and the spit of my tongue into your
   heart.

Vii, o verim soŋe o verid andam.
At last, I give you my blood for your blood.

To hear this chant, visit: http://www.christinefeehan.com/members/.

3. THE GREAT HEALING CHANT OF THE CARPATHIANS

The most well-known—and most dramatic—of the Carpathian healing
chants is ***En Sarna Pus* (The Great Healing Chant)**. This chant is reserved
for recovering the wounded or unconscious Carpathian's soul.

Typically a group of men would form a circle around the sick
Carpathian (to "encircle him with our care and compassion") and begin
the chant. The shaman or healer or leader is the prime actor in this healing
ceremony. It is he who will actually make the spiritual journey into the
netherworld, aided by his clanspeople. Their purpose is to ecstatically
dance, sing, drum and chant, all the while visualizing (through the words
of the chant) the journey itself—every step of it, over and over again—to
the point where the shaman, in trance, leaves his body, and makes that
very journey. (Indeed, the word *ecstasy* is from the Latin *ex statis*, which
literally means "out of the body.")

One advantage that the Carpathian healer has over many other shamans is his telepathic link to his lost brother. Most shamans must wander
in the dark of the nether realms in search of their lost brother. But the
Carpathian healer directly "hears" in his mind the voice of his lost brother
calling to him, and can thus "zero in on" his soul like a homing beacon.
For this reason, Carpathian healing tends to have a higher success rate
than most other traditions of this sort.

Something of the geography of the "other world" is useful for us to
examine, in order to fully understand the words of the Great Carpathian
Healing Chant. A reference is made to the "Great Tree" (in Carpathian:

En Puwe). Many ancient traditions, including the Carpathian tradition, understood the worlds—the heaven worlds, our world and the nether realms—to be "hung" upon a great pole, or axis, or tree. Here on earth, we are positioned halfway up this tree, on one of its branches. Hence many ancient texts referred to the material world as "middle earth": midway between heaven and hell. Climbing the tree would lead one to the heaven worlds. Descending the tree to its roots would lead to the nether realms. The shaman was necessarily a master of movement up and down the Great Tree, sometimes moving unaided, and sometimes assisted by (or even mounted upon the back of) an animal spirit guide. In various traditions, this Great Tree was known variously as the *axis mundi* (the "axis of the worlds"), Ygddrasil (in Norse mythology), Mount Meru (the sacred world mountain of Tibetan tradition), etc. The Christian cosmos, with its heaven, purgatory/earth and hell, is also worth comparing. It is even given a similar topography in Dante's *Divine Comedy*: Dante is led on a journey first to hell, at the center of the earth; then upward to Mount Purgatory, which sits on the earth's surface directly opposite Jerusalem; then farther upward first to Eden, the earthly paradise, at the summit of Mount Purgatory; and then upward at last to Heaven.

In the shamanistic tradition, it was understood that the small always reflects the large; the personal always reflects the cosmic. A movement in the greater dimensions of the cosmos also coincides with an internal movement. For example, the *axis mundi* of the cosmos corresponds with the spinal column of the individual. Journeys up and down the *axis mundi* often coincided with the movements of natural and spiritual energies (sometimes called *kundalini* or *shakti*) in the spinal column of the shaman or mystic.

En Sarna Pus (The Great Healing Chant)
In this chant, ekä ("brother") would be replaced by "sister," "father," "mother," depending on the person to be healed.

Ot ekäm ainajanak hany, jama.
My brother's body is a lump of earth, close to death.

Me, ot ekäm kuntajanak, pirädak ekäm, gond és irgalom türe.
We, the clan of my brother, encircle him with our care and compassion.

O pus wäkenkek, ot oma śarnank, és ot pus fünk, álnak ekäm ainajanak,
pitänak ekäm ainajanak elävä.
Our healing energies, ancient words of magic and healing herbs bless
my brother's body, keep it alive.

Ot ekäm sielanak pälä. Ot omboće päläja juta alatt o jüti, kinta, és szelemek
lamtijaknak.
But my brother's soul is only half. His other half wanders in the
netherworld.

Ot en mekem ŋamaŋ: kulkedak otti ot ekäm omboće päläjanak.
My great deed is this: I travel to find my brother's other half.

Rekatüre, saradak, tappadak, odam, kaŋa o numa waram, és avaa owe o
lewl mahoz.
We dance, we chant, we dream ecstatically, to call my spirit bird, and to
open the door to the other world.

Ntak o numa waram, és mozdulak; jomadak.
I mount my spirit bird and we begin to move; we are under way.

Piwtädak ot En Puwe tyvinak, ećidak alatt o jüti, kinta, és szelemek
lamtijaknak.
Following the trunk of the Great Tree, we fall into the netherworld.

Fázak, fázak nó o śaro.
It is cold, very cold.

Juttadak ot ekäm o akarataban, o sívaban és o sielaban.
My brother and I are linked in mind, heart and soul.

Ot ekäm sielanak kaŋa engem.
My brother's soul calls to me.

Kuledak és piwtädak ot ekäm.
I hear and follow his track.

Saɣedak és tuledak ot ekäm kulyanak.
Encounter I the demon who is devouring my brother's soul.

Nenäm ćoro, o kuly torodak.
In anger, I fight the demon.

O kuly pél engem.
He is afraid of me.

Lejkkadak o kaŋka salamaval.
I strike his throat with a lightning bolt.

Molodak ot ainaja komakamal.
I break his body with my bare hands.

Toja és molanâ.
He is bent over, and falls apart.

Hän ćaδa.
He runs away.

Manedak ot ekäm sielanak.
I rescue my brother's soul.

Alədak ot ekam sielanak o komamban.
I lift my brother's soul in the hollow of my hand.

Alədam ot ekam numa waramra.
I lift him onto my spirit bird.

Piwtädak ot En Puwe tyvijanak és sayedak jälleen ot elävä ainak majaknak.
Following up the Great Tree, we return to the land of the living.

Ot ekäm elä jälleen.
My brother lives again.

Ot ekäm weńća jälleen.
He is complete again.

To hear this chant, visit: http://www.christinefeehan.com/members/.

4. CARPATHIAN MUSICAL AESTHETICS

In the sung Carpathian pieces (such as the "Lullaby" and the "Song to Heal the Earth"), you'll hear elements that are shared by many of the musical traditions in the Uralic geographical region, some of which still exist—from Eastern European (Bulgarian, Romanian, Hungarian, Croatian, etc.) to Romany ("gypsy"). These elements include:

- the rapid alternation between major and minor modalities, including a sudden switch (called a "Picardy third") from minor to major to end a piece or section (as at the end of the "Lullaby")
- the use of close (tight) harmonies
- the use of *ritardi* (slowing down the piece) and *crescendi* (swelling in volume) for brief periods
- the use of *glissandi* (slides) in the singing tradition
- the use of trills in the singing tradition (as in the final invocation of the "Song to Heal the Earth")—similar to Celtic, a singing tradition more familiar to many of us
- the use of parallel fifths (as in the final invocation of the "Song to Heal the Earth")
- controlled use of dissonance
- "call and response" chanting (typical of many of the world's chanting traditions)

- extending the length of a musical line (by adding a couple of bars) to heighten dramatic effect
- and many more

"Lullaby" and "Song to Heal the Earth" illustrate two rather different forms of Carpathian music (a quiet, intimate piece and an energetic ensemble piece)—but whatever the form, Carpathian music is full of feeling.

5. LULLABY

This song is sung by a woman while a child is still in the womb or when the threat of a miscarriage is apparent. The baby can hear the song while inside the mother, and the mother can connect with the child telepathically as well. The lullaby is meant to reassure the child, to encourage the baby to hold on, to stay—to reassure the child that he or she will be protected by love even from inside until birth. The last line literally means that the mother's love will protect her child until the child is born ("rise").

Musically, the Carpathian "Lullaby" is in three-quarter time ("waltz time"), as are a significant portion of the world's various traditional lullabies (perhaps the most famous of which is "Brahms' Lullaby"). The arrangement for solo voice is the original context: a mother singing to her child, unaccompanied. The arrangement for chorus and violin ensemble illustrates how musical even the simplest Carpathian pieces often are, and how easily they lend themselves to contemporary instrumental or orchestral arrangements. (A wide range of contemporary composers, including Dvořák and Smetana, have taken advantage of a similar discovery, working other traditional Eastern European music into their symphonic poems.)

Odam-Sarna Kondak (Lullaby)

Tumtesz o wäke ku pitasz belső.
Feel the strength you hold inside.

Hiszasz sívadet. Én olenam gæidnod.
Trust your heart. I'll be your guide.

Sas csecsemõm; kuńasz.
Hush, my baby; close your eyes.

Rauho joŋe ted.
Peace will come to you.

Tumtesz o sívdobbanás ku olen lamt3ad belső.
Feel the rhythm deep inside.

Gond-kumpadek ku kim te.
Waves of love that cover you.

Pesänak te, asti o jüti, kidüsz.
Protect, until the night you rise.

To hear this song, visit: http://www.christinefeehan.com/members/.

6. SONG TO HEAL THE EARTH

This is the earth-healing song that is used by the Carpathian women to heal soil filled with various toxins. The women take a position on four sides and call to the universe to draw on the healing energy with love and respect. The soil of the earth is their resting place, the place where they rejuvenate, and they must make it safe not only for themselves but for their unborn children as well as their men and living children. This is a beautiful ritual performed by the women together, raising their voices in harmony and calling on the earth's minerals and healing properties to come forth and help them save their children. They literally dance and sing to heal the earth in a ceremony as old as their species. The dance and notes of the song are adjusted according to the toxins felt through the healer's bare feet. The feet are placed in a certain pattern and the hands gracefully weave a healing spell while the dance is performed. They must be especially careful when the soil is prepared for babies. This is a ceremony of love and healing.

Musically, the ritual is divided into several sections:

- **First verse**: A "call and response" section, where the chant leader sings the "call" solo, and then some or all of the women sing the "response" in the close harmony style typical of the Carpathian musical tradition. The repeated response—*Ai Emä Maγe*—is an invocation of the source of power for the healing ritual: "Oh, Mother Nature."
- **First chorus**: This section is filled with clapping, dancing, ancient horns and other means used to invoke and heighten the energies upon which the ritual is drawing.
- **Second verse**
- **Second chorus**
- **Closing invocation:** In this closing part, two song leaders, in close harmony, take all the energy gathered by the earlier portions of the song/ritual and focus it entirely on the healing purpose.

What you will be listening to are brief tastes of what would typically be a significantly longer ritual, in which the verse and chorus parts are developed and repeated many times, to be closed by a single rendition of the final invocation.

Sarna Pusm O Maγet (Song to Heal the Earth)

First verse
Ai, Emä Maγe,
Oh, Mother Nature,

Me sívadbin lañaak.
We are your beloved daughters.

Me tappadak, me pusmak o maɣet.
We dance to heal the earth.

Me sarnadak, me pusmak o hanyet.
We sing to heal the earth.

Sielanket jutta tedet it,
We join with you now,

Sívank és akaratank és sielank juttanak.
Our hearts and minds and spirits become one.

Second verse
Ai, Ëmä maɣe,
Oh, Mother Nature,

Me sívadbin lańaak.
We are your beloved daughters.

Me andak arwadet emänked és me kaŋank o
We pay homage to our mother and call upon the

Põhi és Lõuna, Ida és Lääs.
North and South, East and West.

Pide és aldyn és myös belső.
Above and below and within as well.

Gondank o maɣenak pusm hän ku olen jama.
Our love of the land heals that which is in need.

Juttanak teval it,
We join with you now,

Maye mayeval.
Earth to earth.

O pirä elidak weńća.
The circle of life is complete.

To hear this chant, visit: http://www.christinefeehan.com/members/.

7. CARPATHIAN CHANTING TECHNIQUE

As with their healing techniques, the actual "chanting technique" of the
Carpathians has much in common with the other shamanistic traditions of
the Central Asian steppes. The primary mode of chanting was throat chanting using overtones. Modern examples of this manner of singing can still
be found in the Mongolian, Tuvan and Tibetan traditions. You can find an
audio example of the Gyuto Tibetan Buddhist monks engaged in throat
chanting at: http://www.christinefeehan.com/carpathian_chanting/.

As with Tuva, note on the map the geographical proximity of Tibet
to Kazakhstan and the Southern Urals.

The beginning part of the Tibetan chant emphasizes synchronizing
all the voices around a single tone, aimed at healing a particular "chakra"
of the body. This is fairly typical of the Gyuto throat-chanting tradition,
but it is not a significant part of the Carpathian tradition. Nonetheless, it
serves as an interesting contrast.

The part of the Gyuto chanting example that is most similar to the
Carpathian style of chanting is the midsection, where the men are chanting the words together with great force. The purpose here is not to generate a "healing tone" that will affect a particular "chakra," but rather to
generate as much power as possible for initiating the "out of body" travel,
and for fighting the demonic forces that the healer/traveler must face and
overcome.

The songs of the Carpathian women (illustrated by their "Lullaby"
and their "Song to Heal the Earth") are part of the same ancient musical
and healing tradition as the Lesser and Great Healing Chants of the

warrior males. You can hear some of the same instruments in both the male warriors' healing chants and the women's "Song to Heal the Earth." Also, they share the common purpose of generating and directing power. However, the women's songs are distinctively feminine in character. One immediately noticeable difference is that, while the men speak their words in the manner of a chant, the women sing songs with melodies and harmonies, softening the overall performance. A feminine, nurturing quality is especially evident in the "Lullaby."

APPENDIX 2

The Carpathian Language

Like all human languages, the language of the Carpathians contains the richness and nuance that can only come from a long history of use. At best we can only touch on some of the main features of the language in this brief appendix:

1. The history of the Carpathian language
2. Carpathian grammar and other characteristics of the language
3. Examples of the Carpathian language (including the Ritual Words and the Warriors' Chant)
4. A much-abridged Carpathian dictionary

1. THE HISTORY OF THE CARPATHIAN LANGUAGE

The Carpathian language of today is essentially identical to the Carpathian language of thousands of years ago. A "dead" language like the Latin of two thousand years ago has evolved into a significantly different modern language (Italian) because of countless generations of speakers and great historical fluctuations. In contrast, many of the speakers of Carpathian from thousands of years ago are still alive. Their presence—coupled with the deliberate isolation of the Carpathians from the other major forces of change in the world—has acted (and continues to act) as a stabilizing force that has preserved the integrity of the language over the centuries. Carpathian culture has also acted as a stabilizing force. For instance, the Ritual Words, the various healing chants (see Appendix 1) and other cultural artifacts have been passed down through the centuries with great fidelity.

One small exception should be noted: the splintering of the Carpathians into separate geographic regions has led to some minor dialectization. However, the telepathic link among all Carpathians (as well as each Carpathian's regular return to his or her homeland) has ensured that the differences among dialects are relatively superficial (e.g., small numbers of new words, minor differences in pronunciation, etc.), since the deeper, internal language of mind-forms has remained the same because of continuous use across space and time.

The Carpathian language was (and still is) the proto-language for the Uralic (or Finno-Ugric) family of languages. Today, the Uralic languages are spoken in northern, eastern and central Europe and in Siberia. More than twenty-three million people in the world speak languages that can trace their ancestry to Carpathian. Magyar or Hungarian (about fourteen million speakers), Finnish (about five million speakers) and Estonian (about one million speakers) are the three major contemporary descendents of this proto-language. The only factor that unites the more than twenty languages in the Uralic family is that their ancestry can be traced back to a common proto-language—Carpathian—that split (starting some six thousand years ago) into the various languages in the Uralic family. In the same way, European languages such as English and French belong to the better-known Indo-European family and also evolved from a common proto-language ancestor (a different one from Carpathian).

The following table provides a sense of some of the similarities in the language family.

Note: The Finnic/Carpathian "k" shows up often as Hungarian "h." Similarly, the Finnic/Carpathian "p" often corresponds to the Hungarian "f."

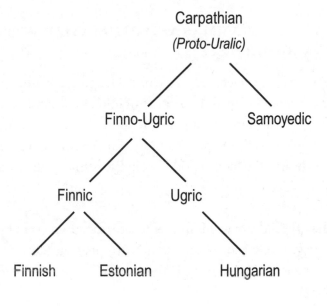

Carpathian
(proto-Uralic)

Finnish
(Suomi)

Hungarian
(Magyar)

Carpathian (proto-Uralic)	Finnish (Suomi)	Hungarian (Magyar)
elä—live	*elä*—live	*él*—live
elid—life	*clinikä*—life	*élet*—life
pesä—nest	*pesä*—nest	*fészek*—nest
kola—die	*kuole*—die	*hal*—die
pälä—half, side	*pieltä*—tilt, tip to the side	*fél, fele*—fellow human, friend (half; one side of two) *feleség*—wife
and—give	*anta, antaa*—give	*ad*—give
koje—husband, man	*koira*—dog, the male (of animals)	*here*—drone, testicle
wäke—power	*väki*—folks, people, men; force	*vall-/-vel*—with (instrumental suffix)
	väkevä—powerful, strong	*vele*—with him/her/it
wete—water	*vesi*—water	*viz*—water

2. CARPATHIAN GRAMMAR AND OTHER CHARACTERISTICS OF THE LANGUAGE

Idioms. As both an ancient language and a language of an earth people, Carpathian is more inclined toward use of idioms constructed from concrete, "earthy" terms rather than abstractions. For instance, our modern abstraction "to cherish" is expressed more concretely in Carpathian as "to hold in one's heart"; the "netherworld" is, in Carpathian, "the land of night, fog and ghosts"; etc.

Word order. The order of words in a sentence is determined not by syntactic roles (like subject, verb and object) but rather by pragmatic, discourse-driven factors. Examples: *"Tied vagyok."* ("Yours am I."); *"Sívamet andam."* ("My heart I give you.")

Agglutination. The Carpathian language is agglutinative; that is, longer words are constructed from smaller components. An agglutinating language uses suffixes or prefixes whose meanings are generally unique, and which are concatenated one after another without overlap. In Carpathian, words typically consist of a stem that is followed by one or more suffixes. For example, *"sívambam"* derives from the stem *"sív"* ("heart"), followed by *"am"* ("my," making it "my heart"), followed by *"bam"* ("in," making it "in my heart"). As you might imagine, agglutination in Carpathian can sometimes produce very long words, or words that are very difficult to pronounce. Vowels often get inserted between suffixes to prevent too many consonants from appearing in a row (which can make a word unpronounceable).

Noun cases. Like all languages, Carpathian has many noun cases; the same noun will be "spelled" differently depending on its role in a sentence. The noun cases include: nominative (when the noun is the subject of the sentence), accusative (when the noun is a direct object of the verb), dative (indirect object), genitive (or possessive), instrumental, final, suppressive, inessive, elative, terminative and delative.

We will use the possessive (or genitive) case as an example to illustrate how all noun cases in Carpathian involve adding standard suffixes to the noun stems. Thus expressing possession in Carpathian—"my lifemate," "your lifemate," "his lifemate," "her lifemate," etc.—involves adding a particular suffix (such as "-*am*") to the noun stem (*"päläfertiil"*) to produce the possessive (*"päläfertiilam"*—"my lifemate"). Which suffix to use depends upon which person ("my," "your," "his," etc.) and whether the noun ends in a consonant or a vowel. The table below shows the suffixes for singular nouns only (not plural), and also shows the similarity to the suffixes used in contemporary Hungarian. (Hungarian is actually a little more complex, in that it also requires "vowel rhyming": which suffix to use also depends on the last vowel in the noun; hence the multiple choices in the cells below, where Carpathian only has a single choice.)

	Carpathian (proto-Uralic)		Contemporary Hungarian	
person	**noun ends in vowel**	**noun ends in consonant**	**noun ends in vowel**	**noun ends in consonant**
1st singular (my)	-m	-am	-m	-om, -em, -öm
2nd singular (your)	-d	-ad	-d	-od, -ed, -öd
3rd singular (his, her, its)	-ja	-a	-ja/-je	-a, -e
1st plural (our)	-nk	-ank	-nk	-unk, -ünk
2nd plural (your)	-tak	-atak	-tok, -tek, -tök	-otok, -etek, -ötök
3rd plural (their)	-jak	-ak	-juk, -jük	-uk, -ük

Note: As mentioned earlier, vowels often get inserted between the word and its suffix so as to prevent too many consonants from appearing in a row (which would produce unpronounceable words). For example, in the table on the previous page, all nouns that end in a consonant are followed by suffixes beginning with "a."

Verb conjugation. Like its modern descendents (such as Finnish and Hungarian), Carpathian has many verb tenses, far too many to describe here. We will just focus on the conjugation of the present tense. Again, we will place contemporary Hungarian side by side with Carpathian, because of the marked similarity between the two.

As with the possessive case for nouns, the conjugation of verbs is done by adding a suffix onto the verb stem:

Person	Carpathian (proto-Uralic)	Contemporary Hungarian
1st singular (I give)	-am (andam), -ak	-ok, -ek, -ök
2nd singular (you give)	-sz (andsz)	-sz
3rd singular (he/she/it gives)	— (and)	—
1st plural (we give)	-ak (andak)	-unk, -ünk
2nd plural (you give)	-tak (andtak)	-tok, -tek, -tök
3rd plural (they give)	-nak (andnak)	-nak, -nek

As with all languages, there are many "irregular verbs" in Carpathian that don't exactly fit this pattern. But the above table is still a useful guide for most verbs.

3. EXAMPLES OF THE CARPATHIAN LANGUAGE

Here are some brief examples of conversational Carpathian, used in the Dark books. We include the literal translation in square brackets. It is interestingly different from the most appropriate English translation.

Susu.
I am home.
["home/birthplace." "I am" is understood, as is often the case in Carpathian.]

Möért?
What for?

csitri
little one
["little slip of a thing," "little slip of a girl"]

ainaak enyém
forever mine

ainaak sívamet jutta
forever mine (another form)
["forever to-my-heart connected/fixed"]

sívamet
my love
["of-my-heart," "to-my-heart"]

Tet vigyázam.
I love you.
["you-love-I"]

Sarna Rituaali (**The Ritual Words**) is a longer example, and an example of chanted rather than conversational Carpathian. Note the recurring use of *"andam"* ("I give"), to give the chant musicality and force through repetition.

Sarna Rituaali (The Ritual Words)

Te avio päläfertiilam.
You are my lifemate.

Éntölam kuulua, avio päläfertiilam.
I claim you as my lifemate.

Ted kuuluak, kacad, kojed.
I belong to you.

Élidamet andam.
I offer my life for you.

Pesämet andam.
I give you my protection.

Uskolfertiilamet andam.
I give you my allegiance.

Sívamet andam.
I give you my heart.

Sielamet andam.
I give you my soul.

Ainamet andam.
I give you my body.

Sívamet kuuluak kaik että a ted.
I take into my keeping the same that is yours.

Ainaak olenszal sívambin.
Your life will be cherished by me for all my time.

Te élidet ainaak pide minan.
Your life will be placed above my own for all time.

Te avio päläfertiilam.
You are my lifemate.

Ainaak sívamet jutta oleny.
You are bound to me for all eternity.

Ainaak terád vigyázak.
You are always in my care.

To hear these words pronounced (and for more about Carpathian pronunciation altogether), please visit: http://www.christinefeehan.com /members/.

Sarna Kontakawk (**The Warriors' Chant**) is another longer example of the Carpathian language. The warriors' council takes place deep beneath the earth in a chamber of crystals with magma far below it, so the steam is natural and the wisdom of their ancestors is clear and focused. This is a sacred place where they bloodswear to their prince and people and affirm their code of honor as warriors and brothers. It is also where battle strategies are born and all dissension is discussed as well as any concerns the warriors have that they wish to bring to the council and open for discussion.

Sarna Kontakawk (The Warriors' Chant)

Veri isäakank—veri ekäakank.
Blood of our fathers—blood of our brothers.

Veri olen elid.
Blood is life.

Andak veri-elidet Karpatiiakank, és wäke-sarna ku meke arwa-arvo, irgalom, hän ku agba, és wäke kutni, ku manaak verival.
We offer that life to our people with a bloodsworn vow of honor, mercy, integrity and endurance.

Verink sokta; verink kaŋa terád.
Our blood mingles and calls to you.

Akasz énak ku kaŋa és juttasz kuntatak it.
Heed our summons and join with us now.

To hear these words pronounced (and for more about Carpathian pronunciation altogether), please visit: http://www.christinefeehan.com /members/.

See **Appendix 1** for Carpathian healing chants, including the *Kepä Sarna Pus* (The Lesser Healing Chant), the *En Sarna Pus* (The Great Healing Chant), the *Odam-Sarna Kondak* (Lullaby) and the *Sarna Pusm O Mayet* (Song to Heal the Earth).

4. A MUCH-ABRIDGED CARPATHIAN DICTIONARY

This very-much-abridged Carpathian dictionary contains most of the Carpathian words used in the Dark books. Of course, a full Carpathian dictionary would be as large as the usual dictionary for an entire language (typically more than a hundred thousand words).

Note: The Carpathian nouns and verbs below are word **stems**. They generally do not appear in their isolated "stem" form, as below. Instead, they usually appear with suffixes (e.g., *andam—I give*, rather than just the root, *and*).

a—verb negation (*prefix*); not (*adverb*).
aćke—pace, step.
aćke éntölem it—take another step toward me.
agba—to be seemly; to be proper (*verb*). True; seemly; proper (*adj.*).
ai—oh.
aina—body (*noun*).
ainaak—always; forever.
o ainaak jelä peje emnimet ŋamaŋ—sun scorch that woman forever (*Carpathian swear words*).
ainaakä—never.
ainaakfél—old friend.

ak—suffix added after a noun ending in a consonant to make it plural.

aka—to give heed; to hearken; to listen.

aka-arvo—respect (*noun*).

akarat—mind; will (*noun*).

ál—to bless; to attach to.

alatt—through.

aldyn—under; underneath.

alə—to lift; to raise.

alte—to bless; to curse.

amaŋ—this; this one here; that; that one there.

and—to give.

and sielet, arwa-arvomet, és jelämet, kuulua huvémet ku feaj és ködet ainaak—to trade soul, honor and salvation for momentary pleasure and endless damnation.

andasz éntölem irgalomet!—have mercy!

arvo—value; price (*noun*).

arwa—praise (*noun*).

arwa-arvod—honor (*noun*).

arwa-arvod mäne me ködak—may your honor hold back the dark (*greeting*).

arwa-arvo olen gæidnod, ekäm—honor guide you, my brother (*greeting*).

arwa-arvo olen isäntä, ekäm—honor keep you, my brother (*greeting*).

arwa-arvo pile sívadet—may honor light your heart (*greeting*).

aš—no (*exclamation*).

ašša—no (before a noun); not (with a verb that is not in the imperative); not (with an adjective).

aššatotello—disobedient.

asti—until.

avaa—to open.

avio—wedded.

avio päläfertiil—lifemate.

avoi—uncover; show; reveal.

baszú—revenge; vengeance.

belső—within; inside.

bur—good; well.

bur tule ekämet kuntamak—well met brother-kin (*greeting*).

ćaдa—to flee; to run; to escape.

čač3—to be born; to grow.

ćoro—to flow; to run like rain.

csecsemõ—baby (*noun*).

csitri—little one (*female*).

diutal—triumph; victory.

džinõt—brief; short.

eći—to fall.

ej—not (*adverb, suffix*); *nej* when preceding syllable ends in a vowel.

ek—suffix added after a noun ending in a consonant to make it plural.

ekä—brother.

ekäm—my brother.

elä—to live.

eläsz arwa-arvoval—may you live with honor; live nobly (*greeting*).

eläsz jeläbam ainaak—long may you live in the light (*greeting*).

elävä—alive.

elävä ainak majaknak—land of the living.

elid—life.

emä—mother (*noun*).

Emä Maγe—Mother Nature.

emäen—grandmother.

embɛ—if; when.

embɛ karmasz—please.

emni—wife; woman.

emni hän ku köd alte—cursed woman.

emni kuŋenak ku aššatotello—disobedient lunatic.

emnim—my wife; my woman.

én—I.

en—great; many; big.

en hän ku pesä—the protector (literally: the great protector).

en Karpatii—the prince (literally: the great Carpathian).

enä—most.

enkojra—wolf.

én jutta félet és ekämet—I greet a friend and brother (*greeting*).

én maγenak—I am of the earth.

én oma maγeka—I am as old as time (literally: as old as the earth).

En Puwe—The Great Tree. Related to the legends of Ygddrasil, the axis mundi, Mount Meru, heaven and hell, etc.

engem—of me.

és—and.

év—year.

évsatz—century.

ete—before; in front of.

että—that.

fáz—to feel cold or chilly.

fél—fellow; friend.

fél ku kuuluaak sívam belső—beloved.

fél ku vigyázak—dear one.

feldolgaz—prepare.

fertiil—fertile one.

fesztelen—airy.

fü—herbs; grass.

gæidno—road; way.

gond—care; worry; love (*noun*).

hän—he; she; it; one.

hän agba—it is so.

hän ku—prefix: one who; he who; that which.

hän ku agba—truth.

hän ku kaśwa o numamet—sky-owner.

hän ku kuula siela—keeper of his soul.

hän ku kuulua sívamet—keeper of my heart.

hän ku lejkka wäke-sarnat—traitor.

hän ku meke pirämet—defender.

hän ku meke sarnaakmet—mage.

hän ku pesä—protector.

hän ku pesäk kaikak—guardians of all.

hän ku piwtä—predator; hunter; tracker.

hän ku pusm—healer.

hän ku saa kuć3aket—star-reacher.

hän ku tappa—killer; violent person (*noun*). Deadly; violent (*adj.*).

hän ku tuulmahl elidet—vampire (literally: life-stealer).

hän ku vie elidet—vampire (literally: thief of life).

hän ku vigyáz sielamet—keeper of my soul.

hän ku vigyáz sívamet és sielamet—keeper of my heart and soul.

hän sívamak—beloved.

hängem—him; her; it.

hank—they.

hany—clod; lump of earth.

hisz—to believe; to trust.

ho—how.

ida—east.

igazág—justice.

ila—to shine.

inan—mine; my own (*endearment*).

irgalom—compassion; pity; mercy.

isä—father (*noun*).

isäntä—master of the house.

it—now.

jaguár—jaguar.

jaka—to cut; to divide; to separate.

jakam—wound; cut; injury.

jalka—leg.

jälleen—again.

jama—to be sick, infected, wounded or dying; to be near death.

jamatan—fallen; wounded; near death.

jelä—sunlight; day, sun; light.

jelä keje terád—light sear you (*Carpathian swear words*).

o jelä peje kaik hänkanak—sun scorch them all (*Carpathian swear words*).

o jelä peje emnimet—sun scorch the woman (*Carpathian swear words*).

o jelä peje terád—sun scorch you (*Carpathian swear words*).

o jelä peje terád, emni—sun scorch you, woman (*Carpathian swear words*).

o jelä sielamak—light of my soul.

joma—to be under way; to go.

joŋe—to come; to return.

joŋesz arwa-arvoval—return with honor (*greeting*).

joŋesz éntölem, fél ku kuuluaak sívam belsö—come to me, beloved.

jotka—gap; middle; space.

jotkan—between.

juo—to drink.

juosz és eläsz—drink and live (*greeting*).

juosz és olen ainaak sielamet jutta—drink and become one with me (*greeting*).

juta—to go; to wander.

jüti—night; evening.

jutta—connected; fixed (*adj.*). To connect; to join; to fix; to bind (*verb*).

k—suffix added after a noun ending in a vowel to make it plural.

kać3—gift.

kaca—male lover.

kadi—judge.

kaik—all.

käktä—two; many.

käktäverit—mixed blood (literally: two bloods).

kalma—corpse; death; grave.

kaŋa—to call; to invite; to summon; to request; to beg.

kaŋk—windpipe; Adam's apple; throat.

karma—want.

Karpatii—Carpathian.

karpatii ku köd—liar.

Karpatiikunta—the Carpathian people.

käsi—hand.

kaśwa—to own.

kaδa—to abandon; to leave; to remain.

kaδa wäkeva óv o köd—stand fast against the dark (*greeting*).

kat—house; family (*noun*).

katt3—to move; to penetrate; to proceed.

keje—to cook; to burn; to sear.

kepä—lesser; small; easy; few.

kessa—cat.

kessa ku toro—wildcat.

kessake—little cat.

kidü—to wake up; to arise (*intransitive verb*).

kim—to cover an entire object with some sort of covering.

kinn—out; outdoors; outside; without.

kinta—fog; mist; smoke.

kislány—little girl.

kislány hän ku meke sarnaakmet—little mage.

kislány kuŋenak—little lunatic.

kislány kuŋenak minan—my little lunatic.

köd—fog; mist; darkness; evil (*noun*). Foggy, dark; evil (*adj.*).

köd alte hän—darkness curse it (*Carpathian swear words*).

o köd belső—darkness take it (*Carpathian swear words*).

köd elävä és köd nime kutni nimet—evil lives and has a name.

köd jutasz belső—shadow take you (*Carpathian swear words*).

koj—let; allow; decree; establish; order.

koje—man; husband; drone.

kola—to die.

kolasz arwa-arvoval—may you die with honor (*greeting*).

kolatan—dead; departed.

koma—empty hand; bare hand; palm of the hand; hollow of the hand.

kond—all of a family's or clan's children.

kont—warrior; man.

kont o sívanak—strong heart (literally: heart of the warrior).

kor3—basket; container made of birch bark.

kor3nat—containing; including.

ku—who; which; that; where; which; what.

kuć3—star.

kuć3ak!—stars! (exclamation).

kudeje—descent; generation.

kuja—day; sun.

kule—to hear.

kulke—to go or to travel (on land or water).

kulkesz arwa-arvoval, ekäm—walk with honor, my brother (*greeting*).

kulkesz arwaval, joŋesz arwa arvoval—go with glory, return with honor (*greeting*).

kuly—intestinal worm; tapeworm; demon who possesses and devours souls.

küm—human male.

kumala—to sacrifice; to offer; to pray.

kumpa—wave (*noun*).

kuńa—to lie as if asleep; to close or cover the eyes in a game of hide-and-seek; to die.

kuŋe—moon; month.

kunta—band; clan; tribe; family; people; lineage; line.

kuras—sword; large knife.

kure—bind; tie.

kuš—worker; servant.

kutenken—however.

kutni—to be able to bear, carry, endure, stand or take.

kutnisz ainaak—long may you endure (*greeting*).

kuulua—to belong; to hold.

kužõ—long.

lääs—west.

lamti (or lamt3)—lowland; meadow; deep; depth.

lamti ból jüti, kinta, ja szelem—the nether world (literally: the meadow of night, mists, and ghosts).

lańa—daughter.

lejkka—crack; fissure; split (*noun*). To cut; to hit; to strike forcefully (*verb*).

lewl—spirit (*noun*).

lewl ma—the other world (literally: spirit land). *Lewl ma* includes *lamti ból jüti, kinta, ja szelem*: the nether world, but also includes the worlds higher up *En Puwe*, the Great Tree.

liha—flesh.

lõuna—south.

löyly—breath; steam. (related to *lewl*: spirit).

luwe—bone.

ma—land; forest; world.

magköszun—thank.

mana—to abuse; to curse; to ruin.

mäne—to rescue; to save.

maɣe—land; earth; territory; place; nature.

mboće—other; second (*adj.*).

me—we.

megem—us.

meke—deed; work (*noun*). To do; to make; to work (*verb*).

mić (or mića)—beautiful.

mića emni kuŋenak minan—my beautiful lunatic.

minan—mine; my own (*endearment*).

minden—every; all (*adj.*).

möért?—what for? (*exclamation*).

molo—to crush; to break into bits.

molanâ—to crumble; to fall apart.

moo—why; reason.

mozdul—to begin to move; to enter into movement.

muonì—appoint; order; prescribe; command.

muonìak te avoisz te—I command you to reveal yourself.

musta—memory.

myös—also.

m8—thing; what.

na—close; near.

nä—for.

nâbbŏ—so, then.

ŋamaŋ—this; this one here; that; that one there.

ŋamaŋak—these; these ones here; those; those ones there.

nautish—to enjoy.

nélkül—without.

nenä—anger.

nime—name.

nókunta—kinship.

numa—god; sky; top; upper part; highest (related to the English word *numinous*).

numatorkuld—thunder (literally: sky struggle).

ńůp@l—for; to; toward.

ńůp@l mam—toward my world.

nyelv—tongue.

nyál—saliva; spit. (related to *nyelv*: tongue).

ńiŋ3—worm; maggot.

o—the (used before a noun beginning with a consonant).

ó—like; in the same way as; as.

odam—to dream; to sleep.

odam-sarna kondak—lullaby (literally: sleep-song of children).

odam wäke emni—mistress of illusions.

olen—to be.

oma—old; ancient; last; previous.

omas—stand.

omboce—other; second (*adj.*).

ŏrem—to forget; to lose one's way; to make a mistake.

ot—the (used before a noun beginning with a vowel).

ot (or t)—past participle (*suffix*).

otti—to look; to see; to find.

óv—to protect against.

owe—door.

päämoro—aim; target.

pajna—to press.

pälä—half; side.

päläfertiil—mate or wife.

päläpälä—side by side.

palj3—more.

palj3 na éntölem—closer.

partiolen—scout (*noun*).

peje—to burn; scorch.

peje!—burn! (*Carpathian swear word*).

peje terád—get burned (*Carpathian swear words*).

pél—to be afraid; to be scared of.

pesä—nest (*literal; noun*); protection (*figurative; noun*).

pesä—nest; stay (*literal*); protect (*figurative*).

pesäd te engemal—you are safe with me.

pesäsz jeläbam ainaak—long may you stay in the light (*greeting*).

pide—above.

pile—to ignite; to light up.

pion—soon.

pirä—circle; ring (*noun*). To surround; to enclose (*verb*).

piros—red.

pitä—to keep; to hold; to have; to possess.

pitäam mustaakad sielpesäambam—I hold your memories safe in my soul.

pitäsz baszú, piwtäsz igazáget—no vengeance, only justice.

piwtä—to seek; to follow; to follow the track of game; to hunt; to prey upon.

poår—bit; piece.

põhi—north.

pohoopa—vigorous.

pukta—to drive away; to persecute; to put to flight.

pus—healthy; healing.

pusm—to heal; to be restored to health.

puwe—tree; wood.

rambsolg—slave.

rauho—peace.

reka—ecstasy; trance.

rituaali—ritual.

sa—sinew; tendon; cord.

sa4—to call; to name.

saa—arrive, come; become; get, receive.

saasz hän ku andam szabadon—take what I freely offer.

sapar—tail.

sapar bin jalkak—coward (literally: tail between legs).

sapar bin jalkak nélkül mogal—spineless coward.

sas—shoosh (*to a child or baby*).

saγe—to arrive; to come; to reach.

salama—lightning; lightning bolt.

sarna—words; speech; song; magic incantation (*noun*). To chant; to sing; to celebrate (*verb*).

sarna hän agba—claim.

sarna kontakawk—warriors' chant.

sarna kunta—alliance (literally: single tribe through sacred words).

śaro—frozen snow.

satz—hundred.

siel—soul.

siel sielamed—soul to soul (literally: your soul to my soul).

sielam—my soul.

sielam pitwä sielad—my soul searches for your soul.

sielam sieladed—my soul to your soul.

sieljelä isäntä—purity of soul triumphs.

sisar—sister.

sisarak sivak—sisters of the heart.

sisarke—little sister.

sív—heart.

sív pide köd—love transcends evil.

sív pide minden köd—love transcends all evil.

sívad olen wäkeva, hän ku piwtä—may your heart stay strong, hunter (*greeting*).

sívam és sielam—my heart and soul.

sívamet—my heart.

sívdobbanás—heartbeat (*literal*); rhythm (*figurative*).

sokta—to mix; to stir around.

sõl—dare, venture.

sõl olen engemal, sarna sívametak—dare to be with me, song of my heart.

soŋe—to enter; to penetrate; to compensate; to replace.

Susiküm—Lycan.

susu—home; birthplace (*noun*). At home (*adv.*).

szabadon—freely.

szelem—ghost.

ször—time; occasion.

t (or ot)—past participle (*suffix*).

taj—to be worth.

taka—behind; beyond.

takka—to hang; to remain stuck.

takkap—obstacle; challenge; difficulty; ordeal; trial.

tappa—to dance; to stamp with the feet; to kill.

tasa—even so; just the same.

te—you.

te kalma, te jama ńiŋ3kval, te apitäsz arwa-arvo—you are nothing but a walking maggot-infected corpse, without honor.

te magköszunam nä ŋamaŋ kać3 taka arvo—thank you for this gift beyond price.

ted—yours.

terád keje—get scorched (*Carpathian swear words*).

tõd—to know.

tõdak pitäsz wäke bekimet mekesz kaiket—I know you have the courage to face anything.

tõdhän—knowledge.

tõdhän lõ kuraset agbapäämoroam—knowledge flies the sword true to its aim.

toja—to bend; to bow; to break.

toro—to fight; to quarrel.

torosz wäkeval—fight fiercely (*greeting*).

totello—obey.

tsak—only.

t'šuva vni—period of time.

tti—to look; to see; to find.

tuhanos—thousand.

tuhanos löylyak türelamak saγe diutalet—a thousand patient breaths bring victory.

tule—to meet; to come.

tuli—fire.

tumte—to feel; to touch; to touch upon.

türe—full; satiated; accomplished.

türelam—patience.

türelam agba kontsalamaval—patience is the warrior's true weapon.

tyvi—stem; base; trunk.

ul3—very; exceedingly; quite.

umuš—wisdom; discernment.

und—past participle (*suffix*).

uskol—faithful.

uskolfertiil—allegiance; loyalty.

usm—to heal; to be restored to health.

vár—to wait.

varolind—dangerous.

veri—blood.

veri ekäakank—blood of our brothers.

veri-elidet—blood-life.

veri isäakank—blood of our fathers.

veri olen piros, ekäm—literally: blood be red, my brother; figuratively: find your lifemate (*greeting*).

veriak ot en Karpatiiak—by the blood of the prince (literally: by the blood of the great Carpathian; *Carpathian swear words*).

veridet peje—may your blood burn (*Carpathian swear words*).

vigyáz—to love; to care for; to take care of.

vii—last; at last; finally.

wäke—power; strength.

wäke beki—strength; courage.

wäke kaδa—steadfastness.

wäke kutni—endurance.

wäke-sarna—vow; curse; blessing (literally: power words).

wäkeva—powerful; strong.

wara—bird; crow.

weńća—complete; whole.

wete—water (*noun*).